Praise for *Bila Yarrudh...*

'There are books you encounter as an ... press into the hands of your younger self. *Bila Yarrudhanggalangdhuray* is one of those books – a novel that turns Australia's long-mythologised settler history into a raw and resilient heartsong.'

Guardian

'A heartfelt story of colonisation and its negative effects … the novel tells a powerful and affecting tale of Aboriginal people's identity, community and deep connection to country.'

Canberra Times

'Engrossing and wonderful storytelling. I really loved these strong, brave Wiradyuri characters.'

Melissa Lucashenko, author of *Too Much Lip*

'A powerful story of family, place and belonging.'

Kate Grenville, author of *A Room Made of Leaves*

'*Bila Yarrudhanggalangdhuray* is a remarkable story of courage and a love of country. The tenacity of an Aboriginal woman, Wagadhaany, is made possible by the deep strength of the earth she walks on. Although Wagadhaany is confronted by the ravages of colonialism, with hope and determination she seeks a pathway home to land and her people, both living and ancestral. Her story is not one of the past alone. It is a story that hums with contemporary resonance. Anita Heiss writes with heart and energy on every page of this novel.'

Tony Birch, author of *The White Girl*

'This is a book to sink into. Lyrical and tender, Anita Heiss's *Bila Yarrudhanggalangdhuray* tells a story of courage, connection and belonging which is both universal and deeply personal, with the river singing through every page. A grand achievement and destined to be read for a long time to come.'

Meg Keneally, author of *Fled* and *The Wreck*

'A heartbreaking story of disruption and loss, and the warmest invitation to share the space of landscape and language, recovery and love. The generous reach of *Bila Yarrudhanggalangdhuray* insists on individual power and an expansive empathy.'
Ashley Hay, author of *A Hundred Small Lessons*

'This is the Australian novel I've been waiting for. Epic storytelling with a deep warmth at its heart, *Bila Yarrudhanggalangdhuray* will break your heart but leave you with hope and a strong connection to the people of the river. A love story not only between people, but between people and country. Anita Heiss has given us a magnificent, gripping read – masterful storytelling which brings the past to life in a way we've never seen before. I just loved it. This story will stay with me forever.'
Pamela Hart, author of *The Charleston Scandal*

'The novel flows like the great Murrumbidgee River itself, with powerful undercurrents that sweep the reader along – I feel it's a book that all Australians should read, to try and understand why our colonial past still causes so much pain and grievance.'
Kate Forsyth, author of *The Blue Rose*

'Anita Heiss is at the height of her storytelling powers in this inspiring, heartbreaking, profound tale that explores the deep, eternal connection to country and the resilience of the human heart. Wagadhaany is a timeless heroine who reminds us of the steps our ancestors walked.'
Larissa Behrendt, film maker and author

'It is a love story, a story of loss, a hopeful story. The river is a guide, but you have to be open to its spiritual lessons.'
Dr Terri Janke

Anita
HEISS

Bila Yarrudhanggalangdhuray

**SIMON &
SCHUSTER**

London · New York · Sydney · Toronto · New Delhi

BILA YARRUDHANGGALANGDHURAY
First published in Australia in 2021 by
Simon & Schuster (Australia) Pty Limited
Suite 19A, Level 1, Building C,
450 Miller Street, Cammeray, NSW 2062
This edition published in 2022.

10 9 8 7 6 5 4 3 2

Sydney New York London Toronto New Delhi
Visit our website at www.simonandschuster.com.au

A catalogue record for this
book is available from the
National Library of Australia

ISBN: 9781761104800

Cover design: Luke Causby
Cover images: © Luke Penrith (Gugar Dreaming); © Grahamec (landscape);
© Luke Causby (cockatoos)
Typeset by Midland Typesetters, Australia
Printed and bound in Australia by Griffin Press

The paper this book is printed on is certified against the
Forest Stewardship Council® Standards. Griffin Press holds
chain of custody certification SCS-COC-001185. FSC®
promotes environmentally responsible, socially beneficial
and economically viable management of the world's forests.

To all the unsung heroes and heroines
who are part of our national story

Prologue

1838, Gundagai

'Not a good place to live, Boss, too flat!'

Wagadhaany looks up at her father as he speaks to a White man with piercing green eyes across the way. She is a wide-eyed four-year-old with a spring in her step and a toothy smile that goes from ear to ear. She is bone thin with dark brown hair that falls in large curls down her back. She loves walking along the river when her babiin is not off with her uncles, and she is interested to see all the new people who are coming to live near them.

Between where she stands and the bila, there are three rows of ganya-galang. She watches the current flow rapidly downstream, then turns to observe different men swinging hammers and grunting with hard work, making their ganya-galang out of wood and stones, not with branches and trees. They are building them next to each other, and it's different to their campsite which is not so straight, and not so boring, she thinks. But these ganya-galang look like they are very strong and won't ever move, ever.

1

Wagadhaany recalls her father and uncles talking about all the White people coming to live on Wiradyuri ngurambang – our Ancestors' country, they always insist to each other. She thinks the stranger across the way is so white and so skinny he could move around like a birig. But she is sure her babiin wouldn't be talking to a spirit like he is a real person.

She is frightened out of her dark skin as the man hisses at them both, 'Go away!'

She is curious and wants to ask so many questions – the who, the what, the when and the how. Mostly she wants to know *why* something is so. 'Why is he so angry?' she whispers as the corners of her mouth turn downwards. She is about to cry.

She is prone to crying. She hates being the youngest of five children. Her siblings are all brothers, and she is often left out of their games because she is a girl, and because she is the baby of the family. She likes being her babiin's favourite but that doesn't always help with the boys, who for some reason enjoy seeing her cry.

Wagadhaany holds her breath as she looks over to the man and sees angry eyes and a furrowed forehead on a tired, pale face. She has heard her uncles talking about not building on the river flats, that it's not the right place to make a home for anyone. That it's not safe to build a house where the water will flood when it rains heavily. They know because even though they camp there and have ceremony there, they move to higher ground as soon as the rain falls hard. But these new ganya-galang won't be able to be moved.

She knows that this place has flooded before, and it will again. She wants to tell the man herself, but she wouldn't dare. That would be disrespectful and the one thing that she must always show Elders is yindyamarra. Even though the man is not her uncle, he is most definitely older than her, by many, many years, and so she keeps her mouth shut.

As she feels her father's body jerk, Wagadhaany immediately pulls herself into his side, wanting in fact to go away, as they have been ordered. She has seen angry White men and angry Black men before, and when they are angry at the same time it is scary. She can feel tears welling at the thought of a confrontation, and as the sun is high in the sky, she doesn't want anyone ruining this beautiful, otherwise carefree day for her and her babiin. Wagadhaany is relieved when her father resumes walking and the man goes back to hammering lengths of wood.

After only a few steps she hears the man bellow, 'Get out of that mud!'

She turns quickly, still holding her father's hand, and sees two boys playing in some wet dirt, the man glaring at them. Wagadhaany wonders if the boys carried the water from the river in the tin buckets she sees nearby, to make the mud. The wet dirt looks inviting. There's been no rain for so long and everything else around is dry – the grass, the dusty path they are walking on, and her throat too. Back at the camp her aunties have been complaining about the dust and commenting on how low the river is getting, and while Wagadhaany often traces the cracks in the earth of the riverbank, she stops thinking about it now, because playing in the mud looks like fun and she'd rather be doing that. She knows she could never go and play with *those* boys – she's never played with White kids before. She wants to ask her babiin if she can make some mud when they get back to camp, but he is looking at the White man, and so she says nothing and just stares as well. Wagadhaany grips her father's hand tightly. The questions start playing on a loop in her head.

Why have we stopped? What are you going to say, Babiin? Who is this man anyway? Are you angry too?

'Silly man,' her father says under his breath as he turns back around and slides his left foot forward and gently pulls his daughter along with him.

Wagadhaany looks up at the tower of the man next to her. The sun stings her eyes and she squints. She grips her father's hand tighter and skips a few steps, wondering what her brothers are doing. Probably fishing, she tells herself. She hopes they'll make mud cakes with her later.

After a few slow strides, her father turns around, abruptly swinging his daughter around with him.

'Here,' he says loudly and clearly to the White man, as he looks from the river to his left and waves his arms from side to side. 'Flood area, biggest rains, the water goes past here.'

He raises his hand up above his head to show how high the water may rise. Wagadhaany thinks that her babiin is very tall, so the water will be very tall too.

The man scoffs as he points to the dry landscape. 'You don't know what you're talking about. We *need* rain. It certainly doesn't look like it's going to flood to me.'

'It hasn't flooded for longest time,' Yarri says. 'It *will* happen again. We know.'

'This side of the river,' the White man says, waving his hand along the right-hand bank of the Marrambidya Bila. 'This is the Crossing Place.'

Wagadhaany follows the swing of his arm. Her eyes rest momentarily on the biggest red river gum tree she has ever seen. She follows the creamy bark of the trunk skyward and among the white flowers she glimpses some movement. It's a koala and

4

her baby sleeping. They make her smile and she wishes she could get to the other side of the river to see them better. But she can't swim, and she knows that even though the river is low, even though she can see the brown earth for some of the way through the water, it is probably still very deep in the middle. And it's cold. She shivers just thinking about how chilly the water was the last time she put her feet in, and how strong the current was, and how dangerous it was, as the aunties told her. She is in her own world, looking at the koalas and hoping the singing parrots don't wake them up, when the White man's voice shakes her.

He points to the ground beneath his feet. 'And right here and around here –' he swings his skinny white arms again and Wagadhaany feels a bit dizzy watching them flailing about '– this is where Gundagai town is going to be built, you'll see.'

Yarri shrugs his shoulders and Wagadhaany follows her father's actions. She expects the other man might do the same but he doesn't. Instead, he slams his shovel down on the ground with a great thump. He puts his hands on his hips. 'It's going to be a service town for travellers and pastoralists between Sydney and Melbourne,' he says, as if he is one of the official men Wagadhaany has heard her uncles talk about at camp. 'There'll be a punt service over at Stuckey's Crossing too.' He points in the direction of the crossing. 'You just wait and see.'

Wagadhaany looks at her father. She has so many questions, because she doesn't really understand what the man is talking about. *Yamawa?* She wants to ask her question out loud. *What for, Babiin? Why is he here and angry, and yamawa are you talking to him? And what is a punt?* There are so many new people, new things happening where they live, and so many new words that sound so different to the language they speak in the camp.

When she looks back at the White man, she sees his eyes flick to her. His bright green eyes are scary-looking, and Wagadhaany is a little taken aback, but she can't look away. She stares at him when he mumbles something about Blacks not being smart enough to understand but he keeps talking to her father anyway.

'I'm building an attic,' he says.

Yarri doesn't respond, so the man goes on.

'That's a room in the roof,' he says sarcastically, 'and we can go up high if there is any flooding, but I'm sure we won't have to.'

Yarri shakes his head. 'Come.' Wagadhaany feels a gentle pull on her hand. 'They never listen, Wagadhaany, never listen.'

'Why didn't you tell him, Babiin?' she asks quietly, not wanting to upset her father any more than he already is.

'Tell him what?'

'What Marrambidya means.' She takes three steps to each of her father's lunges. 'That it means big flood, big water.' Wagadhaany looks up and smiles at her hero, hoping that he is proud that she remembers the stories he tells her.

'No matter what you say, or how many times you say it, ngamurr, some people, especially White people, they just won't listen.'

The sun beats down on the camp as Wagadhaany sits at her father's feet in the shade of a eucalyptus tree. She listens intently as he tells the other men of his exchange with the White man that morning.

'Things are changing. More White people, more White people's animals, White food and White sickness. Things will change for us too because of that,' Yarri says, and Wagadhaany hears the worry in her father's voice. 'I don't know how long we can stay on this land, our land. They have marked the land over that way already.' Yarri points in the direction he and Waga-dhaany had walked earlier that day, towards the sun.

'They are making their own homes, like ours, but they will not be moved on, not like us. Their way is different, no campfire for everyone to gather around to talk – no sitting like this, and it looks like no sharing.' He motions around the circle where all her uncles and some of her aunties and cousins sit, preparing their catch to share that night, and shakes his head. 'They do not understand the land and river like we do, and they don't care that they should not build on the flat earth there, that it will flood again, one day.' He looks to the sky, then pats Wagadhaany on the head. 'As sure as day becomes night and night becomes day again, things will change. And it *will* flood.'

Yarri recounts the morning's events to the other men as they show Wagadhaany's brothers – Jirrima, Yarran, Euroka and Ngalan – how to gut a kangaroo. Wagadhaany moves to squat on her haunches, watching, happy that she only has to look on. Her brothers are in the thick of the gutting and she turns her nose up at the smell of the raw flesh and internal organs. She likes it much more when the wambuwuny is cooked. She is fascinated by the way her brothers participate with precision and enthusiasm, and even though she usually prefers to be with the women, weaving and looking after the younger children, right now she is staying where she is, hoping that they can all go make mud cakes together soon.

'They don't understand what it is capable of,' her uncle Dyan responds, as he points to the river. All her mamaba-galang are smart, but Mamaba Dyan might be the smartest. 'That bila has already taken so many people, he will again.'

All the men nod. They know the truth about the strength in the flowing Marrambidya.

'They don't understand the land, they just keep chopping down trees to build their ganya-galang,' Mamaba Dyan says, as he removes the main organs of the kangaroo. 'Some of our men are helping them. To get flour and sugar and tea.'

'They build roads too, and those roads are changing this place,' Mamaba Badhrig says, as he holds the hind legs of the animal down to make the dismembering easier.

'And the new animals, those cows and sheep, they are changing the land too,' Yarri says. 'And our men, they are being asked to help work with those cows and sheep. I reckon I could ride a horse better than they do,' he adds confidently.

'And ride 'em well,' Mamaba Badhrig says.

'We could teach them a lot, if they just listened,' Yarri adds.

Wagadhaany watches her uncles all nod in agreement, but her attention to the man-talk is waning, she wants to play.

She knows her babiin is watching her through the corner of his eye as she walks off towards the bila. Sometimes she thinks he has eyes in the back of his head because he always knows where she is, sometimes before she even gets there. When she reaches the sandy riverbank she plops down on her bubul, crosses her skinny brown legs and starts mixing earth with water. She waits impatiently for her brothers to come down and fish.

As she moves her hands through the wet sand, she thinks about the looks on the faces of the young boys she saw earlier that morning and how they were giggling as they played in the mud. She giggles too and wishes her brothers would have fun with her instead of always leaving her out. Sometimes she wants to scream at them that it's not her fault she's a girl. Wagadhaany

waves over her younger cousins and other camp kids who join
her and she shows them what to do with the sand and water.
Together they make mud cakes and their chuckles rise up the
bank to where her balgalbalgar-galang are drinking tea and
talking. Now that the wambuwuny is on the fire they can rest
a while. She wishes she was an Elder and could drink tea too,
because they seem to laugh a lot when they are talking together
around the fire.

As the day draws to a close and dusk settles in, Wagadhaany
and her brothers and cousins, who have formed one big group
along the bank after several hours of throwing mud at each other,
are oblivious to time. But the sun is about to set and the kuracca-
galang are screeching along the river.

'Beware the waawii!' Wagadhaany's gunhi sings out.

Wagadhaany looks up at her mother with worry on her face,
as do the others. They are frightened of being gobbled up by the
scary bunyip. All the Wiradyuri kids know the story about the
bunyip, having been told it many times, even though once was
more than enough. It's why they aren't supposed to go too close
to the water, and although Wagadhaany has never seen a bunyip,
she's positive she never wants to.

'I saw the waawii once,' Jirrima says.

'Don't lie!' Wagadhaany screeches, shaking her head with a
quiver in her voice.

'I did too, he was like a strange water creature in the shape of
a star,' Yarran says, using his hands to show the shape and size
of what he claims he saw.

'No, I saw him, and he was like a big snake with a long, wide
face and a flat nose with big fangs,' her brother Ngalan says. He
seems to be enjoying making the smaller kids cry.

'Nah, *I* really saw the waawii come out of the water and walk right up the bank and he was taller than Babiin with Mamaba Dyan on his shoulders. He was like a giant with big claws and a head like a dinawan,' Jirrima adds.

Wagadhaany tries not to think about this monster with an emu head. 'Stop it! Stop it!' she cries.

She takes flight back up the bank to her gunhi who is waiting, expecting the tears and fears, because inevitably the boys manage to upset their baby sister around the same time every day. Wagadhaany can hear her brothers laughing behind her, and her round brown face is soaked in tears when she buries her face in her mother's neck. It is the place she feels most safe, most protected, most at home.

'Ngamurr, your gumbal-galang don't mean harm, but you will have to be strong around them.'

'Are all boys like that?' she sobs.

'Not all, but most.'

Wagadhaany can almost hear a giggle in her mother's words and is confused. She cries louder when her brothers call out again. She doesn't understand what they are saying but she knows they are still making fun of her. Her mother releases her from the tight hug just long enough to sing out to her sons who are still by the water.

'Your babiin will speak to you,' she calls down to the river. 'Now get up here.'

She pulls her daughter close again. From the corner of her eye Wagadhaany can see the boys taking short, slow, almost shy steps up the bank. She smiles slyly to herself because she knows that even though the bunyip might not get them tonight, their father will not let them get away with anything. She is his favourite gudha and they all know it.

'Show yindyamarra to your sister, to everyone,' says her babiin. 'The bunyip knows everything, so always be respectful.'

Yarri is serious and they all feel it. Wagadhaany is still clinging to her mother as her brothers are being spoken to. She watches them staring at the ground and kicking dirt around, waiting till their babiin has finished. Sometimes he is scarier than the bunyip.

'Come!' Her mother puts her down, takes her by the hand and walks her to the women who are teaching the young girls to dance. 'Waga means to dance,' she reminds her daughter. 'You are our little dancer, Wagadhaany, always remember that.'

She looks up to her mother, feeling special, as though she has an important role, a place with the women, with all her family. And she starts to move her feet, gently kicking up the earth as she watches the older women's moves, mimicking them as best as her little body can. She likes being their little dancer.

In the ganya that night, Wagadhaany nestles closer to her younger cousins – Ngaayuga, Gandi, Yiri and Yirabiga – and they lace their legs through each other's as much to keep warm as to have fun.

'What's a bunyip?' Ngaayuga asks.

Wagadhaany sits upright, almost breaking her cousin's leg as she does so, which results in a loud screech, drawing the attention of the Elders outside by the fire.

'Way!' Yarri calls out for them to be quiet. 'You girls go to sleep.'

Wagadhaany puts her finger up to her lips to shoosh the others, then slumps back down and leans in to her little cousins. 'The waawii is a very, very, very scary creature that lives in the

Marrambidya Bila,' she whispers. 'When you see the water go around and around in circles, that's when you know he is there.'

She waves her hand in the air in circles and makes a whooshing sound as her cousins look and listen intently.

'How do you know it's a boy?' Gandi asks.

'Because only boys are scary and would hurt children,' Yirabiga responds.

They all nod in agreement.

'Gunhi says that if we go down to the river alone and get too close to the water then . . .' Wagadhaany pauses, letting her wide eyes and a shake of her head suggest what will happen. She sees the fear in her cousins' faces and stops. She's not like her older brothers who enjoy scaring young kids. 'So, we should always have an adult with us near the river, especially at night.'

Chapter One

The Great Flood – 24 June 1852, Gundagai

Wild wind and torrential rain thrash the Bradley home. The pitter-patter of the first drops to fall has been quickly replaced with a pelting that hits the windows so hard it risks smashing them. Wagadhaany shivers with fear as a bitterly cold draught comes through a gap in the door frame.

'We need to sandbag,' Henry Bradley says forcefully, his role as patriarch of the family never more tested than now. 'Others have already done it. We're going to lose everything if we don't take action now!'

It's an announcement and an order in one, his four sons jumping to attention instantly, as does Wagadhaany, waiting for her instructions as their servant.

Henry Bradley's bright green eyes are as scary to her today as they were the first time she saw them. Little did she know back then that the man she encountered building this house would be the man she would end up in servitude to.

13

Many of the White families have domestic help, young women to clean, cook and help with children, and young men to help on the sheep and cattle stations. In some ways she feels lucky that she and her father work for the same family, but she often wonders if her babiin remembers the day they first met Henry Bradley all those years ago. She's been with the Bradleys for four years and never has she seen any warmth in Mr Bradley's eyes.

'No!' Mr Bradley's wife, Elizabeth, has never raised her voice in their home and her challenge to her husband comes out with a tremble. She is fighting back tears and is visibly shaken by the torrential rain that is drenching their town. 'We should just leave now, we should go to higher ground.'

She looks pleadingly at her husband as she keeps a firm grip on her Bible and prayer beads, shivering in the winter cold as it has been impossible to keep the living-room fire alight.

'Some families have already moved to safety. Mr Johnson said some of the natives from the camp on the flood plain moved to Mount Parnassus this morning,' David Bradley says.

Wagadhaany knows that her family would have been in that group and her heart skips a beat waiting for her boss's next words.

'They led anyone who wanted to go up to the hills,' David adds. 'Andrew and I could take Mother to safety.'

'No, we stay together as a family.' Henry Bradley doesn't look up. 'I don't think it will come this far into town.'

'Sheridan Street is less than half a mile away from the river and the water is rising fast, Father, and we are not on the high end of town,' James says with urgency in his voice.

His father ignores him.

Elizabeth Bradley's lips are turning blue as she starts crying. 'Why didn't you listen to Mr Johnson when he came by on his horse? He told you to leave, but you never listen,' she says, chin quivering. 'Never listen.'

By the look on Henry Bradley's face, he isn't happy being chastised by his wife. Wagadhaany is reminded of her father saying *White men never listen* on the day that she first saw Mr Bradley.

So much has changed in the fourteen years since – the size of the town, the number of shops and houses, so many new townsfolk, and more Aboriginal people working for White families. Her own father is one of many men who have become stockmen and shepherds on the Bradleys' and other local stations, riding horses with skill to herd cattle and sheep, like her Uncle Badhrig said they would. The one thing that doesn't seem to have changed is Henry Bradley's refusal to listen to people who know better. Wagadhaany has vivid memories of her father saying it was a bad idea to build here. Her ears are filled with his wise words as the rain continues to fall without mercy.

She hopes the Bradley patriarch will not be his usual stubborn self. Without realising it, she looks pleadingly at him as well. *Will you get your family to safety soon? Will you take me with you?*

'Only those families in the lowest part of the town, over on the north bank of the river, have moved,' he responds, looking at each family member in turn, but bypassing her altogether. 'We are fine here, I think. Those living above shopfronts are still there.' He strains to see the lights on buildings either side of their home. 'The river will *not* reach us.'

Wagadhaany thinks her boss sounds confident but his face defies his voice. He looks worried, and she is positive she is not the only one in the room who notices this. She is fighting back tears of fear for many reasons, but first and foremost, because she cannot swim well, not like her brothers. She rarely fished with them, and her confidence could never match the current that would often pull them downstream. She has seen the rushing water outside, and she is certain she will not have enough strength to keep herself safe if the house is flooded and she is caught. She looks desperately at Henry Bradley, completely at his mercy. She swallows the tears back because she knows he will not tolerate seeing her cry. He never has, not for as long as she can remember working for him. And for that matter, tonight is the first time she has seen Elizabeth Bradley cry in this house that has been stifled by manners and decorum for too long.

The four Bradley sons move in silence as they follow their father outside, falling naturally into order of age from eldest to youngest. The bossiest, James, she believes to be twenty-six years old. The physically strongest, David, is only a year younger. Usually the chattiest of the four, Harry, is twenty-two, while the kindest of the brothers, Andrew, she thinks is probably only a couple of years older than she is, but she can't be sure. Andrew is the son always by his mother's side, though all four of the brothers adore their mother.

With her own safety at the forefront of her concerns, Wagadhaany steps gingerly in the direction of the window so she can see what the men are doing. When she touches the glass she realises her fingers are numb, and she doesn't know how long they have been that way. She rubs her hands together as fast as she can, and then down her thighs, but they are frozen too. She panics, thinking that if she doesn't drown she might freeze to death. She hears the men yelling over the rain and watches them start to position the loaded wheat bags and other hessian bags they have managed to get their hands on earlier in the day. They set to work filling them with sand, anticipating that the rain will continue to fall. She is surprised to watch the labour of men who hardly lift a finger around the house.

'I don't think we have enough gunny sacks,' Harry sings out to no-one yet everyone. 'We need to get more!'

His brothers don't respond, perhaps because there are no more bags to be had. Wagadhaany continues to watch the men quickly but carefully placing the sandbags lengthwise and parallel to the rainwater that is already flowing past their home and rising by the minute.

'Faster! Faster!' James orders.

The others do as they have been instructed, but Wagadhaany sees a look of contempt on David's face, as if he hates to be ordered around by his brother. If anything, though, James appears to be the only one who knows what he is doing.

As the men work on protecting the house, Elizabeth Bradley works through her prayer beads, one at a time. Wagadhaany stands in a corner, watching her and waiting for instructions. She asks Biyaami to keep them all safe – the Bradleys, her own family, the townsfolk – and without wanting to be selfish, she asks twice for herself.

The Bradley brothers re-enter the house, shouting at each other about what they should do next. David Bradley paces furiously back and forth, back and forth, back and forth, as if he is in a trance and doesn't know where he is. His brothers notice but no-one says anything because they are still arguing about whether they should stay or leave.

Wagadhaany wants to leave and get back to her family, but she has no right to say that, to say anything. She is without a voice in this house. Her job is not to offer an opinion, or even to have one. At the camp it is different. There she has a voice and a purpose. There she is a woman, and her role is to nurture the little ones. Her life at the Bradleys' has no real meaning, no real purpose. Her job is to clean, cook, sew and be of assistance wherever and whenever Mrs Bradley requires her. Mostly she is invisible to the men, only necessary to them in that she prepares their meals and washes their clothes and is an aide to the matriarch of the family. While they have rarely taken much notice of her, Wagadhaany has often observed their egos, and tonight is no different.

When Henry Bradley finally returns indoors, the men continue to debate how to manage the flood. Elizabeth Bradley looks to Wagadhaany for support but she knows that her husband would never consider what the Black girl might think they should do, and tonight will be no different. Support, humanity, friendship . . . These are not qualities that have existed between the two women before, but tonight Wagadhaany recognises that she and Mrs Bradley are essential to each other's survival.

'We are not leaving the house!' James Bradley says. Known to share his father's stubbornness and temper, he thumps his fist on the dining table.

There is shocked silence in the room.

'Well, I am,' David declares, and he stops pacing the room he has walked around and around in for hours.

'You are not going ANYWHERE!' Henry Bradley grabs his son by the front of his shirt. 'We are a family and we will stay together.'

The other men step in to defuse the situation, prying their father's hands from their brother's body and forcing them apart. Father and son have their eyes locked in rage.

All Wagadhaany hopes is that in Mr Bradley's demand to stay together, she is included. Even though her own family is at the front of her mind, she does not want to go out into this harsh weather alone. She can hear the miilgi continuing to thrash the town, and the sound makes her even more anxious.

'Please, David, please don't leave. We must stay together, your father is right. Please stay with me,' Mrs Bradley pleads with her son.

Andrew moves to her side, gently resting a hand on her shoulder. As she leans forward and weeps loudly into a linen handkerchief, he crouches to his mother's ear and says, 'The doorways are sandbagged, Mother, but if I am forced to leave I will take you with me.'

She looks up to her son with tear-filled eyes and soaked cheeks.

'Make some tea, Wilma!' Henry Bradley barks.

And in a most uncharacteristic response, her own emotions rising like the water level, Wagadhaany responds just loud enough to be heard, 'My name is Wagadhaany, *wogga-dine*.'

She turns swiftly, shocked at her behaviour, but also angry that even after years of Henry Bradley giving her orders he still can't use her name. She knows she will pay for the disobedience; Henry Bradley has only slapped her once, but there is nothing to say that he won't do it again. But before anyone in the room can comment, the crash of a tree against the house captures everyone's attention and the conversation turns to that.

As she walks to the kitchen she wonders if being called her proper name even matters. If she is going to die, she may as well be Wilma. Tears fall down her cheeks almost as fast and full as the torrential rain falling outside. She thinks about her family, but she doesn't worry as much for them as she does for herself and the Bradleys. This place has flooded before and her clan have always survived. They know when and where to move, how to listen to and act on the messages from the weather. She is certain that as soon as they saw the river begin to rise and the current flow faster, her babiin and uncles would have moved the women and their campsite to higher ground. They may be cold and wet, but they will be safe.

She puts a pot of water on the wood stove to boil. She notices the warmth in the kitchen compared to the living room and even though it would be cramped, she wonders why the Bradleys aren't huddled in here. Her hands shake and the cups rattle as she prepares them on a tray. She tries to be as normal as she can with fear for her own safety racing through her veins and her heart beating at a pace she's never felt before. 'Keep us safe, Biyaami, please keep us safe,' she whispers as she wipes her face on her apron and pours the steaming water into the teapot. She has to believe that everything will be all right or she will never stop crying.

It is rare that she has to pour tea for the entire family at once and she is nervous on top of being scared, especially since she has been rude to Henry Bradley. Careful not to drop the overloaded tray, she walks slowly into the room where there is silence apart from the sound of miilgi lashing the home. The Bradleys are fortunate their house is made of stone, when so many in town are made of wood or weatherboard, with shingle roofs that would never withstand the rain. That the Bradleys' house also has an attic speaks of their privilege.

As the skies continue to open, the four brothers and their father put their disagreements aside and huddle together closely, heads down, as they strategise their next move. Wagadhaany hears the odd word: flooding, safety, Mother. The men all look towards their matriarch, knowing that she is their number one priority.

James finally speaks. 'We should've known this was going to happen. The flood of 1844 claimed two lives. All that damage, we should've learned.' He walks to a window while his family looks on.

Wagadhaany stands still in the corner, waiting for further instructions, never acting without direction or approval. No-one has touched their tea. She wishes desperately that the rain was not falling and she was sitting around the campfire with her family, her parents, her brothers and cousins. Her mind is racing as fast as her heart.

'We tried, James,' David reminds his brother, angrily. 'We petitioned Governor Gipps to relocate the town, remember?' He starts pacing again, and turns abruptly. 'It's not like we didn't try.'

'I remember only too well,' James nods. 'I remember his mouthpiece, the Colonial Secretary, telling us we bought for better or worse, like our future lives and any threat to the towns-folk meant absolutely nothing. We were simply to be tamed by his words. Nothing more than that.'

David shakes his head. 'They never listened to us.'

Wagadhaany's babiin was right. None of them ever listen.

'The thing is,' Harry finally interjects, having been unusually quiet, 'is that everyone said the big one was behind us, but I don't think it is.'

He looks out the window into the darkness of the night, then they all do. Wagadhaany can see very little. Her vision is blinded by rain beating against the glass, and with the decrease in visibility comes an increase in fear. She hears yelling from outside. 'The banks have broken! The banks have broken!'

The water will be rushing through the town within minutes, she knows. The surrounding flood plains will soon be well and truly under water. She remembers this happening before and the floodwaters being strong enough to carry heavy carriages and houses downstream.

'The banks have broken!' James frantically repeats, and his voice reverberates throughout the house and Wagadhaany shakes with fear. Her heart beats so hard she thinks she can hear it. She wants to scream, but her lips barely part as tears begin to fall again.

As Andrew races outside, she imagines his face being hit hard by the icy rain. Winter in Gundagai is brutal enough without stormy weather. She can see that the wind is forcing him to put his hands up to his face to protect it. 'Hey,' he calls out to a lone figure, who is still yelling, 'The banks have broken! The banks have broken!'

As James and David move to the door, Wagadhaany strains to see what is happening. A man pushes his body against the wind, back towards Andrew Bradley. 'The banks have broken,' he yells again, leaning into Andrew's ear before a gust of wind pushes him away from Andrew and the house.

Andrew's face is ashen when he re-enters the room.

'What is it?' his mother asks as he puts his arm firmly around her.

He shakes his head, forcing out words. 'A boat crossing the river has been swamped.' He pauses. 'He said five children drowned.' He exhales, closes his eyes briefly and then adds, 'The boatman too.'

Everyone in the room drops their head in shock. There is an unplanned moment of silence until Henry Bradley commands, 'Everyone to the attic, now!'

Wagadhaany moves as fast as the Bradleys, even though it's not clear that she is included in the order. Andrew holds a wooden chair firmly on the large dining table, as James helps each onto the table, then carefully onto the chair and through the opening in the ceiling into the attic. When Wagadhaany reaches James there is a moment of awkwardness. For the first time she looks directly and desperately into his cold eyes. He says nothing, just motions for her to climb, and she does. Andrew assists her and then follows. Finally, James uses all his upper body strength to lift himself through the opening, just as there's the crash of water in the room below. He is visibly disturbed as he looks down to see furniture tossing and turning, the torrent ruining their belongings. His face is ghostly white and when he looks back to his family, his troubled expression makes Wagadhaany even more nervous than before.

Anxiety runs through her veins, her heart begins to race and she feels dizzy. She is overwhelmed by the sound of the miilgi pelting the roof, and she can't understand how the miilgi that brings so much life to the river, to the land and to all living things, can now be causing so much devastation. She turns her thoughts to the animals that will not survive. The normally noisy kuracca-galang and the mulyan-galang that will most likely be flushed from the trees to their death. The flood will take all the land animals with it too. *Where will the animals find refuge? And what of the townsfolk who don't have attics to climb into?*

She fears for her own family too but tells herself they will have moved fast enough to avoid the flooding. In her heart she knows that her babiin and her mamaba-galang will have prepared everyone in time; the Old People, the women and children will have been made safe, because Wiradyuri people know better than anyone what the river is capable of.

In the dead of night, Wagadhaany thinks about those who have already been swept away by the floodwaters that continue to rage past them. No-one is speaking. Henry and James are keeping watch from the roof but not reporting back what they can see. Wagadhaany wonders if whole buildings are being swept away, washed out of town, out of sight. She wonders if every other person in town is as terrified as she is.

Through a small window Wagadhaany sees flashes of light across the way. A lantern is being waved slowly by someone in a tree, a man. The light moves from side to side as if he is signalling for attention. She can just make out that with his other arm he is clinging to a branch.

Can anyone else see him? How long he has been there? Where is his family? Maybe he is not a strong swimmer either. But no amount of strength would be useful tonight, no human can win against the flooding streets.

Suddenly the light disappears. The lantern has been dropped or, worse still, the man has fallen into the icy, raging water. Wagadhaany gasps out loud. She can't bear to think what has happened. Reluctantly, she imagines his body twisting and turning in the current, and how fear must be choking him, how he may never see daylight again. She hugs her legs as close as possible to her body and closes her eyes tightly, overwhelmed with the fear of falling into the river. Her tears begin to fall again. She sits silently, desperately trying to ignore the blisteringly cold air coming through every crack in the roof. She rocks back and forth slowly, quietly whispering to Biyaami, *Please keep us safe, please keep us safe.* The Great Spirit is her only hope.

The hours pass and the cold is too cutting for her to do anything but listen to the rain pelting on the tin roof. It is loud and unrelenting. The attic is like an ice box, and while Waga-dhaany is shivering, she is at least dry. She wonders how the men are coping outside. She turns from her lonely place near the window and watches Andrew, the devoted son who has not left his mother's side. She wishes someone was there to comfort her also. She looks at David, who is mumbling under his breath. He appears to be praying, the son who always takes himself to church every Sunday without any reminders. Wagadhaany closes her eyes and as the wind and rain continue to hammer against the house, she pleads with Biyaami again. *Please keep us safe, please keep us safe.*

Not for the first time she wishes that the rains had started falling when she was at camp with her family. If the rain had started during her weekly Sunday visit, she would've been safe with her family on higher, safer ground, with much less uncertainty than she feels right now in the Bradleys' attic.

It seems like hours before James climbs through the hatch from the roof back into the attic. Wagadhaany is hopeful when she sees him. Perhaps his view of what is happening outside is better than hers through the tiny window. Her optimism is shattered when he declares, 'It's time. We need to move to the roof now. Andrew . . .' He nods to his younger sibling to support their mother in climbing through the small opening that will lead them into the storm.

One by one they awkwardly make their way out. Rain whips Wagadhaany's face. It feels like it is cutting into her skin. The force of the wind knocks her backwards into the arms of David, who catches her. She doesn't have time to consider whether it is simply reflex or concern on his part, she is grateful, but still it is an uncomfortable moment.

'I've got you,' he reassures her, holding her arm firmly.

It takes a few seconds for both of them to find their balance. She watches as David grips onto a branch overhanging the roof, and together they sit down close to Mrs Bradley and Andrew. The four link arms and anchor themselves against the gale. She feels safe for the moment.

'We'll be fine, we just need to wait for the rain to stop,' Harry says to his mother. 'I'm sure it will ease up soon and then the water will drop and we can head back inside,' he continues, as if chatting about a normal situation.

But he is not convincing anyone. There is no reason to believe the sky will stop crying for some time yet.

Wagadhaany does not understand weather patterns but she thinks Harry is outrageously confident given the chaos of what is happening all around them. Then, only seconds after he stops speaking, there is a heart-wrenching screech, the sound of a woman in distress, and not far away. There follows a howling chorus of screams and cries of women and children. Everyone's ears are filled with the terror the river is inflicting on the towns-folk. Mrs Bradley weeps uncontrollably and as Wagadhaany grips onto David like a frightened child, he makes an attempt to shelter them both from the elements under his jacket. She is grateful for this, but his efforts are in vain. Everyone was soaked to the skin within seconds of climbing outside.

'I can't swim well,' Wagadhaany cries, looking directly into David's eyes. It's the first time they've made proper eye contact, ever. 'I'm not strong enough.'

There is pleading in her voice. There is no time for shame tonight, not when her life is hanging by a thread. She needs him to understand the terror that is gripping her mind, the fear that is numbing her to the core. She is panic-stricken by the thought that she may end up in the river and be swept away like the man and his torch, that *her* screeches may be the next to be heard. She doesn't want to die. She doesn't want anyone to die. But Wagadhaany can't see any response in David Bradley's eyes, so she turns away, hangs her head and calls upon Biyaami again.

When she opens her eyes she sees that David is praying too. She hopes his prayers are answered. She knows his is a Christian God, but they need all the help they can get tonight.

'Hold on to me this way,' he orders, raising his arm up for Wagadhaany to link her arm through his, more comfortably and securely, as Andrew moves across to the chimney, his arm firmly linked with his mother's.

She feels David pull her firmly against his body, tighter and tighter. It feels strange to be so close to any man, but being anchored to him makes her feel safer.

They sit and wait. As time passes, Wagadhaany loses feeling in her feet and her hands. Her teeth chatter uncontrollably. Being weighed down by David gives her some sense of security, but it does nothing to stop the feeling of horror she experiences every time she hears a scream for help.

In the numbing cold and darkness, her mind controls her emotions and her heart. She rises slightly from her seated position and screams whenever she hears the crash of a building nearby. Her imagination evokes a terrifying nightmare of what dreadful things must be happening to families in the town, and reminds her of the fear she has for her own family, wherever they are.

Chapter Two

The Wiradyuri people know to move to higher ground. They have done it many times before, and they will probably do it again. Camping and having ceremony on the flood plain is their way of life, but so is understanding the ways of nature, the flow and power of the Marrambidya, and when to get out of his way.

As the waters begin to rise rapidly, Yarri and the other men move their women and children swiftly to Mount Parnassus. There is no doubt in Yarri's mind that the centre of Gundagai town will be under water eventually, so the tasks are divided into looking after their own women and children and going to help the towns-folk. Yarri, a shepherd on the Bradley Station, is desperate to get to his daughter, but by the time he has the chance to even look for her, the town is submerged. All he can hope for is that his boss has taken care of her, and placed her on high ground also.

'I do not have a favourite gudha,' he tells his wife. 'But . . .' He pauses, takes a deep breath and sighs.

Yarri's desperate concern for his only ngamurr and youngest gudha is causing his heart to beat faster than he can mumble his words. He thinks of the young woman whose eyes, nose and mouth mirror his own, and whose gentle temperament is the opposite of her mother's. Yiramiilan, his fiery Wiradyuri wife, has been anxious since the rains began falling heavily. She has not let her grandchildren out of her sight, and he smiles weakly at his grandsons huddled around Yiramiilan, as if protecting their grandmother. When she looks at her husband, Yarri sees the desperation in her eyes.

'Find her,' she says gently.

Yarri takes this as an order. He understands his obligation to his wife, to his daughter, to all of them. He nods and leaves the new ganya built only hours earlier to protect them from the miilgi they know will continue to fall. The Wiradyuri men know this weather won't end soon. There has been talk that the miilgi will fall for days.

'Let's go!' Yarri nods to Jacky Jacky, who has a flat-bottomed boat provided by a local White man who's heard the two are going out to rescue locals. Yarri hopes Jacky Jacky will be able to manage the river. Having been raised by a White man after his mother was speared, his knowledge of the river is not as vast as Yarri's. But he believes Jacky Jacky's will to help rescue people in distress is as big as his heart. Together they carry their rafts towards the turbulent waters, determined to help in any way they can. Word has spread that lives have already been lost, and they don't want any more deaths on their ngurambang, on their bila.

With no thoughts of his own safety, Yarri paddles his bark canoe, leading the way with purpose, and heading out to help save as many of the townsfolk as he can.

Yarri is strong and his mind is a powerful tool, and while used to mustering sheep, he now needs to muster all the mental strength he can to help him face the physical challenges of chilling temperatures and raging waters. He must ignore the fact that the water feels like liquid ice. He must put aside his own fear and any concerns for his own safety as he embarks on his mission. There is no Black and White tonight; there is just life and death.

As they head out in search of those stranded, Yarri is conscious of the strong current pulling them downstream. He keeps watch of Jacky Jacky as they both do their best in the dark, with only the faint moonlight to guide them. Yarri expertly dodges an enormous log that could easily have knocked him off his canoe, then nods to Jacky Jacky as each paddles in a different direction, following shrieks and shouting.

The night is filled with eerie cries, disturbing howls and pleas for help. These mix with the frightful sounds of houses crashing apart before drifting downriver. Piercing screams come at Yarri from all directions and his ears ring. The sight of people clinging to trees and sitting on rooftops is inconceivable and he is relieved his own mob are safe, protected from the flood and the sights and sounds he is witnessing. Yiramiilan would be distressed to see what is happening in the town, and he always struggles when she is angry or sad. He is glad she has been spared from witnessing this devastation.

As he fights to cross the river, he sees a man and a woman clinging to a tree, about to lose their battle against the turbulent river.

'Help me, help, please!' the woman screams.

Thoughts of his daughter in danger flash into his consciousness, but even though he aches to find Wagadhaany, Yarri can't ignore this woman. The fearful desperation in her voice urges him to paddle faster. Eventually he reaches the tree and grabs hold of a wide branch. He coaxes the woman towards him, using as little English as required, and as much as he knows.

'Help me, help, please . . .' she repeats. Her voice sounds tired as she falls across the canoe and struggles to secure herself.

'Thank you, thank you,' she says breathlessly.

The woman's gratitude is obvious to Yarri as he watches her manoeuvring herself into an almost comfortable position. He refrains from helping her, unsure whether touching a White woman would be acceptable, even at a time like this. They do not speak as Yarri paddles to a place on the riverbank where men have gathered to assist people back to safer ground. He paddles his canoe into a spot where he can lodge it, drags the canoe out, and is joined by townsfolk who swiftly get the woman to safety.

The townsfolk are grateful. Even amid their exhaustion and trauma, they are appreciative, but still they beg him to go back for other family. They offer bribes where possible, but Yarri doesn't take them. Besides, he knows that after tonight they will have very little to give.

He wastes no time in relaunching his canoe into the river, and heads back for the man. To his relief he sees Jacky Jacky only metres away, and he knows that this man too will soon be safe.

Yarri's canoe can only carry one passenger at a time, so it's hard work going back and forth getting those in need to safe ground. He navigates the treacherous waters methodically, working with the current as best he can, and understanding what is required to get close to those he needs to assist. Although he is not thinking about anything beyond the task at hand, he focuses with the strength and determination of a man destined to be a hero.

The people he is rescuing are unknown to Yarri. He knows nothing of their stories. All he cares about is that a human life is a human life, and all he wants to do is save as many people as he can, and find his daughter safe.

The river has been flooding now for a day and a half. It's early morning but with no sunlight and a sky full of dark clouds, it's hard to tell. Yarri's muscles are aching and he is mentally exhausted from having to concentrate so hard on dodging debris and staying afloat. There appears to be no end in sight as the miilgi continues to fall, and it's clear that most of the town's houses have been swept away with the flood. He paddles his canoe with less ease than the day before but with more urgency as he frantically looks for Wagadhaany and the Bradleys.

His eyes dart from left to right with determination. He watches with concern as a man climbs from a floating rooftop into a tree. The skilful move impresses Yarri, who manoeuvres his canoe towards the tree, dodging floating rubbish as he paddles. The man repeats, 'Thank you, thank you, thank you!' as Yarri steadies the canoe for him to climb in. Yarri paddles him to safety and resumes his search for Wagadhaany. For the first time he allows doubt to fill his mind, and the extreme fear of not finding her alive flows through his veins as rapidly as the river flows through the town. He feels a pang in his heart and almost loses balance of the canoe before he steadies his thoughts and the craft, and paddles towards the sounds of shouting further ahead.

With rainfall slapping his face he finds it hard to see properly, but in the distance, Yarri has a blurred view of a naked White man up a tree, where the fruit bats nest on what the townspeople call Bat Island. Yarri paddles and paddles until he reaches the island. He recognises the man as the punt keeper. He's heard the same man is also a surgeon, a respected man in the town.

'Thank you, thank you,' the punt keeper says with enthusiastic gratitude. 'I swam as far as I could.' He attempts to cover his genitals with his hands in a show of modesty. 'The river ripped my clothes off.'

Yarri nods in acknowledgement of the man's efforts. 'Here,' he says, motioning to where the man should hold tightly to secure himself.

Yarri doesn't know what else to say, and he is too exhausted to speak anyway. But as the canoe floats with effort to the shore, Yarri thinks about the two men there together; a naked White man and a barely clothed Black man are nothing but two men stuck in the midst of a devastating flood. He knows he has the power to save this man's life. *A life is a life*, he says over and over in his mind, knowing that the weather, the rain and the river don't care what colour anyone is right now, and that in this moment they are equal. Yarri takes a deep breath and works his arms harder than he ever has, willing them to bring both men to shore, and wishing they were both equals every day.

Chapter Three

The sun has risen and set again behind the rain clouds and Wagadhaany is exhausted. There has been no talking for the long hours that she and the Bradleys have clung to life and each other on the roof. She cannot feel her limbs, and she does not attempt to move for fear of falling into the river that continues to rush by. She doesn't know if anyone has slept and she keeps her eyes closed to protect them from the wind and rain. Just as she starts to think about her gunhi she hears a painful, long cry, forcing her to open her eyes.

Mrs Bradley is slipping from the tin roof of the house. It appears the weight of the water on her long, layered dress has added to the difficulty of holding on.

'Nooooooooooo!' Wagadhaany screams.

In a split second Mr Bradley, Andrew and Harry follow her, all yelling at the top of their lungs. It's hard to tell if they have slipped too, but Wagadhaany believes they were hoping to rescue their wife and mother. No sooner has Wagadhaany stopped screaming than the four Bradleys have disappeared.

James and David are yelling uncontrollably in the dark of night, their words making no sense at all, muffled by the wind and miilgi. Wagadhaany and David are still clinging to each other; his arm remains linked to hers. She feels their bodies jolt forward, as if David has thought to lunge into the bila as well. But he doesn't. Something holds him back, and her gratitude is silent but overwhelming.

As the seconds and minutes pass slowly, she comes to understand the sheer luck that sees them still secure, while the other four Bradleys have been carried away, surely to their deaths. There can be no confirmation, not yet, but she can't imagine that anything will be able to save them from drowning.

When the brothers stop yelling, silence follows as grief sets in. Hunger and sleeplessness drain all her energy, and she cannot even imagine speaking. Besides, what would she say?

The waters continue to rise through the town and, aside from the sound of miilgi that continues to fall, the three sit in sombre stillness. Wagadhaany's heart aches at what she has witnessed, and what she knows the men have lost.

Her tears mix with raindrops when she sees remnants of Mrs Bradley's dress caught on the tree closest to the house. Ripped straight from her person as the water carried her away. She hopes James and David can't see it. Her own short, calico housedress is so light that it is like a layer of skin on her thin frame. If it were any heavier the weight of the soaking wet material might drag her away also.

Her quiet weeping is private and goes unnoticed by the men. She thinks they are crying too, grief-stricken for their parents and siblings. Her fear dissolves into grief for the family that has been a significant part of her life for the past few years, even if they would never consider her in the same way. Sorry business is sad business, and as the time passes, she wonders what ceremonies they will have.

She thinks of Mrs Bradley, who had been the only other female in a house full of loud men. She doesn't want to think about where Mrs Bradley is right now, but she is sure that Andrew is still by her side.

Wagadhaany opens her eyes when the rain stops and she notices the water level dropping around them, but she continues to concentrate on holding onto David. Her right arm aches at the elbow where it loops and grips his. His other arm is still looped around the tree branch. She has no idea how long it has been since anything has been said, but the unspoken is accepted. As she waits, Wagadhaany allows her thoughts to drift back to her family, to where her father, uncles and brothers fish, to where her cousins Ngaayuga, Gandi, Yiri and Yirabiga wash and play when the adults are around. Her mother is also there, the marradir of the family. She knows her beautiful mother will be worried about her, about all her children, but especially her. She wishes she could dance with her now, with all the bamali-galang.

She thinks about the power of the bila, of the stories she heard growing up, and wonders what has happened to the waawii in the flood. *Is he awake and waiting for those who drown?*

She recalls her father telling her many times that the Marrambidya is strong, that it is always to be respected, and while she knows its name means big water, she can't remember the Wiradyuri word for flood. The word has been said over and over again in English by the two brothers who, she now realises, have stopped checking to see if she is all right.

As daylight breaks and her head jerks as she nods with fatigue, Wagadhaany thinks she sees her father approaching. Is she imagining it though? She is weak, tired, so hungry her stomach hurts, and she cannot feel her lips at all. She is not even sure if she is alive or not. She squints, and then she is positive she is there, and her babiin is almost there too.

She can only manage to softly mouth the word. 'Babiin?'

David sits up taller as she speaks. She wonders if he knows the word. She feels his eyes turn to her but she remains fixed on who is in front of her. From the corner of her eye she can see David turn and look into the dawn.

'Yarri!' he attempts to yell, but his voice too is a soft call into the wind.

'Babiin!' Wagadhaany shouts, louder this time. 'Babiin!'

The third attempt is almost loud enough for her father to hear.

'Yarri!' James finally yells at the top of his lungs.

'It's one of our men,' David says, and when Wagadhaany hears 'our men', it feels like he means they own his father.

Yarri is on his knees, crouched low in the bottom of his bark canoe. Wagadhaany can see how strong the current is. She is worried that at any moment the canoe will tip and her father will be swept away, just as so many others already have. He looks exhausted but the muscles in his slender arms still look capable. As he gets closer, Wagadhaany can see the worry in her father's eyes.

Wagadhaany's mind is racing. She wants to ask him everything. *Where is my gunhi, my gumbal-galang, my wunaagany-galang, my miyagan? Is everyone safe? What has he seen on the river already? How many have been swept away?* The questions are there but they are not as important right now as getting off the roof to safe ground.

'Come,' her father beckons.

Wagadhaany looks to the Bradleys, confirming it is all right for her to go first. Neither challenge her. As Yarri holds on with one hand to the same tree that David and James are clinging to, he reaches out to his daughter with the other. His legs are forced to grip the canoe as best they can. David has to forcefully unwrap Wagadhaany's arm from his. Her fear of slipping away is strong, but after some coaxing she reluctantly lets go of him, squealing like a young girl as she does.

'It's all right,' her father says gently. 'I've taken many like this already, we can do it.'

David holds tight to Wagadhaany's forearm and slides her off the roof and into the barely balanced canoe.

'Mandaang guwu,' she whispers into the night, thankful to him for keeping her safe, keeping her alive till now.

'I'll come back,' Yarri says to the men. 'Soon. I'll be back.'

Wagadhaany sits in the front, gripping both sides of the canoe as her father steers as best he can to the nearest bank. She is thinking only of how her arms ache from clutching on to life for what seems like forever. She doesn't turn to look at her father, for fear of losing her balance. Facing forward, she waits only for the sight of land.

As the shoreline approaches, her heartbeat slows and she weeps with relief. Safety is only a few feet away. Her father gets out of the canoe and drags it up the bank, while Wagadhaany still holds on tightly.

Once on shore, Yarri hugs her so tightly she is almost breathless. For the first time since she and the Bradleys climbed into the attic, she feels some warmth in her body. It soon dissipates as they walk to the place where all the townspeople are gathering. Yarri leaves his daughter there, saying he will go back for the Bradleys.

In the hall there are murmurs of acts of heroism and stories of those who have lost their loved ones. Even in her exhausted state, Wagadhaany can't help but assist a mother with young children; they remind her of the gudha-galang at camp. They are all crying. She learns that their father is missing, and he is only one of many. This is sorry business like she has never seen; so much grief, so much weeping, so much chaos.

She does not know how much time has passed when she sees David Bradley again. *He's been saved!* He looks to her, his eyes dark with sadness, and she thinks there is an attempt at some warmth in a slight upturn of his mouth. She knows then that her father has saved him. She watches as David walks directly to the local publican, Mr Sheahan. She's overheard that Mr Sheahan has been helping to move people from the Sir George Tavern, where more than thirty townsfolk were safe until the floodwaters began to rise. The tavern was destroyed, valuable goods and personal belongings lost, but all of the people were saved. She learns that some were rescued by the man known as Long Jimmy from their camp, and she feels pride rise within her.

'He is a brave man,' the woman says through tears.

Wagadhaany thinks she is talking about Long Jimmy but soon realises she is not.

'Mr Sheahan has made five perilous trips out in his boat to get people here to safety. But my husband, he is still out there somewhere.' She breaks down, weeping again. Her children are asleep on the ground, exhausted and oblivious to how different their lives will be when they wake up.

She watches in silence as townsfolk lament lost family, missing friends and respected community members confirmed dead. It's a small town and everyone who lives here knows everyone else, and no-one is unaffected by these deaths.

Concern for her father, her uncles, for everyone out in the miilgi waiting to be rescued or trying to rescue, overwhelms Wagadhaany, but she takes comfort being the only Wiradyuri person in the hall. She sees this as a positive sign, that no-one in the camp needed rescuing.

This is the first time Wagadhaany has been in a place with so many White people. Today, though, she seems to be the only one noticing her difference. Everyone else is consumed by their own misery. A desperate feeling of sorrow engulfs Wagadhaany when she sees James and David Bradley hugging in a corner. She watches the rise and fall of the men's shoulders, the emotion gripping them, their tears. She doesn't try to imagine, nor does she want to, what it might be like to lose your parents and brothers. The Bradleys are distraught, and the overflow of their grief falls to her by default of being their servant, by having been there with them in the final moments of their parents' and brothers' lives. The ordeal has made her wonder if she too was part of their family. They kept her alive even when they couldn't keep their parents and siblings safe. She feels a pang of guilt at the thought. *But what else could they have done?* They couldn't simply have left her in the house, which flooded as soon as they reached the attic.

She is confused, exhausted, disoriented. She shakes her head to dispel the mayhem in her mind.

When she sees her father arrive back at the hall, he is helping another man to a seat. Once he has positioned the man, her father walks directly over to her.

'Is that Mr Tester?' she asks.

Her father nods.

'Can't find his family. Maybe they are here.'

They both look around the hall, searching until they hear a man moan as if punched in the stomach. The hall quietens immediately.

'Mr Lynham,' someone whispers loudly nearby. 'His family has been swept away.'

Wagadhaany immediately pushes herself into her father's chest, sobbing. 'How many people have been swept away, Babiin, how many?'

He holds her the closest she remembers ever being held.

'They say between eighty and a hundred people are gone, the bila took them.'

That is a large number of the town's population and she shudders with the thought of so many floating to their deaths like the Bradleys.

'Stay here,' he tells her. 'Until the rain stops, there is no way home.'

Wagadhaany does as her father says, sitting quietly, watching as people continue to enter the hall, to cry, to hug, to grieve. Only when the announcement is made that the floodwaters are draining out of the town does she make her way back to her miyagan, her father close by her side.

Chapter Four

The sun is high in the sky but the air is crisp. The campfire has been burning overnight and Yarri, Jacky Jacky, Long Jimmy and Tommy Davis have gathered together to share painful stories of the days just gone by. They have not returned to the flood plain. It will be days before they can do that again. Rather, they sit on higher ground with tins of hot black tea in their hands. The women sit beside them and the gudha-galang are restless at the adults' feet. Wagadhaany and her mother sit with arms entwined, having not left each other's side since Wagadhaany returned home. Eventually she knows they will go back to the riverbank and build new ganya-galang, but for now they reflect solemnly on all that has happened.

Only Wagadhaany and the men know the full extent of what has transpired for the townspeople of Gundagai over the past few days. The devastation of the raging river ripping families apart, tearing humans from buildings and trees and homes and businesses from their foundations, will be torturing her father and uncles as well. That knowledge, the recurring images in her mind, and the memories of the desperate screams of men, women and children in the dark of night have created knots in her stomach, and although the men do not voice it, she has no doubt they feel the same way. It may have been townsfolk who died, but the loss of any life is always felt by all in the camp, because grief is a shared human experience.

'So many gone,' Yarri tells the group. 'So many lives.' He shakes his head, rests it in his hands.

Jacky Jacky looks to Yarri with sympathy. 'Gudha-galang, women, animals, so many gone, just washed away.'

'That bila will always be stronger than man, so we must show yindyamarra always,' Long Jimmy says as he looks towards the river.

The entire group hang their heads in sadness and out of respect. Wagadhaany has tears rolling down her face as she thinks of Elizabeth and Henry Bradley and their two sons, now confirmed dead.

'I tried,' Yarri adds. 'I tried to get one young migay. She was tied to a tree with a belt. But too many branches in the way. I tried to get her.' He sighs deeply. 'But she panicked. And then she screamed, she let go of the tree, waving her arms around. And . . .'

He inhales deeply through his nose, then breathes out heavily through his mouth. The kids giggle at the breath they can see due to the cold morning air.

'She waved her arms around and the belt broke. It just broke, just like that. And she fell into the water. I couldn't save her. Water was too fast. She was gone, just like that.' He waves his hand from left to right in a fast sweeping action. 'I didn't save her. I *couldn't* save her.'

He rests his head in his hands again as Wagadhaany rubs his back. Two of the children push in front of her and start rubbing Yarri's back too.

'Look!' an energetic gudha says. 'Gabaa-galang come visit.'

All the children spin in excitement and the expectation of seeing White strangers in their camp. Some jump to their feet. The little ones curl under their mothers' legs. Wagadhaany observes as the older boys look to the men to see what action they will take and if they should follow.

'It's the Mister Bradleys,' Yarri says.

He stands slowly, his body still aching from the long days and nights fighting against the river. Wagadhaany thinks the Bradleys look even more drawn and unkempt since the night in the hall.

They both nod in acknowledgement at the group gathered around the fire. Yarri shakes the possum skin from his shoulders and walks to the men. Jacky Jacky follows him and stands behind. They hold their hands out in an unusual greeting between White and Black men.

'Mister Bradley,' Yarri says to each one, and he hesitates before extending his hand to meet theirs, an unfamiliar courtesy. He nods his head in an added show of respect.

'We are sorry,' he adds, turning to his family, acknowledging that they too feel the Bradleys' pain. 'About your family.'

The brothers nod in response. 'Thank you,' James says automatically. 'We were told we could find you here.'

He looks around the camp with hollow eyes and Wagadhaany wonders what he might be thinking. She has never seen the Bradleys so raw with emotion. They look to Wagadhaany and the others and attempt to smile with gratitude. She smiles back as best she can.

'I'll be back to the station, boss,' Yarri says quickly.

Wagadhaany wishes he wouldn't assume he has to go straight back to work. After all, he saved their lives.

'It's all right,' David says, placing a hand on Yarri's shoulder, another rare act of kindness. 'The other men are taking care of things. We know you must be tired. We won't expect you for a few more days. But we do need you back to take charge again.'

Yarri nods.

Wagadhaany is grateful to David Bradley and his gentleness towards her father, her hero, *their* hero.

'For your family.' David hands a wheat bag to Wagadhaany, looking at her only briefly with dark eyes. 'Just a few oranges from our trees. Everything else has been stripped bare.'

Yarri opens the bag and takes the oranges, then turns around to hand them to the group of kids waiting to accept whatever is in the wheat bag that once held sand. The kids don't know or care what's in the bag. A gift is a gift and they are excited about this one from these gabaa-galang.

'We need Wagadhaany,' David says, turning to look at her then back to Yarri. 'We can't manage the house without her. Without Mother.' He chokes back emotion. 'We need her to help us get the house back in order, please.'

'You saved my daughter's life, you kept her alive, of course she will help you.'

Yarri turns to Wagadhaany. The gratitude she hears in her father's voice is heartbreaking, but she desperately wants to scream out, *But you saved their lives too, Babiin. They should be grateful. YOU are the real hero.*

The sound of mud squelching beneath her feet annoys Waga-dhaany, but the annoyance disappears as her thoughts are drawn to what she sees in front of her, or what she doesn't see. The town has almost disappeared. The buildings, the shops, everything gone. It's no longer a town but a shell. The bare foundations of some stores remain, but the main street is soulless.

She looks at the place where the school used to be. Nothing is left but the bell tower and a large rose bush growing against its wall. Everything else has been uprooted, turned on its side or washed away.

On the footpath filthy with upturned dirt and rubbish she finds a broken doll, naked, caught in between some rocks. The force of the water has ripped the clothes from its porcelain body and cracked its face. She pulls the doll to her chest as emotion rises in her throat. *Where is the little girl this belongs to?*

People are walking sluggishly through town, carrying what is left of their belongings in their hands. No cases, no bags, just the clothes on their backs and some food salvaged from pantries and ice boxes.

There are only three houses left complete; one of them is the Bradleys'. They are lucky theirs is stone slab as the brutal weather has destroyed most of the shops, the school and church, all built from timber and now lost to the flood.

She pauses out the front. Some wooden floorboards are propped against the wall to catch the first sunlight of the day, needing to be dried out. Around the side of the house is Mrs Bradley's vegetable garden, completely ruined. A single potato lies in the mud.

Wagadhaany is overwhelmed by the thought of walking into a home where only two family members have survived. The rotting smell becomes too much for her, and she collapses to her knees, overcome by the sudden realisation of what has happened and how everything has changed for so many. Weeping in the street, anywhere public, is normal in Gundagai now. There is no shame in the emotions sweeping over the townsfolk, so she cries until her tears dry up. She wipes her face on her apron, presses her hands down the front of her flood-damaged calico dress, and shakes the sorrow from her head as best she can. There is noise coming from the house and although she has no idea what time it is she knows the Bradleys will be waiting for her.

The door is ajar, for no other reason than it can't be closed properly. The flood has expanded the timber and it no longer fits the frame. When Wagadhaany gently pushes it open she sees the brothers tearing up the floorboards. No words are spoken, the only sound is the pulling of nails. She watches silently, waiting for the right moment to declare she is there, back to work. She scans the room, which is full of light as the curtains are down and the windows that aren't broken are wide open. A strong, chilly breeze is passing through. As David lifts one of the damaged boards upright he sees her standing in the doorway. There is sadness but also relief on his face, almost as if he is glad to see her.

'Hello,' he says with what seems a forced half-smile.

It's the first true smile he has ever shown her, so she responds with a warm smile in return. The devastation of the great flood has left huge scars on these two men. She knows that life in the house will never be the same. But she is grateful, and assumes he is too, that they are both alive.

'You're here, Wilma, good.' James is cold, direct. The flood has not changed his demeanor towards her at all. If anything, he is more cranky, more bossy.

'Look in the linen cupboard. The door stayed shut during the flooding, so the linen might well be salvageable. If so, wash it. The walls need to be scrubbed too. Then see what we can salvage in the kitchen. We've gathered what we could find in the garden and street. Everything needs to be boiled before the rot sets in.'

'But . . .' Wagadhaany begins, knowing there will be no dry wood to light a fire to boil any water.

She doesn't want to argue or get in trouble though. And even after everything they have been through, the fact that he still calls her Wilma and not her proper name upsets her. She takes a deep breath, closes her eyes and imagines what her mother would say and think right now. She can hear her voice. *Be loving, they have just lost their parents, their miyagan.*

'And the clothes, they can be burned,' James orders, interrupting her thoughts.

He keeps listing the chores he has for her. He is talking fast, as if it is a race to finish what he is saying. 'And Mother's chair . . .' He points to the upholstered chair Mrs Bradley had been sitting in the night she died. He moves to upturn it. 'I want this cleaned up properly, like it was before . . .' He pauses, swallows hard.

'And you should try and rebuild Mother's vegetable garden. Yes, she would want that,' he adds, looking around the room as if to seek out more chores for her. 'We will need to be growing our own food immediately, as supplies will be low.'

Wagadhaany is dumbfounded that he expects so much of one person.

Be loving, they have just lost their parents, their miyagan.

David walks up behind his brother, takes the hammer from his hand and steers James to the yet-to-be-cleaned chair.

'Not everything has to be done today, James, or this week.'

48

David looks at Wagadhaany. She is trying to focus on caring thoughts, but she knows her face tells a story of distress and concern. She is unsure of how to behave as a servant girl now that the woman of the house is no longer there and the man newly in charge is grief-stricken and not coping, full of orders, and *still* can't say her name properly.

'We don't have any dry wood yet to make a fire to boil water or sterilise or clean anything,' David says, to Wagadhaany's relief. 'I will work on that, and Wagadhaany will sort through the linen press.'

She realises this is the first time that David Bradley has referred to her by her proper name.

'The clothes . . .' James blurts out. 'Anyone's clothes you find, burn those too, when you get some dry wood. Burn them!'

James is determined and angry, but David closes his eyes and bites his lip. Wagadhaany isn't sure what he is thinking but she believes the clothes should go to those families in town who've lost everything. Even her own mob could use some of the shoes and warm jackets the Bradleys used to wear. But she says nothing, because while everything has changed for the townsfolk, she feels like absolutely nothing has changed for her. And though she is trying to be understanding through their grief, she resents still being spoken to as the servant, the cleaner, the cook. She hates being the Black woman who just has to do what the White people tell her. She is grateful to be alive, but she hates that being alive reminds her that she is still powerless in her own life.

David looks at Wagadhaany, points his chin to the door and, taking her gently by the elbow, walks her to the kitchen. She is suddenly reminded of how her arm ached the night of the flood.

'There is no rush, but we do need to get all those tasks completed.' He nods, and Wagadhaany nods back in agreement. 'James is suffering. We are both suffering. And the clothes, do not burn them. We will give them to the townsfolk in need.'

He pauses and places a hand on her arm. She feels awkward about this show of intimacy that has never happened before and it makes her uneasy. There are no raging floodwaters now, and he has touched her twice already today. Her thoughts are broken when he speaks again. 'If you could clean our rooms first, please, we will work in here.'

By 'our rooms' she knows he means his and James's rooms. Her room, a square, dark cell off the kitchen, can wait.

In the weeks that follow Wagadhaany works harder than she has ever had to. Even though there are only two Bradleys to cook for when a fire can finally be made, the physical exertion required to get their home back to some semblance of its past condition takes its toll. The beating of rugs leaves her arms aching. The scrubbing of walls for days on end makes her back burn. The many trips she makes to the site set up to assist townsfolk impacted by the flood, where she takes some of the Bradleys' clothes that have escaped water damage, leave her legs tired. And her head throbs constantly. There is less than usual to eat, and her sleepless nights are riddled with nightmares.

As she walks through the town each day fulfilling any and every errand that James Bradley gives her, Wagadhaany notices the changes. Slowly the streets are being repaired and rebuilt. The grief and sadness of locals has shifted to blaming officials for allowing the town to be flooded, for not being better prepared. People are reliving the history of previous floods and talking about how it should not have happened again. She feels like a witness without a voice. She was there, she lived through the horror of the flood, the fear, the physical exhaustion, the loss of those she knew. But no-one asks how she is, what she thinks or knows, or how she feels. It is only when she hears the Bradley brothers speak to each other that she learns the real news of what is happening in town, and she takes what is relevant back to the camp any chance she gets. The latest news is that the townsfolk are going to petition the government to swap their land for lots on higher ground, but there is no mention of what will happen to her family's camp.

David and James sit in the living room reading a newspaper from Sydney. It's been just over two weeks since the flood, since the entire Bradley family sat in the same room, waiting for the rest of their lives to be determined, not knowing they'd be changed forever. It has been a week since the bodies of their parents and brothers were found and they had to identify each one over the course of a few days. Wagadhaany has been preparing nightly meals that are hardly touched. She's watched James Bradley drink a lot of whisky. Through the brothers, she has seen the ways some White people deal with sorry business. She recognises the same human emotions of sadness and grief in the two men that she has seen in the men of her miyagan during times of death and loss.

'Settlers have lost all their wheat, and nearly all the town's horses were swept away. Seventy-eight townsfolk have been interred at Gundagai, and there are more bodies than that – there would have been travelling miners in town at the time, on their way to the goldfields.'

David reads snippets to James in a monotone, and Wagadhaany listens in with interest. The newspapers are the only way to get information about what has happened and what might be planned for the future.

'The news reports can't even tell us how many,' James says. 'I've heard that the body count they are telling us can't possibly be correct. Some say eighty-nine drowned. There are probably many more than that.'

'Shhh,' David urges his brother, as he continues to read.

'There will be special services held in Sydney for the relief of those suffering in the country.'

'What good will that do? It won't bring anyone back,' James says angrily.

'No, but it will bring *some* peace to *some* people, James. I am going to the service in town tomorrow. You will come. We will pay our respects to Mother and Father, and our brothers. We will do this together, and we will behave in the manner the Bradleys always have, with dignity.'

'Why?' James asks. 'What does it matter now?'

'Our parents worked hard to give us the life we live, the one we all had together. They moved here to build a legacy, our station is that legacy. And that is why we will always stay here, no matter what happens.' He looks to his brother for a response, but there is none. 'And our mother was well respected by the other women in the church community. She would expect us to be there, and you know it.'

James mumbles something incoherent.

'And you will go, do you hear me?'

James looks at his brother with defeat on his face then turns his gaze towards a dirty window. Wagadhaany expects him to shout and order her to clean it, but he doesn't.

The next day is overcast as the men walk with purpose towards the makeshift church with Wagadhaany in tow. She was surprised that so many of the clothes survived inside closed cupboard doors, even if they were covered in mud. She has cleaned their suits as best she could because although she has never been to church she has been told you must look your best and be respectful in the house of the Lord. Though the original building is no longer there, she knows the Bradleys' holy space is sacred, just like Wiradyuri ceremonial spaces. She is glad to have been invited, but feels strange wearing Mrs Bradley's leather gloves and hat, and the olive green, woollen dress is too big for her slight frame.

'I'm glad you chose something from Mother's wardrobe, she would want that, and it looks good on you.'

Wagadhaany is not sure the late Mrs Bradley's clothes look good on her, or if it is appropriate for David to comment on her appearance, but she feels warm – so very warm – in the woollen dress. She has never worn anything like it and she wonders what her family would think if they could see her now.

The townsfolk have acted differently towards Wagadhaany since the flood. Many know that it was her father and uncles who saved the lives of their family and friends, so today they nod to her in acknowledgement, and they look at the Bradley brothers with compassion. Wagadhaany wonders where the other Aboriginal servants are. Maybe they are still cleaning up, or maybe they don't have houses to clean any more.

At the service the foreign smell of incense invades Wagadhaany's nostrils and she sneezes constantly. She wonders if this is like the cleansing smoke of the gum leaves she is more used to. She is embarrassed and hopes she's not annoying anyone. She dares not leave her seat, though, for fear of drawing attention to herself and the clothes she is in.

The priest is a short, bald, round man with pale skin and rosy cheeks. He speaks with a very a thick accent and Wagadhaany has to listen closely to understand every word. She hopes to learn something about the religion and the God that she has heard so much about at the Bradley house. She looks around. While people appear tired and sad, they are holding onto their Bibles and prayer beads just like Mrs Bradley was doing the night she passed. She wonders why White people have to get dressed up and go to church to worship and pray if, as they say, God is everywhere. She always speaks to Biyaami late at night before she goes to sleep.

Wagadhaany is tired from all the standing up and sitting down over and over again, and is grateful when the priest instructs them to sit again. She crosses her legs like the other young women as the priest continues.

'A reading from Ecclesiastes chapter seven verses one to thirteen.

A good name is better than precious ointment,
and the day of death than the day of birth.
It is better to go to the house of mourning
than to go to the house of feasting,
for this is the end of all mankind,
and the living will lay it to heart.
Sorrow is better than laughter,
for by sadness of face the heart is made glad.
The heart of the wise is in the house of mourning,
but the heart of fools is in the house of mirth.'

The priest's words confuse her. *How can it be better to go to a house that's mourning than one that is feasting on wambuwuny or fish or damper? And how can sorrow be better than laughter?* She is sure this priest is telling this story wrong.

Wagadhaany slowly looks around to see if she is the only one who thinks the priest is crazy. That maybe he is reading the words backwards. But everyone else has their head bowed, including the Bradleys. So she turns to face the front again and listens to see if he makes any more mistakes or any sense.

'*Better is the end of a thing than its beginning . . .*'

No, he has not changed his line of thinking! Is he saying that death is better than birth? This can't be the case, because people are joyful when a baby is born, and right now the entire town is grieving because of the end of so many lives. Wagadhaany misses the next line because her mind is all twisted around beginnings and endings, but she hears a few lines later.

'*Consider the work of God: who can make straight what he has made crooked?*'

If the work of the flood was the crooked work of God – and Wagadhaany isn't sure it was, though the rain did fall from the sky, and that's where she's heard God in heaven is – then the Whiteman's God has a lot to answer for.

When the service ends and they are walking back to the house, Wagadhaany fidgets with her clothes and is surprised when David says to James, 'I feel like I got some answers today.'

Wagadhaany's eyes dart to James, wondering if he feels the same. Is she the only one who found the priest confusing?

Chapter Five

'*The scenes ... are truly distressing. At every step you see someone lamenting the dead. Here and there the sorrowing remains, of what three days before was a large and thriving family.*'

James Bradley is reading aloud from *The Sydney Morning Herald*, which has already been in the hands of a number of people in town. For the last few weeks, most people have focused on their own sense of loss, but slowly the locals are completing a picture of what happened. With no local newspaper, any news reports they receive are from the outside, and many feel they are not getting the whole truth or the full details of the flood. Sometimes word of mouth is not enough to placate the anger so many feel at being so unprepared. Stories in *The Goulburn Herald and County of Argyle Advertiser* and newspapers from Sydney only worsen their pain, serving to justify their outrage at the authorities. As the townsfolk understand more clearly what happened in Gundagai, everyone is looking to ensure that those who are to blame are found accountable.

'It's the government's fault,' James says. 'No-one should have been allowed to build on the river flats. Their bloody short-sightedness caused all this death.'

He collapses into one of the leather chairs that have been salvaged and weeps, not knowing that Wagadhaany stands in the doorway, waiting for directions about her chores for the day. Mrs Bradley had always been the one to administer her tasks, and since her passing there has been little structure in her days.

David walks behind his brother and lays a gentle hand on his shoulder. She knows they only have each other now, and the toll of losing their parents and brothers has left them not only full of rage but also without much direction.

'So many dead, and those who didn't die have their lives in ruin. We're just lucky that most of our livestock survived thanks to the drovers moving them from the river, and that this house withstood the flood. The river was trying its darnedest to tear it down. Imagine, only three buildings in town left standing and our home was one of them. God was looking over us, no doubt,' David says quietly.

'I guess you are right, but still . . .' James pauses and exhales deeply.

For Wagadhaany, the house has become one of deep sighs and tears. She has witnessed emotions she has never seen before in the men – in any man.

'We could be in a bark hut like most of the other towns-people,' David adds, 'but at least we are here, in our home, warm of a night. And for that we should be grateful.' He looks to the fireplace, which has been stocked with wood, and he appears to be watching the dancing flames. 'I feel guilty that we still have a roof over our heads.'

James stares at the ground, motionless.

'Many are carrying their water in buckets from the river. That water is not even safe.' David shakes his head, looks to his brother for a response. But there is nothing.

David's words force Wagadhaany to think of her own family. Not for one moment has David thought about how the local Wiradyuri people live and will continue to live after this flood, with none of the luxuries that the Bradleys rely on. Neither brother realises that what the White people in town are experiencing right now, and what they consider as hardship, has been the life of Wiradyuri people forever. Living off the land with little shelter is all they have ever known. Managing the elements is difficult in the cold months, but the land and their knowledge of how to use it has provided them with the tools for survival and the sustenance to live well. Her babiin has told her that Wiradyuri people have prospered and lived in harmony with the bila for many, many, many years.

David runs a grey handkerchief over his face and clears his throat. 'Did you hear about the Marshall children?'

'No, what happened to *them*?' James finally looks up at his brother, his tone suggesting he expects he is about to hear another tragic story of loss.

'The boy dipped his bucket into the water and was scared to near death by a big black water animal. Apparently it had wild, glaring eyes and rose out of the water like some kind of monster.' David tells the story with a trace of animation in his voice.

James scoffs. 'How ridiculous! That just sounds like kids making up stories. Though I guess you cannot blame them, the flood has made us all a little crazy.'

David shakes his head in disagreement. 'I believe it to be absolutely true, James. I'm told there was a bellowing sound that scared the children – and I daresay many of the adults – and it was heard by locals a distance away, so . . .' He looks for some acceptance of this account from his brother. 'What would be the purpose in making up such a story right now, with so much real-life tragedy for people to deal with?'

'If it's true, and I am not saying I am convinced, then what the hell did the floodwaters bring?' James asks, with a look of concern on his face.

'The waawii!' Wagadhaany says out loud, neither thinking nor realising that both men can hear her.

They turn in her direction.

'What's that?' James asks bluntly, noticing for the first time she is nearby. 'What did you say, Wilma?'

'Nothing, Mr Bradley,' she responds nervously, not moving from the doorway, as she has not been given permission to enter the room and she would never enter any room without a specific request or order. 'I . . . um . . . I have cleaned the breakfast dishes. What would you like me to do next?'

'Today we are going into town for a special ceremony for the heroes of the rescue. You will come with us,' David orders.

'Yes, sir.'

Her mind is full of questions again. She has never been to a ceremony other than ones by the river, corroborees, when there is mayilgan and yinaa-galang business. She hopes this is a happy gathering, but mostly she hopes to see her parents again. It is the end of the working week and maybe the Bradleys will let her go back to the camp with them earlier, so she doesn't have to wait until Sunday. She is not brave enough to ask, even though she misses her family more than ever, especially being in a house with only men, and a lot of grief and anger.

When the brothers stand and move towards the doorway, she rushes to get out of the way to let them pass.

The three of them walk into town, Wagadhaany a few feet behind the men who take quick, purposeful steps. There is a large crowd gathered near where the hotel once stood. It is as if everyone left in the town has turned up. She is sure this is going to be a happy ceremony.

As they get closer, Wagadhaany's heart beats faster as she sees her gunhi and much of her miyagan. She looks at David, the more approachable of the two brothers, for permission to stand with her family. He nods his approval and she runs to be at their side. Her gunhi hugs her tightly and they huddle with their miyagan in the cold, separate from the White townspeople. Regardless of the heroic acts of the Wiradyuri men during the flood, it has always been a given they are not part of Gundagai town. They are fringe-dwellers on their own land. Wagadhaany looks around the crowd, the Black people and Whites standing some distance away from each other, and understands that even today, as they celebrate the heroes who saved many White lives, the local Wiradyuri people are still valued much less, if they are truly valued at all.

Both Jacky Jacky and Yarri stand in front of the crowd in old suit jackets that Wagadhaany imagines are borrowed, their long dusty pants held up by pieces of rope. Wagadhaany is full of pride in the men. She wonders where Long Jimmy and Tommy Davis are, and looks around to see if they are up the back of the crowd. They were so brave and strong, caring for others during the flood when they could have died themselves. She is reminded of her own safety, and she looks to her father with a heart full of love and gratitude. He was her hero before the flood. Now he is everyone's hero too.

The town hasn't got much to smile about, but she is grinning because this day is a celebration, and there is excitement in the air. She reaches down to a toddler at her ankles and picks up her baby niece, Yullara, sitting her on her hip. She rocks her from side to side. She plays with the child's ears and giggles, knowing her name means long-eared bandicoot. Wagadhaany hopes the other cousins don't pull the little one's ears to make them any longer. She stops rocking and giggling as soon as the speeches begin.

Jacky Jacky and her babiin smile widely as they stand next to a smartly dressed official in a dark suit and hat. In a very deep, loud voice the official announces, 'It is with honour that I present Yarri and Jacky Jacky with brass breastplates for their bravery during the flood. We appreciate your courage and we are grateful.' He says that Jacky Jacky saved nineteen lives and her father saved forty-nine more and the crowd applaud with gratitude.

Wagadhaany doesn't know who the man speaking is but he presents a breastplate to Jacky Jacky first, placing the chain over the man's head. The breastplate rests high on his bony chest, which he is proudly pushing out as much as possible. The crowd moves in close to see what is etched on the metal plate and Jacky Jacky proudly shows them. One at a time they slowly approach and consider the drawing of the flood at the top of the plate, with a man perched high up in a tree above the swirling waters. Below is an image of a man in a bark canoe rowing towards the stranded man. It is Jacky Jacky, but she knows it is her father, Long Jimmy and Tommy Davis also, because they were out there, somewhere, in the dark of night too.

She wonders if the White people understand that most Wiradyuri men know how to work with the river and the land, even in times of flood. That the Marrambidya is not something to be afraid of. Rather, the bila is to be respected and relied upon for food, for transport, for life. That the men have been brave *and* smart.

When they repeat the presentation to her father, Wagadhaany is bursting with pride.

It takes Wagadhaany a long time to get to sleep that night. She wonders why, if the town is so proud of and thankful to Jacky Jacky and Yarri, they don't they give them and the people on the river some more blankets and food. The breastplates will not keep them warm from the frost that continues to settle in each night and early morning. They have possum-skin cloaks, of course, but they could have more blankets too, and shoes, and maybe even some extra food for the times that hunting does not always bring enough for the entire camp. The Bradleys think furniture and sheets and warm coats are important; maybe they could offer the heroes and their families some of those things as thanks.

When she finally dozes off, she tosses and turns in her bed, crying in her sleep. Her mind is riddled with nightmares; reliving the horrifying scenes of the flood, the screams of women and children, the sounds of branches breaking and buildings crumbling, horses being swept away never to be ridden or groomed again. She relives the moment she saw her father and the fear in his eyes when she was trying to get onto his canoe. The risks he took to get her, the Bradleys and many other townspeople to safety.

She wakes in the dark of night and there is complete silence. No wind, no rain, no movement in the Bradley house. Her eyes are open, but with no windows in her sleeping quarters there is nothing to be seen, just blackness. So, she slowly allows her eyelids to close and chooses to think about happy moments in time; about her childhood, her family living back on the river-bank where it is safe. She imagines the children cuddling up close and tight in the ganya-galang, like she used to do with her cousins. She pictures everyone enjoying the shared food they hunt for themselves. She can see them all sitting around the fire telling stories and she desperately wishes she could be there too. Finally, she thinks about the absolute selflessness and courage of her father on the night of the flood, and it is the pride she has in him that soothes her. She knows that material things like blankets will keep most people warm, but it's the love of her miyagan that will always keep her alive.

'Wogga, wogga, doinarn!'

James Bradley is yelling something that vaguely sounds like her name. He has never said it properly, or in full, or even really tried to, and this morning's attempted struggle with the pronunciation is embarrassing for both of them. She can't determine his tone but fears she is in trouble. In a rush to get dressed and into the kitchen as fast as possible she falls off the bed. She imagines she must have slept in, which has never happened before either.

It will be a morning of firsts if that is the case. She hasn't even got time to think what will greet her outside the door.

She pulls on her calico tunic, runs her fingers through her hair and opens the door onto the kitchen.

She steps through, closes the door behind her and stands to attention. Immediately she notices that the fire is already lit and a pot of water is boiling on the stove. Both Bradley brothers are seated at the table, and look like they have been there for some time. Maybe they found it difficult to sleep last night too.

'Yes sir?' she says sheepishly.

James looks to Wagadhaany, points with his head in the direction of his brother. David has a newspaper in his hands. She thinks he is attempting to smile but she cannot gauge the expression on his face so just stands there. Between James's attempt at pronouncing her name and David's smile, she feels awkward for the three of them.

'There is something in the newspaper about the flood and your father. I thought you might like to know about it.' David says. 'I'll read it to you.'

So, she isn't in trouble. She grins in response, as relief rushes through her. 'Ngawa, dharraay,' she says, nodding.

Both brothers frown. She had been told in her early days with the Bradleys that she was not to speak her traditional language in the house, or anywhere for that matter.

'Yes,' she says quickly and enthusiastically. 'Yes please, Mr Bradley.'

David turns to the front page of the paper. 'This was published on 28 August, so that's five days ago. It's *The Goulburn Herald*. A man by the name of James Riley wrote a poem titled "The Gundagai Calamity". I'll read you the fifth verse only as I think it says the most.' He flicks to a page inside and speaks almost as if he's giving a sermon:

'*Again, Australia's sable son,*
With vigour ply their frail canoe;
Right well hast thou already done
But much, O much, is still to do.'

Wagadhaany's grin grows wider. Her father is in the newspaper! She thinks this is wonderful and can't wait to tell all the family, because she is sure they will not know about it. She listens to the poetry, to the words, but because she is so excited, she doesn't hear exactly what David is saying, or understand it. To her ears, the English language seems much more complicated than Wiradyuri.

'Here,' he says, when he has finished, handing her the paper. 'It says your father saved forty-nine lives in the flood. That includes ours. Take this to your family.'

She reaches for the newspaper with the enthusiasm of a child receiving a sweet from the local shopkeeper. Even though no-one at the camp can read, it doesn't matter. They too will be eager to hear about the mention of her father's bravery in the big flood. When David hands the paper over, he rests his hand on top of hers for a second, and she retreats quietly.

Later that day, when her tasks are completed, Wagadhaany walks quickly through town and down to the river. She is overwhelmed with pride and excitement about sharing the story with everyone there. She can't wait to hold up the paper. However, as she approaches, she realises that a ceremony is being prepared. She can see the cleansing smoke and people walking through it. Because she lives with the Bradleys, she is often late to receive news. Immediately she panics and starts searching for her gunhi, babiin, balgabalgar-galang, anyone who can tell her what is going on.

She sees her gunhi sitting in a circle with the other women, all the children scattered between them and around them. When it is clear to Wagadhaany that everyone is in mourning she starts running. Someone has passed, but she has no idea who. She feels nauseous and frightened. Is it one of her gumbal-galang or wunaagany-galang, her babiin? *Who is it?* She looks around desperately to see who is missing from their camp. Her head is spinning, trying to work it out. Her gunhi rises from the ground, shoulders hunched over. She looks tired, helpless. When Wagadhaany reaches her they hold each other tight and tears fall freely for the lost one, and because they cannot always be together as a family, even during times like these.

'What happened?' she whispers in her mother's ear as they hug.

But her mother cannot speak. She is inconsolable. Within seconds Yarri appears and his daughter turns and asks him the same question. 'What happened, Babiin?'

'The weather, too cold and too wet for Long Jimmy. The medicine we needed was on land Whites are building on, we dared not go there, we are not welcome there. We couldn't help him. And now he is gone.'

Wagadhaany can feel the weight of pain and anger in her father's voice. She can feel it in his hug as he pulls her close to his heart, which is racing. She starts to cry. She doesn't know if anyone in town offered to help Long Jimmy, and she knows that asking will not bring him back. But she wonders if a White person would die from the cold and wet, like he has. And how many more Wiradyuri will die from not being able to get medicine from their own land.

That day she dances with her gunhi, with her bamali-galang, and she mourns for the hero who passed too soon.

Three months pass and as the weather changes, the town shows signs of rebirth and rejuvenation. The colours of the landscape are no longer those of dull winter grasses covered in frost but of lush greens and vibrant spring florals. When summer finally sets in, the heat sees Wagadhaany's family fishing and enjoying river life on the long, warm days. But the one thing that hasn't changed is the memory of losing Long Jimmy. It is accepted now that it was his exposure to the bitter winter weather that killed him. Wagadhaany's anger has bubbled inside her since, knowing that it was the Great Flood that eventually took his life. A heroic man who was out saving the lives of White people in a country where White people did not value his Wiradyuri life at all.

Although she is back in her usual role with the Bradleys, cooking, cleaning, doing any job she is required to do, she is still without a daily plan. As she goes from task to task, increasingly she thinks about the value of her own life, in the eyes of these two men. She doesn't see any pay, and though she doesn't know why, she does know that it has always been this way. For her father too. He only ever got rations, clothing and on the rare occasion some coins that he would use for extra food for his miyagan.

At no point have the Bradley men said anything to her about Long Jimmy. She wonders if they know of his passing, and if they would even care if they did. She has become increasingly aware that the White people live very separate lives to each other, and even the simple sharing of food among families is not common. They look after themselves first. Wagadhaany works in one world, while trying to live according to the values of the Wiradyuri world where she belongs, where everyone is accountable to other people, and where she'd rather be.

As the days and weeks pass, she notices that the conversations in the house shift from what is happening on their station – the cattle, the sheep, the staff, the impact of the flood – to talk about moving to Wagga Wagga. She knows that Wagga Wagga means the place of dancing and celebration, and that her parents named her Wagadhaany because it means dancer. Maybe her kinship ties go as far as this new place, wherever it is. Whatever the connection, she is excited and feels a warmth in her heart as she imagines what her life might be like after the Bradleys leave Gundagai for the place of celebration, and she can go back to living with her family again.

Chapter Six

'It's time to leave Gundagai,' James says without emotion, refusing to face his brother.

The December sunlight is streaming through the window and six months after the flood there are still reminders all around them of the dreadful night when they lost both their parents and their brothers. The cracked walls and water stains are insignificant in comparison to the emotional scars they bear.

'But the government has only just agreed to exchange all the allotments at risk of flooding for land on higher ground. It's a good offer. People in town are happy with that progress.' David sounds positive. 'Though I don't think we'll ever flood again . . .'

'Happy? People *aren't* happy!' James is angry and yelling, his temper shorter than it has ever been. 'And it's too little too late, for too many people.' He walks to the mantelpiece and pours a whisky into one of the few glasses that survived the flood. 'Mark my words, it *will* happen again.' He paces the room.

'Have no doubt, it *will* flood again, *and* again *and* again.' He looks David square in the eye, as if challenging him to argue back. 'And the Murrumbidgee isn't the only thing that will flood this town.' He gulps the whisky. 'We'll be flooded by gold diggers soon enough.'

David points to the glass. 'It's a bit early in the day for that, isn't it?'

'Don't judge me!' James snaps back. 'In the blink of an eye we can be gone.' He clicks his fingers. 'Just like that! So, if I want a whisky in the morning I will have it. And if I want to drink it in Wagga Wagga, then by God I will do that as well.' He pours another, takes an unceremonious mouthful, looks at the near-empty glass and puts it down.

'Why Wagga Wagga? Why there? Why move at all?' David starts pacing, as Wagadhaany's seen him do when he's anxious. 'You're behaving like a bloody madman this morning. And how could we even start another run?'

This is the first time Wagadhaany has heard David curse, and she nearly drops the teacup she is placing in front of him. But she recovers from the fumble quickly and goes back to pouring tea, hoping that the disagreement between the Bradley brothers doesn't turn physical.

'Wagga Wagga has been gazetted for four years, it's growing and it's got potential,' James retorts, pouring his third drink. 'We can get a run in Wagga Wagga under the same Squatters Act that Father used for our run here. But we must move swiftly. My people tell me that pastoral occupancy is spreading.'

David rolls his eyes as James takes another mouthful of whisky.

'There is a lot of potential there, a lot of potential, I tell you.'

'Potential for what?' David demands.

Wagadhaany's heart begins to race as David's voice gets louder. Anger is not something she is used to.

'Well, for a start, it could be a city one day, a big booming city.' As James stretches his arms apart to suggest a large size, a few drops of whisky spill from his glass. 'Oh dear.'

David shakes his head and steps back.

'You see,' James says with rising sarcasm in his voice as he steps towards David, 'Wagga Wagga has a chief constable *and* a court-house. It has hotels. And although many people have already left the town for the goldfields of Victoria, you mark my words –' he pokes David in the chest '– They will be back with more money. And then businesses will boom.' James gestures with his hands to suggest an explosion, spilling more whisky onto the floor. 'Oh dear, what a waste.'

'James!' David yells, losing patience.

Wagadhaany is surprised when James appears to ignore his brother's anger and instead takes another mouthful.

'The town is between Sydney and Melbourne, so it is the best place for markets for produce,' James continues.

David takes the glass from his brother's hand. His movements are calm but his face is contorted, as if he is struggling to hide his anger. 'The truth, and you know it, James,' he says through gritted teeth, 'is that Wagga Wagga is no better placed than Gundagai, which is on an already well-known route between Sydney and Melbourne.'

Wagadhaany leaves the room with the empty tea tray but lingers in the doorway. She hopes that the brothers don't end up in a physical fight, because even though David is generally the calmer one, she can tell that he is agitated by his brother's comments. David is holding the empty whisky glass and pacing the room again. She wishes she wasn't the only woman in the house.

'Look,' James says, clumsily sitting down, the whisky affecting his balance. 'I've thought about this, David. You and I both know it's going to take a long time for Gundagai to recover, and we aren't getting any younger. We need to reclaim our lives, rebuild the business, build a new station. Father worked so hard to give us a good life.'

'And that good life is right here,' David argues, 'where Father chose to bring the family.'

But James will not listen. 'There's more potential in Wagga Wagga. The land is better there, the plains are ideal for grazing. We could have the largest of all the sheep and cattle runs there, and one day, I'd like to move into farming pigs. I can't see the same future, that same opportunity, for us here, not now.' James looks up and offers his brother a sad smile. There's a hint of humanity in his expression, and Wagadhaany wonders if he is suppressing his grief or if the whisky has influenced his mood.

David walks to the window, strains to see out as the sunlight streams directly through the glass. He pauses, then unexpect- edly spins around, violently, almost losing his balance. 'For goodness sake, there are floods in Wagga Wagga too, James,' he declares, raising the empty glass. 'You know that! The Murrumbidgee is nine hundred miles long, and runs down- stream from here to Wagga Wagga and beyond. I know you've read the *Gazette*. You want to relocate from one flooded town to another? It makes no sense, and I'm not going to be part of your reckless plan.'

The challenge is set. James stands immediately, uneasy on his feet. Eventually he is fully upright. 'You *will* go.' He moves his feet further apart, attempting to stabilise himslf. 'We are family. I am the eldest and you will do as I say.'

'You are the eldest only marginally, James,' David responds calmly. 'And age doesn't necessarily bring wisdom with it.'

As David starts to walk towards the doorway, Wagadhaany retreats swiftly to the kitchen sink and pretends to fuss with the dishes. Within moments, David is standing behind her, close. He reaches around and puts the glass he is holding in the sink. She expects him to move away but he doesn't. Rather, he moves closer so his body touches hers. Immediately she feels trapped as his body gently pushes against her back. She says nothing, speechless with fear, her heart racing.

To her shock he grips her hips firmly and turns her around to face him. Her head spins as a memory she has forced to the darkest recesses of her mind resurfaces. She sees Mrs Bradley enter the kitchen as David has her pinned against the sink like today, and she hears the words, 'DAVID! Step away from the girl this minute.' Wagadhaany remembers the shame on his face that day as he moved away from her at his mother's orders, while a furious Mrs Bradley hounded him, making him promise he would never in his life behave that way again.

Wagadhaany stands there frozen, conscious that David's breathing is heavy, and she sees a different look in his eyes. She is terrified and it takes all the courage she can muster to voice the words, 'What would Mrs Bradley say?'

David stands as if in a trance. His eyes leave hers and he looks off into the distance remembering, she is sure, that same moment. She can nearly feel the shame filling his body. A tear escapes his eye and suddenly, as if repulsed, he lets her go and turns away.

Never before has Wagadhaany been so grateful for David Bradley's respect for his mother.

'David!' James calls from the living room.

David leaves the kitchen. It is some minutes before Wagadhaany can breathe calmly again. When she does, she decides to erase David's actions from her mind. While she doesn't know much about who David Bradley is on the inside, she does know how much he loved his mother, and she trusts that the memory of his mother will protect her.

She moves quietly to the doorway to listen as the men continue their conversation.

'Moving to Wagga Wagga isn't going to make us forget the pain of losing Mother and Father. Or our brothers.' He chokes back whatever is rising in his throat. 'Moving towns and houses isn't going to change anything at all. What can be better about life over there?' David crosses the room and throws his arms in the air. 'Answer me that! Just tell me, because none of your arguments really hold any water for me.'

He waits for James to look at him directly. When he does, David seizes the brief moment of connection. 'This is where we belong. Right here. This is where our parents chose to settle our family, and this is where we have buried them.' His voice chokes, and it takes almost a minute for him to compose himself. 'This is where we should stay.'

'Here? In the house and town that flooded? The place where a flood took the lives of everyone we love? The man who built this house for us and the woman who bore and raised us, who kept us together as a family? This is *not* where we belong anymore.' James takes several deep breaths and attempts to relax, rolling his shoulders backwards and breathing out, as if the whole conversation has been a physical effort. 'We can get a large run in Wagga Wagga, build a new life, a bigger life, leave a legacy our parents would be proud of. We can come back to visit their graves, if that is what you think connects you to this place.' He sighs, as if exhausted from the arguing, and likely too from trying to forget the night of the flood, just as Wagadhaany herself has tried. 'I am tired of thinking about the future, about forgetting the past. I am tired of feeling so sad.'

There is a moment of silence.

'You say you have thought this through, but what about all the things that moving would entail?' asks David. 'What about the labour, stockmen, farm help? Are you planning to use Chinese indentured labourers?'

James is indignant. 'Look, I know the Chinese are building roads and railways these days. But I am *not* like the great Coolie importer McLeay! I will use Blackfellows, not Chinamen. The Blacks make good stockmen. You know that. I've seen a Blackfellow thrown from his horse and land on his feet like a cat. They have skills that the Chinamen won't have.'

Wagadhaany hasn't heard James talking about her people in this way before, with some sense of praise and recognition. She listens harder, waiting to see if he mentions her father's name.

'And they know the land. They are good guides in the bush,' James continues.

Wagadhaany is proud of the way Wiradyuri men are thought of as stockmen. Heroes with horses. And knowledgeable.

'And they only need a few rations, we can save money there.'

With that, however, Wagadhaany is reminded of how the Black men aren't paid the same for their work as the Whites, even though they are often better at their jobs.

'The only problem,' James adds, 'and it shouldn't affect us if our property is out of the centre of town, is that I hear the Blacks frequent Wagga Wagga in large numbers.'

'How is that a problem?' David frowns. 'We've had no problem with them here. And Yarri is the best worker we have.'

While Wagadhaany is grateful for the recognition of her father's skills, the conversation is making her uneasy.

'Do not fool yourself, the Blacks are an annoyance to most of the townspeople here. Yarri is good, yes, but he is different. He knows how to behave properly, probably because he works for us.'

Wagadhaany wonders what behaving properly means, what behaving properly involves, and how her babiin is different to the other Wiradyuri men who work for the Bradleys.

'I am sure *she* has taken a penny here and there,' James continues with a slur.

Wagadhaany is horrified at the suggestion that she has stolen money. She desperately wants to defend herself but holds her tongue.

'I do not believe her to be a thief,' David replies, 'and she is the only person who can manage this house without Mother. And Mother thought her to be a kind soul, I am sure.'

'Ha, a kind but *stupid* soul. Though maybe smart enough not to steal, she knows I would have her locked up if she did.' He stands up, pours some whisky into a fresh glass and takes a sip. 'Anyway, what would she spend it on? Not smart enough to know that.'

James is still angry, and Wagadhaany doesn't know why. She can feel her heart race and considers what it would be like to pour scalding tea all over James Bradley. That would give him something to be cranky about.

'Didn't you hear that Jenkins found nine head of cattle dead, killed by the natives? He has other stories of his cattle speared by the Blacks on his station. We are just lucky *our* Blacks toe the line,' James continues.

Our Blacks? They don't own us, we are not theirs! Wagadhaany wants them to leave Gundagai because then she will be free from their beliefs and her servitude. She turns from the doorway and moves back into the kitchen. She doesn't want to hear any more, but they are loud and she still hears everything.

'So, will we take Yarri with us then, and the others?' David asks. 'Is that what you are proposing?'

'I'm not taking anyone with me. There are enough natives, we can get more down there. They are cheaper than the Chinese labour anyway, so we will benefit financially. Everybody wins.'

Everybody wins? Wagadhaany asks herself. She will win, and her family will win when she goes back to them. 'Everybody wins,' she whispers to herself.

'You are no better than a Coolie if you are happy to treat the natives as slaves. And we owe Yarri, and what about . . .'

'Leave the girl out of it. We owe her nothing. We kept her alive, we give her a roof, and I know she eats our leftovers, so she is doing better than most of them.'

The contempt in his voice is painful for Wagadhaany to hear, and she wants to tell him that she only ever takes the leftovers that she knows Mrs Bradley would have given her.

'Just as her father kept *us* alive,' says David. 'You should never forget that. We might not owe her, but we *do* owe him!'

Wagadhaany appears in the doorway just as James Bradley is putting both hands on the arms of his chair and pushing himself up. He walks across the room and looks David directly in the eye.

'I just want to leave a legacy, in memory of our parents, for us.' The room is silent for a long minute before he adds, 'For a son I hope to have one day.'

'I want the same thing, James, a son, a legacy. But I want it here in Gundagai.'

'No! I will have a son, and his future is NOT HERE!'

Chapter Seven

Louisa Spencer, a widow of the Great Flood, lost her new husband and all of her family when the raging waters rushed through their home that fateful June. It has been eight long, lonely months since then and she is still grieving. A young widow, she is slowly finding some emotional strength and regaining a sense of purpose. Even though her wealth means that material things have been repaired or replaced quickly, her heart remains broken.

Each morning she watches the vast number of parrots that gather around her home at Morleys Creek, which, thanks to her family's wealth, was rebuilt quickly. She feeds the birds crumbs of homemade bread, believing the spirits of her lost ones are in the tiny creatures. Without knowing it, her hand often moves to her heart as she thinks of the husband she barely knew but loved nonetheless, and on most days she cries for hours on end.

This morning is slightly different though. It is the first time since the tragedy that Louisa is to make a public appearance, at a local horse-racing event on the north bank of Tenandra Flat. She has been vague since the flood, lost without the guidance of her Quaker parents. But today she is reuniting herself with the work of the group with the goal of creating a legacy in her parents' memory. In the wake of the flood, her Quaker sense of human rights and social justice, of peace and community life, now requires reinvigoration. She knows she must refocus her faith and the desire of the Quaker family to see equality for the Aborigines of Australia and fair treatment of convicts brought to the new colony. This was the reason they had come to Australia from England two years prior. And it is the reason she will continue to rise each day, and move forward with her life.

Louisa has also found a new love of wildlife since being left alone, and she is concerned to see that all animals are treated well, including the horses, especially after so much animal life was lost during the flood.

A woman of means, she can afford to wear the latest fashion when out in Gundagai, but Louisa has always been modest in her dress, and in recent months has rarely had cause to wear anything but her day frocks. Today she wears one she has sewn herself. Under the plain dress are layers of petticoats, creating a bell-shaped skirt. She doesn't like the excessive layering but it is the norm in town. A bonnet covers her hair and there is barely any flesh to be seen, as she protects both her modesty and her pale English skin from the harsh February sun.

She stands under a plain white parasol near the starting post, which is fixed on the riverbank. Although she can't see far into the distance, she gazes in the direction of the finish line about two miles away. Today she is the guest of Mayor Robertson. It's an important invitation she could not be so rude as to decline.

And she thinks perhaps the event might provide some opportunity to raise the issue of animal welfare. She is aware that the mayor recognises her personal wealth – born from the family's chocolate business still booming back in England – and that she could potentially influence and support some of the rebuilding of the local town and economy. He has told her so, in a variety of ways, but she has made no commitment and does not intend to do so.

Louisa stares at the track and waits for the first race. She is oblivious to what is going on around her. She wonders if she is the only person there who believes horseracing demonstrates man's capacity for animal cruelty for the sake of human pleasure and profit. The expression on her face gives away nothing of what she is feeling, or of the disgust she feels at any form of mistreatment. Like on most days since June, she is shrouded in an unintended air of mystery.

She notices a distinguished gentleman, in a day coat and top hat. She believes him to be the station owner James Bradley, but can't be sure. She is not interested in finding out either. Any man betting on the horses is not a man she is keen to speak with.

From the corner of her eye, she sees him exchange pleasantries with some local punters before introducing himself to William Guise, owner of nearby Cunningham Station. They are standing within earshot and Louisa can't help but hear every word.

The men share stories about riding racehorses as young boys. James rode with the permission of his father, and William as a wayward child, needing the reins to be pulled in on both him and the horses. She is certain both men are here today for the profit to be gained, and understands that their bets have been laid in plenty of time for the first race.

When the starter gun for the race goes off there is a loud cheer among the crowd, and when a chestnut thoroughbred sixteen hands high crosses the finish line first, James bellows his approval so loudly that Louisa turns around. She frowns and glares at him, while trying to save her face from the direct sun. She tilts the parasol and refocuses her vision so she can see him. So he can see her displeasure. But when Louisa's eyes meet his, she feels a tingling in her chest as if all the broken pieces of her heart are suddenly knitting themselves back together. The moment feels magical and she wonders if he feels the same sensations.

Louisa's heart skips a beat as James's eyes take in her petite, feminine frame. She feels both uncomfortable and excited at the same time. A hot rush through her body makes her face flush red. She can see he is taken by her; his smile covers his entire face. She watches as he turns to William and, in what he must think is a whisper, requests to be introduced.

'You know she's a Quaker,' says William, rolling his eyes.

It has been the same since her family first arrived. Catholics and Protestants were acceptable in the town, but those of other faiths – like the Quakers – well, they had always been frowned upon or mocked. But it had been water off a duck's back for her family; not because the family thought themselves better than anyone else, but simply because their faith reminded them every day of their purpose.

'I'm not sure I know what that implies,' she hears James admit, not taking his eyes off her.

'She comes from a very controversial family. They are on the side of the convicts and natives. That's all her father used to talk to me about. Of course, I listened, or pretended to. They have a thriving business back in England. Chocolate money, and money is money, regardless of religion or if it's chocolate.' He chuckles.

Louisa's heart sinks at the mention of her father. She turns her eyes away, to the mayor, who is chatting nearby. She really should speak to him – it is why she came here, after all.

'Used to talk to you? He doesn't anymore?' James asks.

'No, sadly her parents and siblings, all of them, lost in the flood.' William shakes his head. 'And her husband. Newly wedded. Very sad indeed.'

'Like my own family,' James responds, removing his hat and running his hand through his thick black hair. Hair that Louisa thinks is quite handsome – she can still see him from the corner of her eye.

'I find her a little . . . unconventional.'

'How so?' James asks.

'Quakers think *anyone* can have a relationship with God directly, and that means churches and clergy aren't necessary. She doesn't come to church *at all*. I find that very strange, don't you?'

William is still talking as James walks towards Louisa. She can see him wiping his hands on his trousers.

By the time William realises, he has to trot to catch up. As James approaches her, with William in tow, she wonders what he will say. He tips his hat and puts it under his arm, before his feet come to a standstill in front of her. There is an awkward silence until William stops alongside James and introduces the pair.

'Mrs Spencer, may I present to you Mr James Bradley of Bradley Station.'

Louisa nods in acknowledgement. Her parasol tilts slightly. 'A pleasure to make your acquaintance, Mr Bradley.' As she extends her hand, Louisa is glad she is wearing gloves as her palms are damp with perspiration. Her stomach flutters with the butterflies she has only ever felt once before, with her late husband.

'The pleasure is all mine,' he responds. James opens his mouth as if to speak again, but there is a pause and she can see that he is struggling to make conversation. 'And that is quite an exquisite parasol, Mrs Spencer.'

'Yes, and it is practical. If I take the handle off it reveals a blade,' she says, with no change to her facial expression. 'For safety.'

'For safety, yes,' James and William say in unison, their eyes wide.

'But of course, I don't believe in weapons, unless completely necessary. My late husband had it made for when I was out alone, you understand, at events like this.' A smile appears on her face for the first time in many months, creating dimples in her otherwise smooth complexion. The men laugh out loud. She and James both sigh with relief that the mood is now less serious, and Louisa is glad for a moment of anything that is not sadness. There follows an uncomfortable silence until a voice comes from behind them.

'Mrs Spencer, the carriage is ready when you are.'

Louisa's coachman stands tall and competent-looking, with both hands behind his back as he awaits instruction. She almost regrets directing him to collect her after the first race but she believed that would've been ample time to speak to the mayor.

'Thank you, Charles, I will be along momentarily.' Louisa turns back to James and William.

'You're leaving so soon?' James asks with boyish disappointment.

'I do not support entertainment resulting from cruelty to animals, Mr Bradley. I had wanted to speak to the mayor about it before the first race, but he has so many guests today, I must now wait for another opportunity. I have seen enough. Congratulations on your win.' Louisa is blunt, honest. She hopes she hasn't embarrassed James Bradley, but she is a woman who speaks her mind.

James looks stunned but responds immediately. 'I do not attend these events regularly, Mrs Spencer, for I tend to agree with you.'

She has no sense that he is lying, but she finds herself suddenly feeling reproachful – not of him, but of herself, that such strong feelings for a man could surge through her so soon after the death of her husband. She walks quickly towards the coach.

'Perhaps we could discuss this issue, and others, over a cup of tea sometime?' James suggests as he walks alongside her.

'Perhaps. Goodbye, Mr Bradley, enjoy the rest of the day.'

A few days later, Louisa arrives by carriage at the Bradley home. When a dark servant girl opens the door to receive her, she is surprised to see the young woman curtsy. Louisa watches as the girl moves quickly. She sees her youthful glow, and her dark brown eyes matching the chocolate colour of her hair, which is pulled into a hair net with a single curl falling down the side of her face. Tall and lean, she is elegant, but her curtsy is completely unnecessary.

'Oh no,' Louisa says, 'that is not necessary at all.' She extends her gloved hand for the girl to take. 'My name is Louisa,' she says with her warmest smile.

The girl appears shocked and smiles nervously, gently taking her hand, and to Louisa's surprise she curtsies again. 'Yes,

Miss Louisa. Mr James is waiting for you in the living room. I am to show you in.'

The girl's manners are impeccable and Louisa wonders where she has learned them. She enters, her huge bell-like skirt requiring the girl to step wide to let her pass.

'And what is your name?'

'I am Wagadhaany, Miss Louisa.'

'Your name is . . . Wog-a-dine?'

'That's correct, Miss Louisa.' Wagadhaany chuckles.

'Is everything all right?'

'Yes, Miss Louisa, it's just that you are the first White person who can say my name properly.'

'Really?' Louisa is surprised. It was no challenge at all for her to pronounce.

'Yes, Miss Louisa.'

'Please, I am just Louisa,' she says, as she removes her gloves. 'What does it mean? Your name, that is?'

'Dancer, Miss.' Wagadhaany smiles, looking proud as she leads the guest into the sitting room and announces, 'Miss Louisa is here for you, Mr James.'

James springs to his feet. 'It is such an honour to have you in my home, Mrs Spencer. Please take a seat,' he offers. 'And I promised tea.'

'Thank you, I hope you haven't gone to too much trouble.'

Louisa can tell that although work has been done to repair any flood damage to the room, there are still faint water stains that must have been too hard to clean or conceal.

'Thank you, Wilma.' James nods to Wagadhaany – his directive to her to prepare some tea – but Louisa is confused by the use of the name Wilma.

'You seem to have good help in Wagadhaany,' she comments. 'I don't have any domestic help. I mean, I don't need help.'

James looks confused. 'Yes, she has been with us since before . . .' He pauses. 'For many years.'

Louisa can tell he is nervous; he is fumbling and perspiring. She has limited experience with men, but she knows well enough that a beautiful woman can turn an intelligent man into a blathering fool. She wonders how much experience he has had with women. Not socialising much, she is not privy to the gossip of the town or any tales of wayward behaviour.

She is well aware of her impact on James, but more focused on her own reaction to him. She feels a heat rise within her, the strong chemistry between them, but she has no intention of saying anything or acting upon it. She believes from their first meeting that James is a gentleman and will not be forward. And as a woman raised to be a lady *and* as a recent widow, she would never be so brash as to even hint at any interest in a man. But whatever the pull is, it is magnetic, as strong as the sixteen-hand horse that brought them together at the races.

As the fluttery and strange feeling returns, she feels she is betraying the husband she lost less than a year ago. Her husband was the man she made vows to as a wife. *Until death do us part. Death. Part.* The words hit her hard as she positions herself on a re-upholstered chair. Suddenly her eyes mist over and she feels slightly faint. She puts her left hand to her forehead as the colour drains from her face.

'Mrs Spencer!' James rushes over and bends on one knee. 'Are you all right?'

Louisa takes a breath. 'I am fine, Mr Bradley, perhaps some water.' She takes a few short breaths. 'I think the warm weather is just a little too much for me today.'

'Of course, of course.'

He rises quickly and strides at pace towards the kitchen. Before she has time to think, he is back in front of her, a determined grin on his face and a glass of water in his hand. 'I hope this helps.'

Louisa sips slowly, eyes fixed on the glass as she tries to ignore James's eyes fixed on her.

When Wagadhaany finally enters the room with a pot of tea and freshly baked biscuits, Louisa looks to her, thankful for the break in the awkward moment.

'Thank you. I am fine now.' She hands the glass back to James.

Wagadhaany places the tray on the table and goes to pour the tea, but Louisa rests her hand softly on the young woman's, stopping her.

'Shall I?' Louisa asks James.

'If that is your wish, Mrs Spencer.'

Wagadhaany nods to Louisa, then to James Bradley, and leaves the room.

'The town gossips will be having a field day, Mr Bradley,' Louisa says as she pours the tea and places a biscuit on a small plate for James. 'I have no doubt many will have much to say about my coach outside your house today.'

'I am sorry, Mrs Spencer. I hope coming here hasn't been problematic for you. I would hate to taint your character. I am simply interested in your thoughts on the issues you raised at the track.'

'It is fine, Mr Bradley. After all, we are simply drinking tea.' She hands him his cup. 'That does not make for very interesting gossip now, does it?'

'I can offer you something stronger,' he says. 'Some sherry perhaps?'

'Oh no, Mr Bradley, Quakers do not drink. We are in the business of chocolate.' She offers a sweet smile. 'Cocoa and sugar are virtuous alternatives to alcohol, which, I am sure you will agree, is the cause of great moral evil.' She looks to him for agreement, but before he can speak she continues. 'I have heard, but have no proof at hand, that alcoholism has also been the cause of some deaths right here in the colony. Temperance is what society needs today, Mr Bradley, don't you think?'

'You are quite right, Mrs Spencer, alcohol is evil, and it is enjoyed only on very rare occasions in our house. I shan't lie to you though, this is a Catholic household and, well, the Catholics are no teetotallers.' He chuckles, and his feeble attempt at humour makes her smile.

Louisa reaches into her purse. 'I did bring you something, for the house.' She hands James a small block of chocolate. 'As I've mentioned, my family were in the chocolate business back in England. We were more fortunate than most others in the south who worked in factories or on the land. We were quite blessed actually. It was the chocolate that afforded us the opportunity to come here to do the work of our Quaker faith,' she says. 'I mean, I still am. Blessed, that is.'

'Yes, I have heard from the town gossips.' He chuckles. 'But I know very little about your faith or how you practise.'

Louisa doesn't respond. She feels no need to explain her faith to James but there is another awkward silence.

'Can I pour you some more tea?' James offers, even though Louisa has barely touched her cup. She puts her hand gently over it to signal no more tea is required. As she takes a sip, she notices James looking at her left hand.

'Louisa, if I may, I see you are still wearing your wedding band, and I am sorry to learn of your loss in the flood. So many wonderful lives, special people, taken from families, from this town.'

She understands that his own family is included in these words yet feels forced to explain her lot. She is on the verge of tears but manages to keep up the appearances that, as a lady, she should. She folds her hands in her lap, so James cannot see that they are now shaking.

'Mr Bradley – James, if I may?' She takes a deep breath. 'I lost everyone in the flood, my parents, my sister and my younger brother.'

James sits still, listening, she believes, intently. She bows her head to gather her thoughts and words, and a few seconds later looks up to meet his eyes.

'And I lost my husband, Oscar. We had only been married a short time.' A lone tear escapes and falls down her left cheek. 'I am all alone. A widow with no-one but my loyal coachman, who kept me safe the night of the flood by taking me to higher ground while my husband and family stayed to protect the property.'

She is aware that her experience is not dissimilar to James's and she sees tears in his eyes. He stands suddenly, turns his back to her, pulls a handkerchief from his pocket, dabs his eyes, clears his throat and then turns to face her again.

'I beg forgiveness, Louisa.'

'You never need forgiveness for sharing your emotions, James. There is no shame in weeping for people we have loved and lost. We have both seen the darkness that death brings to those left behind.' Louisa stands and walks over to him, as if it is the most natural action. She places her hand gently on his forearm and whispers softly, 'I am here for you.'

'Hello, Miss Louisa.'

Wagadhaany appears to open the door cautiously. Louisa wonders if it seems unusual that she has returned to the Bradley house so soon after her first visit, but feels she connected not only with James over their cup of tea, but also with Wagadhaany, and she is desperate to spend time with another woman, given that since the flood her days have been spent mostly alone.

'I'm sorry but Mr Bradley is not here right now. He has gone to Wagga Wagga with Mr David Bradley to look at land.'

'Yes, I understand as much. James did tell me. But I came to see you. To bring you these.' She lifts a linen cloth from the top of her basket to reveal homemade biscuits. 'I enjoyed your treats the other day,' she says. 'I too like to bake. In fact, I bake all the time, and I can't possibly eat all of these alone. May I share them with you?'

'I am not used to hosting guests while the Bradleys are not here,' Wagadhaany explains. 'But I am sure that Mr Bradley would be happy to have you sitting in his living room again.' She steps aside to let Louisa pass. 'I will make you some tea.'

When she places the tray on the table and begins to pour, Louisa notices there is only one cup.

'Where is your cup?' she asks.

'I do not drink from these cups, and *never* in here, Miss Louisa.'

'That is absurd.' Louisa frowns. James Bradley doesn't call his servant by her name, doesn't allow her to drink from the same cups and share in a basic daily activity. She has heard about the mistreatment of the Aborigines but thought that living in the same house meant there would be some shared level of humanity. What was she thinking in getting close to him? How can she find James Bradley attractive when he treats such a beautiful young soul like Wagadhaany in such an appalling way?

'Please get yourself a cup, Wagadhaany,' Louisa requests.

While the girl goes to the kitchen, Louisa is left alone with her thoughts. Being in the Bradley home again reminds Louisa that, coming from a Quaker background, her family would never have enjoyed the benefits of indentured labour provided by either Aboriginal people or convicts. Her parents were not the only citizens in the town to have enlightened views of the local Aborigines, and they had spoken of other families who dined with their Black friends. She had thought that most people were like her, but her experience in town generally was lacking, and moreso since the passing of her husband and family. Perhaps the truth was that most men were like William and James.

Meeting Wagadhaany in this setting, Louisa realises that she has never had any real connection with the local Aboriginal people of Gundagai. Her father and mother, although keen to work with them, had yet to establish firm roots in the town. In that moment, as Wagadhaany re-enters the room, looking nervous holding a teacup that she will drink out of for the first time, Louisa sees the young woman as the perfect conduit for her work from now on; the work of finding equality for the people she has only ever known to have lived on the fringes of town. She was only hoping for some female companionship, but now she will focus her Quaker work through Wagadhaany.

'Please, sit with me,' Louisa requests gently, as Wagadhaany looks uncertain and nervous.

'Yes, Miss Louisa.'

'Wagadhaany, please call me Louisa. I would like to be your friend. I thought I could share some of my recipes with you, if you would like that.'

As Wagdahaany sips tea from a china cup for the first time, Louisa watches the woman she hopes to befriend, and believes that something good will come of her meeting James Bradley after all.

Over the next weeks, as the Bradley brothers travel to and from Wagga Wagga in preparation for their eventual relocation, Louisa visits Wagadhaany every other day, sharing recipes and spending time baking with her. When James is there, it is obvious that the connection between them is growing, that she is losing her heart to him, that she enjoys and feels comfortable in his home. She can see how easy it could be to make the Bradley house her own home. But while he is always pleased to see her, Louisa becomes aware that he is not as happy to see her spending so much time with his servant.

'Louisa,' he takes her hand and holds it in his own, 'it fills my heart with joy to see you in my home. Your presence, your smile, bring happiness and hope back into my life.' He kisses her hand and keeps hold of it. 'But I am concerned about whatever it is you are doing with Wilma.'

'Wagadhaany,' she corrects him. 'Her name is Wagadhaany. And what I am *doing* is being a friend. She is my very gentle and *kind* friend.' There is a hint in her tone that James's treatment of the girl should be much better, and she is determined to teach him ways to be an improved man, and a finer citizen.

'Yes, dear, but you do realise you cannot be friends outside of these walls, don't you?'

Louisa frowns and releases his hand. 'Don't be so silly, James. I can be friends with whomever I choose.'

'I am not being silly, Louisa. It is against the law for us to be in the company of their kind in New South Wales. We can go to gaol for doing so.' He looks at her, confused, as if she should already know this.

Louisa's blood is boiling at the kind of language James is using. She feels tension rise in her body. '*Their kind?* What do you mean by *their kind?* And who are the *we?* What law can possibly exist that tells human beings who they can and cannot be friends with?'

'*We* are the we!' he says, sounding as silly as Louisa had suggested. 'The White people are the we. And the law is British law. It is legislated, Louisa. It is the law, and I am not a lawbreaker. And nor should you be.' James appears agitated. 'I need you to know that what you are doing with Wilma – being *friends* – well, it is against the law.' His tone has changed to one of concern and he takes her hand again.

'No law will *ever* tell me who I cannot speak to or be friends with, and no *man* will either,' Louisa declares, unpeeling James's hand from hers and attempting to move away from him on the settee. It is a show of strength that she has not had to exercise before, but since losing her father and husband, she has had little choice but to be her own protector.

When James responds, there is panic in his voice. 'Please, Louisa, it's not me, I want you to be happy, and if Wilma . . .'

'Wagadhaany,' Louisa snaps. 'Wog-a-dine. It really isn't that difficult, James.'

'Yes, of course. If she makes you happy, then that makes me happy, but please be careful. Promise me you will not go out gallivanting around with her.'

'Do not offend me, James Bradley. I do not gallivant!'

'No, you don't. You are a lady, and that is why I fell in love with you.'

It is the first time that James has declared his true feelings for Louisa, and while her own emotions are strong, she is reluctant to voice them. But his words have set her heart on fire, and she allows him to kiss her. She is surprised at his passion, and at how much she delights in it. When he releases her some seconds later, she still says nothing. She is falling in love and the attraction is strong. But still, she has a lot of work to do to change James's mind about her friendship with Wagadhaany, and more importantly his lack of respect for the young woman.

'How often do you see your family?' Louisa asks one morning as she kneads dough to make bread she intends to share among the townsfolk. It is a simple way to contribute, and baking with Wagadhaany means she is less lonely as well. Besides, she finds she wants to be at her own home less and less, as everything about the place reminds her of her late husband.

'On Sundays when Mr James and Mr David go to church, I go to the camp. Sometimes Mrs Bradley would tell me to stay the night there, but now I have to come back the same night. I must always be here to make the tea and serve the porridge in the morning.'

Wagadhaany responds matter-of-factly, as if there is nothing unusual about her role with the Bradleys, as if this is how all White households function. Louisa kneads a little harder, upset that her new friend is constantly being kept from her family, that she is treated like a slave. She realises that this must be more common than she thought, and wonders how many other families in the new colonies use indentured labour.

'Where do you sleep, then?' she asks, unaware that she is making Wagadhaany uncomfortable and that no-one, even the Bradleys, ever asks about her quarters.

'In a room through there.' Without looking up from the tray she is preparing to put the dough on to rise, she points to a door off the kitchen. Louisa looks to the door and back to Wagadhaany, who appears to be disinterested in talking about her accommodations.

'May I see?' she asks. 'Perhaps we could sew you some new curtains.'

'Oh no, Miss Louisa, I don't need curtains, there are no windows,' Wagadhaany advises.

'No windows means no natural light and no fresh air!' Louisa is outraged, and stops short of saying what is on her mind, that the room sounds like a prison cell. She thinks Wagadhaany must be either naïve or too scared to complain about her lodgings. 'My family never had servants at all. Quakers believe we are all equal, and that we should serve each other. And for you to have so little freedom and no natural light . . . well, that is simply unacceptable.'

Louisa punches the dough hard without a word. She is angry. She *must* make changes for Wagadhaany. It is her duty.

She places the dough on the prepared tray. 'Next we place calico over the dough and put it on the windowsill and wait for it to rise. Once that is done, we will knead it again, then lay it out for a second rise, and then into the oven to cook.'

Wagadhaany is watching and listening with interest. Louisa checks to make sure there is enough wood near the stove.

'Right, what do you think about baking bread?'

'I think it is like making damper,' Wagadhaany says. 'We cook something similar at the camp, but we cook it in the ashes of the fire. The flour is made from seeds of the spinifex bush, and we grind them up really good to make the flour. It's a bit browner than the flour we get from the shop here in town. We add water and salt and then make it flat and cook it in the ashes. It's a bit faster cooking our way too, and we don't have windowsills for it to rise either. Then, when it's cooked we all share.'

'Windowsills aside, I think we might have a lot of things in common. Sometimes we just need to look for them,' Louisa says thoughtfully, acknowledging that Wagadhaany is self-sufficient and comes from a place of sharing also. 'Bread or your damper, each is one of the basic necessities of life, which we all need to survive.'

When the bread is baked, she leaves the Bradley house, content that she is finally establishing a real friendship, an intimacy with another woman, the first she feels comfortable with in Gundagai. Her relationship with James now seems almost secondary to the one blossoming with Wagadhaany, who she is investing all her time with. Still, James's talk of moving to Wagga Wagga concerns her. *Is he smitten enough to take her with him?* She hopes so. She would go with him in a heartbeat.

A new life, a new chance at love, and a new friend. The thought of so much newfound happiness is almost too much for her to contain and she smiles to no-one but herself. Her only concern now is that she wonders if Wagadhaany might be suspicious of her, but she is confident that things will become easier and more relaxed, with trust growing between them the more time they spend together.

Chapter Eight

It is Sunday and while the Bradleys are in town Wagadhaany is at the camp holding the latest baby in her miyagan. Gandi has had her first son, who Wagadhaany is only just meeting, and the newest family member is being smothered with love. All the other children want to look and touch, and they reach in with varying degrees of gentleness to kiss their cousin on the forehead. It is the most precious bundle she has ever held, and she wonders if the life she currently leads will ever allow her to be a mother herself.

A fire burns brightly and a feast is being prepared following the return of the men from days away hunting. She feels at home again, in a place where she can be herself, feel at peace. Although more and more people are moving to the camp and away from their original land, there is always a welcome fire, and enough to share. And even with the fancy biscuits and Louisa's company in recent weeks, she is never truly content unless she's eating the food caught and cooked by her miyagan.

As the clan enjoy a meal of wambuwuny, nothing is wasted; every part of the kangaroo is eaten and appreciated. While everyone relaxes with full bellies, including Wagadhaany, she takes the opportunity to tell the Elders about Louisa and how she has been kind and caring, cooking with her and wanting to make curtains for the room without any windows. She immediately notices the Old People, mainly the women, looking at each other sideways. They don't say anything in words, but their facial expressions communicate enough. She knows they are suspicious, but she doesn't ask why. If they want her to know something they will tell her.

When the feast is over, she cuddles the small children whose eyes are wide and bright whenever she is there. She laughs as they fight over space in the humpy, just as she did in her own joyful childhood with her cousins.

Her heart is heavy when she has to leave them all again and go back to her tiny room in town. She'd rather be five to a bed with family than alone in that dark box of a room. Leaving is a routine she has endured for a long time, but every time she departs it's as miserable as the last.

Yiramiilan walks Wagadhaany to the edge of their campsite, where Yarri is waiting to escort his daughter to town. Mother and daughter hug tightly and before she lets Wagadhaany loose from the embrace she says sternly, 'Don't be telling that woman about our life here. We don't trust any strangers, *any!*'

Some days later, when Wagadhaany returns from the grocer to the Bradley house with milk and tea, there is a festive mood.

James is grinning from ear to ear and Louisa is flushed in the face. They are doing some kind of dance, which she watches from the doorway. She wonders if they have both been drinking, even though she hasn't seen James touch any whisky since Louisa first visited, and she has never seen Louisa drink at all.

'Wagadhaany! Come!' Louisa says, breaking from James's arms and doing a half-skip towards her. 'I have the most wonderful news.' Louisa's smile is so broad, Wagadhaany cannot help but grin as well. 'James has asked me to marry him.' She hugs Wagadhaany tightly. 'And of course I have said yes to living as Mrs Bradley, happily every after.'

She twirls to look at her betrothed and smiles, spinning back around in one smooth motion. Wagadhaany claps with happiness for Louisa, and for James, but mostly for herself. She knows that when they eventually leave for Wagga Wagga, as husband and wife, she will be able to go back to her family, and then they can *all* live happily ever after. She tries to stop her mind spinning around with excitement, and focuses on Louisa.

Louisa holds Wagadhaany's hands. 'You must help me prepare, although it will be a very small event.'

The bride-to-be steps away and back to James, who takes her hand, where a very modest gold band sits on her wedding finger. Wagadhaany sees his beaming face, and imagines what it must be like to find such joy in another human being. She wonders what the mysteries of married life hold, what the warmth of another human next to you in bed might feel like, a human that isn't one of your many young cousins. She basks in their happiness as Louisa shoos James away, and the two women sit down and start making plans.

Three days later, after a flurry of activity and Wagadhaany's excitement about being part of her first English-style wedding, the two women prepare for the ceremony, which will be held in the Bradley home. Louisa prefers the intimacy of a small wedding – only David and the minister will be there – and it also ensures that they can marry quickly.

'What *is* this?' Wagadhaany asks Louisa, as she helps her dress for her nuptials. Louisa is gasping for breath and Wagadhaany is afraid.

'It's called a corset, it helps to flatten my stomach.' She runs her hands down the front of her body. 'I need you to lace it up the back for me, as tight as you can, please.'

'But why? Your stomach is already flat. There is almost nothing there.' She continues to lace the garment but is completely confused about what she is squashing Louisa into. 'What is it made of?'

'Whalebone,' Louisa says, almost breathless. 'It's made from a whale. Pull tighter please,' she says, gasping. 'Tighter.'

Wagadhaany doesn't know what a whale is but she can see how much smaller Louisa's waist is becoming when she pulls the whalebone corset tighter. She is frightened that she may be breaking some of Louisa's own bones in the process, but she does as she is asked.

'A bit more, tighter, just a bit more . . .' Louisa's voice fades a little with every tug on the laces.

Wagadhaany is pulling as hard as she can. She's almost as breathless as Louisa, and cannot imagine enduring such pressure on her own stomach for any reason. 'It is so tight, Louisa, doesn't it hurt your binbin?'

'My binbin?'

'Stomach, your stomach. Doesn't it hurt? It hurts me just looking at you, and I am not the one wearing it!'

'Don't make me laugh, I have no room for laughter in here.' Louisa runs her hands around her girth, looking at herself in the mirror at the same time.

Wagadhaany is confused as she struggles to keep hold of the cords. 'I don't know any other woman who would wear this.'

If only the bamali-galang could see this happening. She is sure they would be suspicious of any woman putting bones around her body to make her stomach smaller. It is a very strange thing to do, when she and most of the women in her family are often hungry and want to make their stomachs bigger.

Louisa walks to the full-length mirror with Wagadhaany in tow, still doing up the laces. 'It gives me better posture, Waga- dhaany. I stand taller, much taller. It doesn't hurt so much as it feels like a really firm hug.'

'Why don't you just stand up taller for yourself?' Wagadhaany asks. 'And you will be married today, why can't you just ask Mr James to give you a really firm hug after the wedding? And then, maybe . . . you can stop doing this.'

Wagadhaany ties the last of the corset and collapses on the bed behind her, as exhausted as if she had been beating the dust out of the rugs. Both women laugh at the folly.

As Louisa regards herself in the mirror, Wagadhaany sees a dreamy look in her eyes.

'We are young women and we do need long hugs, Waga- dhaany. I have desires too, of course, and I want to have a family with James. He desperately wants a son, and I want to give him one. And today is the beginning of that new journey. I will marry my love and as soon as we have the right property for what James and David want to do with their business, then we will move to Wagga Wagga and have a beautiful family and life together.'

As Louisa's eyes glisten with tears of happiness, Wagadhaany is fascinated by the ceremony and exchange of vows between her friend and James Bradley. She looks on, dressed in one of Louisa's frocks, feeling elegant and pretty like never before, but also uncomfortable. She's wearing lots of petticoats and layers and the dress is much heavier than her normal tunic. And Louisa has given her fancy shoes to wear too. Wedding attire, she had called it.

She looks at the smile on Louisa's face and believes that getting married to a man you love must make a woman happy. She catches David staring at her. His left eye twitches and he smiles, but she doesn't know what this means. *Is it some secret thing that happens at weddings? Is she meant to twitch her eye back at him?* As she attempts to understand the ceremony, David reaches into his pocket and pulls out a slim band of gold, handing it to James. As he slips the ring on Louisa's finger, the minister advises that now they are man and wife. *But if he is a man, then she must be a woman?* Wagadhaany is baffled, but the ceremony has moved on. *Does marriage mean that the woman has a role but the man only has to be a man?* She is not convinced that this marriage ceremony is good for the woman, and yet Louisa is glowing and her smile is so bright it lights up the room.

David Bradley gives her the eye-twitch again and she is relieved when he walks off to escort the minister out of the house, as

James and Louisa sip champagne from the crystal glasses she had washed and polished earlier. The wedding is over, and she has so many more questions she wants to ask Louisa.

'These are from my family home.' Louisa unrolls some brightly coloured fabric in what is now her marital bedroom. 'I'd like to hang them here, so if you can help me take these old ones down . . .' she reaches for the deep cerise curtains hanging over the main window, 'we can put these ones up.'

This bedroom once belonged to Elizabeth and Henry Bradley and has not been used since their deaths. But it is the only one big enough for a couple, so it is where Louisa and James will now sleep. The two women remove the old curtains and hang the new, and together unpack Louisa's belongings, which have been delivered from her former residence. They push a large, heavy box under the bed.

'They're books,' says Louisa. 'Books for children.'

Wagadhaany nods but doesn't ask her to explain.

There are two cushions covered in deep gold velvet with tassels on the corners that Wagadhaany particularly likes. 'These are beautiful,' she says, running her hand across the fabric.

'I will use them until I get new ones,' Louisa says. 'And then you can have them for your own room, if you like.' Louisa looks pleased with herself. 'I'd love to share some of my furnishings with you, my friend, so that we can make a beautiful home together in Wagga Wagga.'

Wagadhaany drops the cushion she has been holding. 'What are you talking about, Louisa? Why would I go to Wagga Wagga?

Especially now that you and Mr James are married – you know how to take care of him better than I can.' It is a statement and a question in one and Wagadhaany is distressed, picking the cushion up and dropping it again. 'I should be able to stay here, in Gundagai, on the river, with my miyagan, my family.' She is pleading, and shaking.

'Oh, you don't want to come to Wagga Wagga? I thought you could come not as a servant but as my friend, my confidante, though we would still work together.'

'No, I don't want to go. Why would you think I would want to leave Gundagai, leave my family?' Wagadhaany is upset. 'I don't understand. You don't need me. You told me you've never had a servant before, your family doesn't believe in servants, so *you* don't believe in servants, you said so, you said we were equal.' She starts to cry.

Louisa cringes then says very quickly, with an air of dismissal, 'It's not up to me really. James and David don't want to leave you behind.'

Wagadhaany looks at her with tear-filled eyes. 'You must talk the Bradleys into leaving me behind then, Louisa. You must,' she urges. 'You said you are my friend, and you want to help me be free.' She takes a breath. 'And so, Louisa, that is what you must do.'

Chapter Nine

As rain pelts the house making an enormous racket, Waga-dhaany is rooted to her spot in the kitchen, standing behind Louisa, who has her head on the table and is sobbing. They are both terrified by the thought of another flood taking everything from them, from Gundagai, again. She rubs Louisa's back because she has no idea what else to do. Louisa keeps mumbling through her tears, 'Not again, not again, not again.'

'Move faster!' James is yelling at his brother on the front veranda, as he and David sandbag the entrance.

A sense of déjà vu engulfs the town. Emotions are heightened as the heavy rain continues to fall and even though the water is rising more slowly than it did the previous winter, the fear of what is possible remains the same.

'We should have moved to higher ground already,' David says, 'when we had the chance. This is history repeating itself.'

'That wouldn't have helped,' James argues. 'Even those who rebuilt their homes on the hills of Mount Parnassus . . .' He puffs from the exertion of lifting and placing sandbags then stands upright. 'Even those homes, like ours, could potentially suffer.'

It's quiet for a few minutes as the men continue loading bag on top of bag. Without looking at David, James stands upright, pulls his aching shoulders back and wipes his brow with the back of his left hand. 'And this is why it's time to leave here.' He bends back down to lift a sandbag while waiting for a response, but there is none.

The men monitor the situation for hours, sleeves rolled up, sweat mixing with rain while the words between them decrease as time passes. Then, as fast as the water had rushed through the town, it leaves.

The men go into the kitchen where Louisa and Wagadhaany have been waiting, too afraid to move. Louisa rises and immediately clings to her husband, leaving Wagadhaany to stand alone by the table. Everyone is tired and the men are drenched. David looks at Wagadhaany with a sympathetic smile.

'It's going to be fine,' James announces. 'We are going to be fine. And we will be more than fine in Wagga Wagga,' he says, looking directly at David. 'The people over there are flood-conscious. And they are better prepared than we have ever been here. Perhaps better prepared than Gundagai will *ever* be.'

James assists Louisa to sit down at the kitchen table and continues to talk about Wagga Wagga. 'The town's commercial premises and industry have moved south to flood-free land. We will settle where it is flood-proof. We will no longer have to worry about this.' He waves his arms towards both the front and back entrances to their home and begins to unroll his sleeves down his bare arms.

David puts some wood into the stove and the fire finds new life.

James takes a seat and says solemnly, 'And the memories here are too painful anyway.'

The pot of stew will be big enough to feed them for the week. Before, it would have held enough food for the entire family for two days.

'Wagadhaany?' David peers into the kitchen where Wagadhaany is peeling potatoes to go into the stew she is preparing for dinner. He has used her traditional name often since the flood and she tells herself it is a show of respect for her father, but she still can't help but feel uncomfortable around him. She turns around with the small knife in her hand to find him standing very close by.

'Yes, sir?' she says with a quiver in her voice.

'I need to speak to your father, but not at the station.' He stops. 'Tell him to come to the house.'

'Yes, sir, I will tell him.' He doesn't say what he needs to speak to Yarri about. And she doesn't ask. Eager, she adds, 'Now, sir? Shall I get him now?'

'No, finish your chores and when you go back to the river on Sunday, bring him to the house with you when you return. It is very important.' He looks directly into her eyes.

'Of course, sir. I will bring him here with me.'

David nods. Wagadhaany nods too and waits for him to leave the kitchen. She goes back to preparing the vegetables, her head full of questions and ideas as to why David would want to speak with her father. Maybe the Bradleys want to pay him in more than tobacco, flour and tea for his work on the station. Maybe they want to give him something for being a hero. Her mind is full of maybes and she's excited and keen to get back to camp, to accompany her father back to the Bradleys' for whatever the good news is.

'I don't know what they want,' she responds to her father, when he asks why he must visit the Bradleys' home. 'Maybe they want to give you something for saving their lives. Or maybe they want to give you some money for being their best worker. It can only be good, can't it? Maybe they want to give you something from the house to say thank you. A warm coat, perhaps? What do you think?' Or maybe Louisa has talked to the Bradleys and they will tell him that they are moving, and she is free to stay, but she doesn't mention that.

'I don't know, ngamurr. When a White man calls on a Black man it is not ever a good thing. Usually they want something, or demand something, expect something.' He stops suddenly, and Wagadhaany understands that what her father is saying is that the White man is in control of everything, even the Black man's freedom.

'But the Bradleys are different, Babiin. They are kind to me, mostly.' Wagadhaany wants to believe that all White people are not the same. She doesn't tell her father about James Bradley's outbursts though, thinking that the alcohol probably made him say things.

'You work hard for them, my girl. You have looked after that family like your own. You spend more time with them than with us. They *should* be kind to you. They *should* feed you well, house you well, give you good clothes – not their mother's clothes.'

She understands the reference is to the dress Wagadhaany wore to the church service. There are no secrets in small towns and even the Whites' gossip is heard in the Black camp.

'Walking around in the clothes of a ghost, that is not right. That is not yindyamarra. That is not showing respect. I do not think they are good people most of the time.'

This is the first time Wagadhaany has heard her father speak ill of the Bradleys in all the years she has worked for them. All the years that *he* has worked for them. She doesn't understand why he is being so unkind when the possibilities of why they want to see him are endless. They walk the rest of the way in silence, Wagadhaany full of hope that something wonderful is happening.

When they reach the front of the house, where a new fence and gate have finally been erected, Yarri stops still, as does Wagadhaany, and they wait for David Bradley to notice them through the window.

'Go to the market and get some eggs,' David instructs Wagadhaany, without emotion.

She doesn't tell him they have plenty of eggs, knowing she needs to go so the men can talk. Suddenly, her hope turns to nerves as she leaves her father alone with David. Something does not feel right but she leaves the house as quickly as she can.

At the grocer's she is shaking, fumbling and dry in the mouth. She is looking around but can't focus.

'Hey!' the man behind the counter bellows. 'What are you doing? You better not be stealing.'

She frowns at him, shocked at the suggestion.

'You Blacks are all the same.'

She feels like crying and wants to run outside, but she can't go back without the eggs. She asks for four and says, 'They are for Mr David Bradley, thank you.'

He snorts. She imagines he is a pig as he wraps the eggs in some cloth. No other words are spoken as she leaves.

She walks briskly back to where the two men are standing in the front garden, where at last some marigolds are blooming and a few potatoes are ready to be pulled from the ground.

'You should stay with your family tonight,' David suggests.

'Babiin?' she turns to her father, concerned about what has transpired in her absence. His look of resignation turns her stomach even more.

Was it good news? Did they offer him something wonderful for his heroism and hard work? Has she finished working with the Bradleys and will she be allowed to go back to helping her mother and aunties with the children? She has so many questions but asks none of them. She knows her father will let her know when she can speak.

'I'll take those.' David takes the parcel from her, as confusion races through her mind. She looks at the two men one at a time, searching for answers to the questions that continue to flood her thoughts.

As they walk back to camp, Yarri explains to Wagadhaany the plans the Bradleys have burdened him with. 'Mr Bradley told me he and his brother and his brother's new wife, Mrs Bradley, they all are moving to Wagga Wagga.'

'They are really going! I knew they would. Louisa is excited, and I am so happy for her.' What she really means is that she is happy for herself – her babiin didn't mention her name, so she mustn't be going. She twirls around like a young girl without a care in the world. She has a spring in her step and wants to sing at the thought of her life joyfully changing just as Louisa's has.

It is some minutes before she realises her father is silent and frowning, and that his steps have slowed.

'What is it, Babiin? Why do you look so sad? Will you lose your work at the station?'

He stops still, staring at the ground.

'What? Tell me?' Her heart races with panic. 'What did David Bradley say to upset you?'

In the softest of voices, he says, 'You are going with the Bradleys when they move to Wagga Wagga.'

'No I'm not, you must've heard wrong, Babiin,' she says confidently. 'They don't need me any more, Louisa doesn't like servants.'

'Mr Bradley said they need you and he wanted to tell me himself. They will take care of you, he promised me.' There is pleading in her father's voice.

'This is a mistake. I'm not going to Wagga Wagga. I am going to live with you and all the miyagan again, yes, that's what is happening.' She is strong in her words, sure of her position and the future ahead.

Yarri takes her face in his hands. 'I am sorry,' he says looking into her eyes. 'They are the bosses, so they say what will happen. You must go with them.'

Wagadhaany is in shock. She feels only anger and disbelief, as if her heart has stopped beating and the blood has stopped flowing around her body. She feels light-headed. It's as if her life has frozen in time, right before her eyes, which are now so full of tears that her babiin is a blur before her. He places his hands on her shoulders, as if holding her up.

'I'm not going anywhere,' she says, trying to yell but without any power in her voice. 'No, no, no,' she repeats. 'They can't make me go. They can't.'

'Wagadhaany, shhh.'

She hears her father's gentle voice, his words without power.

'You told him no, didn't you? Did you tell him no?' She is pleading, desperate for her father to be on her side, to have him be her hero again, to keep her with her clan.

When Yarri doesn't answer she becomes even more agitated. 'Did you say I *would* go?' She pushes his hands from her. 'Why would you agree that I would go?'

Her voice is raised, and angry. She has never spoken to her father this way, and she knows it sounds disrespectful, but she is confused beyond comprehension and feels like her life has just been pulled from under her.

'I won't go, I won't go.'

She falls to her knees, weeping, punching the earth. It's as if the long months of grief and loss within the Bradley house have finally caught up with her, and combined with this news it is too much for her heart to take, too much for her mind to decipher, too much for her to cope with. She sobs uncontrollably, as if wailing the death of someone she loves, and in some ways she is, she is grieving the loss of her life with all she loves; her miyagan, her dancing.

Yarri reaches down and pulls her up close to him, holding her tight and breathing heavily. She wants to resist, but she is already too emotionally drained to do anything but fall into his chest. He waits a few moments then says, 'We have no say.

You have to go. And I must stay on with the new owners of the Bradleys' station. It is what they want. It is what they have said will happen.'

Wagadhaany begins to sob harder. 'What about what *we* want? I don't understand. Why do they even want me to go? I am nothing to them. I am no-one.'

'Don't ever say that. You are not nothing. You are a strong Wiradyuri yinaagang. You are your mother's and my daughter.' He places his hand under her chin and gently moves her head up so her tear-filled eyes meet his, now also full of tears. 'You are our hope as life continues to change for us all.'

Wagadhaany can barely hear her father through her howling. She tries to speak, but her words are garbled, lost in her distress at the thought of moving when David Bradley originally said he didn't even want to go. 'How is moving away with White men a life of hope? My life will not be better without my miyagan. I don't understand.' She sobs harder.

'Daughter, you must go with them. Mr Bradley told me there is something that is law called the Masters and Servants Act. It is different to our lore, our ways of doing things, our stories and customs on how we are to behave. Their ways, the White ways, they have governments who make orders and commands. He said that Aboriginal people are the servants and White people are the masters, and it is the law.' He shrugs his shoulders. 'This is what they have told me. How can I argue against the law? And I need the rations from the station work for the family, now we can't always hunt where we used to. He said he will make sure I still have work. And I need to look after your gunhi and the miyagan. You understand, don't you?'

Wagadhaany doesn't understand and wonders if her father

believes the words he is saying. 'What about *our* ways of doing things? What about what the Ancestors have taught us about how to live? Why are we living the White man's way, what they call law?'

Yarri doesn't answer her questions but continues. 'He said there are not enough workers because so many have gone to search for gold. They need you to help them,' he pauses, 'and he reminded me that he saved your life.'

'But, but . . .' She is crying so hard she can't get her words out. She wants to scream to the world that her father is the hero, that he saved *all* of their lives. 'You didn't just save *my* life that night but you went back out and saved theirs too. Mr James's *and* Mr David's.'

She wants to mention all the other lives her father saved, but she can't. The words are stuck in her heart.

Yarri takes both her hands in his and holds them firmly. 'They saved your life, Wagadhaany. I will never forget the night I found you, your arms linked in theirs. Without them you would not be here with me right now. I will always remember that, and I will always be grateful. Biyaami was there with you, but their sheer strength and willpower kept you anchored to that spot. We cannot ignore that you are alive because of them.'

'And they are still alive because of *you*.' She says softly, collapsing to the ground again.

'I don't want to go,' Wagadhaany is distraught at the thought of leaving her family for good, to go to a place she knows virtually nothing about except that there are other Wiradyuri people there. 'I belong here, this is my home,' she says with tear-filled eyes, as she talks to her parents.

'You will always have miyagan around this country, your Wiradyuri country. I think Wagga Wagga is many days away, but the Ancestors will be with you wherever you walk, and even though we won't be there in body, you will always have us in your heart.'

Yiramiilan puts her hand on her daughter's chest as she speaks, and Wagadhaany feels some comfort in the wisdom of her mother, the matriarch for all the men in their lives, and for her. But Wagadhaany is not consoled by her mother's words. She wants to live with the kin she knows, the cousins she grew up with, the nieces and nephews being born here, in Gundagai. She is not remotely interested in anything that James Bradley has said about the benefits of them moving away. There is nothing about *his* benefits that will translate to her life being better. There are no benefits to be had for her. There is nothing to be gained at all by being separated from her miyagan.

Wagadhaany's oldest aunty, Bamali Gari, moves to her niece's side, puts her arm over her shoulder and pulls her around to face her. 'Never forget the meaning of your name,' she says in the young woman's ear. 'Wagadhaany, you know your name means a dancer. So, this new place, it is your place also. Waga Waga, the place to dance, the place to celebrate. My heart hopes it will be a good home for you, my girl.'

She thinks back to her childhood, the first time her mother told her she was their little dancer, the pride she felt. It still sits within her heart, even though her giiny breaks right now.

All the women have gathered around the gunhi and ngamurr now and they begin to sing as Bamali Gari continues. 'You will dance our stories down the way there.' Her aunty points towards the new place. 'And when your feet hit the earth, we will feel it here.'

'Gari?' Wagadhaany says her bamali's name as a question, because she knows it means truth. She wants to know if her aunt is telling her the truth.

'Gari!' her bamali confirms. Taking her niece in her arms, she whispers in her ear, 'White man's way, the distance is not so far, but we always feel distance in our heart when we are forced to be apart.'

Wagadhaany begins to weep, convinced that this will be the last time she will see her mother, father, brothers, aunties, uncles and cousins. Spending time with them briefly each week was barely enough to sustain her over the past few years, but the unknown before her, and the reality of being so far away from them, is too much for her to bear.

Am I dreaming? Is this a nightmare? Wagadhaany's thoughts are blurred, her emotions smothering her, twisting everything in her mind. She is crying and her breathing becomes gasping and erratic as she asks herself these questions over and over again.

The older women have moved in closer around her, trying to absorb her distress. Their own hearts are aching with the pain of seeing the young woman so distraught, so miserable, so heartbroken. The men are preparing a fire, to smoke her and themselves, to cleanse away all the worry, the concern, the fear they share about her leaving the clan. The children walk to the centre of the circle and hand Yarri some small branches of eucalyptus leaves, which they have pulled carefully from low-hanging branches, knowing that they are only ever to take what comes easily to them, what the land wants them to have.

As the mob fall into a formation around the fire, they are unified in their love and concern for Wagadhaany, and she feels this intensely. The collective strength shared around the circle makes her stronger, and yet somehow more vulnerable at the same time. This sense of togetherness is something she has experienced all her life, but she can hardly believe it exists anywhere else. *How can it be?* This way of being a family is not what she witnesses at the Bradleys.

Her mother begins to sing a powerful song, and one by one they join in, eyes closed, hands moving to the sky, to the earth, to their bodies, over and again. They sing a song of thanks to Biyaami and in pairs walk to the sacred fire, breathing in the smoke, washing it over their bodies, cleansing themselves not only of the pain of saying goodbye to Wagadhaany, but also of everything that has ailed them in recent times. Each individual carries their own scars from life, many created by the changes that are occurring for them in their Wiradyuri country. And many still grieve for Long Jimmy, as if his passing were only yesterday.

Wagadhaany walks into the middle of the circle with her cousins, the women she has grown up with, become a woman with. Ngaayuga, Gandi, Yiri and Yirabiga are all crying as they hold hands and walk to the fire together, shoulders slumped, the weight of sadness falling heavily on each of them. Simultaneously they gently release hands and lean in or kneel at the fire. Wagadhaany is slow, considered, focused. She waves her hands to draw the smoke towards her, she fills her lungs at the same time. Her spirit needs it. She closes her eyes and takes three deep breaths. She stands again and turns so the smoke washes her back and legs. She lifts her feet and allows the smoke to cover those as well. At that moment, the words of her mother strike her clearly: everywhere she walks her Ancestors will continue to walk with her. With that thought she feels an inner strength. Her faith and trust in the wisdom of her Elders, and knowing that her Ancestors will always ensure that she will never be alone spiritually, mean that while she doesn't want to leave, she knows she will survive. She looks up to the sky, acknowledges Biyaami, and walks back to the rim of the circle.

When the ceremony is over, there are no grand speeches like she heard at the church service after the flood, or at the presentation of the breastplates to Jacky Jacky and her father. There are only the strong arms of her Elders holding her, one by one. And there are warm cuddles from the children who don't understand what is going on, but love their Bamali Wagadhaany.

When it's time to say goodbye, her mother embraces her youngest child and pulls her as close to her own heart as possible. They breathe in time and as she pushes some hair from her daughter's ear, she whispers, 'Be strong, my girl. Know we love you, my girl. Come back to us, my girl.'

One by one, each of her brothers approaches her, hugs her and tells her he loves her. The scene rips at her giiny. She considers each of the men and thinks about the countless times they found joy in tormenting her. Now she sees they are the tormented ones as she leaves them for the unknown. She hopes they never have to face this kind of unknown themselves.

As Wagadhaany and Yarri walk away from the camp, the women start to wail. She thinks it sounds like the wailing when someone dies. She is not dead but it feels like she has died inside. She has no idea when she will see her miyagan again, and she has no power to decide this either. She knows she is not the first to have been forced to leave and work for White people, and she knows she will not be the last. When she turns briefly for one last glimpse of the camp, she sees the women holding the children closer, tighter than ever before. She knows her grief is shared by them all; they are grieving the breaking down of their most treasured miyagan.

As she turns back and continues to walk, she thinks of the gudha-galang huddling into each other and their mothers and aunties. She knows they'll be fussing over who can get closest and wrap their arms and legs around the women the tightest. She wishes they understood the significance of staying close to their parents, always.

A few of the older children chase after Wagadhaany and Yarri, and call out lovingly, 'Take us with you! Take us with you!'

They are too young to understand where and why she is going, or what her departure will mean to her, to all of them.

But she is glad for their naivety; it makes her smile even though it breaks her giiny at the same time. She wonders if she will ever have children of her own. If she will ever find the love she sees between her parents, the love she sees in Louisa's eyes for James.

As they walk further away from camp, the calls from the children fade then cease altogether. Wagadhaany takes her father's hand, tears streaming down her face, her stomach in knots. She does not turn around again for she cannot bear the thought of seeing her family still watching. More importantly, she does not want her mother to worry any more than she already is. She knows she must be strong, for her family and for herself. So she continues to face forward, putting one foot in front of the other until they reach town.

The sky turns from burnt orange to dark mauve as the sun sets over Gundagai. These colours usually soothe Wagadhaany's heart, but tonight there is no colour or skyline that can do that. As she and her father reach the Bradley house, she looks up to see Louisa's silhouette against the dim light of the main bedroom. She appears to be folding clothes, no doubt packing for the journey ahead. Something in the pit of Wagadhaany's stomach shifts, weighing her down.

They stop at the front gate and stare at the door ahead. Once she walks through it, she may never see her father again. Something is gripping her giiny so tight it's as if it is being ripped right out of her chest.

'You will have a new life, a different life now,' Yarri says, regret in his voice.

'I don't want a new life, Babiin. I don't want to be a different person,' she says. 'I want to be me, here, with you.' She falls into her father's chest. 'I want to be me, and I belong here.'

She can feel her babiin's giiny beating fast. He takes a deep breath and gently pushes her back so he can look in her eyes.

'You will always be our daughter, Wagadhaany. You can never become someone else. Your identity will be the same, our dancer. But you will be a dancer in a different place. The same, but different.'

Wagadhaany is confused. How can she be the same but different? She shakes her head, crying, and Yarri grips her firmly.

'You must be strong. You must come back to us. We love you more than all the miima-galang in the sky.' His words echo her mother's. But she doesn't need words. She has always understood the depth of her father's love. Right now she can see the fear and heartache in his eyes as he says goodbye, letting her go. She can imagine his guilt but understands it is out of his control. It is not his fault. It is not her fault.

As she hugs her father what she feels is so intense that even though she has the words to express herself, there is no power in her throat for her words to rise out. It is as if the Bradleys have stolen not only her life but also her ability to speak.

She looks into her father's eyes and sees his tears and her giiny shatters. He kisses her forehead and steps back, nods and looks towards the door. Involuntarily, she turns and walks towards it. In that moment something new, something powerful, rises in her, so overwhelming she feels her hands form fists. She realises it is hate. Hate for James Bradley. Hate for David Bradley. And in this moment she feels less respect for Louisa too.

Wagadhaany does not sleep that night. Instead she thinks about everything other than the trip to Wagga Wagga: the beautiful sky as she walked into town with her babiin, the young children chasing and calling after her, her mother and aunties wailing as she walked away, the tears in her father's eyes. So much pain, so much suffering. *Why do humans do this to each other?* If the Bradleys let her stay, everyone would be happier.

She dozes off but it seems like only minutes later that she is woken by the sounds of the horses and the bullock dray being brought around. She knows it is very early in the morning because she hasn't heard the roosters yet, her usual wake-up call. She breathes in deeply, her eyes crusty from crying in her sleep.

It's time, she tells herself, and she swings her legs over the side of her bed as if it is a normal day and she is about to go into the kitchen and make the tea. Without any more thought, she dresses in the dark. She strikes a match to the kerosene lamp and as the flame takes hold she pulls together her few belongings. Into a small calico bag she places some undergarments and a pair of shoes Louisa gave her, a pair she calls Sunday shoes, though she's not sure why she can't wear them on other days of the week. Safely inside is a Quaker Bible that Louisa also gifted her, even though she cannot read. Between two pages she has hidden a headband from her mother, made from string and the feathers of a guinea fowl. She wants to wear it now, but knows that the Bradley men will neither understand nor permit her to do so. She promises herself she will wear it whenever her spirit is homesick.

She looks around the tiny space. This will be the last time she wakes in here, the dark room with no air, no natural light, no warmth. She never wanted to live in this house and now, in a strange turn of events, she realises she never wants to leave.

A knock on the door startles her, and she drops the bag and her things tumble out.

'Yes?' she asks, nervously, bending to collect the items.

'It's just me,' Louisa says softly. 'Are you ready?'

Wiray, she says in her mind, shaking her head. *No! I am not ready.* She will never be ready to leave her family behind. But cautiously she responds, 'Yes.'

She checks the items in the bag, turns down the lamp and opens the door.

As the two women step into the carriage, both are silent. Wagadhaany feels strange. Something she can't control or describe is taking over. Her chest feels tight and she is having trouble breathing, but she dares not say anything. She knows that James Bradley would be very angry if she were to stall their departure in any way. And so she sits, cramped, pushed to one side of the carriage with Louisa close to her, a blanket across their laps and some of Louisa's essentials that she didn't want to travel without crushed at their feet. The men sit opposite, looking out each side of the carriage. Occasionally Wagadhaany catches David Bradley looking at her, expressionless, and wonders if he too wishes he were back in Gundagai.

She focuses on breathing as quietly as possible and clutches her calico bag. She wants to put her headband on. She wants to sing to Biyaami and ask her for protection on the journey ahead. She does so in her mind, knowing that she will still be heard. And while her eyes are open, she can't see anything through the tears that tumble down her cheeks. It is some time before she notices the carriage is moving.

In the carriage, Louisa sits upright, conscious of the awkward silence between her and Wagadhaany, brought about by her friend's soft but constant sobbing. Louisa wishes Wagadhaany would stop crying, and that she could be happy and positive about what lies ahead. She hopes that in time her friend will feel grateful about leaving Gundagai.

As James snorts in his sleep, Louisa has a fleeting moment of guilt at having married him so soon after Oscar's death. But what was she to do? She was alone, and she needed to be filled with hope again. She believes that moving to Wagga Wagga will allow her to finally let go of the pain Gundagai has brought her, the sorrowful memories of her family and her late husband. Her heart is already lighter thinking about starting afresh, building a future, having a family.

She smiles at her husband, closes her eyes and thinks about what the first day of her new life in a new town might bring. She imagines meeting other Quakers and feels more motivated about continuing the important work of helping the convicts and the Aborigines. While she didn't mind James using convicts on their station as a way of giving them some employment, she is against the outright exploitation of them for the hard labour of building roads. Many convicts were sent to the colony for minor crimes, and she detests the fact they are treated as if they're all murderers. If she can set up a Quaker group in Wagga Wagga then perhaps collectively they can assist current and ex-convicts to live more morally, and help them to rebuild their lives through gainful employment in the town.

In recent days, Louisa has given a lot of thought to Wagadhaany, trying to rationalise taking her with them to Wagga Wagga. She needs to turn the guilt she feels at upsetting her friend into a better outcome for both of them. As Wagadhaany's silent sobs mix with the sounds of the Bradley men snoring, she looks at David Bradley, grateful that he has been so support-ive of Wagadhaany leaving Gundagai with them, although not sure why he was. She imagines it may have been simply to be in opposition to James, who didn't want Wagadhaany to come, but she doesn't mind. As long as her friend is with her, she is happy.

Louisa thinks about how Wagadhaany could play a key role in connecting her with the local Aboriginal people and guiding the work that needs to be done. She doesn't know how it might eventuate, but she is determined to ensure that the Blacks have equality with White people. She has so much to learn, and so much to do, but with Wagadhaany by her side every day, teaching her, she is certain change is possible. It simply must be.

As much as Louisa tries to find reasons for Wagadhaany to be positive about leaving, she knows that her crying is born from the heartache of already missing her family. Louisa prays that taking Wagadhaany away from them will lead to a better life for her; better living quarters, freedom to move around with or without Louisa by her side, spending time doing things together in a bigger town. She can live a life of equality if she stays with Louisa.

The carriage pulls to a halt for the second time as Wagadhaany, utterly grief-stricken, is ill by the roadside. James is impatient and annoyed, mumbling under his breath, while David tries his best to calm his brother and check on the wellbeing of the girl at the same time. When he rests a hand on Wagadhaany's shoulder, Louisa notices the intimacy in his gesture, but brushes it off as a sign of caring that her husband is incapable of showing her friend. She is embarrassed by James's cold-heartedness while Wagadhaany is so physically unwell and emotionally distraught.

Back on the bumpy road, Louisa links her arm through Waga-dhaany's to comfort her. Louisa is desperate to take some of the misery from her friend. 'Please, please stop crying,' she begs. 'You are not alone. I am here, we are here together, and you still have your family.'

But there is no response.

'You have not lost your family; not like *I* have. Not like James and David did,' she whispers, as both men appear to be sleeping. 'Your family are alive and well and you will be able to visit them. I will go with you, won't I?' She holds Wagadhaany's hand tightly.

Over the four-day journey, they stop many times to feed the bullocks and to ensure they have enough water and rest. Occasionally, Louisa discovers joy in the rolling hills and open woodland. She recognises the yellow box trees James had pointed out to her back in Gundagai, and feels that some sense of their past life will stay with her.

Wagadhaany finally stops crying but is silent for the rest of the long journey. Louisa keeps their arms linked as she closes her eyes and notes every bump as the carriage rattles along the dirt road. As she relaxes into its rhythm, she lists in her mind the possibilities that lie ahead: her new life with James, her new purpose and, one day, her own children to care for.

Chapter Ten

As exhaustion grips her, Wagadhaany is pale and listless from being physically sick during the journey. She has lost track of how many days they have been travelling, as one teary day blurs into another, and she has no interest in eating, in being alive. Coupled with the emotional drain of saying goodbye to her world in Gundagai, she is weak, vague and disinterested in whatever Louisa is saying. She shakes her head to clear the fog in her mind and realises that not only does her heart feel numb, so do her ears.

The horses travel faster than the dray and arrive at the new property before the Bradleys' possessions. As they move slowly up a bumpy path to the new homestead, Wagadhaany finally notices the landscape. It is the same but somehow different to Gundagai. A vast green expanse that goes on and on. The land around Wagga Wagga at first sight appears flatter than the countryside they have left, but in her mind it is unmistakably Wiradyuri.

When the carriage finally comes to a stop, she is grateful to be able to place her feet on solid ground and breathe in the clean air. It takes a few seconds to balance herself, as she is unsteady from sitting for so long and in need of some sustenance. She closes her eyes and silently lets her Ancestors know she is there; she acknowledges the Ancient Ones, the Old People who have been there before her and have passed on, and she asks Biyaami for protection while she is so far from her miyagan. As a slight breeze washes over her she knows she has been heard and she is not alone. Only then does she begin to relax.

She turns around slowly, taking in the views of the Marrambidya plains, overwhelmed by the expanse of what she understands comprises the Bradley property. The size of the building that will be their home takes her by surprise. She has never seen a house so large, so white, and with so many windows, and enormous windows at that. She is already considering the effort it is going to take to keep them clean. At least, she tells herself, maybe here she will have a window of her own, some natural light, a room the sun can shine into and warm in winter. Where she can look at the land from a place that is private. And maybe even somewhere to hang the curtains that Louisa had offered back in Gundagai.

As Louisa and James walk towards their new home she falls behind, trying to guess how many rooms are inside, how much linen there will be to wash, furniture to dust. The work is too much to contemplate right now, so she turns around and looks at the countryside behind them, wondering which direction her family are in. She considers the minor bumps in the horizon before her. Her eyes are weary and unfocused but she searches anyway for the family she left behind, wondering if they are looking into the distance for her as well.

'James!' Louisa declares. 'This is breathtaking!'

'This, Louisa,' he says, sweeping his hand from left to right to take in the extent of the property, 'this is known as Quakers Hill. The name called me to it, just as I was drawn to you that first day at the Gundagai races.'

Wagadhaany is surprised to see this different side to James, one that suggests his heart, his emotions, may have played a role in the move, that business had not been the only thing on his mind.

'Let me assure you though,' he continues, looking to his brother as if he knows what's on everyone's mind, 'it may have a connection by name, but don't think for a minute it's not the best business decision I've ever made. We've ever made. You were with me on the trips here, my brother, so you know the benefits of this property. The river is to the east.' James points and the others look in the direction of his arm. 'And the centre of town is that way,' he says, pointing to the south-east, and Louisa moves her entire body as he speaks, opening her arms wide as if she is going to hug the entire landscape to her body.

'This is beautiful,' she says, twirling around and around and around.

Wagadhaany is dizzy simply watching Louisa and wonders how she has the energy to move that way at all after such a long, tiring journey. She is lethargic and desperate for sleep.

'Your new home, my love,' James says, placing his hand on the small of Louisa's back just as she comes to a stop. 'Only the best for you. Rest assured this is one of *the* most significant properties in the area.'

Louisa hugs him, pulls back and then looks at him adoringly. 'I never really paid much thought to what our home might be like, James, and I don't care about having the best of anything, that has never been a concern of mine. I don't care about bricks and mortar. You should know me better than that by now. Fancy was not the way I was raised.'

She pauses, casting her eyes away from James. Wagadhaany wonders if Louisa is thinking about her family also. James moves closer to Louisa's side as she takes in a deep breath and swallows both the air and her emotions.

'But this is just beautiful,' she says warmly. She places a hand over her heart. 'And I am so very happy.'

Before the last word has left her lips, he draws her close to him and their lips touch gently.

'Come,' he says, taking her hand and walking with her across the property. 'Tarcutta Creek is there,' he explains, gesturing, 'and it meets the Murrumbidgee River there. So, we are in the best position for managing the property.'

Louisa turns and nods for Wagadhaany to follow. Wagadhaany looks to the river and her mind carries her back to Gundagai. The ancient trees lining the riverbank, the dry grasses for weaving, the peacefulness of the bila – it's the same as she remembers back home. She can see the strength of the current but it is going the wrong way. Even if she could swim properly, there's no way she could rely on the river to take her back. She turns to look at David, who is standing close behind her, his hands firmly in his pockets, staring at the river as if he is willing it to do something other than be a home for Murray cod and garfish. She wonders if he is thinking about how the rising waters of the river might flood Wagga Wagga one day too.

With long, relaxed strides, James walks to his brother and slaps him on the back, snapping him out of his thoughts. 'We are in proper cattle country now, David. We will make this a pastoral run like no other. We can use the river and the creek for cattle and sheep, and the Blackfellows can sleep nearby too. There's a lagoon beyond those trees. It's even better than I could ever have imagined.'

James appears pleased with himself and with what he has already managed to attain towards ensuring the Bradley legacy.

The conversation between him and David is suddenly drowned out by the screeching of cockatoos. It's as if the birds have appeared from nowhere. But Wagadhaany knows her mother's totem is always there in the big gum trees. Cockatoos are never a surprise to her, least of all at dusk.

She smiles for the first time in days because it is obvious that her mother is there with her. And while she has no idea how life is going to unfold for her in Wagga Wagga, she knows that the call of the kuracca at sunset each day will remind her that she is never alone.

As the kuracca-galang swarm the area she feels great delight, her spirits lifted, but the three Bradleys are astonished. None of them has seen so many cockatoos in one place at one time, and they stand in awe, mouths agape, enthralled by the sight. At the peak of their calls, Louisa puts her hands over her ears as if they need protecting.

'I'll have the men do something so that noise doesn't bother you again, Louisa,' James says. 'It's not a racket we need every day now, is it?'

As he pecks his wife on the cheek, Wagadhaany's hate for him resurfaces.

Over the weeks that follow, under Louisa's direction, Waga-dhaany assists in setting up the new home and determining the chores that will be shared between them. In a heated argument with James when they first arrived, Louisa had insisted that she would do chores alongside Wagadhaany. She doesn't know why Louisa is so desperate to cause trouble with her new husband.

She has noticed James's look of disdain whenever the two women are together, enjoying each other's company. She supposes he wishes his wife was spending her time with the women in town, rather than doing domestic duties.

'We did not bring her here for nothing,' James growls at Louisa one evening, as she cooks their dinner. 'We had an agreement.'

He looks to David, who sits waiting for his meal. Wagadhaany doesn't know where to look.

'She should be cooking our meals.' James has venom in his voice but David says nothing. He simply looks at Louisa.

David Bradley offers little to most conversations; rather, he comes and goes from his room, at times leaving the house for meetings in town or other parts of the countryside. Wagadhaany has no true understanding of the younger brother's role, she only knows that when he is not handling the financial side of the family's affairs, he is quiet. *What is bubbling away inside you, David Bradley? Is it hatred, because in your heart you did not want to come here either? Or something else?*

Wagadhaany can feel her own hatred setting in, taking over. She hates being spoken of as if she is not even there. She has no idea what agreement was made and she doesn't know what she has ever done to make James Bradley dislike her so much.

When James is not making his displeasure known, he is busy managing the labour for the cattle run. Soon the station is functioning, buzzing with life. Cattle are grazing, stockmen are gathering and Wagadhaany sees groups of Aboriginal men for the first time since leaving Gundagai. She wonders if they are her kin, if they know her family or who she is, and where they are from.

Are they Wiradyuri? Have they heard of my babiin and Jacky Jacky? Did they experience the floods that washed over Gundagai many times? And where are all the women – their wives, daughters and families?

She always has so many questions, but there are no opportunities to ask them of anyone, so there are no answers. As she hangs the clean linen along a length of rope at the back of the house, she sees some of the Aboriginal men by the river down from the house. A pang of loneliness and homesickness washes over her as she thinks of her father, and her uncles and brothers, who are working on other stations now too. She is carried back to her old life on the river in Gundagai, thinking of her gunhi and bamali-galang dancing, where she should be. She breathes slowly in and out, in and out, and forces back any sadness and longing that threaten to cause her to weep.

That night she hears James Bradley's voice from upstairs. She knows he has started drinking again, and suspects that now he has taken Louisa as his wife, he feels his abstinence is no longer necessary. There is scuffling on the floorboards and her heart rises to her throat when she hears Louisa yelp. It is the only sound Louisa makes before there is sobbing and Wagadhaany knows he has his hands on his wife. She is frozen with fear, and with disappointment, because in the morning she knows Louisa will face the day as if nothing happened.

It's weeks before there is any rain in Wagga Wagga and when it finally falls, it comes in giant drops that hit the dry ground with force. The rainfall is welcome but so heavy that there is fear of flooding. When Wagadhaany hears Louisa and both Bradley brothers express their concerns, she is worried. They all knew that Wagga Wagga was at risk of flooding too.

As the Marrambidya begins to slowly rise, the Black stockmen camped along it move up the bank, but there is no urgency to do anything at the house on the hill. Wagadhaany is conscious of the tension between the brothers, and believes that David is waiting for any opportunity to prove that Wagga Wagga may turn out to be as dangerously flood-prone as Gundagai. He has taken to giving her glances that suggest he is now an ally, or at least not the enemy. He is a Bradley, a man who gives her an eye-twitch and a strange smile occasionally. She knows she can't trust him, and she is always careful when he is around. And while she might not feel as much loathing for David as she does James, he was the Bradley brother who spoke to her father. She is sure he was the one who decided she would leave Gundagai with them. He can't truly be her ally, not now, not ever, she tells herself.

As the three Bradleys stand on the veranda looking at the flowing river through the downpour, Wagadhaany watches from the doorway.

'We are just as much at risk of flooding here as we were back home!' David says sharply, turning on his heel and walking past Wagadhaany, back inside.

Wagadhaany moves to sit at the dining table and busies herself peeling potatoes, feigning disinterest in anything other than preparing the nightly meal. Louisa sidles up next to her and gently takes her hand.

'It's going to be all right,' she says. 'We are safe here.'

'I know,' she responds, thinking of her father rescuing her, the Bradleys and so many townsfolk during the Great Flood. Having survived the horrors of that night, she firmly believes the Ancestors will always keep her safe. 'I know.'

Wagadhaany stands and walks to the kitchen stove, Louisa following. As she puts the potatoes in a pot of water above the wood fire, Wagadhaany speaks softly. 'Rain is life, Louisa,' she says, remembering what the old women back home used to tell her.

'Of course it is,' Louisa responds.

'And . . .' Wagadhaany wants to say more, she wants to share the wisdom of the Old People with Louisa, but she is hesitant. For as much as Louisa tries to include her and make her feel at home, she is aware of how things are for Black people, and James Bradley is a constant reminder that she is not really welcome in their house, and she is never going to be their equal.

Louisa pushes the younger woman. 'Go on, Wagadhaany, what is it? Tell me what you know so I can learn. How can I *help* Aborigines if I don't listen and learn from you?'

Her eyes are warm and caring, and her voice is soft, softer than usual, and Wagadhaany thinks it's hard not to like her. But she cannot imagine that her husband would in any way support his wife *helping* Wiradyuri people, given how much he appears to detest Louisa being friendly with just one Wiradyuri yinaa.

She looks through the doorway into the sitting room where both Bradley men are in quiet conversation. She stands close to Louisa and says matter-of-factly, 'It's simple. The earth gives us rain for water to drink, and food from the land to eat. This is how she shows she loves us. In return we must always show respect. If we respect the earth and sky, they will respect us back.'

Chapter Eleven

Yindyamarra, a young Wiradyuri man, stands in front of James Bradley, ready to work. He listens to the instructions and warnings.

'This is Charlie, he is the head stockman you are to answer to,' James announces to the men he has employed to work with his cattle.

Yindy looks from one man to another.

'Charlie is in charge, and you will follow his orders in regards to the cattle run. You will do *everything* he says.' James looks at Yindyamarra and then at the other lean, dark men standing around. He turns to a few White labourers, many of them former convicts, standing to his left.

Yindyamarra notices they stand separately, just as they live.

'Charlie will report to me, and I will know your every move.'

It's a warning that Yindyamarra has heard before. This is not his first job as a stockman, and while he is well known for his skill with horses, he is trusted less than the White men, and his work, while better, is worth less due to the colour of his skin.

As James walks back towards the homestead, Charlie addresses the men. 'You can call me Red, because of my hair.'

Some of the White men laugh and point to Charlie's flaming hair, while the Black men just shake their heads. Yindy thinks Charlie's hair is more the colour of the orange fruit he's seen occasionally. But he is happy to call Charlie Red for the blotches on his fat, white face. Yindy wonders if he will ever understand the White man's humour, but he doesn't really care. He's not there for fun, he's there for the rations and the tobacco he takes back to camp. And because it's the only sense of freedom he has, riding across the land for days at a time. And it's one way he can keep alive the memory of his own father, killed in a riding accident when he was a young boy.

When Charlie doesn't get a reaction from the Black men he goes on attack. 'So, you lot are gonna be like that, are ya? Well, I tell ya what, if this was *my* run, I'd never have employed you wild tribe. As far as I'm concerned, you're nothing but lazy savages.'

Some of the White men nod in agreement and Yindy hears whispers of words like 'vagrants' and 'savages' but he doesn't react. He has heard them all before.

'But *you* cost less than *those* men.' He points to the group to his left. 'And even less than the Chinese who could've done some of the work you'll be doing here. But as Bradley just said, I will report back to him your *e-v-e-r-y* move.' He spits on the ground in front of him and the Black men take a step back.

Yindyamarra is wide-eyed at the speech he's just heard. He's not sure who this red-headed fella is, but he's wrong about the Black men being lazy. They've been working the longest days for as long as he can remember. They have worked to help the White men build properties on their own Wiradyuri land. They have built fences on their own land to keep cattle in and themselves out. They have done a lot of things that are strange, in his eyes, but they have always worked hard.

He looks at the other Black men, their sleeves rolled up above their elbows, exposing their lean but muscular arms. Their shirts are tucked into working pants, many pairs held up by second-hand leather belts, some with rope, while their hats show the wear and tear of time spent in all kinds of weather. The men are dusty and look older than their years.

'And let it be known that I won't tolerate any insolence from you lot either.'

Charlie continues his insults as the White workers offer menacing stares towards the Black workers in support of the man they will only call Red from now on. And while Yindyamarra doesn't know the words 'wretched' or 'sinister', he does understand Charlie's tone when he spits them out. He also understands his place in the working team, but he will not let another's hatred impact his love of riding, or his desire to be the best stockman this side of the Marrambidya.

'Right, we need to get down to business,' Charlie says, motioning at the men to move in closer and form a ring around him. 'Bradley's given me a list of things we need to get to as a matter of priority.' He looks at a sheet of paper with handwriting on it, reads it quickly, folds it up and puts it in his back pocket.

'So, how many of you have done this before?' he asks, scanning the group as nearly all the men raise their hands in the air. 'Right! Good! You know then that you have to be confident with the cattle, but you need to be careful too. And mark my words,' he pauses and looks directly at the Black men. 'I know exactly how many there are, and I'll know if any go missing or have been mistreated. Do you understand?'

He waits for each of them to make eye contact, tilt their head in a nod, tip their hat, or make some other show of acknowledgement that they understand what he is saying: that he does not trust them. 'So, don't even think about stealing any for dinner down by the river with the other natives, because if you do, it will be the end of you, in more ways than one.'

Yindyamarra doesn't know why Charlie is threatening the men. They all know better than to steal, and they prefer wambuwuny anyway, because fresh kangaroo on the coals will always taste better to Wiradyuri men than any new meat the White men eat.

Charlie continues with his instructions. 'You'll need to check the animals for injuries, check their teeth if they are old, feed them, brand them, tag them. Some of you will be required to castrate them. Do you understand what that means?' Again, he looks to the Black men, expecting them to know or understand less than the White men. 'Do you know what I am talking about? To cut their balls off!'

He says it so aggressively that most of the men grab their own crotches. Some wince and some chuckle. Yindy can't help but snicker. None of them imagines that any male – human or otherwise – wants their testicles removed, or to be responsible for taking another's. He is sure of that.

'Yes, boss. We know what it means to cut the balls off,' one sings out.

Charlie nods to acknowledge the response and goes on. 'Sheep will arrive soon, and they will need a different level of care, including help with birthing. Can you do that?' he asks, looking to the Black men again, as if they are the only ones who are expected to do any work on the Bradleys' station and need special instructions.

'Yeah, I'm really good at it, Boss,' one yells out, and another mimics putting his arm inside an animal's backside.

The men guffaw, humour the one staple in their survival since White men arrived and changed their lives, their landscape, their future. This light-hearted moment is an appreciated change.

For a moment even the head stockman smiles, and then he composes himself so swiftly it's as if no joke ever happened, as if they had not been connected by laughter. 'Enough of the jokes, we are here to work and the Bradleys mean business. I know some of you are used to just walking around a lot, lying under trees, doing nothing, but this is *work*, this is what *real men* do. This is how life on the land *really is*.' He looks around the group, staring down as many of the Black men as he can, not understanding that *they* are the real men of the land, that they know what real work is, and how to survive on the land better than anyone else.

Yindy doesn't like the way he is being spoken to but this is the way his life is now. Although every Wiradyuri man and woman has an equally important role to play, in the White society there are bosses who are men, and the bosses are always more important than the workers. And on the cattle stations, the White workers are nearly always considered more important than the Black workers. But having more power doesn't mean having more intelligence, Yindy knows, so he is neither worried nor intimidated by Charlie. He knows he is skilful on the horse and as good as, if not better than, any other man in the region. And he believes that most of the Black men working for the Bradleys are just as good as well.

'You men,' the boss says to the White men, 'your quarters are down the back of the property.' He points in the direction of some huts.

'And you lot,' he says to the Black men, 'I guess you'll be happy to stay down near the river.' He points to where there's recently been a campfire. 'Or, if you go to sleep with your tribe, wherever they are.' He rolls his eyes and nods to the White workers in solidarity, adding, 'Make sure you are back here by sunrise. And do not take any of the horses off the property unless you are droving. Do you understand?'

'Yes, sir,' they say in unison.

'All right. Be back here tomorrow.'

A few of the men, who are choosing to stay by the river near the station, quickly set about stripping sheets of bark from some nearby trees to build their shelters. Most of them have moved along the river many times through displacement and for work, and can build a ganya at lightning speed.

'Where're you from?' one of the Black stockmen asks Yindy.

'Along the Galari – the Whitefellas call it the Lachlan now – but we moved here, more work for the men with more cattle. I live with my miyagan, that way, at the big camp on the wetlands.' He nods to the east. 'And you?'

'I was born on the Wambool Bila.' He looks towards the sun to determine north-east and points in that direction. 'Whitefella call it Macquarie River. All the rivers of this country, they are our lifeline.'

Yindy nods, thinking about the Macquarie fella he's heard of, the one who made some of the White laws they live under now. 'You were moved here?'

'No, I came for the work. This was the only way to be able to move, you know, under the White man's law.' He tears strips of bark from a box gum.

143

Yindy looks at his countryman, to the direction of the Galari and the Wambool, and then to the Marrambidya, and thinks about the three bila-galang of Wiradyuri country, firm in his belief that as long as he can live on his own land, he can survive.

The next morning, Yindy arrives at the Bradleys' station before sunrise, as instructed. The White men are still asleep. He heads to the stables and looks for his horse. The horse had not been given to him. It had *chosen* him. When he first entered the stables a few days before, a handsome animal snorted the minute he walked near, and the seasoned stockman knew the sound was a call. As he enters again today to take his partner out, Yindy can feel that the connection between them has grown, that trust and companionship are already there.

Yindy knows that he and the horse he has named Mudyi need to work as a team, as long, tiring days and many months in the saddle lie ahead. He trusts that his youthful body can take the exertion, but he wants to prove himself to the red-faced fella, and his relationship with Mudyi will be paramount to his success.

The horse stands at seventeen hands high, his reddish-brown coat matched by a mane and tail that are slightly lighter in colour but rougher in texture. In the middle of his forehead is a white patch, which makes his dark brown eyes more prominent. Yindy runs his hands over the silky torso and down the length of his strong legs. All the while he is whispering, 'Mudyi, Mudyi, Mudyi.' As he gently moves his hand along the horse's back, ribs and hindquarters, he whispers again, 'Mudyi, you *are* my friend, aren't you?'

The horse neighs and throws his head back and forth.

'Ngawa?' Yindy asks. 'Is that a yes?'

The horse neighs again and the stockman knows they understand each other. Their friendship is born.

In the weeks that follow, Yindy quickly settles into life as a stockman on the Bradleys' station. He works the cattle on the unfenced property by day and at night sometimes sleeps by the river near the station but most often walks to the camp to sleep with his extended family further along the river.

After one long morning of branding the cattle, the men are ready for their midday meal. Yindy has heard that rabbit stew and damper are waiting, and he walks with purpose towards the homestead where he sees two women standing outside. Yindy knows one to be the station owner's wife while the other, no doubt, is the servant girl. The White woman supervises the serving of the meal, directing the men where to stand, while the dark younger woman ladles the stew and hands a bowl to each of the men. Yindy notices that she never makes any eye contact with the stockmen, but focuses on the task at hand. He assumes she doesn't want to draw any attention to herself from these hungry men needing to be fed. He knows the different kinds of hunger that can overcome the men he is working with. In the weeks she has been serving their food, she has never looked up once. He hopes today she will.

When she passes the bowl to him today, she does look up, and when Yindy sees her dark brown eyes, framed with the longest eyelashes he has ever seen, he smiles. The young woman smiles back. He thinks her face is as perfectly round and bright as the sun and he is immediately filled with warmth. Her cheeks have a hint of pink in them, as if she is blushing. He doesn't want to take his eyes from hers, but his male instincts take over and his eyes dart swiftly over her lean frame. She is tiny, he thinks to himself, and wishes he could fatten her up with some fresh wambuwuny. He would catch it especially for her.

When he looks into her eyes again, her smile is so warm it melts his heart. A few loose curls fall down the side of her face and he wishes he could touch them. More importantly, he wishes he could hear her voice. He wonders what it sounds like, how her full lips might pronounce his name.

Their hands hold the bowl in the air for too many seconds. Yindy's heart skips more than one beat before someone in the back of the line bellows, 'Hurry up, a man could die of starvation waiting for you Blacks.'

The young woman lets go of the bowl instantly, and although Yindy is conscious that they have been watched, he doesn't care. He takes in her slender fingers and wishes he could touch her hand, just for a moment. He wants to speak but he has no words. He sees embarrassment on the young woman's face. He is expected to move on, to take his bowl and walk away from the table, but his feet are rooted to the ground, as if they have been there for centuries. He doesn't want to move on, he doesn't want to step away from this woman. He hopes that she is feeling the same excitement that he is. Butterflies flutter from his stomach all the way to his loins. He tries to look into her eyes again, but she is staring down at the next bowl, which she fills before handing it to the next man in the queue. Disappointment falls heavy on him. He feels his shoulders slump. He lifts his feet, slowly making his way to where the other men have gathered in the shade of a grey box gum. Maybe she didn't feel the same.

Yindy is mesmerised by the beauty of the one who is now too many feet away from him. He is aware of his racing heartbeat and breathing and tries to slow both. He looks at his food and realises that while it's a gift to have had her prepare it, his appetite seems to have disappeared. But when he sees the other men devouring their meals, he starts to enjoy his own, as if she has made the stew just for him. He savours it, imagining her warm, wide smile in every mouthful.

Some of the men are going back for second helpings, others are lying down, hats over their faces, trying to get a short kip in before the long afternoon's work that awaits them. Yindy smells tobacco smoke, but is not interested in rolling a cigarette like most of the other men do every chance they get. He leans back against the trunk of the tree and tilts his hat just enough to shade his eyes and hide the fact that he is looking at the Aboriginal servant. She is pretty, he thinks to himself, and wonders if the other men are admiring her too. He thinks they must be reading his mind when they start talking about women.

'She's all right,' Johnno, one of the White stockmen says, just loud enough for the men to hear. 'The boss's missus, that is. She's all right, eh?' He seems to be seeking endorsement from the others.

'Yeah,' 'Suppose so,' 'Reckon,' come the replies.

'I saw her down there by the river one day,' he continues. 'Her ankles were . . . my God,' he adds, wiping his forehead as if the thought of Louisa's legs had caused him to break out in a sweat. 'It was a hot day and she didn't know I could see her.' He leans in to the men closest to him and lowers his voice. 'And she unlaced her boots, slid off her stockings . . .' He looks around to check that only the stockmen are within hearing range. 'And put her dainty little feet on the sand.' He uses his fingers on the ground to demonstrate her movements. 'I tell you, her ankles, they were the most beautiful ankles I have ever seen.'

There is laughter. 'Ankles?' 'I'd want more than ankles.' 'What, did she slide her bloomers off too?'

'Nah, kept her bloomers on. But I tell you, those ankles were enough to . . .' He pauses. 'Well, you know,' he says, breaking into laughter, one hand on his crotch.

'Bradley will have you hung if he ever hears you were doing that over his missus,' Frank says.

'I tell you,' Johnno says, ignoring Frank, 'it was hot enough to scald a lizard. I had sweat dripping off me, and I wanted to cool off in the river but I couldn't because . . . well, she was there with her ankles, so I just sat under the tree.'

'Don't you mean behind the tree?'

'Yeah, so I sat behind and under the tree, melting, and I looked at her and those damned ankles and she looked like a glass of cool water. I tell you, I just wanted to drink her.'

'But that's not all you wanted to do, is it?'

'Ah, stop it,' Frank says firmly. 'Don't be speaking about Bradley's wife like that.'

Yindy doesn't want to hear what the men are saying about Mrs Bradley, but no-one can escape it. He has never spoken to her even though he has seen her out on the property looking busy in the garden.

'It's all right for you, you've got a woman at home. You can drink her or do whatever you want with her any time you want,' Johnno replies.

Frank shakes his head, half in disbelief, half in disgust. 'You men are the reason no good woman in town will go near a stockman. You've got no-one to blame but yourselves for being lonely.'

'Lonely? I'm not lonely, I'm thirsty –' Johnno laughs '– for that long cool drink I saw.' And he looks across to the serving table where the women are clearing up.

'Ah, you better aim lower than the likes of Louisa Bradley, mate, or you're gonna be thirsty for a long time to come,' Jack, another stockman, advises.

'What about that Black gin?' Johnno suggests, nodding towards Wagadhaany, who is stacking the metal bowls to wash. 'She looks like a decent piece of meat, and I reckon them natives would be wild in bed.'

He looks to Yindy, to see if he will take the bait. Yindy's heart is racing and his blood is boiling, and one of the other Wiradyuri men is already on his feet.

'Don't you be speaking about our women like that. We aren't animals, you know.'

'Calm down, darky, we're just joking. Ain't no gin jockeys here,' he says.

But he doesn't convince Yindy, who looks angrily to the other Wiradyuri men, each of them waiting. If one moves an inch, they are all in.

Yindy waits for the signal to act, to deal with the disrespect to the woman without a name, and to Mrs Bradley as well. He reminds himself of the meaning of his name – respect – and that he will always defend the honour of Wiradyuri yinaa-galang, because his parents, who named him, would expect it of him.

But he also knows that there are different rules for Black men. The White man's word would always be taken over the Black man's, and he knows that any dispute is a chance that he could lose his job as a stockman, be locked up, arrested or worse. He has seen war on Wiradyuri country, most of it started by men like these, and he knows that in any conflict, there will be no repercussions if a Black man is killed.

Yindy knows he needs to be smart, and to trust what his belly is telling him. He lets the comments go.

It's a long day, but the afternoon seems less exhausting as Yindy gets through the cattle branding with his mind only half on the job. He thinks about the woman he almost met. Although he knows she is a servant, she held his gaze long enough to suggest she is a woman that knows her own mind. A woman who is consuming his mind right now with thoughts that help to drown out the painful cries and lurching of the calves when the branding iron hits their ears. As much as he loves being a stockman, he hates some of the jobs he has to do. His strength is also tested when branding the steers, whose pain is played out with kicking. He narrowly misses a number of kicks, but others don't, and Yindy almost falls over laughing when a steer kicks Johnno in the balls.

At the end of the day, after the horses are returned to the stables, the White men return to their lodgings on the property and most of the Black men return to their families on the wetlands by the bila. Yindy walks silently in a trance, thinking about the migay who has stolen his thoughts. He fears that with so many laws restricting what he can do as a Wiradyuri man, he may never get close to her. Will he ever get the chance to speak to her properly, to get to know her?

He doesn't even try to stop thinking about her, for his pre-occupation with how beautiful she is is too strong. And so he rides the wave, not knowing where his thoughts and wishes will lead, or whether his many questions will be answered. *How far has she travelled to be on this station? Is she Wiradyuri? Where are her family?* And, most importantly, *When will I see her again?*

It is weeks before Yindy sees Wagadhaany again because he is sent droving almost immediately after their first meeting. But he never stops thinking, imagining, hoping. He feels differently about the world since that day, that fleeting moment with the brown-eyed girl. He is feeling something deep for the migay, a feeling in his heart and loins that he hasn't known before. With long days and nights alone, and nothing but his mind and thoughts for company, Yindy starts making up stories about a life he could lead with the woman he hopes is not already married to another man. He starts thinking of her as his mamadin.

It is nightfall when he finally returns to the station. He is too tired to walk back to the camp and decides he will sleep by the river near the homestead.

He rolls his shoulders, pulls his head back, stretches his neck and tries to give his body some reprieve from the pain the days of riding have inflicted on his spine. His body aches all over and he has blisters on his feet from boots that are too big for him. The dampened bark he pushed into the toes offered some relief but not enough. He feels both pleasure and pain when he eases himself into the river that evening. The cold water at first stings then soothes the blisters, and the dirt drifts away with the current.

As the moonlight hits the surface of the lagoon, he slowly sinks and lets the world above wash over him. It is so peaceful, he wishes he could hold his breath and enjoy the serenity for longer. But his lung capacity soon reaches its limit and he pushes hard on the sandy bottom of the river, grateful not to have hit a sharp-edged rock. He leaps high out of the water, enjoying the moment and splashing around like he did as a young child. He flicks his long, wet hair from side to side and chuckles to himself at the simple pleasures to be had at the end of a hard day. As he calms down and the water settles around him, he notices a female silhouette on the other side of the river. At first all he can make out is a lean figure. A woman has been bathing alone and he knows he has startled her as she seems to be rushing to cover herself. He imagines she feels shame, just as he does at his splashing around like a crazy duck. The last thing he wants to do is frighten a naked woman in the same water he is in. And then his mind blurs. A woman, naked.

He refrains from speaking for fear of making the situation worse. He decides not to move either. He plants his feet firmly in the sand of the riverbed, wriggles his blistered toes and waits – for what, he's not sure.

He tries not to stare, but it's difficult not to. Then, as the moonlight catches the woman walking up the bank towards the homestead, Yindy instantly knows it is the migay, *his* migay.

He desperately wants her to know it is him, the one who held the bowl with her for too long that day. The one she smiled at with her beautiful mouth and deep, dark eyes. But he can't say anything. He is mute. But he is also grateful. It is enough for him to know she has been naked, nearby, in the same water as him. And with that thought there is a simultaneous tug in his loins and his heart.

He lowers himself back into river, the water reaching his chin as he tilts his head back and looks to the full moon.

As he lies in his swag that night his thoughts swirl. He closes his eyes under a cloudless, black blanket of sky and drifts off to sleep, scripting what it will be like the next time he sees her.

When next they meet, he will not be splashing around in the river like a crazy duck.

'You,' Charlie says, pointing at Yindy. 'I'm told you know this country best. Can you get the cattle across the border to Victoria?'

'Yes, boss,' Yindy replies. He doesn't remotely know where the border is, but if he can find out the Wiradyuri name of the place he must get the cattle to, then it will be easier.

'Can you do it without having the cattle fall off any cliffs?' There's sarcasm in the boss's voice, but Yindy chooses to ignore it. He is going to take on this challenge and prove he is the best stockman of them all.

Days later, Yindy sets off in charge of the group tasked with moving a small herd to the sale yards across the border. He's proud of being appointed the leader. Two White men in the party, however, aren't so happy.

Charlie has shown him a map and told him the direction they are to travel and how far it is between where they are and where they must go. He feels confident when one of the other Black drovers says that it is Yorta Yorta country, where it meets Wiradyuri country in the south.

'The border is Victoria, we are in New South Wales,' Charlie says.

'All right, boss.'

It is just another instance of the White people changing the names of Aboriginal land. He nods, acknowledging that he understands what is ahead of him.

'The Bradleys want to start building a name for themselves in the marketplace and this is the beginning. You are to start off at daybreak.' Charlie leaves the men to prepare for the days ahead.

Early next morning, they start droving the cattle. There's a hint of orange in the sky.

Sitting upright on Mudyi, Yindy feels strong, in control, somehow empowered even though he is anything but. It's working with the cattle, riding Mudyi, and travelling across the countryside that gives him the sense of freedom that the clans left by the river lack.

On the first long day the heat is overwhelming. The cattle need to be rested often and given adequate water. And so do the men. Yindy is determined to carry out Charlie's orders, but he's also conscious of making sure the men are all right. They set up camp before it gets dark, and while it is still warm enough to wash in the river.

The men take turns watching the cattle while the others sleep. Yindy lies facing the blanket of stars across the blackest sky he has ever seen. He searches and searches, squinting at times to focus his eyes, until he finds the gugurmin. When he finally makes out the outline of the dark emu, he squints harder, trailing his gaze from the emu's beak and head, and following its long neck down to its body. The feathers appear to him in the shadows, backlit by a full moon. He takes a deep breath as he thinks of his family back on the Marrambidya wetlands, sharing the same night sky. He wonders if they are looking at it right now too. *And what of my migay back at the Bradley homestead? At this moment, is she bathing under this constellation?*

The night sky reminds him of the distinctive, three-pronged emu footprints he saw earlier in the day, the sky always mirroring the land, as the Old People told him. He decides that before they leave in the morning he will set some traps, hoping to catch an emu once they are gone, for him to find on their way back. When it is his turn to sleep Yindy closes his eyes, the gugurmin etched into his mind.

At first light, he is up before the others. He dresses, puts the billy over the fire and checks the cattle are all accounted for. He wastes no time in tying nets made of stringybark between a number of trees where he has seen the emu tracks. Once done, he stands with his hands on his hips, confident that he will be able to take some tucker back to his family along the river.

Chapter Twelve

The weeks have passed slowly since Wagadhaany shared that special moment with the stockman, and she keeps recalling how she was moved by the depth of his eyes. Over and over in her mind she has replayed the moment she handed him his bowl of stew, and the impact his smile had on her. She knows her smile was not innocent. It was born out of a longing she had not felt before.

She is lost in thought as she hangs the last sheet out to dry. When she turns to go back into the house, her heart skips a beat as she glimpses the same young man riding up to the other stockmen. The chestnut horse he rides is so tall she fears for his safety should he fall. His posture reminds her of her father, and she imagines he rode the same way when he was young. But she never saw her father ride, never saw him working, only knew that he was often away from the camp, giving everything he could to the Bradleys so he could bring home rations for his family.

As the stockman dismounts, Wagadhaany feels a flash of

gratitude in seeing the stranger again. She imagines he follows the same routine as her father back upstream. Her face softens and the corners of her mouth turn upwards. Like the kuracca that greets her at the end of the day, this man is a reminder that her people are everywhere, in the spirit and in the flesh, and even though they have not properly met, he represents a connection to her mayiny. She thinks he has the look of the Wiradyuri.

Wagadhaany realises she has been staring at him for some minutes, wondering where this stranger comes from and where he lives, where *all* the other Wiradyuri people live. She hopes they are nearby, and that she will get to meet them soon, so she might feel less homesick, feel part of a family again. When he dismounts, she notices his long hair, muscly arms and lean legs as he pulls the reins over the horse's head. His strong body does not go unnoticed, and she considers him to be handsome. She can hear the women back home whispering marambang ngulun, handsome face. And she smiles.

She watches him whisper in the animal's ear, look deep into its eyes and run his hand down the centre of the horse's face. She has seen this deep love and respect for animals before, as totems, but not for animals she knows arrived with the White people. The corners of her mouth turn upwards again. He is so focused. Her grin remains for some time after.

The long, lonely days turn into weeks and months for Waga-dhaany. The routine of life in the homestead without contact with any other Aboriginal people – aside from brief sightings of the stockmen at meal times – starts to take its toll. Her life hasn't changed for the better. Now she is helping Louisa prepare meals for many men, not just the Bradley brothers. And the house is much bigger, with many more windows to clean and beds to make and a bigger garden to tend to. She has extra work without any chance to see her family. She feels constantly sad, homesick, heartsick.

As she is charged with beating the dust from rugs, she imagines she is hitting James and David Bradley, although she doesn't know where that impulse for violence has come from. It has never been part of her life. At times she feels as if her actions are separate from her intentions and she finds herself calling on Biyaami for guidance. At other times, she looks for the young man, desperate for connection, for his smile, for the way he looked at her that first day. The handsome stockman swings in and out of her thoughts at regular intervals and she wonders if he ever thinks of her. She understands through overheard conversations that the 'young native stockman' has been driving cattle to better land for grazing and to market.

Depression weighs heavily on Wagadhaany most days, and because it's getting cooler, with grey skies and cold nights, it's hard for her to get up most mornings. She accepts that she has no choice but to be here, the law says so, but surely things can't be like this forever. An eternity away from her miyagan is not an idea she is willing to entertain at all.

As they settle more and more into their domestic routine, she notices James's drinking only become heavier, and though by day Louisa pretends all is as it should be, Wagadhaany knows she has started to challenge her husband at night. On many evenings, when Louisa and James are upstairs, arguing about his drinking and her not being the socialite wife he wants, Wagadhaany worries, especially when she hears James's voice get louder and angrier, and the sound of feet shuffling as if Louisa is trying to physically avoid him. But she does nothing. What can she do?

Instead, she tries to settle her anxious thoughts alone, staring out the window at the night sky and wearing the feathered headband her mother gave her, calling on Biyaami to connect them. On those nights, tears fall as her heart sinks. Sometimes she wishes she was with her Ancestors in the spirit world, and not on a station so far from her miyagan. She wonders how many other women like her are heartsick and missing their families too.

One cool, windy afternoon, Wagadhaany is sweeping the back veranda as she does at the end of every day, and desperately seeking some distraction not only from the chores but from her homesickness. Her heart is heavy, and it is constantly being called back to Gundagai. She hears a man yelling in the distance and looks towards the stockmen's quarters where two men are wrestling but laughing at the same time. She wonders if any of them have wives, and if so, where they are. *And what about gudhagalang? Where are the children?* That question carries her back to Gundagai where there were always lots of children, everywhere, and the thought of them having fun without her seeing it brings a tear to her eye.

She rests her head on the broom handle and closes her eyes. She sees her cousins – Ngaayuga, Gandi, Yiri and Yirabiga – and thinks about their childhood, playing together by the river, sleeping in the same humpy. She misses the laughter, the squeals of the young ones when her brothers would tell scary stories. She is overcome with emotion when she thinks of the young men back there now, no longer around to tease her, or to talk to. *What are they doing now? Are they still living at the camp, working as stockmen, or have they been moved on too?*

The tears begin to fall as she remembers her mother, her mother's face the day she left the camp for the last time, and the wailing of the women that followed her as she walked away with her father. She recalls her mother's final words: *Be strong, my girl. Know we love you, my girl. Come back to us, my girl.* The words should lift her, fill her with the security of knowing that all those miles away she is being thought of, is missed, that she is still deeply loved. But her spirits are not raised. Instead, she feels as if someone is standing on her heart and it can't beat properly, that it is being crushed by a power stronger than anything she has ever known.

Wagadhaany drops the broom, causing a thudding noise as it hits the veranda. She doesn't realise how loud the sound is so is surprised to see Louisa appear on the veranda, looking concerned. Wagadhaany is still sobbing, holding her apron up to her face, her shoulders hunched over.

'Oh no, what is it?' Louisa rushes over and puts her arms around Wagadhaany and hugs her in a way that no-one else has since she left Gundagai. The close contact, the affection shown, only makes her cry harder.

'Tell me,' Louisa says, 'please tell me what's wrong.' Her voice is shaky. 'Why are you so distraught, my friend?'

'Home,' Wagadhaany says, gasping. 'I want to go home.' She looks into Louisa's eyes, her vision blurred.

'Oh, Wagadhaany. Why aren't you happy here?'

When Louisa steps back to look directly in her eyes, Wagadhaany simply shakes her head gently, left, right, left.

'I've tried to make this a home for you too. I don't know what else I can do.'

Wagadhaany wipes her face on her sleeve, sniffs hard and swallows. 'How can I be happy away from my family?' She shrugs her shoulders in defeat, knowing nothing in Wagga Wagga can lift her spirits. 'I miss my parents and my aunties and uncles. I miss my brothers. I want to know what they are doing, if they are healthy. I want to see Jirrima, Yarran, Euroka and Ngalan, even though they nearly always tease me. They are my blood, my kin. I hope none of them have been sent away like me. I would hate them to be this unhappy, to feel this hopeless.

'And my cousins,' she hesitates to say their names, but she does so to bring them to life again, even if briefly. 'Ngaayuga, Gandi, Yiri and Yirabiga, we were so close.' She pats her chest to demonstrate they were close to heart. 'We had each other, and I had all their beautiful children to cuddle too, and now I have no-one. I am all alone.'

She looks to Louisa with eyes full of tears, and then squeezes them tight to clear them. 'Why are you looking like that?' she sniffles, confused by the shocked look on Louisa's face.

'I had no idea your family was so big. All those cousins and second cousins.'

Wagadhaany gives a weak laugh. 'That's not big, they are just *some* of my cousins, I have many more, and aunties, uncles. Everyone is related through kinship so we are all a family. And I miss them all. Every single one of them.' Her voice breaks and she gulps down further tears.

In that moment it dawns on her that she's never heard Louisa or the Bradleys talk about anyone in their families apart from their siblings and parents. They never talk about their Old People or Ancestors, and there are never any children around with their games and laughter. She thinks it's odd that Louisa and other White people choose to leave family, and country, and to forget them. Surely Louisa must have cousins, aunties and uncles.

She wonders how the two of them can ever really be friends when Louisa doesn't understand the sense of loss she feels being away from her clan. When she doesn't see that her grief is tied to her disconnection from her family, from not being able to dance at ceremony, from not being able to walk on the land where she was birthed and raised. How can she explain to Louisa, whose family *chose* to live on other people's land, that she feels robbed of her sense of identity, that everything that makes her Wagadhaany, the dancer, has been taken from her? How can this White woman ever understand her, or be able to help her?

She pities Louisa at that moment, realising her own life is rich in ways that cannot be measured by heads of cattle, or pennies, or acres of land. Wagadhaany feels her body heating, the emotion rising within. She closes her eyes and starts moving her feet slowly to the sound of nothing but the breeze in the trees, as if every grey gum is singing to her. She breathes in the scent of eucalyptus and imagines being with the women back home, dancing around the ceremonial fire, her feet following the steps of those who have danced the country for tens of thousands of years before her. She knows the Ancient Ones are with her again.

'Wagadhaany!' Louisa says, breaking her trance. 'What are you doing?'

She opens her eyes, realising that this is the first time she has danced for a long time, and that she has never danced in front of a White person before. She knows that James Bradley would be very angry if he found out she was dancing instead of sweeping, but she can't stop. She doesn't want to stop.

'I miss dancing with the women,' she replies, her feet still moving, wishing she was on her sacred ground back home. 'My name,' she continues, patting her chest with purpose, 'my name means dancer. I told you that the first time we met, don't you remember?'

She wonders if Louisa has ever listened to her, if her claims of wanting to help Aborigines are true. If, when Louisa refers to her as a friend, she really means it.

'It is who I am, Louisa. I can't forget who I am. I don't want to forget. I *won't* forget.' She is conscious of her louder-than-acceptable voice, of her tone with the woman who is still her boss, and she corrects herself immediately. 'I *must* dance, Louisa,' she says softly. 'It is in me, part of me, it is my spirit, my life.'

'But what about your new life here? Isn't *this* a better life?' Louisa looks around the property, at the large station and beautiful home, as if these things make up for a lack of family contact and of love. 'Don't you like your room?'

'This is not me,' Wagadhaany stresses, her bottom lip trembling again. 'A room cannot replace my family or their love. This property is *you*.'

Wagadhaany realises this is the first time she and Louisa have been completely honest with each other. Maybe they are almost equals in friendship, if nothing else.

As quick as she catches a glimpse of equality, she sees it disappear when Louisa's tone changes to one of authority. 'You mightn't see it, Wagadhaany, but you have changed, I have seen you change. You are not the same person as you were back in Gundagai.'

Wagadhaany feels challenged. 'I have not changed.' She is adamant, remembering her father's final words, that people don't change but become a different form of their original self. 'I'm *not* different. I am the same Wiradyuri yinaa I have always been.'

She boldly uses her language, and places her hand firmly on her chest, reclaiming an identity the Bradleys have tried to take from her since she was first forced to work for them. 'A new town, and a new home, even a new window does not make a new me. That is just silly. I am Wagadhaany, I will always be me. A new place and things won't change that.'

It is as if in her misery she has found an inner strength. She has become fearless, unafraid of challenging Louisa. 'My life looks different to you because I have a window and curtains, and a better dress and shoes, but,' she continues, patting herself again, 'I am the same on the inside. In here.'

Louisa looks hurt, disappointed. Neither of the women know where to turn, as if looking at each other would be even more unsettling. But while Wagadhaany wants Louisa to understand what she is trying to explain, the last thing she wants to do is hurt her feelings. She is, after all, the only person she has to lean on here in Wagga Wagga. She is beginning to realise that Louisa needs her too, not just to help around the house, but as emotional support, since she has no other female companionship.

In the uncomfortable silence, Wagadhaany bends over and picks up the broom. She looks at it for a moment, considers its long handle and smiles, having found a way to explain what she has been trying to express to Louisa. She will try one more time.

'Touch this,' she says to Louisa, who looks perplexed. 'Go on, touch it, please.'

Louisa runs her hand along the upper length of the broom handle.

'What is it made of?'

Louisa frowns. 'Wood, of course.'

'Yes,' Wagadhaany agrees. 'And where does wood come from?'

'Well,' she says, looking at Wagadhaany suspiciously. 'It comes from trees.'

Wagadhaany can hear the frustration in Louisa's voice at having to answer such basic questions.

'So, the handle is made of wood, and wood comes from trees, and so you could say that this handle is a tree, in a different form.'

Louisa considers the words, looks at the broom handle, touches it again. She looks back at Wagadhaany.

'The tree hasn't really changed, Louisa, it's just in a different form now.'

Louisa nods.

'I am the tree, Louisa. I am still the same, just a bit different here because of how I live, but that hasn't changed who I am inside, who I am as a person. I am still the Wagadhaany I was the day you met me, and for all the years before you met me. And I will be me for all the days ahead.'

Just as her father had said she would be.

Over the following days there are long periods of silence between the women. Wagadhaany feels stronger in herself but no less homesick. She can feel the hatred bubbling inside her again – for the Bradley brothers for keeping her in Wagga Wagga, and for Louisa for allowing it.

She is quiet, walking alongside Louisa as they enter the general store in the centre of town. Her mind is in conflict, thoughts of home competing with visions of the stockman she served at the homestead – his gentle face, his broad smile, his strong-looking arms. How she would love to have them around her. She feels a hot rush as memories of their first meeting turn over and over in her head, and her body experiences unfamiliar sensations.

On the other hand, she is surprised at how full of life Louisa appears to be. Mumbling about her shopping list, she walks at a brisk pace a few steps ahead, having a one-sided conversation about picking up seeds for the vegetable garden at the homestead, which Wagadhaany wishes wouldn't get any bigger. She doesn't comment on Wagadhaany's lack of interest and almost bounces through the doorway of the store as if to prove, after their difficult conversation the other day, that life in Wagga Wagga is a happier one than in Gundagai.

Wagadhaany walks slowly into the shop but her mood changes unexpectedly when she looks up and sees another young Aboriginal woman. She has no idea who the woman is or where she is from, but is certain the Ancestors have brought her to the store today. She is overwhelmed with gratitude even before their first words are spoken.

Louisa moves swiftly and excitedly towards the shop owner, taking no notice of Wagadhaany's quick, quiet steps in the other direction. It's as if some greater force is carrying her to the other woman, who watches warily as she approaches. Without hesitation, Wagadhaany stands as close as possible to her while trying not to cause any fear or awkwardness.

'Wagadhaany, Wiradyuri yinaagang,' she says softly, pretending to be interested in the soap.

She turns slowly to check that neither Louisa nor the shop owner can hear her. Wagadhaany is not convinced that she would be happy for her servant to be mixing with other Black people in Wagga Wagga.

The young woman beams, responding with one hand on her chest, 'Yiray, Wiradyuri yinaagang.'

The two women smile at each other, and Wagadhaany feels her hopes rise. Louisa is not the true friend she claims to be, but maybe this woman could be.

'I work for the Bradleys,' Wagadhaany whispers, 'on their station, over that way.' She points in the direction she and Louisa have just come from. 'They have cattle. I clean and cook with Mrs Bradley,' she adds, looking in Louisa's direction, then she pauses. 'She's a good White person.'

Yiray nods. 'I work in the Hansen homestead. They have sheep. I cook and clean too. I think I might know one good White person, but she is not my boss.' She shrugs her shoulders. 'I haven't seen you in here before.'

'I don't leave the homestead very often. But I'd really like to. It's strange to live and work in the same place every day, and not see any other of our people.' She looks towards Louisa again. She is in an intense conversation with the shopkeeper. 'Except for the Black stockmen who work with the cattle there.'

Wagadhaany has the smallest hint of a smile as she thinks of the handsome young man on the chestnut horse.

'You live in a house?' Yiray asks, surprised. 'The same house as the White people?'

'Yes, I have my own room, with a *window*!

Yiray opens her eyes wide, and Wagadhaany realises how impressed she sounded, talking about her window. She quickly moves on. 'So, where do *you* live?'

'By the river, with my miyagan, that's my home now. We've been moved around a bit, but now we live together in a camp by the river. Most of us, anyway, live together there.'

Yiray's answer falls heavy on Wagadhaany's heart, as memories of her own family surface and homesickness settles in her belly again. No window in any fancy house with one good White person in it is *ever* going to make her feel like she did when she was back home with her kin, her cousins, the children, the fishing and dancing and ceremony. She wants to be with her family, like Yiray.

She sighs out loud, then whispers softly, 'I miss my miyagan so much.' Tears begin to form and she swallows hard. This is not the place to lose control of her emotions. Louisa may have forgiven her outburst back at the homestead but it is unlikely she would do the same here. 'It feels like I haven't seen them in forever.'

'Come to the river,' Yiray whispers. She looks cautiously around the store. 'There are many of our people all round here.' She moves her eyes in every direction. 'From across Wiradyuri ngurambang. They come for work too. Some of the men are at the Bradley station. We all share everything. It goes further. Not this though,' she adds, screwing her face up at some potatoes she has already purchased. '*Our* food is better.'

Wagadhaany hasn't had any wambuwuny since arriving in Wagga Wagga. She wants to be more like the woman in front of her, more like she was back home. She wants to be connected again, to be one of the tribe, to share food. She doesn't want to be different, be like a White person, without a big family, without her songs and dancing.

'Good day,' Louisa says, joining the two women.

Both look guilty, like two children up to mischief.

'I'm Louisa Bradley,' she says, extending her hand.

Yiray is taken aback at the show of courtesy that is not common between White landowners and Black servants. Wagadhaany notices the shopkeeper's frown when Yiray wipes her hand on her tunic and awkwardly takes Louisa's hand, shaking it weakly.

'And you are?' Louisa asks in a friendly tone.

'I am Yiray,' she says, and curtsies.

'Oh no, don't curtsy, please,' Louisa says, reminding Wagadhaany of the first time they met at the Bradley house in Gundagai. 'Yiray is a lovely name.' She swings around to Wagadhaany. 'Look what we have,' she says enthusiastically. 'Some seeds and fruit stones for planting at the homestead. Soon we will be able to grow all our own fresh foods.'

Before Wagadhaany has the chance to consider Louisa's comments, or to register how she refers to them as 'we', Louisa returns her focus to Yiray.

'Do you live nearby, Yiray? Are you on a homestead like ours?' She nods to Wagadhaany, who now feels uncomfortable because it sounds like she is more connected to the Whites than the Blacks. She wishes Louisa would stop saying 'we'. She wants to say, *This is not* our *homestead. It's* your *homestead, the Bradley homestead, and I just clean it!*

Yiray looks at the Wiradyuri yinaa with concern in her eyes. Wagadhaany recognises that look. When White people ask questions, they do so with a tone of superiority. And most questions about location are either to remind the Blacks they are not free to move about, or to lay blame on them for something that has happened in a particular place.

'Umm, I must go. Mrs Hansen will be wondering where I am, and I am never to dawdle.'

Wagadhaany has never heard the word dawdle before but she is too embarrassed to ask what it means.

The next day Wagadhaany and Louisa work for a long time in the sun creating an even bigger vegetable plot. They turn the soil, measuring as best they can the spaces between each dropping of seeds. Louisa hums quietly as she plants, while Wagadhaany loses herself in thoughts about Yiray. In her mind she is reliving their few exchanged words over and over again. She needs a plan so she can get to the river to meet everyone; maybe Yiray's miyagan is her family too. Wiradyuri people have travelled the land for many, many years. They have married and grown their miyagan, so it is possible that some of her extended family are here too. Her heart swells at the thought of being with some of her own people again.

She wants to ask Louisa about going to the river, but is aware that she has never left the property alone, and knows that James Bradley would never approve of it. She needs to enlist Louisa's support, without her taking over. As she turns the soil, she carefully tries to engage Louisa in conversation. 'Is that a church song?' she asks of Louisa's humming.

'Oh, no, Quakers don't have hymns. Singing gets in the way of worship, Wagadhaany,' she explains. 'I'm just humming some sounds I hear in my head. I do like to sing though.'

Wagadhaany doesn't know how to respond; she doesn't know the right questions to ask about Louisa's religion and God, and why singing is not part of worship. Her miyagan sing all the time, the women, the men, the children, everyone sings for Biyaami to show thanks and praise. They have songs for all ceremonies, to welcome people, to lay people to rest when they pass over, songs of thanks. But she doesn't say any of that. She doesn't want to show up these White people for not having as rich a spirituality as the Wiradyuri. She stays quiet, says nothing, and pretends to focus on the garden while she waits for another burst of inspiration. She only wants permission to go to see Yiray, to meet the tribe by the river and maybe talk with them about her home.

'Louisa . . .' She coughs, not quite sure what she is going to say next, but desperate to say something.

'Yes?' Louisa is looking down, concentrating on the task at hand.

'The girl we met yesterday, Yiray.' She's still unsure about what she should say and how much she can trust Louisa with her hopes and plans.

But Louisa looks up immediately, her interest apparently piqued. She stops pushing seeds into the soil and stands up. She rolls her shoulders back and rubs the nape of her neck with both hands. 'Yes,' she says. 'I have been thinking about what the young woman might be able to do to assist in the Quaker mission. The two of you together could help me. It's time, I think.'

Wagadhaany is shocked that Louisa has been thinking about Yiray. She decides she must be especially careful about how much she gives away, and casts around for something to say without saying much at all. She remembers Yiray's look of surprise when she told her about the window in her room.

'Yiray lives by the river but works on a station like this. Why do I live in the house, Louisa, and not on the river too?'

'Because,' Louisa says, wiping her hands on the front of her apron, '*I* am your family now.'

She pulls Wagadhaany into an embrace that is both awkward and startling. It's the second hug they've had in only a few days and it makes Wagadhaany uneasy.

Wagadhaany thinks about her miyagan constantly, but never has she thought of Louisa as family. It is a revelation to her that the White woman standing before her thinks of her that way. It makes some sense though. The loss Louisa must have felt when her family died in the flood would have left her longing for family, just as she herself does. It bonds them as women, as suffering humans who loved and still love those closest to them, even though they may no longer physically be there. They want to hold their family, share their days with them, say 'I love you'.

The sense of privilege Wagadhaany feels makes her feel incredibly uncomfortable.

There's been silence for an uncomfortable length of time and both women feel it. Louisa finally speaks. 'It's not only that I think of you as family, I think we – you and me – and your new friend Yiray, that we should all have the same things in life. Some people . . . *some* people think that being from England makes us better than being from here, in New South Wales. And that if you have fancy clothes and lots of cattle and a big house, then you are a better human being.'

Louisa is looking at Wagadhaany as if expecting a response, but Wagadhaany doesn't know what to say or do. She wonders if the *some people* Louisa is talking about includes her husband, James.

'And it is true, as you would know, that *some people*, especially the people in power, in the government, think that we – people like me – are better people than people like you.'

'You mean White people with houses are better than Black people who live by the river?' Wagadhaany asks, wanting to be clear about what she is hearing.

'Well, yes. But you know that *I* don't believe that, *I* don't think that.' Louisa takes Wagadhaany's hand. 'Please, tell me you know I don't think like that. I never have and I never will.' Louisa is adamant.

'Yes, Louisa,' she says, because it is true that Louisa has always treated her differently from how other Whites have. Since the very first time they met and Louisa called her by her proper name, invited her to drink tea with her, Wagadhaany has mostly been treated with respect and kindness.

Because Louisa has declared Wagadhaany's place in her new family, the Wiradyuri yinaagang thinks she should seize the moment and ask about being free like Louisa is to move around, about going to the river. Before losing her nerve, she simply blurts it out. 'I want to go to the river and meet Yiray's miyagan, I mean, family.'

She stops abruptly and holds her breath, hoping she hasn't spoken out of turn or in a way that will render her in trouble. Even if she is Louisa's family, she is still the Bradleys' servant.

Waiting anxiously, she is taken completely by surprise at Louisa's reply.

'That is the best idea I have heard in a very long time. We shall go as soon as possible.'

What? We? What does Louisa mean by 'we'? She is confused but Louisa is vigorously brushing the soil off her hands and mumbling about how she can start to get back to her mission, her purpose, about why her family came to New South Wales in the first place. Wagadhaany's head is spinning. She did not mean for them to go together. She does not want Louisa to go at all. She saw the look on Yiray's face when Louisa asked where she lived. She is positive that Yiray does not want this White woman visiting her by the river.

'Louisa . . .' Wagadhaany pauses, realising she is having a conversation that is almost unheard of, one that has probably never been had between a White woman and a Wiradyuri woman before. She decides to approach the matter gently. There is always the risk that she will not return, and she knows Louisa is probably thinking of that.

'Maybe . . .' She pauses, gathers her confidence. 'Maybe I should go to the river first, to meet the women, alone, without you.' Wagadhaany is nervous and can tell that the words in her head and the words that are falling from her mouth are not necessarily the same, but she continues. 'It's just that . . .' She stops.

Louisa frowns.

'I don't remember any White women ever coming to our camp in Gundagai. It would have been a strange occurrence and might have made us feel suspicious.' Yes, that's the word she wanted. Hoping Louisa will understand the point she is trying to make, she continues. 'So . . . perhaps it would be good for me to go alone at first, as a friendly Aboriginal face. We wouldn't want to make anyone suspicious, would we? Because that won't help you with your work, and maybe then, later, if you want to . . .'

Wagadhaany stops. She has no idea what Louisa wants to do with her and Yiray, how she intends to make them and all Aborigines equal, or what her 'work' actually involves. But she thinks this is the only way Louisa may let her go alone.

Relief washes over Wagadhaany when Louisa smiles and says, 'Of course, of course, you are absolutely right. You should go and meet everyone, make friends. Talk to people and then it will be easier for me when we go together. I know that the English can be a bit overbearing at times. I don't want to scare anyone off, I want to help people, remember? Maybe I can teach them English, to read and write, and then help them go to school.'

Wagadhaany isn't sure if Louisa is asking her or telling her, but is pleasantly surprised at how easy that was, and that Louisa is happy for her to go meet Yiray.

'And when you are there, maybe you can just tell them that I will visit with you next time?' It is a statement and a question rolled into one and Wagadhaany isn't sure if she is meant to answer or not, but Louisa asks, 'Could you do that, do you think?'

Wagadhaany is so happy. Louisa has not only said she can go to the river and meet Yiray's family, but also that she is going to let her go alone. She is so excited she *almost* hugs Louisa back, but she stops herself, simply saying, 'I can do that.'

Chapter Thirteen

It seems like an eternity of waiting before Wagadhaany finally gets to meet Yiray at the store again.

On their fourth visit in as many weeks, her hopes of seeing Yiray aren't high, and so she walks despondently into the store, expecting nothing but more disappointment. When she sees Yiray, her beaming smile is mirrored back, as if they have known each other for a lifetime. As if they had grown up together as miyagan. As if they *both* have been desperate to see each other again.

'I've been looking for you, waiting to see you again,' Yiray says, to Wagadhaany's absolute joy.

'Can I visit with you, please?' she blurts out immediately.

Yiray nods. 'I need to . . .' She looks at her basket and to the grocer and moves away. 'I'll meet you down the road a bit,' she says, and nods towards the south before moving off.

Louisa has been standing back, as if she has a new sense of self-awareness, and has allowed Wagadhaany to speak to Yiray alone.

'Can I go with Yiray today?' Wagadhaany turns to ask Louisa softly.

Louisa smiles her approval and hands her the baked bread. Wagadhaany leaves the shop swiftly and walks with speed down the road, not knowing how far she should travel before stopping to wait. She sees a scar tree on the other side of the road and crosses, recognising the shape of a guluman that has been cut from its bark. She takes this as a sign and waits. When she sees Yiray walking towards her, her heart races with excitement, with the possibilities of what might happen next.

Even though it is a long walk, Wagadhaany has a spring in her step all the way back to the Hansen homestead. She feels like she is with her cousins again, and notices that Yiray's hair is dead straight and jet-black like Yirabiga's, unlike her own mass of long, dark curls. She remembers how much fun they had as kids trying to make Yirabiga's hair a little wavy by twisting wet paperbark through it. *How much time has passed since then? How long is Yirabiga's hair now? Does Yiray do that with her hair too?* So many questions are spinning in her head.

'Wait here,' Yiray says. 'I must give this to Mrs Hansen before I can leave for the day. I might have to do some more chores before I can go, but she usually lets me leave before dark.'

Wagadhaany is shocked that Yiray might have to work late and then walk home in the dark. The differences in their lives are becoming clearer.

Wagadhaany has no idea how long she sits there but it is long enough for her to watch a dyirridyirri bouncing around near her. The willie wagtail reminds her of home, and she is lost in tranquil thought when Yiray returns.

'Come, we have a way to walk still.'

Looking at the sun and trying to remember the direction she has come from, and the direction of the Bradleys' homestead from the Hansens', she knows she is heading north-west from town.

When they reach the campsite in the wetlands by the river, Wagadhaany immediately thinks of her family. There are ganya-galang with small fires near them, and one larger fire that must be a communal one. Suddenly, children rush the women, only beaten by mirri-galang barking wildly, as they did in Gundagai, warning everyone of a stranger approaching.

'Who is this, Aunty?', 'What's your name?', 'Can you play with me?'

The children tug on Wagadhaany's hand and tunic and she loves it. It reminds her so much of her life back in Gundagai, and when the dogs finally stop barking she smiles.

With all the chatter and laughter from the children, her heart sings just as it did each time she went back to her own camp. It made her feel she'd been missed, that she mattered. Today she feels the same sense of welcoming, the same sense of belonging. She smiles at Yiray, knowing her face says more than any words can. Yiray returns the look and for the first time since leaving Gundagai, Wagadhaany feels she has a sense of family and home again.

'This way.'

Yiray takes her hand and walks towards the women, who are preparing a meal. Wagadhaany recognises the smell of fowl and her mouth waters.

'Gunhi,' Yiray calls out. 'Gunhi, this is Wagadhaany, the yinaagang I told you about, the one I met at the store.'

Yiray steps back so her mother can consider her. 'This is my mother,' she says proudly to Wagadhaany.

'Dancer,' the old woman says, 'your name means dancer.'

'Ngawa, it does.'

Wagadhaany is so excited that she can barely control her emotions. But she waits until the time is right, until Yiray's gunhi makes it clear she can speak. She was always taught to listen twice as much as speaking, a lesson reinforced by her own gunhi.

'You like to dance?' the older woman asks.

'Ngawa. I would *always* dance back home, with the women, my gunhi, my bamali-galang, and my cousins, by the river, for ceremony, sometimes for fun, and always for the Ancestors.' She reminds herself that she really should listen and look more than she speaks, but she can't help herself. 'I miss dancing, I miss my miyagan, I miss home.' She looks at the women around the campfire all smiling back at her.

'Come,' Yiray's mother says, 'sit with us. I am Bagabin, my name means –'

Wagadhaany cuts in. 'It means blue flower,' she says proudly.

'Ngawa, it does. My gunhi, she loved blue flowers, she named me. She is with the dead ones now, but she is here too, with us, as we weave.' Wagadhaany looks around the circle, where some of the women are weaving mats to sleep on. 'Sit,' the older woman points to the ground. 'Who is your miyagan?'

'My father is Yarri and my mother is Yiramiilan. My family are in Gundagai. I had to come here to work on the Bradley station. I had no choice.'

'None of us has a choice, this is our life now. The men, they work for the White man, go where the White man says, we live where the White man tells us to live.'

'They are no good, the White people,' a grey-haired woman says, as she joins them.

'Eh, you can't say that, Giigandul,' Bagabin says, chastising the other woman.

'It's true, you know it,' she replies then turns to Wagadhaany. 'She knows it's true. I would not trust a White person as far as I could throw a fat wambad, and that's not very far.'

Wagadhaany wonders if anyone would ever throw a fat wombat anyway.

'Who be throwing wambad-galang around then?' asks a third aunty who's sitting at the fire and has only heard part of the conversation.

'Shhh, Mulbirrang, no-one be throwing a wambad anywhere.'

'Oh, your gunhi should've called you gurgur because you can't hear anything proper, never could,' Giigandul says sarcastically.

'I'm a colourful rosella, not gurgur at all,' she replies. 'And I can hear just fine. And why you always so cranky? That's why your name means prickly.'

'It means prickly silver wattle!' Giigandul retorts.

'What's that? I can't hear you. I'm gurgur, remember?'

And with an outbreak of laughter the tension disappears. The sound of the women finding humour and joy in the simplest of moments, and seeing them all so happy, relishing each other's company, hits Wagadhaany hard. It's the same kind of laugher she grew up with back home. These women could be *her* gunhi, her grandmother, aunties and cousins. These could be *her* miyagan. She remembers the words of her own gunhi the last time she saw her. *You will always have miyagan around this country, your Wiradyuri country. I think Wagga Wagga is many days away, but the Ancestors will be with you wherever you walk, and even though we won't be there in body, you will always have us in your heart.*

'Where you live now, migay?' Bagabin asks. 'Yiray says you live in the White woman's house, in your own room, with a window.'

Wagadhaany instantly wishes she could go back in time and have that first conversation with Yiray again. She would not mention the window, she would not mention anything that makes her different to the other Wiradyuri women with her right now.

'Well?' Bamali Giigandul asks.

Wagadhaany thinks she really is a cranky, prickly woman and that she must answer the question, and quickly. She moves her feet slightly, nervous, and looks to Yiray who smiles warmly, knowing this is all part of the welcome to any camp.

'Yes, Bamali, I live in the Bradley house. I take care of the chores, but Mrs Bradley, she takes care of me. She lost her family in the big flood in Gundagai and she says that *I* am like her family now.' Saying it out loud somehow makes her believe it more, feel it more, and she thinks that if the women believe it too, maybe they won't be so suspicious.

'She gave me a room in the house and we do the chores together because she'd never had a servant before she married Mr Bradley. She doesn't believe in servants. Not like Mr Bradley. He is different, he has always had servants, and he treats me like a servant too. But he and his brother, they both saved my life in the flood. They let me hold onto them until my babiin came and rescued us all. My babiin says I owe my life to them, but they owe their lives to him. So, I think nobody owes anybody anything anymore.'

Wagadhaany can hear herself rambling but she can't stop talking, and she realises it's because other than with Louisa, she's had no conversation since leaving Gundagai. No language, no

181

stories, no dancing, no sharing. She wonders how she can still live without so much that is important to her. She looks around the circle where the women are weaving and knows they must all be listening, because no-one else is talking.

'Miss Louisa, she is different,' she continues. 'We cook together and garden together, she wants to help us.' She motions to include the women. 'She wants all of us to have the same things as White people, like being able to read and write and go to school. I want to help her do that,' she says, though she's still not sure if she truly believes it, or even knows what it entails.

'Be careful, my girl,' Bamali Bagabin says. 'We helped the White people when they first came here. Our men, they helped them find food and helped track their animals. They helped build their homes. But they made us move off our land, and built fences on our land around those homes, and now we all have to live here together. Our own land fenced off from us. We are the custodians of this land. We are responsible for looking after it, taking care of this place. How can we do that when we are fenced off from the land, and when their big, fat animals are running all over it?'

Of course, it's not right, but Wagadhaany doesn't know how to respond or what she can do to change that. She doesn't have the chance to say anything before Bamali Prickly speaks.

'And their animals, them cows and sheep, they drive away our wambuwuny-galang, the ones that are left, and they ruin our tucker on the ground when they run all over it. That is not right now, is it? What do they expect us to eat if we can't eat our own food?'

Bamali Prickly shakes her head and looks to the sun, which is only partially covered by thin clouds.

'There's been fighting across this land too, up that way, and down that way.' She waves in both directions. 'The Whites just kill our wambuwuny-galang and wilay, not for food, we don't know why they just shoot as many as they can, and then there is nothing left for our people to eat. But when *we* kill their animals to live, to survive, then they become violent, and we cannot win against their guns.

'Threatening our lives, threatening to kill us, to make sure we do what they want, don't you forget that. And it means we are *always* afraid, always watching and waiting.'

Bamali Prickly doesn't sound cranky this time, she sounds sad, and her words fall heavily on Wagadhaany's heart.

'Has there been a war here?' Wagadhaany asks, with worry in her voice.

'Not right here but that way.' The old woman raises her thin arm and points in the opposite direction to the sun. 'A place called Bathurst, there was much fighting and violence for many years, and many of our people died, were murdered.' She shakes her head slowly in sorrow. 'They were led by a hero named Windradyne. He was so strong it took six White men to capture him. After being held for a long time with chains on his legs, they finally released him, and he continued to fight for his people and his land, *our* Wiradyuri land. There was more death, more violence, more White men with guns. And they killed many of his family. So much pain for him. For our people. We know he died of a broken giiny.' She puts her hand on her heart and hangs her head.

Wagadhaany remembers her uncles talking by the fire when she was young. Their stories didn't make sense then, but listening to Bamali Prickly now, it is all coming back to her. Their words about the enemy, their enemy, and the massacres.

'Our people can be shot by Whites and nothing will happen. And we cannot even protect ourselves with a gun. Aboriginal people cannot have guns, the White man's law says so. They don't trust us with guns. And I don't trust *them* with *anything*! Always remember my girl, be careful of who you trust.'

Wagadhaany recalls the stories of Wiradyuri people being shot at, women and children too. Some for taking potatoes along the Macquarie River.

'All right, that's enough! This girl is Wiradyuri miyagan, we need to make her feel welcome, not fill her with fear.'

Bagabin stands and motions for the women to join her.

They move to the side, form a circle and hold hands. Bagabin starts to sing, and the other women join in, as does Yiray. Wagadhaany doesn't know this song but she understands the words. When she recognises the repeated lines, she sings them and slowly the women all move their feet in time. As soon as she starts to dance, her heart swells. It is full from being around her people, from hearing and speaking her language, and from the smell of guinea fowl on the fire. Before she knows it, the sun has fallen behind a hill in the distance. Her heart is beating differently, more slowly, as if in rhythm with the songs her Old People used to sing on the river back at home.

Wagadhaany's sense of tranquillity is soon stifled by the realisation that she has been away for many hours and the Bradleys will be angry. Even if Louisa forgives her, James Bradley won't if he finds out. She starts to panic and her heart begins to race.

When she returns to the homestead the sky is a blanket of

darkness. It is so black she feels scared as she takes her final steps towards the house, because she can barely see in front of her. She follows the dim light coming from the front windows but she can see no movement through them. The curtains are yet to be pulled for the evening, a task she usually tends to. James Bradley will be furious that she has not prepared his dinner, and Louisa will be upset and no doubt concerned about her. She has been away far longer than she should have, she knows that. But how could she have left any sooner? Every second was a precious gift which she will thank Biyaami for later.

She gingerly walks in the back door, tiptoeing as if arriving quietly will make some difference to the fact that she is late. Louisa is sitting in the living room, reading, and Wagadhaany coughs softly to announce she is back.

'You're home, good, come, sit,' Louisa says, looking up. She runs her hand along the settee and pats it twice. 'Tell me everything.' Louisa is like a child, eager to know a secret. 'How many people are there? Are there children? When can I go meet them?'

Wagadhaany is confused. *Why isn't Louisa angry? Where is James Bradley? And why so many questions?* She feels overwhelmed, pressured by Louisa, and still doesn't understand her interest in meeting the mob by the river. Her afternoon was special, it was for her, it is not something for White people to have too. *Why do they want to take everything?*

'Well?' Louisa asks again. 'Oh sorry, you must be tired and hungry. Shall I make us some tea?'

Wagadhaany thinks about the billy tea she had at the river and the taste of the guinea fowl the bamali-galang made her eat before she left. They fussed just like the aunties back in Gundagai and she loved it. She doesn't want any English-style tea now, or possibly ever. Billy tea made her feel normal again, more herself, less different to the other women. It reminded her that she may have changed a little, but she has not really changed at all.

'Oh, I don't need anything, Miss Louisa, really. I am fine.'

Wagadhaany doesn't realise what she's done until it's pointed out.

'*Miss Louisa*? Why are you calling me that again? You haven't called me that since the first time we met.' Louisa sounds suspicious and disappointed at the same time.

'Oh.' Wagadhaany shakes her head and thinks on her feet. 'It must've been because Yiray talked about her employer, Mrs Hansen . . . when she talked about her work.'

'Tell me about them, I want to know everything,' Louisa says emphatically. 'Absolutely everything.'

'Well, I only met Yiray's mother and some of the aunties. They are mostly Wiradyuri people living at the camp, but there are others who have travelled to work here too, on stations nearby.'

'And children? Are there children?' Louisa asks enthusiastically.

'Yes, there are children, there are always lots of children. We have big families, remember?' She looks at Louisa suspiciously, wondering why she is so obsessed with children, and remembers Prickly Aunty's warnings. 'They are all well looked after, if that is what you are worried about.'

'Oh no, I wasn't worried at all. I see how beautifully you were raised, I am sure all Aboriginal children are raised the same way.' Louisa puts her hand to her stomach. 'Wagadhaany, I just love children,' she says, her eyes twinkling. 'I hope to be a mother. I want to have a family one day, a big family. Not as big as yours,' she laughs. 'I don't think I could manage that. But I really want children.' Louisa stops abruptly, no doubt aware that she has reminded Wagadhaany that she is so far away from her own family. 'When James is ready, of course. And when *I* am ready. I have so much work to do first.'

After days of being hounded, Wagadhaany finally agrees to take Louisa to the river. To meet the aunties and all the children she keeps asking about.

When they walk into the camp together, the children rush Wagadhaany but steer clear of Louisa. She is the whitest person they have ever seen, and Wagadhaany can hear them saying in their language: 'Is she a birig?', 'Has she never been in the sun?', 'Why are her cheeks red?' The dogs bark noisily and Wagadhaany can't help but laugh.

'What are they saying?' Louisa asks.

'They want to know if you're a ghost, you are so white.'

They find the women weaving and cooking. Yiray isn't home from the Hansens' station yet but Wagadhaany doesn't feel uncomfortable at all. It reminds her of walking into her own camp back home. Bamali Bagabin looks up, and waves both women over to her side.

'This is my . . .' Wagadhaany stops herself from introducing Louisa as her friend. 'This is Mrs Louisa Bradley,' she says, 'from the Bradleys' station.'

She sounds almost cold, but is conscious of what the older women had advised her when they first met. The group in front of her cannot hide, nor do they seem to be trying to hide, their distrust of Louisa. Their eyes and facial expressions are anything but welcoming.

Wagadhaany sees the suspicion in their eyes and doesn't blame them. In the past, their generosity has been exploited and their land stolen by the White settlers. Louisa is married to one of those settlers. And her own family took land too.

Since meeting these women, Wagadhaany has understood that the Bradleys must be the beneficiaries of land being taken from some of the Wiradyuri people. *How else could they have that property? And who was living on that land before? Maybe even some of those living in this camp.* Even so, she still wants to believe that Louisa is different to the other White people, including her husband, and that there is truth in her words, that she wants to help these women and children have equal rights with White people, whatever that means.

The women are looking to Wagadhaany for some sign, some surety that the waadyin before them can be trusted. For her part, Wagadhaany wants to make the women feel at ease, for them to understand that she has the trust and friendship of a good White person, because surely they can't *all* be bad. She decides there is pride to be had in having a good White friend, and so she introduces Louisa again, touching her arm.

'Louisa is my friend, she has been taking care of me. Well, we take care of each other, I guess. And she doesn't make me do all the chores in the house myself, we do them together.'

This is the first time Wagadhaany has seen Louisa appear nervous and uncomfortable. As she stands holding a basket of baked goods, small beads of perspiration form on her brow. Wagadhaany urges her forward gently because someone else needs to speak and right now the women are just glaring at them both.

'F ... f ... for you,' Louisa stammers. 'We baked them together,' she adds, motioning to Wagadhaany. Louisa considers it an important act of friendship, a token gesture of kindness, a way of demonstrating her generosity. For Wagadhaany, food has *always* been shared among her people, not as a gesture of anything. Sharing came from understanding that another was hungry. Sharing food was just the Wiradyuri way.

'Yes, we did,' Wagadhaany endorses.

She's hoping one of the women will smile, even slightly, and soften the mood, making them both feel welcome, because at this moment she knows that her presence is tainted simply by being there with Louisa. She starts to feel that this may have been an incredibly bad idea, bad judgement, disrespectful even. The bamali-galang had warned her about trusting White people, so why did she bring Louisa here? She is cranky with herself for not listening, for not understanding and practising yindyamarra.

While the bamali-galang demonstrate no interest in Louisa at all, it's hard not to notice their eyes focusing on the basket in her hands. She is sure the aroma of baked scones is making their mouths water. Their eyes all look in the direction of the basket and Louisa lifts the calico cloth to reveal some pumpkin scones, freshly baked, and bright orange in colour. Their eyes widen at the sight of this new food. They have only had white damper before.

'Scones are a bit like damper,' Wagadhaany explains, 'but these are made from pumpkins. We grow them ourselves. The pumpkins, not the scones.'

Wagadhaany panics when she sees an entire row of raised eyebrows in front of her, but then half laughs because they are exactly the same faces her mother and aunties pull back home. But she doesn't know why they are looking that way. Then it hits her. She remembers hearing stories back home about White people lacing damper with a poison, something called arsenic, and leaving it out for the Aboriginal people to eat. Many had died. She feels sick to the stomach because she knows this is probably why they are wary.

She reaches into the basket and takes a scone. 'Actually, Louisa, I think I need one right now,' she says, taking a bite, then handing it to Louisa to take a bite too.

Louisa and the women are all shocked. Blacks and Whites don't share food, especially if it is poisoned.

Wagadhaany frowns at Louisa and whispers, 'I'll explain later, take a bite.'

Louisa breaks a small piece off the scone and puts it in her mouth, watching the women the whole time. Once she has swallowed, the women relax their brows and all reach into the basket and take a scone. They relish every bite, making sounds of pleasure as they devour them within seconds. Wagadhaany breathes a sigh of relief.

'Of course, next time we will bring lots of fresh vegetables from the garden,' Louisa says.

Any relief turns to concern in a split second. Louisa just can't help herself. *Next time? Next time?* She wishes Louisa would just let them get through this *first time* without the Old Ones banishing them both forever. She steps in quickly. If nothing else, she wants to save her own place with the women, even if she can't save Louisa's. She is so homesick and their undeniably Wiradyuri expressions this morning have just made things worse. She has missed the laughing and the gossiping of the women back home, and how they could never hide their feelings. The women can and will always let you know what they are thinking without words. *It must be a Wiradyuri yinaa thing, to wear your feelings and thoughts on your face at all times.*

Wagadhaany feels ill to the stomach. 'Louisa is a Quaker,' she says. 'They want to help Aboriginal people, to make sure we are treated properly by the government and by other White people.'

The women furrow their brows again. They look at Louisa, then back to Wagadhaany. There are still no words from any of them though, which makes Wagadhaany feel very uncomfortable.

'Her people, Louisa's people, they are from England. They are called Quakers, that's right, isn't it?'

She looks towards Louisa to confirm she's correct, desperate for the conversation to become more friendly as fast as possible.

'Her people are what?' Bamali Giigandul says in her cranky way, flicking a hand towards Louisa then putting it on her hip.

'Quackers,' says Bamali Mulbirrang. 'Quack, quack, quackers,' she says, making all the women burst out laughing.

When they all start quacking, the children come running back to be part of the fun. They crouch on the ground, trying to waddle, pretending they are ducks. When one bamali gets down and tries to be a duck too, there is an outrageous roar of happiness. At first Louisa looks terrified, imagining they are making fun of her and disrespecting her religion. She doesn't know what to do. She looks to Yiray, who has just arrived and is laughing, and then to Wagadhaany, who has her hand over her mouth, giggling. When Louisa looks down and sees a small child clinging to her leg, facing upwards and trying to be a duck, and with the widest grin she has ever seen, only then does she begin to chuckle as well.

When all the joviality dies down, Wagadhaany relaxes. It appears that Louisa may actually be made welcome.

Bamali Bagabin nods in the direction of a woven mat, and the women move to sit in a circle. Some of the younger girls join in, and they continue with their basket weaving and start talking among themselves.

'Like this,' Wagadhaany says, as she gets Louisa started, remembering when she first learned to weave, taught by her mother when she was very young.

'Tell us about your Quacking tribe,' Bamali Bagabin says, and a ripple of laughter begins again.

Louisa looks to Wagadhaany for confirmation that it is all right to speak. She hopes Louisa will use the raised eyebrows and other facial expressions of the women as cues from now on. They have always helped her. She leans in and whispers, 'Aunty asked you to speak, so you can speak, you *must* speak. At other times, just listen.'

'We are a small group,' Louisa starts. 'We don't call ourselves a tribe, but maybe we are.' She shrugs her shoulders. 'We believe in a simple life. A peaceful life.'

The women nod as if their lives are the same, or at least were before their land was invaded. Wagadhaany focuses on their eyebrows for any hint of movement.

'Treating people equally and caring for everyone in society are very important to us. We believe everyone should have the same things, the same chance for a good life.'

The weaving continues, with whispering among the older women, while Yiray and Wagadhaany sit close and compare their handiwork.

Wagadhaany feels content, at home and safe when sitting in the circle. It's just as it was with the women back in Gundagai. She loses herself in memories of those times, and wonders if the women ever think of her, miss her in their circles, in their dances. A wave of warmth rushes over her. It's the love she felt back then flowing through her now as she reminds herself that she must be missed, and not only by family who love her. Everyone in every dance, every ceremony, has a role, a place, she would *have* to be missed. She notices that even though she feels homesick today, the tears haven't welled. Instead, for the first time in a long time, she has been able to think about her miyagan and not get upset. She looks around the group to the women, the children, and her friends, Yiray and Louisa, and she wonders if they truly are her new family. If Louisa was right.

'Talk,' Bamali Giigandul says, without looking up. 'Tell us about your people.'

Louisa rests her weaving in her lap because she wants to look at the women as she speaks. Most of them aren't looking back though.

'Well,' she says, waiting to see if anyone will acknowledge her. When they don't, she continues. 'We don't have sermons or masses like some of the other religions here. We just come together for a meeting, in the name of God, of course. And we sit in a large circle just like this.' She moves her hand to demonstrate. 'But men and women sit together. Sometimes, most of the time, we don't speak at all. But we can if we want to.'

Yiray's Bamali Mulbirrang is the only one looking. It appears there is some truth in her being hard of hearing, and she is watching the way Louisa's mouth moves. Louisa focuses on this aunty who appears to be listening. Some of the other women look back quickly while they weave, but others don't look up at all, completely focused on their hands.

'And?' Bamali Giigandul says in a cranky tone, without looking up. 'Is that it? Is that all? What's your spirit? What you believe?'

'We believe that spirituality is everywhere, wherever we are, so we don't have to go to church like the Catholics or the Protestants. And we don't have long sermons.'

Her last comment sees a number of eyebrows move as foreheads furrow, and Wagadhaany is grateful when Louisa goes on to explain what she means.

'We don't have one man talking for a long time about God and what we should think, and how we should behave.' She looks to the women for some recognition that she has made sense, but she sees only blank faces.

'Many Christians, like the Catholics, the Anglicans and the Protestants who have come here, I am sure that they think that we, the Quakers, are strange.'

At least two of the aunties raise eyebrows and glance at each other as if to suggest that they too think she is strange. Wagadhaany notices but Louisa doesn't see them and continues. 'We don't judge other people, we just focus on our own values of equality, and so sometimes we are political.'

Wagadhaany is getting annoyed. *Doesn't Louisa know that English is hard enough for Aboriginal people without using words like that? How would a word like 'political' ever be relevant to Wiradyuri people?* She's heard the word before in the Bradley home but isn't sure what it means. The fact that most of the women are now whispering among themselves suggests they have stopped listening too because they don't understand much of the language either, and she doesn't blame them. Louisa's enthusiasm is often overwhelming, but now that she is talking on and on about her religion, and using words they don't understand, it is pushing the women away.

But one of the older women speaks abruptly. 'We know the missionaries,' she says, looking to her sisters for support.

There are pursed lips, nods and raised eyebrows.

'That's right,' another adds, 'and most White people think

194

we are strange too, they must, because they treat us like we are strange.'

And the circle comes together as one again, as if there is some sudden, miraculous connection among the women, that being 'strange', rather than just being women, or even just humans, has somehow united them.

'Come!'

Bamali Bagabin takes Louisa's hand and moves to one side. She calls Wagadhaany to stand to the other side. All the women slowly rise, helping each other up off the ground.

'Let's dance,' Bamali Bagabin says.

Wagadhaany knows this is her cue, the role she has always played in ceremony, in women's business. The place in the group she was given when she was first welcomed by the women who told her she had a family with them, that she should never feel alone while they were near. She stands to the side so that Louisa can see her, and they all wait as she slowly takes off her boots and stockings.

'This dance welcomes you to our ngurambang, our land,' she says to Louisa. 'Our way, when we visit other people's country, other people's land, is to always let them know we are there in peace, and we wait to be welcomed.'

For the second time since she arrived in Wagga Wagga, the place that holds her name, Wagadhaany's heart feels light, and her spirit feels grounded. She watches and follows the movements of the women near her. This is a different dance to the one that welcomed her to this place. But all dancing feeds her soul. She loves bringing her name, herself, to life. As her bare feet kick up dust, the dancing lifts her spirit, reminding her that the Ancestors are there in her fluid movements.

It is obvious that the dancing has moved Louisa and she wipes a lone tear from her flushed cheek. She is a little breathless and Wagadhaany realises she has never seen Louisa out of breath or even close to exhausted from exercise before. Aside from gardening and cleaning, Louisa doesn't do much to get flushed.

'How can I thank you for teaching me your dance, showing me your traditions?' Louisa asks.

The women respond with shrugs because it is not their way to expect anything in exchange for sharing, or to expect any generosity from White people at all, even if they are connected by strangeness. Louisa looks to Wagadhaany for some ideas and support, but she too is at a loss. Then, to her shock, Louisa moves in to hug them all. She is awkward, trying too hard to be liked, to fit in, to show she cares. Wiradyuri people are warm and affectionate, but they are not used to having such soft, pale arms around them. The women are kind though, and let her lean into them with her hug of thanks.

'Maybe,' Louisa says, her eyes hopeful, 'I could teach some of the children how to read.' She motions the opening of a book. 'Oh,' she says, reaching into a cloth bag, 'maybe I could teach them to read this.' She hands one of the women a Bible. 'It's the word of God,' she says proudly. 'I am not a trained teacher, but I could try to teach them, if you like.'

Eyebrows are raised all round and Wagadhaany is deflated at the sight of the Bible and by Louisa's suggestion. The women have already told her about the missionaries. They have their own spirituality, beliefs and creator spirits. They don't want White people telling them they should believe in their God. She recalls the mass she went to with James and David Bradley and how she thought the word of the Lord, who is apparently the son of God, was all wrong and backward. She still thinks Louisa's religion, White people's religion, is very strange.

Wagadhaany feels shame and looks to the ground, wishing the long silence would end. When she looks up again, she can see worry in Louisa's eyes as the women frown.

'Louisa,' she says, remembering the box of books they pushed under the bed first at Gundagai and then at Wagga Wagga. 'Do you think maybe some of the books with pictures you have back at the homestead might be better for the children here?'

'Oh, of course, Wagadhaany. I have much better books for the little ones,' she assures the women. 'We brought them out from England with us. I loved them as a child. I am *sure* the children here will too. They have pictures of children playing and having fun, just like your children.'

Louisa beams and Wagadhaany breathes a sigh of relief, and she wonders if the books have pictures of children fishing by a river, hunting, weaving and dancing.

Chapter Fourteen

Watching every aspect of Louisa and James's marital life isn't easy for Wagadhaany. Nor is it remotely interesting. For the most part, she doesn't want to witness their romantic moments, and she is uncomfortable when she hears their arguing. But there she is, with an intimate view of their daily lives, often with nowhere to turn or hide.

'I worry about you when I'm away,' James says to Louisa one evening. 'But business is business and I need to be there when the cattle arrive into Victoria.' He looks out towards the horizon as if he is pondering life's mysteries. 'They should be nice and fat for sale after grazing the lush lands of the Riverina.' He turns back to his wife. 'I will also meet with another businessman there, about backing me in my desire to be mayor. And David will be there, making sure our financial stability is known by all the right people.'

He pulls his wife in close as if the thought of power and money will make him more sexually attractive to her. Louisa smiles and giggles like a schoolgirl, and Wagadhaany rolls her eyes at how lovesick Louisa can be at times.

'I don't like you being here alone,' James whispers in Louisa's ear as they embrace on the veranda early the next morning.

Mist is still rising from the frosty ground as he nuzzles into her neck. Wagadhaany watches and listens through the window from the kitchen. Increasingly, she dislikes seeing James at all, and watching him being loving with Louisa makes her skin crawl. One minute he is angry, the next minute he is trying to kiss her. Wagadhaany wishes she could understand what makes a man so mixed up in his behaviour, but she is just grateful that he is going away again today, and taking David with him.

Louisa pulls away from him gently. 'I worry about you too, darling, but I will be fine, I have Wagadhaany. It's one of the reasons we brought her here, to keep me company, remember?'

Wagadhaany shakes her head. She must have heard that wrong. Surely she wasn't dragged against her will to Wagga Wagga just because Louisa needed company. *No*, she tells herself, *that can't be right*.

'So,' Louisa says, fussing with her hair, 'she will look after me. We will look after each other.'

Wagadhaany calms a little, hearing Louisa speak of their mutual caring, but she almost laughs out loud as well because she knows how much James Bradley hates hearing about their friendship. He is not the caring type, except for caring about what people in town think of him, and caring about whether or not he will become mayor.

She chuckles to herself, also knowing that his wife has been deceptive, that he is completely ignorant of the fact that Louisa has spent time with the local Black women. She knows how much he would detest that also, and attempt to forbid her from doing it again.

'So, we will both be fine here.'

Louisa tries to hug him, but James withdraws. *Here we go*, Wagadhaany thinks. *From loving to furious in a split second.*

'Humph!' James is not pleased. 'Louisa, you know *she* is not the person I want looking after you. I want to be mayor one day. The people you associate with, the people *my wife* associates with, will come into the equation when the town judges my character. *She* will not help my political aspirations *at all*!'

'Don't call her *she*!' Louisa chastises James and steps back, letting her arms fall to her side. 'Wagadhaany is a woman, like me, and when you speak ill of her you hurt both our feelings.'

'I don't mean to hurt you, Louisa, you know that. But I have spent a lot of time and effort building business relationships here in town, garnering interest in who we are as a couple and trying to earn respect from men in power. I will need that support when I run for mayor.'

Louisa appears uninterested, as if she is bored with talk about her husband's dreams and the important men he 'needs' in his life.

'Perhaps you should garner more interest and support from me, James, spend some time and effort on *our* relationship. And given that former convicts have become notable men of civic standing in this town –' she knows he understands the references to George Best and Charles Thompson '– I am sure you won't have *too* many problems becoming mayor, James.'

She doesn't mean for it to sound like James is a criminal, but she doesn't amend her words either.

James looks offended, like a child who has been chastised. He takes both Louisa's hands in his.

'Please don't argue with me when I am about to leave for days on the road.' And he spins from angry to loving again.

Wagadhaany feels dizzy watching his change of moods and can't help but feel he is playing with Louisa's emotions.

Louisa sighs and moves closer to her husband again. Wagadhaany shakes her head. Even with all his faults, James still has Louisa's heart.

'James,' Louisa says, 'I love you but sometimes you are completely unreasonable.'

Wagadhaany wants to walk away but is rooted to the spot. It's as if she is watching something that she must remember for all time, a lesson on life, with a moral, like the stories her aunties would tell her as a child to teach her a lesson. And then she realises she is getting an education in why you should never fall in love with a White man, and how not to look lovesick silly like Louisa. And so she stands there, a student of the Bradleys, and waits for the next part of the lesson.

'I feel safe with Wagadhaany here, all day, every day. Would you rather one of those stockmen, one of the former convicts you are exploiting? Would you prefer one of those men were keeping me company?' She sounds serious as she turns and looks towards the shacks at the back of the property. 'There's always *that* option!'

Wagadhaany thinks Louisa is playing with fire if she's trying to get James jealous, because he will, and then he will get angry. There have been a number of times when James has manhandled Louisa. Though she has not seen it, she has heard it. And yet, Louisa sounds like she is issuing a threat, which is exactly how James Bradley has heard it.

'Absolutely not!' he replies angrily. 'Those men are too crass and crude to be anywhere near you.'

He is clearly agitated, his fists clenched with anger. Louisa pulls him close to her, nuzzles into his chest and stays there until his temper subsides, his fingers loosen. Wagadhaany knows that Louisa is using her femininity, her body, as she often does, to defuse the situation. She doesn't judge her; this is quite possibly the only way for Louisa to negotiate on those occasions when James's anger could easily turn to something more sinister.

James breathes in deeply, then exhales. Gently he takes Louisa's face in his hands. 'You're my English rose, my perfect lady. You are so delicate and soft, and smell *so* sweet. You're precious to me.' He kisses her softly on her pale pink lips.

'And you are my English prince.'

James gently kisses Louisa's neck. At first Louisa giggles, then a quiet whimper of pleasure escapes. Wagadhaany feels her stomach shift and she knows she should move, but she can't. Watching Louisa and James is both disturbing and compelling. It's impossible to turn away.

'You do realise when I met you, I had very little experience in making small talk with a beautiful woman. And you,' he pecks her lips, 'were the most breathtaking woman I had ever seen.'

'Oh stop it, James, I find that hard to believe. You were a worldly man when I met you.'

'The truth is, I worked on our family station as a child. Our mother schooled us, so there were very few opportunities for me – or for any of my brothers – to develop any talent in communicating with the fairer sex. Look at David. Have you ever seen him trying to talk to a beautiful woman? He has no clue. He will never marry, I am sure of that. And trust me, that day we met, I wished I'd had some clues.'

Louisa is blushing and Wagadhaany feels ill watching James swoon, even though it's over her friend. She thinks he manipulates Louisa to get what he wants, but his wife still believes in the romance of her marriage.

Within minutes of waving her husband off down the dusty path, Louisa ushers Wagadhaany upstairs, speaking as she walks.

'That man can make me crazy, I tell you. We are different beings in many ways, but he pulls on my heartstrings.' She turns to Wagadhaany and smiles cheekily. 'And he makes me feel warm all over, without even trying.'

Wagadhaany cannot see what attracts Louisa to James Bradley, and she doesn't even try to understand as they enter the master bedroom.

'Help me please, Wagadhaany.' Louisa gets to her knees and struggles to pull a trunk out from under the bed. 'We must sort the books out, for the children, ready for our next visit.'

Together they drag the heavy brown box into the middle of the room.

When she opens it, Louisa rushes to pull piles of books out and places them on the floor in no particular order. It's obvious she's looking for anything appropriate to take to the river and read with the children.

'What's this?' Wagadhaany holds a book up, unable to read herself.

'That's about medicine. It gives advice about things like fevers, or rashes, in case there's no doctor around. My mother made her own ointments and tonics when we got sick.'

This is the first time Louisa has spoken about her mother, and Wagadhaany wants to hear more about her and the rest of Louisa's family. But Louisa is too preoccupied with the task she has set for herself, and rather than sharing more childhood memories of grazed knees or insect bites, she says, 'Oh that reminds me, we need to restock the medicine chest too. We will do that next time we go into town.'

For a fleeting moment, Wagadhaany is aware that Louisa has not spoken with any emotion about her mother, and wonders if all English people are so very different to the Aboriginal people, with their big families sharing everything, with proper mourning and grief so important in their lives. The way Louisa talks about the Quakers, it sounds like they are very focused on their families, but maybe not. She doesn't ask; she was not raised to pry into things.

'Oh, how I loved this as a child!' Louisa looks dreamily at the cover of a book before gently opening it, as if it is a precious treasure. '*Cobwebs to Catch Flies*,' she reads the title out loud, as if she has an audience, then starts turning the pages. 'Actually, Wagadhaany, this really is the *perfect* book to teach the children reading. And I think they will like the illustrations, don't you? There are pictures of children playing. What do you think?'

She hands the volume over.

It is only the third book Wagadhaany has held. She wasn't aware there were so many different kinds of books, and that they all look so different. The Bible Louisa gave her, the medicine book and now this book with pictures. She opens it and sees a drawing of a garru and gets excited.

'A garru,' she says, showing Louisa. 'Garru.'

'That's a magpie,' she says. 'In English, we say magpie.'

Wagadhaany points to another picture. 'Dharang,' she says. 'We say dharang.'

'That's a viper, a kind of snake,' Louisa responds, eyebrows raised high, as if she is using them like the old aunties she met by the river. 'This will be the perfect book for teaching English, don't you think?'

Wagadhaany shrugs her shoulders. She's never seen anyone read books to their children.

Over the following days, the women go about their daily chores, as do most women living on the land. The tasks are repetitive and mind-numbing for both of them. Wagadhaany usually does the more laborious tasks, like beating the carpets and rugs and washing the clothes and linen in the copper, while Louisa bakes and prepares the meals for the two dozen men who work for the Bradleys.

Wagadhaany notices that Louisa is no longer doing anything too strenuous on the station. But she is not in the least bit worried because while she is doing the harder cleaning jobs alone, it gives her time to think about the man she hasn't seen for a long time.

Occasionally, she enquires about the droving teams: how many men have gone, how long they will be away, how far will they travel. She is only ever interested in tracking the young drover's movements, and by the smile on Louisa's face each time, Wagad-haany knows that she must have been watching that first time they met. If she understands one thing about Louisa Bradley, it is that she is aware of everything that goes on around her.

When the two of them head into town a few days later they stop at the post office, where Louisa regularly collects mail from the main Quaker group in Tasmania. The visits have become regular and the conversations repetitive. But Louisa goes whether or not she is expecting or sending mail, because the post office is a hub of activity, the place where most of the townsfolk go to catch up. It's become apparent to Wagadhaany that Louisa takes pleasure in this opportunity for meeting up with others in the town, and that yarning in the post office is a little like the yarning by the river, except that the townsfolk do it standing, which is not very relaxing at all.

Wagadhaany stands just behind Louisa as she makes small talk with another well-dressed local woman.

When they have said goodbye, Wagadhaany turns to Louisa. 'That lady spoke very differently from you.'

'Yes, we would say that she had a plum in her mouth.'

'I think the bamali-galang would say she had a quandong in her mouth.'

'I think they would,' Louisa laughs.

'Is she an English rose too?' Wagadhaany chuckles.

'What?'

'I heard Mr Bradley. I hear most things,' Wagadhaany says matter-of-factly, looking straight ahead.

Louisa blushes as they leave the store.

'I thought we were going to the general store,' Wagadhaany says, as Louisa begins to walk in a different direction. 'And who are all these strangers? They don't look like they belong in town. They must be visitors to Wagga Wagga, do you think? Of course, all the townsfolk are strangers to me, but these people, they are even stranger strangers.'

'You're a funny woman,' Louisa says warmly. 'I believe they are on their way to the goldfields in Victoria. I imagine they are here picking up supplies. James says it's good for the businesses here, and with all the extra profits the town is really prospering.'

'Louisa!' There's a tone of command in Wagadhaany's voice for the first time since she and Louisa met. Overcome with a new sense of confidence, and wanting to explore the idea of being equals, she is sure she has the right to question her friend, to speak her own mind on certain matters, to challenge Louisa's choice of language.

'*Goldfields? Profits? Prospering?* Do you ever think about the words you use, words that aren't even in my own language?'

'I'm sorry, you are right.' Louisa appears genuinely apologetic. 'I'll explain.'

'Not now.' Wagadhaany feels annoyance bubbling up inside her. She doesn't want a lesson after the incident, she wants Louisa to understand her behaviour before the incident happens. 'Right now I just want to look at all these strangers. Some of them look like you and Mr Bradley, but others have very different-looking faces.'

'Some are English, no doubt, but the other people are Chinese, Wagadhaany. From a country called China. They have come here for the gold, I believe.'

'Chinese. China,' Wagadhaany repeats. 'And where are we going now?' she asks Louisa, disappointed in the change of route, which put an end to any hope of seeing Yiray.

'To the *new* general store. I think they will have everything on our list.' Louisa reads the list out loud. 'Cotton wool, bandages, scissors, needles and cotton, tweezers for splinters, ointment, and of course a thermometer. What else do we need?'

Wagadhaany shrugs her shoulders in frustration. She wishes Louisa could understand that she doesn't know what most of the things on the list actually are.

David Bradley has been staying around the homestead this morning, and before he leaves for yet another meeting in town with the bank manger, Wagadhaany sees him lurking near the kitchen. It's as if every time she turns around he is there, standing close, staring at her. When Louisa appears, he departs immediately.

'When you are finished there, we need to prepare the meal for the men.' Louisa takes metal plates out of the cupboard and places them on the bench in front of where Wagadhaany is counting the cutlery. She is to carry the plates for the midday meal out to the veranda where the meals are served. 'They're always so hungry after bringing the cattle.'

Although Louisa says she wants equality, for Wagadhaany to have the same rights and power as she does, she is still in charge and she still gives the orders. Wagadhaany is used to it, so she turns and smiles at Louisa as she walks out. In moments like these, she feels as if she is merely a servant, even if she does like feeding the men, because meal times give her some hope that she will see the Black man with the big white smile again.

'When you've done that,' Louisa calls, 'you can start peeling the potatoes from the garden for the stew. I've started on the damper.'

The instructions continue, but they wash over Wagadhaany like the breeze coming through the window from the vast Wiradyuri landscape. She and Louisa have their own roles, and they work well together in the kitchen because Wagadhaany chooses to ignore the fact that she is the servant. They yarn about the expected rain, what new vegetable seeds they should plant, and when they might go back to the camp to visit Yiray and the other women.

'I really want to teach the children to read, it is so important,' Louisa says. 'Then when they are older, they will be able to read the newspaper, go to school and who knows, maybe even get a job in town, or even own a cattle station.'

Louisa is full of contradictions. Why doesn't she suggest that Wagadhaany learn to read, go to school, work in town or own a cattle station? Doesn't Louisa understand that the women she met at the river aren't even allowed to live on their own land?

Louisa leans over her shoulder and says, 'It's time.'

That's the cue for Wagadhaany to ring the dinner bell. Louisa never rings it, which hasn't gone unnoticed by Wagadhaany either. *Maybe it's not something English roses do*, she says to herself with a smile.

She takes the metal triangle outside and bangs it with a small metal stick. The truth is, she doesn't mind ringing the bell. She loves watching the cattle raise their heads and look in her direction, as if they too know it's meal time. And when the men lift their heads and tilt their hats back, knowing that after their hard work, they will be fed, she knows she is appreciated for at least one thing, even if it is never voiced. Mostly she likes ringing the dinner bell because it's the one thing that might bring that handsome man back to her. The weather has cooled down and the seasons are changing, so it must be many long weeks since he left.

As she rings the bell today, her heart beats faster and faster when she sees him in the distance. His long strides, his strong legs, his lean yet muscly arms tight against his shirt. He walks looking at the ground, before raising his head towards the house, and her. She can't see his eyes at first, but when she does, she knows he is looking straight at her as the broadest smile forms across his sun-darkened face. When he pushes his hat back he is still looking directly at her, and she thinks there's a change in the way he walks, taller, with a swagger she hasn't noticed on any other man before. But there is no change in his smile. That wide grin is infectious, and she mirrors it. Her hands suddenly feel clammy. She wipes them on her tunic and hopes no-one notices.

'Here we go,' Louisa says, breaking into her thoughts as she walks past with a huge pot of stew. But Wagadhaany is rooted to the ground and doesn't move. 'Are you all right?'

'What?' Wagadhaany has missed Louisa's words.

'I need you to go in and get the damper.'

But Wagadhaany doesn't move. She can't, and more importantly she doesn't want to.

'Now!'

Louisa doesn't yell, although her sharp tone suggests an order. But Wagadhaany only half hears because it's as if all her senses are numb except for her sight, which is consumed by the vision of the man walking towards her.

Louisa is losing patience. 'Wagadhaany!'

'Yes, of course, I'm getting it,' she says, moving inside.

After collecting the damper she checks her hair in the brass jug on the sideboard, and by the time she gets back to the serving station he is there, waiting. For her? Or is he just waiting for the damper? She doesn't care. She just wants that big smile to be a bit closer to her.

'Yiradhu marang,' he says as he gets closer. 'Yamandhu marang?'

She smiles at the language she misses so much, and when she answers in English, 'Good day, I am very good,' she immediately regrets not responding in their language, so she quickly thanks him again, in Wiradyuri. 'Mandaang guwu.'

He is Wiradyuri, and he knows she is too because they share a langugage. She wants to stand there and just smile, but she is cautious. There is very little that Louisa misses, and Wagadhaany doesn't want her interest in this man to be taken over like her time with the women down by the river.

Chapter Fifteen

James Bradley has come and gone from the property many times in recent weeks, and Wagadhaany has watched Louisa's moods change with every departure and arrival. Today he is due to return again, and Louisa wants to have her English prince to herself. She hasn't said it out loud, but Wagadhaany understands enough about desire and longing to understand what Louisa really wants.

With the time she's been given away from the house so they can have some privacy, Wagadhaany goes back to the river, to Yiray and the women. The anticipation of returning to the camp reminds her of when she was allowed to go home on Sundays back in Gundagai, and of how much those weekly reunions fed her spirit. Today there is a sense of freedom in her steps.

On the long walk to the camp she relishes the time alone to think about the man she now refers to as her Budhang Nyiwarri, imagining that one day he might actually become her true Black Sweetheart. She is under his spell, completely consumed by thoughts of him since their most recent meeting. His long absence until recently has been noticeable, and now she wants to see more of him, to stand close to him, touch him. But for the time being, the fleeting moments seeing his smile when she serves his meals are enough to sustain her.

As she approaches the camp she can hear the words of a mourning song she hasn't heard since Gundagai. She knows immediately there is sorry business and a ceremony happening. It is not near where they sleep, but in a separate place, specifically for ceremonies like this. Camp dogs bark at her as she approaches and she shoos them away. Yiray greets Wagadhaany as she heads in the direction of the wailing. Yiray is distressed and sobbing and tells Wagadhaany that one of the women has lost a child at birth. A girl. There is no greater loss for a mother, she knows that. Everyone is hurting.

Yiray falls into Wagadhaany and she supports her friend's body while she continues to weep. When Yiray finally composes herself, Wagadhaany gently pushes the hair from her face and looks into her swollen red eyes. She is overcome with a sense of responsibility as an older sister, with the need to nurture and protect.

'Minhi, I am here for you. Come.'

She takes Yiray's hand and together they head to a red stringy-bark tree to get branches for the smoking ceremony. She gently pulls at a branch but it doesn't break easily, so she knows that it is not ready to be removed. She takes her time, slowly searching for the right one, the one that *is* ready, all the while aware of the leaves rustling in the breeze around them. She pulls gently on another small branch and it comes away without effort. Waga-dhaany wraps her arms around the tree in a firm hug, giving it as much love as she can, thanking it for the leaves that will form part of their cleansing ceremony.

Just as happens back home, the sad news has travelled across Wiradyuri country, and people are arriving from far and wide, walking into the camp from all directions, including some of the stockmen she recognises from the Bradleys' station. They are all coming to pay their respects to the baby that has not had the chance to know that so many would have protected her. That she is still loved even though she is not there in the flesh.

As she walks to where the Elder women are gathered, Wagadhaany sees her Budhang Nyiwarri. They exchange glances but there is no smile for either of them today. The sorrow around the death of any miyagan always hangs heavily, but the death of a newborn brings palpable trauma and sadness. No amount of infatuation for this man can alter that right now.

As the women prepare to dance, they run ochre across Wagadhaany's face and chest. She remembers when she was young, her mother telling her the story of the rainbow serpent, how it had travelled across country, lost its scales, and those scales then turned to ochre. She considers the scales of the rainbow serpent on her skin now, the stories that her parents shared with her, and how those stories come to her at the times when she needs them. A wave of sadness rushes over her, as she turns her thoughts and feelings towards the lost soul who will never hear the stories of her people.

When the women begin to dance, Wagadhaany moves to join them, and in that moment she is strong. Dancing reminds her of her inner strength, and the power in her Wiradyuri identity.

The songs move through her body, from her ears down her limbs and to her bare feet. She dances with all the passion she can muster, wishing she could dance every day, sing her songs every day, speak her language to everyone. She loses herself in the moment, thinking about the baby who will never know the beauty of the Wiradyuri way of life she was to be born into.

When the sorry business rituals are complete, when the songs are sung and there is no more dancing, all that is left is a heavy sadness weighing on the shoulders of every single person there. All that can be heard are the sounds of mirri-galang barking, which at times is drowned out by women wailing and children playing, children who must still be allowed to enjoy their youth.

Night falls suddenly, bringing the dew and cold. Several fires have been built near ganya-galang, to keep everyone warm. A big fire in the centre of the campsite is being used to cook food and provide light for the families to see each other, talk and mourn.

Near one fire there is a waadyin with her child sitting in her lap, as if they are part of the extended miyagan. Wagadhaany is sure she is speaking language too, and thinks that maybe Louisa is not the only good White person in the town, or maybe this woman is just pushy like Louisa.

As Wagadhaany stares at the waadyin, trying not to be too obvious, a camp boy approaches her from behind and taps her on the head with a pair of clapsticks.

'Ouch,' she says grumpily, rubbing her head as the child giggles. 'That's not good. Don't hurt people.'

The child pouts as if suitably chastised and then wraps his tiny, thin arms around her in a hug, and plants three kisses on her left cheek. He nuzzles into her neck, then whispers in her ear, 'Ngurrbul ngindhu.'

It's the first time someone in Wagga Wagga has said they love her. The words touch her heart. She looks at the child, leans in and repeats the words back to him.

'Ngurrbul ngindhu,' she says, and gives three gentle kisses on the child's left cheek, before taking the clapsticks from his hand. 'Now, where did you get these?' she asks, admiring the beauty and craftsmanship of the two sticks made from black wattle. They look exactly like a pair her babiin had made for her gunhi. The pair her gunhi always used in ceremony.

'Mamaba Yindyamarra,' the child says, pointing to his uncle.

When Wagadhaany turns around to see who the uncle is, her eyes immediately lock on her Budhang Nyiwarri. He now has a name – Yindyamarra. It has the meaning of respect and she is impressed by that. He stays with the men, but signals towards the clapsticks and then to her, and she knows that he is giving them to her.

Her Budhang Nyiwarri is Wiradyuri, he dances, and he has given her some clapsticks. She offers a hint of a smile for the man who makes her feel better about being so far away from her home, makes her feel differently as a woman. Seeing him has transformed her sadness and homesickness into something quite different.

'Yamandhu marang?' Yiray asks as she sits down beside Wagadhaany, who places the clapsticks beside her out of Yiray's sight.

'Ngawa, mandaang guwu,' she responds, because now that she has seen her Black Sweetheart she does feel good.

'Who is that waadyin with the gudha?' Wagadhaany asks.

Yiray looks over to the woman and child. 'The waadyin is Jane. She works with me on the Hansen Station. And that's her boy, Darcy.'

'Why are they here?'

'Jane knows everyone here. When she was pregnant she had no-one to help her at the birth, so the aunties took charge.'

Wagadhaany can easily imagine Yiray's aunties taking full control at any moment they needed to.

'They made a bed of fresh eucalyptus leaves for her to lie on and kept her safe.' Both women know that the oil from the leaves would have sterilised the birthing site. 'She is miyagan to most of us, like your Louisa is to you, I guess.'

Yiray's words give Wagadhaany pause for thought; Yiray sees a waadyin as her family too. As she looks back to the woman, Jane, she sees Yindyamarra and holds his gaze long enough for Yiray to notice.

'Who are you looking at?' she asks. 'Is it Yindy?'

'Yindy?' Wagadhaany pretends she doesn't know who Yiray is talking about, but she is grateful for the opportunity to ask about him.

'Over there.' Yiray nods in his direction. 'The one who thinks he's the best-looking man this side of the Marrambidya. That's Yindy.'

'That fella is Yindy?' Wagadhaany pauses, thinking he *is* the best looking man this side of the bila. She's also not quite sure what she wants to ask next or if it is even appropriate.

'What, mingaan? Is everything all right?'

'Ngawa,' she stalls. 'That fella over there,' she repeats herself, 'his name is Yindyamarra.'

'Yindy,' Yiray says again, far louder than Wagadhaany wants her to. 'Yindy, he's my gaagang-gumbal.'

Wagadhaany slinks down as low as she can, even though she

is sitting on the ground. 'He's your older brother?' Now *she* is louder than she wants to be.

'Ngawa, what's wrong? Did he do something? Tell me.'

'No, he did nothing wrong, nothing at all. I've seen him at the Bradleys' station. I have served him meals, that's all.'

'Of course, that was a silly thing to say. I know my gaagang-gumbal and he would never do anything like . . . anything like that.' After a moment, Yiray continues in a whisper. 'Waga-dhaany, can I ask you something?'

'Of course, anything.'

'The men at the Bradleys' station . . . Do they touch you?'

Wagadhaany sees fear and shame in her minhi's eyes but before she can respond, Yiray continues. 'I mean, do they do things that they shouldn't?'

Wagadhaany immediately thinks of David Bradley. Though his behaviour, his staring and his lurking and his standing much too close, frightens her, she feels as if her own fear is nothing compared to what she can see in Yiray's eyes. Again she thinks back to Mrs Elizabeth Bradley, and again she finds herself more grateful than she can ever say for David Bradley's enduring respect for his mother.

'I am fearful around one of them,' she says, 'but I haven't been touched. I am lucky.' She waits for Yiray to say something, and when she doesn't reply, asks, 'What about at the Hansens?'

Yiray takes a deep breath then swallows. 'Many of the women have been . . . raped. Some have had babies, but the White men do not own them. They are loved here though, but the women are never the same.'

Wagadhaany doesn't know what to say, what to do. She puts her hand on Yiray's. 'And you? Are you all right?'

'Don't tell anyone, ever, my gumbal Yindyamarra, he will want to kill someone for touching his sister.'

Wagadhaany moves closer and puts her arm around Yiray, concerned for her safety, and knowing that her own gumbal-galang would do exactly the same.

Chapter Sixteen

Yindy can't recall the moon ever being brighter. He stares at its perfect round shape and the patches of shadow and wonders if anyone is staring back at him, and if its fullness is drawing in others. The stars are flickering at odd intervals and he walks slowly into the river, as he always does, to wash off the dust from the day and to clear his mind.

He slowly immerses his tired body into the cool water, breathing deeply and disappearing beneath the surface for a few seconds. As the water fills his ears he feels safe, as if inside a cocoon. He thinks of the young one who passed over, the ceremony only days before, and he hopes her spirit is at rest.

The river brings him such peace after a long day working on the station or out droving. In the Marrambidya he can be himself without having to try to impress any of the White men he works with. Here, in its waters, there is no fear of retribution for saying the wrong thing or for simply being a Black man. In the river he can dream of being completely free. In the river he *feels* completely free.

As he slowly rises above the surface of the still water, Yindy lets out a long sigh, almost a groan, only to hear a gasp from across the river. He turns swiftly, wondering who is there. He is both surprised and thrilled to see it's the Wiradyuri migay from the station, the one he saw at the mourning ceremony. The one he saw at the river that night. The one known as Wagadhaany, the dancer. A smile bursts across his face.

He tries desperately to see her in the moonlight, already convinced, even though he has not travelled far from this place, that she is the most beautiful creature ever to walk this country. It makes sense, he tells himself, that she is Wiradyuri. She has that look the men talk about, the look that all Wiradyuri women have, that other Black men travel across the land to see.

Still dressed in her work tunic, Wagadhaany is yet to step into the water. She moves her hands awkwardly across her body, demonstrating her modesty, even though she is still clothed. Yindy panics, not wanting to scare her, not wanting her to be afraid of him. He imagines that she is not used to being around men like this, alone. He watches as she scurries up the riverbank, his heart beating so loudly he is sure she can hear it. He places his hand on his chest and is tempted to press hard on it to make the beating stop. Instead he rests it there and nervously calls out, 'Yuwin ngadhi Yindyamarra. My name is Yindyamarra.'

Wagadhaany stops, turns. She has heard him. Perhaps she already knows his name, or at least what it means. He hopes so. He has never been more desperate to impress in his life, but at this moment he's not sure how. He is naked in the water. She is at the top of the riverbank, where the sand meets the grass. They don't know each other.

He moves slightly to his left, she moves awkwardly to her left. They are both trying to see the other more clearly in the dark.

Wagadhaany is squinting, he can see that much. When she moves back down the bank a few steps, they are at last in each other's direct line of sight. He is simultaneously excited and nervous, frightened his body might follow his heart's lead, that he might run right out of the water and up to her.

He tries hard not to stare but he's struggling, wanting to gauge some recognition in her eyes. Without words, he can't decipher what she is thinking, feeling, wanting. At least with the aunties back at camp, he can always rely on their facial expressions to give everything away. But this woman, she is too smart, or too young, to raise her eyebrows in any way.

All that Yindyamarra knows for certain is that this moment, under the perfect moon and blanket of stars, is his, and he can't let an opportunity to get closer to this woman slip by. He has admired her from under the brim of his hat. He has felt the thrill of her touch when she lightly brushed his hand at the station at meal time. He has seen the way she moves her hips when dancing. He has played her words from the homestead over and over in his mind, the sound of her voice a soothing melody in comparison to the rough words of the men he works with. She has melted his heart and left him blind to any other woman he has seen or spoken to since. And he wants her to know that. He wants her to know that he made the clapsticks just for her, in the hope he would be able to give them to her one day. He wants her to know the effect she has had on him as a man, and how many times he has dipped below the surface of the river and allowed himself to dream of her. How many nights she has guided him to sleep without even being there.

There is too much silence, too many unsaid words, and so he has no choice but to speak.

'I'm Yindyamarra,' he finally repeats, desperate for her to stay, to talk. 'My grandmother named me.' He acknowledges the matriarch of his family, who named all her grandchildren.

When there is still no response, no words from the woman before him, he wants to retreat. He feels shame. A voice in his head tells him she does not want to talk to him, she is not interested in his name. She has not thought of him at all since seeing him at the camp.

'Respect. Honour,' he adds desperately, patting his chest with each word. He wants her to know what his name means and that he is a man who is true to that name. And it is his one last attempt to get her to speak.

'Yes,' she finally responds. 'It also means to be kind and gentle.'

And with those few sweet words, the anxiety of trying to impress vanishes. He feels a wave of warmth wash over his entire body. *Is it relief, gratitude, love?* He isn't sure, but the blood running through his veins seems to pump faster, making its way to his loins. She is beautiful, she understands his Wiradyuri language, she knows the meaning of his name. He feels his nyinmaay rise beneath the water but tries to ignore it, hoping she can't see anything, and that by continuing to talk, he can keep her there longer.

'I have Wiradyuri belonging from here and from the Galari – the White men call it the Lachlan River.' He sees her nod; she knows his birthplace. 'My mother, she is from here, from Wagga Wagga, the land of dancing.' He places his hand on his chest. 'My totem is the gugaa.'

He looks towards her, entranced by her eyes. He wants to know who she is, but how? He's standing in the water thinking while she remains on the riverbank. He wants her to speak more.

He wants to hear the sound of her sweet voice, even though she emanates an air of serenity and temptation. He needs to know if he should stop dreaming about her. *Should I just ask her? Why isn't she speaking? Please say something.* In his mind he wills her to speak because he has run out of any words that might help him right now.

'I am Wagadhaany,' she finally says, softly.

The sound of her voice in Yindy's ears is as soothing as the water on his skin. 'Dancer,' he says.

The slightest of smiles forms at the corners of her mouth. 'Yes, but some White people call me Wilma, I don't know why.' She shrugs.

'Because they can't speak our language, even though we have to speak theirs.'

There is silence again, and he doesn't know if she is shy or just uncomfortable. As much as he'd like to, he can't get out of the water and try to make the awkward moment feel any easier.

'I get Yindy for short, but I don't mind that.'

He recalls how many times he's heard the men make fun of his name, struggling to pronounce Yindyamarra properly. He can't understand why it's so hard, when he can say theirs easily.

'Look!' Wagadhaany points to a shooting star moving across the dark sky.

Yindyamarra follows her gaze, reminded of the Wiradyuri story of the Milky Way.

'The stars in the sky are the campfires of my people,' he says. 'Our people.'

'My father told me that story too,' she replies. 'My father is a spiritual man,' she adds. 'He worships Biyaami and every day he gets up and says good morning to the sun. But I also think that it's because my mother's name is Yiramiilan.'

'Sunrise,' they both say together.

'Ngawa,' she says, nodding.

'What is your father's name?' he asks, wondering if the name will sound familiar to him.

'Coonong Denamundinna,' she says proudly. 'But most people know him as Yarri. Or James McDonnell – that's what a lot of the White stockmen call him on the station where he works. He's a shepherd at the Bradleys' old place, near Gundagai, where I have come from. That's where my miyagan are.' And then abruptly she adds, 'I have to go.'

She turns and disappears quickly up the riverbank.

Yindy is confused and disappointed, not sure what has led to her sudden departure. He wants the chance to talk more, to learn more about her family, to know everything about her, but mostly he just wants to keep her there longer, to look at her. He moves through the water towards her side of the bank but it's too late. She is gone. And he is still naked.

'Goodnight, my dancer,' he says under his breath. He dips below the surface of the river again, his heart still racing, his loins aching and his mind thinking that in the morning he will greet the sun like his dancer's father.

Wagadhaany lies awake, her stomach stirring. Her Budhan Nyiwarri, Yindyamarra, has unnerved her. He has knocked her off her axis, made her feel like that shooting star travelling across the night sky. Her heart feels strange and she cannot stop the tingling in her flesh. And she doesn't want to. When she closes her eyes all she can see is the outline of his body in the moonlight. How she had wanted to reach out and touch the droplets of water on his chest, feel the muscles in his arms, know what was hidden beneath the surface of the water.

The few words they exchanged play over and over in her mind. His voice was deep but warm, with a hint of shyness. The physical reaction she felt being near such a good-looking man made her nervous, as she has never felt such stirrings before. All she could think to do was to run off, but now her head spins with questions. She wants to see Yindyamarra again, to speak to him some more. She hopes he wants to speak to her again too. Most importantly, she wants to know if he is true to his name. Only time will tell. Only seeing him again will tell.

She closes her eyes, her lids heavy from a hard day cleaning the house, polishing the silver, washing the bed linen and pressing shirts for the Bradley brothers. When she finally drifts into a deep sleep, she dreams of Yindyamarra with her in the river. There are no awkward silences, only shooting stars and moonlight.

'I saw a man last night by the river,' she confides in Louisa next morning, as she takes the boiling water from the stove to wash the dishes.

Her tone is calm as she tries to hide the excitement that is stirring within her tiny frame. She is grateful that neither James nor David are at the homestead so she can speak to Louisa freely.

Louisa spins around. '*That* one?' she asks, eyes wide. 'The one I have seen you flirting with?'

'What is flirting?' Wagadhaany asks.

'It's the way you behave with someone you like, someone you are attracted to. I saw you act differently with that stockman, Yindyamarra,' Louisa replies with a cheeky grin.

'You know his name? And you saw us? But we hardly spoke.'

'I know *all* the men's names, and I see *everything*, Wagadhaany, especially when it's right in front of me. I saw the way you two looked at each other. *Everyone* saw.' Louisa has a huge smile on her face.

Wagadhaany is shocked and embarrassed. *Who else saw? What do people think? Did anyone at the camp notice? Did anyone see or hear us at the river last night?* Her excitement is at risk of being overshadowed by panic.

'He *is* handsome,' Louisa says. 'And a good worker. That's why he is sent droving so much. He's the best we have.'

As hard as she tries, Wagadhaany can't help but smile. He *is* handsome. There are some facts in life that cannot be ignored: that she must work eleven hours every day, that her family are far away, that the bamali-galang at the camp make her smile with their eyebrows, that James Bradley does not like her at all, that David Bradley makes her feel uneasy. And yes, that Yindyamarra is very good-looking. She is already proud of the man she barely knows. He is the best the Bradleys have. Her father was the best they had in Gundagai. He is the best, like her father.

Louisa takes her hands from the dishwater, dries them on a cloth and motions Wagadhaany to the kitchen table.

'Sit,' Louisa says, taking a seat opposite.

This is a show of friendship and tenderness that Wagadhaany is learning to feel more comfortable with, and today she is grateful for another woman to talk to.

'Tell me everything!' Louisa insists in a warm, excited voice. 'Did you speak? Are you in love?' Louisa is wriggling in her seat like a child waiting for a treat, desperate for any crumb of information.

Wagadhaany doesn't know what it feels like to love someone who is not your miyagan. She's never before been *in love*. She stares at Louisa, dumbfounded by the question. There is so much she doesn't know about life, about people, about men. She realises she must be pulling a face like the aunties at the camp.

'I am sure I am a little older than you, Wagadhaany,' Louisa starts. 'That doesn't necessarily mean I know more than you, but I do have some experience, being married.' She takes Wagadhaany's hand. 'Well, twice married,' she adds.

Wagadhaany understands now that the joining of hands is offered not only as a sign of friendship, but also of solidarity between women.

'Talking about our men, Wagadhaany, it's what we should do on life's journey together, how we can support each other,' Louisa explains earnestly.

'There are many different kinds of love. There is romantic love between a man and woman, like James and me. There is love of family, for our parents and siblings. And there is the love we have for friends. And they are all important.'

Wagadhaany listens intently. Her father would tell her he loved her, but that is not the same as romantic love. She knows that all parents love their children. And she loves her nieces and nephews. And she loves the land and the Marrambidya.

But can we choose who we love and can someone choose to love you? What then? What do women do then? What did my mother do? Did my father choose her?

Louisa leans in, lowering her voice, bringing an even greater intimacy to the conversation. 'James and I married because we needed each other. We were lost souls, our hearts broken from the deaths of so many that we loved. Sometimes I think we fell into each other's lives, rather than falling in love.

'We shared our grief. We then shared a bed. But as time goes by I can see that there is not much more that we share,' she says sadly.

Wagadhaany feels that Louisa is revealing a lot more than she needs to, that her married life with James Bradley should be a private matter between them. But maybe this is what women do as they get older, when they are friends, when they talk about men and love. Maybe this is what the aunties also talk about while weaving. Maybe she will need to share private things with Louisa one day too.

'I loved my first husband, Oscar. He was my first love. I didn't think I would ever love another man, but it is true, I do love James now. You will learn too that love can blossom out of extraordinary circumstances.'

Wagadhaany doesn't know how to respond to these revelations.

'So, there are different kinds of love,' Louisa resumes. 'You can love someone differently to someone else, and it can still be significant, important to you both. Do you understand?'

Wagadhaany is trying hard to understand. She is keen to listen, to learn as much as she can about love, particularly between a man and a woman. She wonders if the reason her heart feels so buoyant when she thinks of Yindyamarra is because she is, in fact, in love. She nods to signal she understands and waits for Louisa to continue.

'James and I love each other, but the sparks are rarer now.'

Wagadhaany wonders if the sparks Louisa speaks of are what she saw in Yindyamarra's eyes as he stood in the water.

'That look, that excitement,' Louisa says, her eyes wide. 'I only see that look when he talks about his political career, or when he wants to have relations.' She slumps back in her chair then, as if by saying those words out loud, the truth of her marriage has become reality. 'He is so focused on wanting to be mayor that he ignores me, like I am nothing in his life aside from the society wife he needs. But I am more than any man's accessory, Wagadhaany. I am a woman with visions for a better country for all people.' Her tone becomes serious. 'I am a woman who would have a lot to offer if my husband allowed me to be more than just a female looking after his basic needs.'

Louisa purses her lips. 'I am not a quitter. I married James because a part of me did love him, and I still do. And it is love that will keep our marriage together. But I cannot, I will not, rely on his love alone. I need more than that, Wagadhaany. And you should keep that in mind as well, with Yindyamarra, or any other man who ignites that spark for you.'

Wagadhaany had been overcome by Louisa's words about love, but the feelings of joy in her heart have been diminished by Louisa's disclosures about her marital life with James. She thinks that Louisa is very good at turning conversations so they focus on herself, and wishes she could go back to thinking about Yindyamarra and the night before, and to dreaming about the nights ahead.

'The flood gave us so much heartache,' Louisa resumes. 'It took the people I loved. It took the people James loved. But it also gave us each other. And in that twist of fate, Wagadhaany, it also gave me you. And the love of good friends is not something that should ever be disregarded either.'

Louisa stands, pushes her chair in. 'And what if in that twist of fate, and in me bringing you to Wagga Wagga, you met the man you will love?'

Chapter Seventeen

A few days later, Louisa is beaming when Wagadhaany enters
the kitchen before daybreak. The kettle is already on the
stove, and she is making them a pot of tea before they start their
daily chores.

'Are you all right?' Wagadhaany asks.

Louisa hums as she moves around the kitchen.

'I'm not a quitter, Wagadhaany, I told you that.'

'Yes, you did, but I don't understand.'

Louisa twitches her eye at her. 'I think James and I will be all
right, I really do.'

'That thing with your eye, that . . .' Wagadhaany tries to
twitch her eye. 'What does it mean? Mr David does it, but I don't
understand.'

'What, this?' Louisa does it again. 'It is called a wink and
it means a joke, or a secret. Or sometimes you might wink in
greeting, but a lady probably wouldn't do that. Sometimes James
will wink at me when he feels like having relations. But that

happens between people who are intimate. I really don't know why David would be winking at you. Maybe he thinks he is being funny.'

Louisa doesn't sound convinced by her own words, and Wagadhaany understands now that this wink is another part of David's behaviour that makes her feel uncomfortable.

'I couldn't stop thinking about what we talked about yesterday,' Louisa continues, 'and the more I thought, the more I understood my feelings and how I need to be considered in any plans James makes for a political career. How our marriage needs to be a priority in his life. How when he is home, he needs to be focused on our relationship, on me.'

Louisa is nearly always direct, clear about what she wants. It's the one thing that Wagadhaany really admires about her, and she wishes she could be more like that herself. She remembers when Louisa first visited the Bradley house back in Gundagai, and how James was a stammering fool around her, changing his way of speaking, fetching whatever she needed. Louisa is the only person she has ever seen James make any real effort for, and Wagadhaany knows it's because Louisa always expected him to do so.

'And?'

'Last night, when James returned, we had a very important conversation.'

She pictures Louisa giving James Bradley a lecture in their marital bed. She has seen the lady of the house use her intellect and moral code to win over her husband at times, and her feminine ways when need be. As long as James is sober, Louisa has every chance of getting her own way. Because although Louisa says there is no spark anymore, Wagadhaany can see the way James still looks at his wife at certain times, the look of longing that she now knows men have for women. The look she hopes Yindyamarra might have for her one day.

'I want to have a family.' Louisa smiles widely. 'And we started trying last night. Today is a new day, and I am confident about the path ahead. I want to be a mother, James wants a legacy for the Bradley name, and so we will be parents. And hopefully soon.' She stands. 'Let's go into town. We will see if there's any mail and get some more fabric. I think I will be making some new clothes for myself very soon.'

Louisa remains confident and positive, until they get to the store and are confronted by a local gossip.

'How many little ones do you have? I see you have help,' the gossip says to Louisa, glancing at Wagadhaany with the same look of contempt many White people have for Blacks who are in public places when apparently they shouldn't be.

At first Louisa appears taken aback at having been asked such a question by a complete stranger, but she quickly regains her composure. 'We have none as yet, but we will. I have been busy supporting my husband's work on our station.'

Wagadhaany hopes Louisa doesn't mention she wants to save Aboriginal people because she can tell by the way the gossip is looking her up and down that such a declaration will not go well. She looks boldly at the gossip, stares straight in her eyes and wishes she could say something about the permanent scowl on her pasty, wrinkled face.

'Well then, you must be doing very well for yourself if you have help and don't really need it,' the gossip responds sarcastically. 'Your husband must be very happy to have all that extra time with you.'

Wagadhaany's eyes dart to Louisa and she hopes the comment

doesn't upset her, given their conversations over the past twenty-four hours.

'Come,' Louisa says, taking Wagadhaany's hand, and leading her awkwardly towards the door.

From the corner of her eye Wagadhaany sees a look of disgust on the woman's face, as they walk away.

When the sun sets and Louisa goes to her room, complaining of a headache, Wagadhaany sneaks down to the river in the hope of seeing Yindy. Since their first meeting she has thought of him constantly. She wants to see his smile, hear his voice, learn more about him. She wants to stand in the river with him and discover what lies below the ripples. She hopes he is thinking the same thing, and that tonight he will choose to sleep near the homestead and not at the camp.

With her sleeping quarters downstairs and well away from Louisa and James's room, it's easy for her to leave the homestead without being noticed. She gently closes the door and makes her way to the same spot she saw Yindy last time. The closer she gets, the faster her heart beats. She is conscious of every footstep, every noise she makes stepping on dry twigs and leaves. She has so many expectations but can't tame any of them. Thinking about Yindy has been her only source of happiness in the last few weeks. Remembering him in the water by moonlight has taken her mind off wanting to go home, and given her some fleeting moments of believing that a happy life in Wagga Wagga may be possible.

As she steps past a grey box gum she sees him. He is sitting alone on the bank with his bare back to her. His broad shoulders and arms look strong, as if he could easily carry her across the river to the other side, from where they could run away into the night. She stops still momentarily, dreaming of having his arms around her. When she takes another step, she stands on a fallen branch and stumbles. The noise startles Yindyamarra. He jumps to his feet and spins, landing in a defensive pose. But when he sees her, his body loosens up and he relaxes into a pose that looks welcoming, that calls her to him.

'Marang yariya,' he says.

Wagadhaany thinks that saying good evening is a bit serious but can't think of anything less so to reply. And so, she repeats it back to him.

'Marang yariya.'

'Here.' He motions her to sit on his horse blanket. She can tell he has given it a good shake.

'I was hoping you might come back. We didn't talk properly last time.' His voice is shaky, a little unsure perhaps, as if he is nervous. 'You were on the riverbank, and me, well . . . I was in there . . .'

He looks into the river and she remembers how handsome he was that night. And now she is right next to him. His rugged appeal stirs her emotions, and she wants to touch him.

'Have you been in already?' she asks, slightly disappointed that she didn't get to see the beads of water on his chest again.

'I have been here quite a while . . . waiting.' He chuckles nervously.

She blushes, wondering if this was what it was like when Louisa first met James. If this is flirting.

'How did you end up here?' he asks.

'I belong to the Bradleys. There's a master and servants law,' she blurts out.

Saying it so easily and honestly reminds her of the lack of freedom in her life. She looks to Yindyamarra, knowing that she should savour every moment she has with him.

'Go on,' he says.

'They lost their family in the big flood in Gundagai. Their parents, and two brothers. I was with them the whole time. It was the worst night of my life.'

'What happened? Who saved you?' Yindy moves closer and she feels her body heat up.

'My father,' she says proudly. 'My father, Yarri, he saved the lives of James and David Bradley. After he got me to safety, he went back out into the raging storm and saved them too. They owe him everything. They wouldn't be here – *I* wouldn't be here – if it weren't for him. But they didn't care, they still made me come here and my father could do nothing about it. I was helpless, I still am.'

Talking about this saddens her. She can feel herself descending again into darkness. For so long it's been like this whenever she thinks or talks about how she came to Wagga Wagga. But when Yindy reaches out and lays his hand gently on hers, the darkness begins to dissipate.

'I heard about the Wiradyuri men in the floods, they are heroes! He is your father?' Yindy seems impressed. 'You must be very proud of him.'

She can't speak. There is burning from her fingertips right up her arm and into her chest, and her mouth is dry. She looks at him shyly. His nervousness seems to have suddenly disappeared and she listens as he speaks, the Wiradyuri and English words falling gently on her ears. She wants to listen to him all night, and she never wants him to move his hand.

'We had floods too,' he tells her. 'The Marrambidya Bila flows here downstream from Gundagai.'

She wonders if the waters she washed in back home ever made their way down to him.

'I have seen terrible things during flood times too, buggies and yarraman-galang swept away by raging waters. I've seen wadhagung-galang climb trees. I've seen mayiny drown, while all the others could do was save themselves and look on helplessly.'

His words bring the terrors of the Gundagai flood back to her.

'And we have our own heroes right here, just like your father. The White people called one Big Peter and they made him King of the Wagga Wagga tribe. He helped a man and saved many women and children from the roofs of houses during one of our floods.'

Yindyamarra's story stirs up so many memories of the Great Flood in Gundagai, but Wagadhaany doesn't get upset this time. Instead, she feels pride for the heroes of these disasters and wonders if Wiradyuri men everywhere are strong and capable, and if the striking man sitting next to her is also potentially a hero, if he would save her life if he had to.

'We have many leaders, many strong men,' he adds, while she listens, mesmerised. 'Yes, Mycotha, Booyarrie, Warange-line, Yallagumie, they are . . .' He pauses. 'The heroes of Wagga Wagga.'

'And you?' she asks, tilting her head. 'Are you a hero of Wagga Wagga?'

'It is for others to decide whether I am a hero or not. To be honest, I'd rather not have any more floods, rather not need to be a hero, ever. And right now, right here, there is no need for me to be a hero.'

Wagadhaany finds Yindy's humility attractive. She turns towards the river, then looks at him with a twinkle in her eye. 'You could be *my* hero.'

And before she has a chance to feel shame about the words she never imagined saying to a man, she stands and walks to the river's edge. As the tide laps at her feet, she removes her tunic and steps carefully into the cold water, feeling her way for debris on the river bed. She is barely wet when he is behind her. His arms are around her belly, pulling her back into him, keeping her safe in the current, and as close as possible to his bare flesh.

She doesn't know why but she trusts Yindy. He is a stranger to her and yet it feels like she has known his body forever, that their souls have been connected since ancient times. She feels safe and secure in his arms, free of the weight of sadness that has plagued her since she farewelled her miyagan. She turns to face him, wraps her legs around his waist, and gently floats, her emotions as light as her body on the water. She closes her eyes. This must be the feeling of being in love that Louisa tried to explain.

The spring air is sweet when she inhales, and Yindy watches the rise and fall of her chest. She loosens his hold on her, takes his hands from her bubul and lowers herself under the water. When she comes up for air, her long, wet curls fall down her front. Yindy moves her hair gently, so it's tucked behind her ears and falls down her back. She likes the way he watches her, as if he is drinking her in. He pulls her to him gently but firmly and they kiss as if this, their first kiss, will be their last. There are no words, only glances and caresses, and she wonders if this is how lovers speak to each other. The night is still. All she can hear is the water lapping around their bodies.

Chapter Eighteen

The first month of spring in Wagga Wagga brings with it the scent of wild flowers and lush grass. Wagadhaany prefers to have the early mornings for herself, some moments of solitude at daybreak to reflect on her new existence. Since arriving in Wagga Wagga she has learned that being alone and being lonely are two different things.

The kitchen is dark but Wagadhaany knows someone is there when she enters before sun-up. She hopes it's neither of the Bradley men, especially David Bradley, who has started drinking regularly. While it is not at the same level as his brother, it still makes Wagadhaany frightened. He is not aggressive like James when drunk, but he rambles and sometimes rants about the life his older brother enjoys compared to his own: the love and affection of a beautiful wife, control over the family estate, his pending role as an official in town. On a number of occasions David has slurred to Wagadhaany, 'He will be unbearable if he becomes mayor, you mark my words.'

'Hello?' she asks softly.

Louisa sits up and gasps in fright.

'Louisa? Are you all right?'

Louisa puts her head on the table and starts sobbing. Her increasingly common mood swings are concerning, and Wagadhaany doesn't know what to do.

'We have been trying to have a baby for months,' she sobs into her folded arms.

Wagadhaany knows that Louisa is desperate to have a child, especially because James is absent a lot. That she feels lonely not only when he is away on business, but also when he is home and focused on everything other than her. Louisa loves children; Wagadhaany can see how much joy it brings her, reading to the children at the camp on the rare occasions she visits. She knows Louisa will be a good mother, but she doesn't know how to help her.

'James is drinking again,' Louisa says. 'He says it's all part of becoming mayor, having to be out with the influential men nearly every night. He comes home drunk, and . . .'

She stops, but Wagadhaany knows what would have come next. She washes his clothes and removes the empty bottles from the house. She hears him yelling. She has known for a while that James Bradley has been drinking heavily again, and that he gets aggressive with Louisa when he is drunk, but she has never said anything about it. She would never want to embarrass Louisa, or make the situation any more difficult for her.

'Did he . . . Did he hurt you?' she asks cautiously. 'Louisa?'

Louisa shakes her head. 'Not last night.'

There are no bruises on her alabaster skin today, but there have been, and Wagadhaany knows it. She has seen the bluish

241

marks on Louisa's upper arms when she has helped her dress, although neither of the women have commented.

There is something upsetting Louisa deeply today, but Wagadhaany is not used to prying, it is not her way. She and Louisa are very different in that respect. But it pains her heart to see her friend so distressed.

'What is it then? Louisa, you can tell me.' She leans over her friend, whose head is on her folded arms on the table. 'If you want to.'

When Wagadhaany places her hands on Louisa's shoulders, she can feel her collarbone through her dress. There is barely any flesh, and Wagadhaany is shocked to realise how thin she has become. She rubs Louisa's shoulders, wondering how she can get her to eat more, and tries to console Louisa and stop her from sobbing.

'Shhhh, whatever the problem is, we can fix it together. I will help you.'

Louisa sits upright, wipes her face on her sleeve. It's the least English-rose behaviour Wagadhaany has ever seen from her, and Wagadhaany finds it endearing.

'I got my monthlies,' she sobs. 'I'm not pregnant. Maybe I can't get pregnant. I'm trying . . . and I think that is why James drinks so much, out of frustration. He wants a son. *I* want a son.'

She falls onto the table again, distressed. Wagadhaany doesn't know what to say or do; this is not a conversation she has ever had. She rubs Louisa's back again, helplessly. This is not something she can help with. Or can she?

'I have an idea,' she whispers. 'Maybe the women by the river can help. They know *everything*. About *everything*.'

'Do you really think so?' Louisa turns her head to the side to speak, as if it would be too much effort to do anything more.

'Do you really think they can help? I know James will be much happier and drink less when we have children, I am sure of that.'

'Trust me, James is not the only person who knows important people,' Wagadhaany reassures her, knowing that the older Wiradyuri women are very wise.

Later that morning, as if Louisa deems it an emergency, they go to the camp and spend hours with the women. The older girls keep the children busy and out of the way, and when the aunties have finished talking with Louisa, her state of mind is calmer. Before she leaves she reads a story to the children. When the book is finished, she asks them to tell her stories and they make some up, right there on the spot. It's as if the morning's tears never fell, as if Louisa will be all right. As if being around children really is the key to her happiness.

It is late afternoon when Louisa leaves the camp, and with her agreement, Wagadhaany stays to wait for Yindy to come back. She finds a secluded spot on the bila where she can be alone and away from the gudha-galang. She sits by the water's edge, thinking about what she's heard from the women today. Their knowledge and wisdom fill her with hope for Louisa becoming a mother, and for herself too as one day she'd also like to have children. She feels the need to dance – something is calling her – and so she stands, shakes off any sadness still resting on her from Louisa's tears that morning, and dances. As her feet gently touch the ground, her soles sweeping from side to side across the earth, she begins to feel at peace again, just like she did in the water with Yindy.

As the sun sets, she sees his silhouette. The backdrop of orange sky sharply defines his lean frame as he approaches but he is not walking as tall as he normally does. Instead, his shoulders look weighed down and his steps are slow. When he reaches her, she stands to greet him, and he is as white in the face as a Black man can possibly be.

'Yindy?'

She catches him as he collapses to the ground, unsure if his lack of strength is from a hard day droving or not enough food. Or perhaps there has been a death. Her heart aches without even knowing what is wrong, and she is desperate to take away his pain.

'Dinawan-galang dead everywhere. Near Eunonyhareenyha.' Yindy weeps, holding his head in his hands. 'They shot them. Dead. For gold.'

He speaks with short breaths as if winded by the greed of his fellow humans killing innocent emus.

'I don't understand,' Wagadhaany whispers. 'Why? Why did they kill the dinawan-galang?' she says angrily. 'And dinawan-galang, they are sacred.'

'I heard they found gold in the belly of one, and so they shot them all, every single one of them.' He shakes his head. 'And . . .' he pauses.

'And what? Tell me. I want to know.'

'They sliced them open, looking for more gold. But they didn't find any. They killed all those beautiful dinawan-galang for nothing. Nothing!'

He puts his head in his hands. This is a different side of Yindy and his broken heart breaks hers. At that moment, she knows she is in love, this is what it must feel like. To care so much for someone, to feel their pain, and to want to take it from them and carry it yourself.

'The poor dinawan-galang.' Wagadhaany sits close to Yindy and starts to cry.

'I shouldn't have told you,' he says. 'I'm sorry. You don't need to know the horror of what the White man is capable of, what he actually does.'

Yindy takes her in his arms. Her heart pains her when she hears these words. She knows Yindy wants to protect her from what happens in his daily life. She knows he wants to be her hero, her strength, when she is so far from her family. But she wants to be there for him too. She thinks of what she can do for him and all she can think of, to heal his spirit, is to dance. And so she stands, and without her clapsticks, which are hidden in her room back at the Bradleys', she claps her hands, softly sings, and dances – for him, for herself, and for the souls of the dinawan-galang. She dances for those whose totem now lies lifeless on Wiradyuri land. She sings and dances for the Ancient Ones, and she asks for strength and guidance. In her words, she voices her gratitude for her own life as she takes Yindy's hand and urges him to dance too.

That night she stays with him. They feast on freshly caught cod and hide in their private place, where she is locked in her lover's arms, unable and unwilling to move. As they lie beneath the bilabang, she thinks about her miyagan going to sleep under the same constellation, the Milky Way connecting them from the sky when they are so far apart on the earth.

'I miss my miyagan, all of them. I miss the bila where I was born. It is the same water, but my feet, my spirit – it feels better back there.' She pauses. 'I feel safe here with you, but I am always sad, every day since the day I was forced to leave. That day my giiny broke into many pieces. And I get sadder now, when you go away.'

Yindy pulls her in close as she begins to cry. 'Ngurrbul ngindhu,' he whispers in her ear, and her heart skips a bit. He loves her.

'Ngurrbul ngindhu,' she whispers back.

There is silence as they stare at the blanket of stars above.

Later, in his sleep, Yindy lets out a snort and Wagadhaany chuckles to herself. Her head rests on his chest and she drifts off again, hoping the dawn will bring a better day for him, for all of them.

By the time the sun is up and Yindy rises, Wagadhaany has long been awake. She is hunched over, vomiting under a tree, trying to hide. The last thing she wants to do is cause Yindy any worry after the terrible days he has just endured. On her last retch, he is there, gently holding her hair back.

She sits back, wipes her face with some paperbark, and looks at him with tired eyes. She hasn't slept much, and she doesn't know how to describe the tightness and discomfort in her stomach.

'Maybe I ate too much. That will teach me to be greedy.' She tries to make light of it.

Days later, she still feels nauseous but doesn't complain. She is already missing Yindy, who is herding cattle south again, and she tries to focus on the tasks at hand. Under the scorching summer sun, she holds a parasol over Louisa's head as she stands in front of a crowd of around two hundred people who are all waiting for James Bradley's wife to drive the first pile into the ground, marking the beginning of the construction of a bridge over the Murrumbidgee River. This new bridge will replace the punt. James, a founding director of the Wagga Wagga Bridge Company, watches with pride as Louisa pulls the string, releasing the drop hammer.

'Three cheers for Mrs Bradley, three cheers for Mr Bradley.'

The crowd applauds, and James and Louisa smile. The event is over in far less time than Wagadhaany had expected, the heat driving the townsfolk away as quickly as they had arrived.

'Louisa, I will see you at home. I am going to the hotel with Baylis and Wallace,' James says warmly to Louisa. 'And tell David to join us when he has finished the accounts.'

She nods, then turns to speak to the wife of a local businessman.

James turns to Wagadhaany. 'Escort Mrs Bradley home, Wilma,' he says quietly.

There is always a change in his tone whenever Louisa is not in earshot.

'After all the drought across the Riverina it's good to see some colour in the street,' Louisa notes as the women walk back to the homestead. 'It's been dusty and dry for long enough, the town really was beginning to look tired. It's going to be a pretty Christmas this year, don't you think?'

Before Wagadhaany has the chance to respond, Louisa continues. 'James was always complaining about how the crops were poor, how everything was wilting, but look now,' she says, pointing to some bright foliage along the roadside. 'I really don't know how we managed to keep our garden alive, Wagadhaany. And the bright red of the Christmas bush, it will make the house look festive, don't you think?'

Wagadhaany feels listless and so unwell she fears she will vomit right there in the street. She holds her stomach and wonders if it is her monthlies coming after a very long time of no blood at all. Louisa is still talking to her but she can't find the words to respond.

As Louisa turns to Wagadhaany, she steps on a loose stone and her footing is unbalanced. She twists her ankle and falls to the ground. The street is empty due to the heat and Wagadhaany is forced to use all her strength to help Louisa to her feet again. Together they hobble to the post office, where the postmaster offers his carriage to take them back to the homestead.

Once home, Louisa asks David to go on horseback to fetch the town's doctor, and to alert James at the hotel. She does not miss him shaking his head at both of them before he leaves the house.

The doctor arrives later that day to check for any broken bones and to administer painkillers. James has remained at the hotel, however, and is noticeably absent. Meanwhile, David lurks and leers in the background.

'I was just walking along Baylis Street, and was so happy to see some bright new leaves on the kurrajong trees,' Louisa tells the doctor. 'I was mesmerised after so many months in this dusty town. Everything was so dry, and my poor garden was looking tired even though I would cart water from the river to revive it.'

That was not completely true, and both the women knew it. It was Wagadhaany and the new women James had recently employed who would cart the water. She did not recognise the Aboriginal women who had started, or the very young White women who did the heavier workloads that the older women couldn't and Louisa wouldn't attempt. She had overheard one of the workers say that Louisa's white skin would not survive the damaging sun, and Wagadhaany knew that James would never approve of his wife carting anything, anywhere. She wondered why Louisa had to be protected from hard work but the Wiradyuri women didn't. And she wondered if that thought ever crossed Louisa's mind, because that made them different, unequal, at least in the eyes of the sun.

'The street needs work but I see the council has called for tenders for the laying of kerbing and pavement,' the doctor replies as he bandages her ankle.

'The work on the street will be a boon for shopkeepers,' David adds.

'And their customers,' says Wagadhaany. 'No more leaping between mud holes in the winter.' She smiles weakly at Louisa.

'Oh yes, that is so true, but sometimes that is fun,' Louisa jokes back.

The doctor's look of shock shows his surprise at the women's banter, and he turns to David to see if he approves.

'There is a lot of change happening in town, even the price of liquor has gone up at the Criterion Hotel,' David adds, always focused on money, prices, the cost of things.

'One would hope that the increase in price would see a decrease in drunkenness,' Louisa says pointedly. 'But,' she continues with a tone of judgement in her voice, 'I hear that rowdiness continues in town.'

David doesn't react. Wagadhaany knows that Louisa hates James going to the town's hotel, or to any hotel, and he is so wealthy that a price rise won't stop him drinking anywhere or as much as he likes.

'I'll make some tea,' says Wagadhaany, noting the other staff are busy doing laundry and cleaning.

She has barely taken a step when the doctor comments, 'Your Black girl is very forward, Mr Bradley.'

But it is Louisa who responds. 'Her name is Wagadhaany, not *Black girl*, and she is like family. No, she *is* my family. Her father saved my James and David in the Great Flood of Gundagai. They owe their lives to Wagadhaany's father.'

'It is true, Yarri saved our lives,' says David, 'but I kept his daughter alive throughout the night, kept her safe until she could be rescued. So, just as we are indebted to her father, she is indebted to us as well, especially to me!'

When Wagadhaany looks up, David Bradley is staring, and he doesn't take his eyes off her. She fidgets with her apron, her hair, and backs out of the room as the conversation continues.

'And Wagadhaany is now my family, as my blood relations all perished in the Great Flood.'

'Yes but . . .' The doctor attempts to speak but is swiftly cut off by Louisa.

'There will be no buts, Doctor. I have only ever known Wagadhaany to be honest and respectful. So too, her family. And all the Aboriginal people I have met here.'

'I didn't mean to offend you, Mrs Bradley,' the doctor apologises. 'Nor you, David.'

'That is all, Doctor, you will not be required any longer,' Louisa says sharply. 'Your bill will be paid as soon as you provide the paperwork.'

Chapter Nineteen

A restless night's sleep has left Yindy feeling lethargic when he is forced to rise at daybreak. His exhaustion compounds his disillusionment at the devastation of Wiradyuri land he sees while droving. As the stockmen move out from the Bradleys' station on what is expected to be a long droving trip, days that may turn into weeks, he takes in the land. Before him he sees the stumps of ancient trees cut down to make buildings; so many burial sites across Wiradyuri country have been ruined by stock-yards and cattle runs, and hunting grounds have been destroyed. He knows some Wiradyuri men helped clear the bush, and that the changes are also in part due to roads being built, tearing up the land. *How much more change is coming?*

There is rubbish in the river where once the water was pure, treated as a precious resource, the source of life. More and more people are moving into town, more people drinking alcohol, more buildings going up. There are fewer and fewer places where his people can be safe, feel free, live in peace. The killing of the dinawan-galang is the latest example of the uncaring and greedy spirit of the White men who will take whatever they want whenever they want. He wants to escape from the selfish ways of these new people, the colonisers and the convicts, and he wants to protect Wagadhaany from the devastating effects of their behaviour too.

He tries to keep track of his thoughts and the cattle at the same time, and is grateful that they continue to move with little effort under his guidance and with the help of well-trained mirri-galang. Without the dogs, the job would be much harder.

As they cross the plains his heart sinks. He remembers the fire-stick farming that he did as a boy, before the White man took over the land. He is old enough to remember the majesty of the country-side before the changes wrought by White greed. This was once a rich landscape for wambuwuny-galang and dinawan-galang and other animals, making it easier to hunt. But it also made it easier for the White man's cattle to graze. When the land was cleared, they moved in, built their houses and took over everything.

He scans the horizon for anything that might break the boredom and something up ahead catches his attention. Pulling on Mudyi's reins, urging him to slow, to almost stop, Yindy is startled by what he believes is a sign: a flock of peregrine falcons flying, swooping, criss-crossing and diving over and around a sloping hill ahead. He knows it's Kengal. The old men told him about this special place created by Biyaami, who left male and female mirrigan-galang there. He knows the story of the two mirrigan-galang lying in wait, who Biyaami turned into the enormous rock.

Yindy slows his horse to a trot, mesmerised by the grandeur of the large birds swooping. He wonders what small animals or birds they might be preying on. One climbs high into the sky, a small bird held firmly in its beak. It is being followed by other falcons. It's breeding season and Yindy knows that many smaller birds will be targeted by more powerful, stronger ones.

The sky is a pale blue, cloudless, perfect. Yindy looks upwards, wondering if the creator is sending him a message. *Is my love being preyed upon? Is Wagadhaany safe from other men who prey like the falcons?* His thoughts are controlling his emotions and he feels distressed, panicked, thinking about the young women he has heard are abused on some stations. Children are being fathered by White men, and not by choice of the Wiradyuri women. He has never had any reason to think in this way about his own sister, nor his love, but he is now fearful of what is possible, what might be happening without him knowing. He can't allow himself to think of the women in his life being raped, their flesh bruised and souls shattered by the violence of the Bradleys and the Charlies in his life. He stands in the saddle and yells at the cattle. Mudyi's trot turns to a canter and he races alongside the herd, forcing them in one direction. He yells out again.

As a stockman, Yindy made a name for himself early on, and he was expected to be a drover. His ability to control cattle is something other men speak of, commenting on his style and skill and his use of dogs. He has always been confident, never shied away when asked to move whatever cattle needing moving, wherever and whenever the Bradleys required it. He learned quickly that being good at something means you are constantly the one turned to, to complete a task, whether you want to or not, whether it is a fair request or not, and whether you are fairly compensated or not.

The team this time includes Johnno and Billy, neither of whom likes riding with Yindyamarra. They are jealous that he can work the cattle much better than any of them, and that he knows the land better than they do. The dislike is mutual though, and they know it. An Irishman by the name of Eddy has joined the team and he doesn't like the English riders either, preferring to keep to himself, or to align with Yindy.

When they stop for a spell in the middle of the scorching day, Johnno chews tobacco and spits it on the ground. 'I don't know why we have to work with Blacks,' he says to Billy, just loud enough for Yindy to hear. 'There's plenty of White men available.'

'It's because they're cheaper than us,' Billy says, rolling a cigarette.

'It's because they're *better* than you are,' Eddy states, not giving the Englishmen the slightest glance, just flashing a sly smile at Yindy, who tips his hat in thanks.

Yindy gets up swiftly and Billy flinches as if Yindy is going to rush him. But he doesn't, he just smiles, knowing he has scared the fool in front of him, then walks away, kicking the earth along the way. The truth is, Yindy doesn't listen to the hateful words anymore. He hears the men's poisonous thoughts, but he doesn't let them taint his spirit, not now, not now that he has Waga-dhaany in his life. Since meeting her, his thoughts have been divided between his role with the cattle and his love back in Wagga Wagga. He wants to protect her, but more importantly he is concerned about her health, and he wishes he didn't have to leave her when she's sick back at the Bradleys'.

With such emotions stirring his mind day in and day out, his train of thought at times takes a different tack. What might his life be like if he stole Mudyi so that he and Wagadhaany could ride as far away as possible from Wagga Wagga, the Bradleys, the stockmen who hate him, and the dinawan-galang killers? What if they could go back to his father's miyagan by the Galari? What if he could mend Wagadhaany's broken heart by taking his love back to Gundagai?

There is nothing more that Yindy wants than to be Waga-dhaany's hero. For her to know that if he could, he would rescue her from her life bound to the Bradleys. That if he could give her the freedom to go wherever she wanted, he would help her in a heartbeat. But he can't. He knows the punishment that would be unleashed upon him, on both of them, if he stole a horse, if they ran away. He has heard stories of men who have tried to escape the shackles of labour, to be free again. Some were arrested, others never seen again.

'Yamayamarra!' he whispers, asking Biyaami for help. 'Yamaya-marra!' he repeats, hoping that the Ancient Ones can hear too.

He feels helpless, disempowered. He wants to control his own life. He wants Wagadhaany to be able to control hers, and he wants Wiradyuri people to have a say in how and where they live. He wants to go back to life before White people came to their land and took it over. A time when his miyagan said his people were happier and healthier.

'Let's go,' Eddy says, and the men rise.

They ride for hours, and by nightfall everyone is exhausted, including Mudyi. Here, he is the closest friend Yindy has. He brushes him down to show his love for the horse, aware of every aching muscle in Mudyi's body.

Afterwards, he walks slowly to where he will rest for the night, away from the other men. As Yindy lays down his swag he notices that the ground is hard, having been trodden by cattle passing through before. His heart pains him at the land being ruined by those who are new to it. They are not taking care of it, they treat it with contempt, as if it is only there for their benefit. And now he is part of that abuse. His job is to move cattle across long distances. He is good at it, but he is in turmoil with guilt.

Droving gives him too much time to think.

One of the cattle dogs barks and Yindy looks out into the dark. He sees the other men get up, look around and settle back down. The dogs have shown good instinct the entire journey, and Yindy is confident that all the cattle that left the Bradleys will make it to market. He walks over to the others who are by the fire. He doesn't sit straightaway, just stares into the distance.

A sand goanna crawls in close to the group.

'Get it,' Johnno yells at Yindy. 'Kill it! You can eat it for your dinner.' He chuckles.

'I don't eat goanna,' Yindy says. 'It's my totem.'

'Ya what?' Billy asks.

'It's that voodoo stuff the Blackfellows talk about.' Johnno waves his arms around. 'I'll just spear it myself, that witchcraft stuff doesn't bother me.'

He lunges at the goanna with his knife but misses and falls to the ground, face first. Billy bursts out laughing, and Yindy and Eddy can't help joining when they see Johnno's face covered in dust. The goanna moves a few feet away then stops, turns around and looks at the dusty White man lying on the ground cursing. It's as if it is mocking him too.

That night by the fire, Eddy sits with Yindy as the White men take to their swags.

'You don't eat goanna, then?' Eddy asks.

'Nah. Everyone has an animal totem that we protect, and that way, no animal should ever disappear. The goanna is the one I protect.'

'Makes good sense,' Eddy replies, staring into the dancing flames as the night dew sets in.

'And I'd never tell him, but you don't spear goannas. If you need to kill for food, you club a goanna.'

'Why's that?'

'Because spearing or stabbing makes all the fat leak out, and that's the part you want. That's what the Old People told me, but I don't know, like I said, I've never killed or eaten one.'

The dog barks again. 'I'll watch for a while,' he says, 'you sleep.'

As he waits for his turn to lie down for the night, Yindy looks around to see if his cheeky totem has returned. He thinks about his role as protector and these thoughts carry him back to his love. He hopes she is resting easy, that she thinks of him occasionally. He stares at the stars, and remembers their first night together.

Chapter Twenty

Wagadhaany's head is foggy with lustful thoughts of Yindya-marra, the man who has stolen her heart, the one she waits for, day in and day out, wanting to be in his arms again. As she sits in her room holding the headband her gunhi gave her, she thinks of her mother's strength through the feathers, and is reminded of the love she still feels even though she is so far from her. She wonders if she will show the same love to her own child. A smile sweeps across her face as she imagines having a family with Yindy, then a hot flush creeps over her as she recalls their secret meetings by the river. In only a short time, she has come to believe they will be together forever, and while she enjoys the thrill of being in love, she is also afraid of what might happen if they are discovered by the other stockmen or the Bradleys. They will not be able to marry without permission of a White official, she knows, and she is not sure if their love will be frowned upon, or worse, forbidden.

Right now, Wagadhaany is more concerned about how Louisa might react, given the strains on her own marriage to James.

It's a rare occasion that they go into town together of an evening, but tonight there is a social dance and Louisa has been excited about meeting some new people. They will be gone for a few hours at least.

To Wagadhaany's relief, David Bradley is on another trip to Melbourne to raise more capital for cattle purchases, so she has not been left alone in the house with him. She has been on edge ever since his suggestion to the doctor that she owes him for keeping her alive. She knows enough to understand that he considers that debt may have to be paid in ways that scare her, though she reminds herself again and again that David loved his mother and would never do anything to disrespect her memory. She tells herself that she is lucky to have Mrs Elizabeth Bradley's protection, she is lucky to be safe.

With the homestead to herself and no-one to check on her movements, she makes her way to the riverbank, seizing the chance to see Yindy. She waits impatiently in their meeting spot, looking left and right constantly, back and forth and back and forth again. She doesn't know when he will be back, but if it is tonight, she will be here, waiting for him.

When she finally sees him approaching in the moonlight, she can tell by his posture that he is exhausted after being away for days. She has lost track of exactly how long he has been gone for, but is glad that she is now feeling less sick than she did when he left. She still vomits in the morning, careful to be out of sight and hearing of Louisa, and she feels strange in her belly most of the day, but she has realised lately she is experiencing what the women back home told her about when she was younger.

'My Budhang Nyiwarri,' she says, throwing her arms around him.

He picks her up with his weary arms and, to her delight, spins her around. She knows his arms and hands must be aching from riding and gripping the reins day after day.

He puts her down gently and looks at her face, feels her forehead, checks for any sign of sickness, and she laughs.

'Yamandhu marang?' he asks.

'Ngawa, baladhu marang.'

She confirms she is feeling good and places his hand on her belly. Yindy's eyes follow their hands and he stares for a long time. There is no response, so she pats both their hands against her belly a few times and waits.

Eventually a smile forms on her lover's face. 'Marganduli?' he asks, wanting to confirm that she is pregnant, that he hasn't got the signals wrong.

'Ngawa,' she says, smiling, 'marganduli.'

She pats her stomach again, his hand underneath hers.

He looks at her belly once more and starts laughing loudly. He picks her up and spins her around, again and again.

When they make love that night there is no hint that Yindy was so physically exhausted he could barely walk only hours before. As Wagadhaany lies naked in his arms, warm under a possum-skin rug, she dozes on and off, lost in dreamy thoughts of bringing a new life into the world. She hopes she can be as wonderful a mother as her own is, and she has no doubt Yindy will be as good a father as her babiin.

It is a close call the next morning when she wakes with the first light of day.

'Yindy!'

She struggles to untangle their twisted limbs, and jumps up when she is free from his legs and arms.

A deep sleep after so much pleasure means she has woken much later than usual, and is at risk of arriving back at the homestead after Louisa and the other servants have already risen. She panics at the thought of being caught out after managing to sneak back so many other times before sunrise. She pulls on her clothes, runs her fingers through her curls to release any leaves and grasses, kisses Yindy quickly on the mouth, and runs as fast as her thin, brown legs will carry her. Wagadhaany hasn't had time to consider what being pregnant will mean to her living arrangements, and she's not sure that it will mean continuing to live in the Bradley house. Might she be allowed to live at the camp by the river, with Yindy? So many questions float through her mind as she races back to the homestead.

As quietly as possible she enters the back of the house and tiptoes to her room, opening and closing the door so quietly she surprises herself. She is panting from running, and leans against the door to catch her breath. She holds her stomach, which feels like it is spinning inside, and thinks about the night before, wishing every night could be spent with her love. She hears movement in the house, rushes to change into her only other work tunic, tidies herself, and hopes that Louisa cannot tell that she looks any different today than she does on any other morning.

When she enters the kitchen she finds Louisa is in a particularly good mood, humming to herself, moving around the table as if she is lighter on her feet. Wagadhaany is pleased to see her friend is in better spirits.

'Good morning!' Louisa says chirpily.

'Um, good morning to you,' Wagadhaany says. She resists

asking Louisa why she is so happy because she doesn't want to have to answer any questions about her own wellbeing. She wants to keep her joy to herself and Yindy, and she doesn't want to hurt Louisa with her news.

Louisa's smile cannot be ignored though. Everywhere she turns, Wagadhaany sees a full set of teeth grinning at her and thinks Louisa's face could light up the whole of Wagga Wagga on this overcast day.

'We have a lot of shopping to do today, Wagadhaany.' Louisa is already writing a list. 'We will head out shortly. I will fetch my coat and . . .'

'I will just tidy the kitchen,' Wagadhaany says as Louisa leaves the room.

She is starving. A newfound appetite in recent weeks means she seems to never get enough food in her belly. She hopes she is eating enough for her and the baby. As soon as she hears Louisa take the stairs she devours a piece of bread in two mouthfuls, checks to see none of the other staff are nearby and puts three pieces of bread in her apron pocket to eat later, then walks briskly back to her room.

As they leave the house, rain threatens but the day remains dry. They walk without speaking, each lost in private thoughts, until they arrive at the small weatherboard store known as the Warehouse. Wagadhaany is grateful that she hasn't felt ill at all along the way.

Inside, it's a hub of activity with locals and travellers buying produce and homewares. Louisa swiftly presents her list to the owner, Mr Thompson, who peers over the top of his spectacles and reads out loud: 'Tea, sugar, salt, soap, pork. You stocking up, Mrs Bradley?'

'I feel like cooking today, Mr Thompson, and we are down on the kitchen basics. While you gather those items, may I look at your fabrics please?'

Louisa still hasn't explained her mood, but if going out with her husband occasionally makes her this happy, then Wagadhaany hopes she goes more often.

Within minutes several bolts of material are laid out for Louisa to choose from, as well as a selection of laces and ribbons. Most of the fabrics are in dull colours – grey, black, bone, brown – but the one or two bright colours capture Wagadhaany's eye. She imagines what it would be like to have money to buy things; food, materials, anything.

'What about this?' Louisa holds up some fabric. 'I am going to make us both new dresses, Wagadhaany,' she says excitedly.

Wagadhaany is surprised.

'Wagadhaany? What do you think? Louisa asks again.

'I've never had a pretty dress.' She carefully touches the lace and ribbon on the counter. 'If I had money to buy things, I would buy . . .' She looks across the choices. 'This one.' She rests her hands on some pink fabric, wanting to ask Louisa why she can't have money to buy things herself. Instead she says, 'I think it would be special to have a dress made by you.'

Her words are sincere. She is touched by Louisa's gesture and her thoughts immediately go to Yindy. *Would he like to see me in a pretty dress?*

As soon as they leave the store Wagadhaany starts to feel ill. Perspiration forms on her forehead and upper lip, and her mouth begins to water. She walks as fast as she can, wanting to get back to the homestead where she can at least hide in the outhouse if need be. But it's too late. She drops the parcel of material and vomits at the same time.

'I'm sorry, I'm sorry, I'm so sorry,' she says, crying. She looks at the brown paper around the fabric. 'It's still clean,' she points out to Louisa.

'I don't care about the material, are *you* all right?' Louisa asks, putting the back of her hand to Wagadhaany's forehead. 'You are sick. We need to get you to the doctor.'

Wagadhaany gets to her feet as fast as she can, because although she feels wobbly and even more nauseous with the hot sun on her face, she cannot risk seeing a doctor. She has no idea what will happen if Louisa and the Bradleys find out she is pregnant. On top of that, the only time she has known an Aboriginal person to go to a White doctor, they did not live much longer.

'No, I don't need a doctor,' she says, wiping her mouth with a handkerchief Louisa has pulled from her purse. 'I am fine,' she says, 'I am.' She tries to think of what to say to explain away her health. 'I am on my monthlies,' she says, using a phrase she has learned from Louisa and since taught Yiray. 'And sometimes my belly goes funny. I'm not really sick, not the kind of sick that needs a doctor.'

Louisa nods. 'I understand, of course. I never vomit, but I know that menstruation affects women differently. Even so, I still think you should see the doctor.'

'Please, no, Louisa. I will be embarrassed to talk about this with a doctor, he is a man. And a White man, and truly, I cannot think of anything worse.'

She wants to be anywhere other than with Louisa right now. Already she is telling too many lies. She never needed or wanted to lie before coming to Wagga Wagga. Maybe she *is* becoming a different person. Her head is spinning in the opposite direction to her stomach, and she doesn't understand the word menstruation either, but assumes it is just another big White word for bleeding.

'The women at the camp, they will know what bush medicines to give me. Can I go and stay there tonight?' she asks, hoping that Louisa will let her go, and alone. All she wants to do is lie down and not think about how sick she feels.

'All right, that is probably a good idea. And maybe you can let me know what they give you, for when I am on my monthlies?'

'Of course.' Wagadhaany agrees, but is annoyed by Louisa wanting to have everything that is shared at the camp. She breathes in and out slowly, in and out, trying to control the nausea, and trying to ignore how Louisa has again turned the situation into something that may benefit her.

She hands Louisa the parcel. 'I will be back in the morning, all right?'

As she walks to the camp holding her stomach, she scolds herself for thinking harshly about Louisa, who has been a good friend to her. A friend who is going to make her a dress – even if she won't fit into it soon because though she is lean, she is going to have a pregnant belly. A friend who worries about her being sick. A friend who is always willing to speak up about how other townsfolk treat the Aboriginal people, and take her to the doctor.

By the time she arrives at the camp her nausea has subsided, and she tells the aunties that Louisa has sent her to read to the children. It is only a half-lie because she does want to read to the gudha-galang, even though that hadn't been her intention.

They quickly gather the books they'd been given and spend the afternoon sharing stories with Wagadhaany until Yindy returns.

The next morning Wagadhaany wakes before sunrise. Yindy has already left and she can hear the gudha-galang playing nearby. She is vomiting again. Tears run down her face with the exhaustion of it. She is hungry and dehydrated. Her nausea is accompanied by a terrible headache and she is confused about where she is. Yiray is by her side quickly with some special tea that her mother has made. She wants to tell her she is margan-duli, but she doesn't want to do it without Yindy there, so she keeps the joyous news to herself.

She is tired of feeling like this. She drinks the tea and prepares herself to walk back to the Bradleys'.

'Where are you going?'

'To the homestead, I have work to do. The Bradleys will be angry.'

'Louisa loves you, she will be worried, not angry. They are different things.'

Wagadhaany is grateful for Yiray's wisdom and knows she is right, but she frets that if Louisa becomes even more worried, she will insist on the doctor even more firmly. But when she stands up and falls backwards against a tree, her dizziness changes everything.

'Mingaan!' Yiray screams, grabbing her by the arm and easing her back to the ground, propping her up against the grey box gum.

The aunties shuffle over from the fire as fast as their bony legs and skinny ankles will allow. By the time they reach the young women, they are shaking their fingers at Wagadhaany.

'You need to rest, my girl,' Bamali Bagabin says, and she nods to her daughter. Yiray helps her lie down.

Bamali Giigandul squints, looking at Wagadhaany suspiciously. 'Look at me,' she says. 'Here in my eyes, right here.' She bends down and pulls her face close to Wagadhaany's. She looks at her cheeks and deep into her dark brown eyes. 'You are marganduli! You are marganduli! I have seen this look many, many times. It is my gift.'

'That and your cranky ways?' Bamali Mulbirrang asks.

'Well, I see your ears are working well today then, Mulbirrang!'

'Is it true?' Bamali Bagabin asks Wagadhaany.

Wagadhaany feels even sicker than before. She did not want to tell them without Yindy. But she cannot tell another lie, and not to his mother. So she nods, keeping her eyes fixed on the ground.

'It is Yindy's, ngawa?'

'Ngawa,' she responds with a tone that says *of course*.

'A mother knows everything.'

The older women's eyebrows say they *all* knew, that mothers do know everything.

'You need to take care of baby now, it's not about you anymore, not about what you want, or what those White people want,' Bamali Bagabin says. 'Lie down, rest, this is where you need to be right now.'

She knows the women are right, and her body knows too. She manoeuvres herself into a comfortable position on the woven mat, and within minutes is asleep again. The sun goes down and rises again, goes down and up again. On the third day she opens her eyes and miraculously feels as if she could swim against the current of the Marrambidya for miles. She doesn't feel sick, or confused, and she doesn't want to be lying down anymore.

As she says her goodbyes and thanks she is reminded of her responsibility to look after herself and the life she is carrying. They all want to see her with a healthy baby, to celebrate, love and raise it together, and Yiray is excited about being a bamali all over again, and is already suggesting names.

She walks back to the Bradleys', the sun's warmth on her face making her believe everything will be all right. But not far from the camp she sees Louisa walking towards her, worry etched across her face.

'I was just coming to look for you, are you all right?' Louisa pulls her close for a hug. 'I was so worried.'

Wagadhaany is again overcome by Louisa's generosity of spirit, her affection and obvious caring for her.

'I'm fine now,' Wagadhaany says, hoping that when she finally tells Louisa the truth, her friend will be happy for her and Yindy.

The kitchen smells sweet when they arrive home. Louisa and her other help have been baking and the aroma turns Wagadhaany's stomach and makes her mouth dry, the usual prelude to vomiting. She swallows hard, closes her eyes and pretends she can will the feeling away. Miraculously, her nausea disappears.

'I'm so glad you are back and feeling better.' Louisa pulls the curtain across and opens the kitchen window. 'Can you tell me what they gave you? Do you think I can take it too, if I need to?'

Louisa's questions are too much for her. Wagadhaany's head is spinning and her stomach is starting to churn again, and she doesn't want to lie anymore. She still doesn't know what the consequences will be when she tells Louisa, but since she has no control of her future situation whether the Bradleys find out now or later, she decides she may as well let go of the lie she has been carrying.

'Wagadhaany?' Louisa takes her gently by elbow and sits her at the table. 'I'll make us some tea. You still look a little pale. Well, not as dark.' She chuckles.

'I'm pregnant, Louisa,' Wagadhaany blurts out. 'I didn't have my monthlies. I am sorry for lying to you.'

There is relief, regret and guilt in her words. She is glad there are no more secrets, even though she feels guilty for breaking her promise to Yindyamarra, but what was she to do?

Louisa drops the cup she is holding and it smashes on the hard floor. 'Pregnant? How can you be pregnant? You and Yindyamarra aren't married!'

Wagadhaany is shocked by Louisa's reaction. She hadn't anticipated Louisa being angry with her. She expected her to be sad, to reflect on her frustrations in creating a family with James. She didn't expect anger, and wonders what a wedding has to do with creating a new life and a loving family.

'I am not married like you and James are married. We did not say words in front of God, but we love each other. We have that love you and I once talked about.'

'But how, and when?' Louisa is confused. 'I don't understand how this happened.' She picks up the pieces of china. 'This was my mother's cup.'

'I am sorry,' Wagadhaany says as she bends down to help. 'I'm sorry I've upset you. I am sorry about the cup.'

Louisa is more than angry, she is furious, huffing and puffing but not saying anything else, and Wagadhaany is afraid of where the conversation might lead.

'I don't know why you are angry with me, Louisa. I am the one who is scared. I am the one afraid of bringing a baby into the world with my own mother so far away.'

She is also afraid of what is going to happen when James Bradley finds out, but she doesn't say that out loud. Right now she just wants to understand Louisa's reaction to the news that has only made Yindy, Yiray and the women down at the river feel joy.

Louisa remains silent until she has finished cleaning up the broken crockery.

'I am not angry, Wagadhaany.' Louisa puts the broken cup in the sink, and walks out of the room.

Wagadhaany is dumbfounded and doesn't know what to do, to follow or to wait. She stands there, motionless. A short while later, Louisa returns with the materials purchased two days before. Her face is still flushed, but her demeanour is calmer.

'I'm sorry for upsetting you,' Wagadhaany tries again, before Louisa has the chance to speak.

'Please, sit. *I* am sorry. It was a shock. I am not upset with you.' Louisa puts the fabric on the kitchen table. 'I am just a little sad, a lot sad. I want to be announcing *my* pregnancy. I still want to be a mother. For me, for James. For all his faults, and I think we both know them, I love him. His mind might not always impress me, but there is something between us that is beyond logic or intellect. I cannot explain it to you, but it is there, and I still want to be the mother of his children.'

Seconds pass as they stare silently at the material before them. 'Well, I guess I'll just have to make your dress a bit bigger than we expected,' Louisa says at last, nodding approval of her own idea. 'And I will make you some baby clothes too, of course.'

Wagadhaany is unsure of what has transpired between the two of them, not convinced that Louisa isn't angry. But she is too scared to ask or say anything now that the kitchen is calm again.

'What on earth are you doing?' James asks Louisa, who is trying on the larger-sized dress she has sewn for Wagadhaany.

Over the last few weeks she has been imagining what it would be like to be pregnant, to experience the nausea, the changes to her body, the joy the news would bring to other people when she told them. She wishes she could go back to the post office and tell that woman that she is having a baby.

Feeling guilty about her initial reaction to Wagadhaany's news, she has spent many hours alone, cursing herself for being so angry and selfish. She hasn't been able to tell her friend that what she was really feeling was pure envy.

Many prayers asking for guidance have helped her find some new strength, and although she fantasises about being pregnant, she is no longer so envious, and is now happy for Wagadhaany. Her words to God have helped, and she wants to support Waga-dhaany as best she can.

'You look ridiculous,' James snarls as he undresses, the whisky on his breath explaining his nastier than usual comments to his wife.

In moments like these Louisa wonders how she ever fell for such a man. Sometimes he acts as if he has venom running through his veins instead of blood.

'We are not poor, you don't have to make such . . . clothes. They are not befitting the wife of the man who will be mayor,' he announces. 'Now, take it off and come over here, to your husband.'

Louisa knows what that means and while she wants to get pregnant, the last thing she wants is to have James's drunken hands on her tonight. When he's intoxicated, he's lecherous, and she can't bear him like that.

When she ignores him he tries to charm her, moving in behind her as she looks in the mirror at the cut of the dress. 'Come,' he says, 'take this off, it is too big for you. I will buy you a new dress, a regal gown. You will be a beautiful English rose.'

Louisa hates that he thinks a few words will pardon the venom he unleashed only moments before. He considers whispering in her ear to be some kind of confession; it is something he does often, especially after drinking, but there is never an apology, never any sign of repentance, never any promise that it will not happen again. And while her own beliefs always lean towards forgiveness, she only tolerates his behaviour because she feels increasingly trapped. So much of her money has gone into the property; all her days and nights are about the homestead and *his* needs, *his* dreams of being mayor.

'I said take it off!' James has reached the point where if he doesn't get what he wants when he wants it, he becomes aggressive, and Louisa has had enough.

Despite the promise she made to herself to protect Wagadhaany for as long as she could, she knows that telling James about the pregnancy will annoy him enough that he will not want to touch her in that way.

'This is for Wagadhaany, she is pregnant.' She says it firmly, without fear. She may feel trapped, but she is not going to let his anger scare her into silence or submission, not this time.

She has let him bully her before, held her tongue on issues that she is passionate about. But she will not be silent out of fear any longer. And she will not be intimate with him ever again when he is disrespectful to her.

She can see the rage flowing through her husband, the result of anger mixed with alcohol. Whatever happens from now on, her first priority will be to protect herself, her friend, and whomever else comes into their lives.

James is livid, his fists clenched. 'She cannot stay in this house, she has to go!'

'Now it is *you* who looks ridiculous. She is pregnant, not a leper.'

'How did this even happen? She is here with you all the time, isn't she?' He peers at her. 'Where have you let her go, down to the river with the other loathsome Blacks? Or does the bastard belong to one of the stockmen?'

'Stop it! Don't talk about Wagadhaany like that, and don't talk about any child like that.'

James isn't listening to his wife. He is getting dressed again and mumbling to himself. 'That *child*,' he says sarcastically, 'will be illegitimate. They don't marry like we do, they won't baptise it like we would.'

'Stop calling the baby *it*!'

James is pacing the floor and huffing. 'I swear, I will be speaking to Charlie tomorrow. If there's been fraternising on my property ... I will not have fraternising happening on my property!'

'Falling in love is not fraternising!'

'Falling in love?' James scoffs. 'No-one is falling in love, every-one knows the native women are easily available.'

'James!' Louisa yells, disgusted.

'What? Why would you think that Wilma is any different?' His anger is palpable. He points at Louisa, poking her in the chest so hard she steps backwards. 'And this is why I never wanted you to become her friend.'

He walks away, then spins around, having just registered her previous comment.

'And don't be so naïve, Louisa. There is no love to be found here in cattle country. Love,' he scoffs. 'I've never heard anything more ridiculous in my life.'

His words bruise Louisa more than his rough hands ever have. She looks at him in disbelief. Is he saying there is no love between them? Where is the man she married?

'Get her out today!' He turns to walk away, not prepared for his wife's response.

'Do not speak to me like that, and for goodness sake, are you *so* useless that you still can't say her name properly?'

He turns, his face red. But Louisa is fuming also and stands her ground. She is not afraid of him.

'And we will *not* throw her out, ever, and certainly not with a child on the way,' she says, her voice raised. 'We will *not* make her life any harder.'

Even though Wagadhaany's pregnancy reminds her of her own failed attempts to conceive, she believes a baby will bring so much love to what has increasingly become a loveless home.

'I will not support the breeding of coloured people here, not in my home. There will be no more discussion on the matter. I am in charge here.'

'This is *our* home! And you are hardly ever here to be in charge. I did not come here penniless, James. I did not come to Wagga

Wagga without means of my own. Other women on the land may be forced to stay with men who treat them badly because they have no choice, but I am not one of those women.'

When she looks at James again, his whole body is tight with contempt, and his face shows his shock at her behaviour towards him. He sits down, wrings his hands, gets up again and walks to the window. He peers to the side of the curtains, grateful that no-one outside has witnessed their performance by the light of the kerosene lamp. Louisa quickly slips out of the dress to lessen the chance of any further conflict and by the time he turns to her she is in her nightgown, seated in a chair on the other side of the room. Her legs are crossed, her hands on the arms of the chair, waiting. The silence in the room is palpable.

James swings around from the window, walks over and grabs her arms, dragging her up from her chair, forcing her against the wall, pushing his face into hers, spitting as he speaks through gritted teeth.

'This isn't my fault. I would have left her behind if I had my way, we can find help anywhere, we don't need her. Remember? I am not the one who brought her here against her will.' He looks directly into his wife's eyes. 'I want to be mayor, and I cannot hope for support if I am housing a pregnant Black woman with no father around.'

Louisa is frightened but she speaks back to him as calmly as she can. 'James Bradley, you will not be rough with me again.'

James ignores her words and asks bluntly, 'Who's the father, does she even know?'

'Yindyamarra is the father.'

'Who?'

'Yindy!'

James lets her go and turns around.

'James, he is one of your head stockmen. He is an honest, good man. You have said so yourself, on more than one occasion.'

Louisa is almost breathless, trying to remind her husband of some basic common decency.

James says nothing, but she hopes he understands that he needs Louisa if he is ever to be a father, and to be the mayor he needs his English rose. And she hopes he understands that her happiness depends on Wagadhaany staying with them. As she watches him leave the room, she rubs her arms, hoping that by morning there will be no bruises to be seen, for both their sakes.

Downstairs in the kitchen, Wagadhaany knows that neither James nor Louisa realises that she has overheard everything. And while she has experienced James Bradley's loathing of her and other Black people in the past, what he said tonight was too much for her. She does not want to bring a baby up in the same house as him and his hate-filled heart. And nor does she want to be the cause of conflict between him and Louisa.

Most interesting has been the revelation that it wasn't James Bradley who wanted her to go to Wagga Wagga with them, which means it must have been David who insisted.

As she lies in bed later that night, hand on her belly, she imagines living with Yindyamarra and their own family by the Marrambidya back in Gundagai.

'I want to live with Yindy,' she tells Louisa the next morning, having found in her sleep the resolve and strength to do so. 'It's best for me and the baby, but also for you and Mr Bradley.'

'No, it's not,' Louisa argues. 'And you can't just leave, you belong here. With me.'

Louisa is upset, on the verge of tears, but Wagadhaany is not going to be pressured. She needs to think about her unborn child. She will not be forced to stay, like she was forced to leave Gundagai. She knows enough about the Quakers now to realise that if Louisa is going to live her faith and fulfil her mission in Wagga Wagga, then she must let her leave. She must not suggest that she is bound to live at the homestead simply because she is their servant. She must let her live an equal life where she makes decisions for herself.

'I actually belong with my own family, Louisa. I always have. And now I belong with the father of my child and my new family,' she says firmly. 'And you need to focus on *your* husband and *your* own life.'

It is as close as she will ever get to saying that Louisa's pre-occupation with her and the local Aboriginal people was just that, a preoccupation, and that nothing had really changed for them.

'I know I will have to work for you, I know about the masters and servants law, but you cannot keep me living here in the home-stead against my will if you honestly believe I am your equal and that I should be as free as you.'

Wagadhaany is feeling strong. She is clear about what she needs to do. 'You have always said you wanted freedom for my people, but you cannot even let the one closest to you have her own. And you need to let me have that freedom. I need to leave here. I need to have my baby in a place where there is only love and where I can be safe.'

'What do mean, safe?'

'Louisa, I haven't told you about David.' She pauses. 'For some time now, he has made me feel uncomfortable by the way he looks at me, the way he brushes past me without any need to. One time, he was so close to me I could feel him against my body. I was frozen with fear.' She takes a nervous breath. 'And I have heard of other girls being raped, on other stations. There are Aboriginal women who end up pregnant to White men. And so I do not feel safe here, not when he is in the house.'

'Has he touched you?' Louisa is clearly angry as she grabs Wagadhaany's hand. 'You must tell me.'

'No, not *that* way. One time, many years ago, Mrs Elizabeth Bradley found him about to . . . She stopped him, and I am careful never to be alone with him. I am sure he knows how he makes me feel. I don't like being near him, with his staring and eye-twitching and the stupid way he smiles at me sometimes, it is not the smile of a friend or family member. He looks at me strangely, and he makes me feel strange. And . . .'

'And what?' Louisa is shaking, visibly upset.

'I do not want to be around James Bradley when he is drunk either, when he is vio–' she pauses. 'When he is angry with you, I know he puts his hands on you. It hurts me to hear the way he speaks to you and to see the bruises on your arms. So, they both make me feel uncomfortable here.'

She moves towards Louisa, who is crying.

'But what about me? What about our life? Please don't leave me.'

'Louisa, your life is not *my* life. You are the wife of the man who wants to be mayor, and maybe if you had friends more like you, more English roses, then maybe he would be happier and you would fight less. Maybe he would drink less too, and he would . . .'

'He would what?' Louisa asks angrily.

'Well, maybe he would hurt you less.'

Louisa hangs her head in shame, as if James's bad behaviour is her fault. When she looks up her eyes are full of tears.

'But I need you. I need your friendship. I need your conversation. I need you to keep me sane in this place whose soul is as dry as the land. You are younger than me, I know that, but you are wise, Wagadhaany, and you make me want to be a better person. What about all the work I want to do with the women, making Aboriginal people equal?'

'Yes, Louisa, what about all the work you wanted to do? Why haven't you done it? Maybe you should just do it, and stop waiting for the rest of the town and your husband to approve.'

Louisa blows her nose on her white handkerchief before speaking again, this time in a soft voice.

'Wagadhaany, please know I am happy for you and Yindyamarra, and I am disgusted with David. I do not even know what to say about him. He has always competed with James, perhaps he thought you could be his . . .' she stops. They both know that no Bradley would ever take a Black woman for his wife.

'I understand you cannot stay here at night anymore but please come back during the day for as long as you can. You are like the sister I never had. I will give the other staff the heavier work so that you will not be as tired.' Louisa's expression is one of sadness as she continues. 'And after the baby is born, well, you can still come back here and work as much as you can. I don't think I could manage if I didn't at least see you regularly.'

Louisa nods as if an agreement has been made. Wagadhaany nods back because she is unsure what else to do.

'And maybe you are right, maybe if I try to be more like the wife James wants, he will be less angry with me. I will try harder.'

Wagadhaany feels sorry for Louisa, as her seemingly independent and spirited friend takes the blame for her husband's behaviour. It is not what she meant to happen, but she is also not responsible for how Louisa feels, or behaves. She needs to focus on her own life now, and that of her own, new family.

Within days Wagadhaany is creating her new life with Yindy. As a proud man, he wants to make a comfortable home for her and builds a ganya to one side of the camp, away from the smoke of the main fire. He also wants privacy from his nosy aunties. At night he makes a small fire to keep them warm. He proves he can take care of her, and makes some pillows for Wagadhaany to rest her beautiful balang on. As she watches her Budhang Nyiwarri work, Wagadhaany hopes she can make their campsite a nurturing place, a home that connects them both to country, where their spirits can feel free.

Even after the comforts that sleeping at the Bradley homestead offered, her spirit finds more peace sleeping by the river with Yindyamarra, the other Wiradyuri people, and even the numerous camp dogs. At night when the men return from working on various properties, they join those who have been hunting and gathering. The food is shared among everyone. It is this way of not living an insular existence that she relishes most.

On some nights she watches Yindy cook wambuwuny on coals and hot ashes in the ground. When the meal is over the fire hole is covered with bushes and branches and huge flames rage, lighting up the whole campsite. On those nights she feels most homesick and yet the most at home. Her mind is carried back to Gundagai, to her brothers and cousins and the laughter they shared growing up. When she looks skyward, she knows that they are all sleeping under the exact same stars, and in that moment they are together.

She returns to the homestead reluctantly, and on one occasion finds that Louisa has made a birthday cake for her, the first she has ever had.

'This is to celebrate the day you were born. English people usually celebrate their birthday every year.'

'How do you know today is my birthday?'

'I don't, but under the circumstances I think we can choose one for you, and today is as good as any.'

'How old do you think I am?' Wagadhaany asks, suddenly enthusiastic.

'Do you have any idea?'

'Mrs Bradley said I was thirteen when I first started with her, but she never gave me a cake.'

'Right, well, we've been here a year, so if we count backwards from now to before the flood, because I know you were with James and his family long before that, my guess is that you are around twenty-one years old. It's hard to tell though because all the Wiradyuri women look so young.'

Wagadhaany smiles. The aunties are always joking about who is the prettiest and who attracts the best-looking Black stockmen. She thinks they would like to believe they look young enough to attract a handsome prince too, like she did.

'Come and eat the cake with me. I've made tea too.'

Working at the homestead and keeping Louisa company continues to be her routine, but as the weeks pass Wagadhaany becomes increasingly tired, so she stays by the river and watches the children. One day, she sees Louisa sitting alone on a log on the fringes of the camp, holding a closed book and looking forlorn. Her heart sinks. How lonely Louisa must be now in the house with Wagadhaany gone and the two Bradley brothers away so much.

Wagadhaany walks over to her, the children and dogs in tow. The smile on Louisa's face grows wider the closer they get. The children haven't seen Louisa for a while, but they start calling out 'Miss Louisa! Miss Louisa!' and running fast towards her. When they reach her, they climb all over her.

'What about a story?' she asks, and their eyes light up.

Chapter Twenty-one

As the months go by, Wagadhaany's body changes in ways she both loves and hates, and the older women take care of her as if she is one of their own. She is grateful to Yiray, who is especially attentive, but her time with Yiray and Yindy's family only makes her heart ache for her own miyagan, especially her mother.

As her pregnancy progresses the nausea subsides but she feels more tired. She is grateful for Louisa's support in preparing food and bringing garments she has made for the baby and other children in the camp. Louisa visits more often now, and each time she visits, she reads a different story to the children. She slowly turns the pages, showing them pictures of people and animals they have never seen before, and the children grow to adore her.

It is the caring and advice offered by the older women that Wagadhaany appreciates most. But although she is grateful for their attention, every time she feels the baby move she wishes she could ask her mother about the kicking that keeps her awake at night. She wishes her mother was there when she makes her way to the birthing spot near the river. And she wishes her cousin Gandi was there too, telling her what to expect when she gives birth, and how to keep her baby safe.

The moon is at its fullest when she finally goes into labour. The children are excited when they see the old women surround her and usher her to the birthing place. They know that soon there will be another little one to play with.

The wise bamali-galang take turns to sit with her, giving her unbroken support as she endures the pains throughout the long night. A possum-skin cloak keeps her back warm and comfortable against the cold rock, and while she focuses on her breathing the women sing.

Just before first light, Wagadhaany gives birth to twin boys by the bila. She is overwhelmed with a love that Louisa had not told her about. A love only a mother can know. Her heart explodes with warmth when she hears her sons cry out for the first time, and a wave of complete happiness washes over her. The women tell her that water and sunshine are all that is needed for life, and that her sons have come from the water of her womb and are now part of the water of the river. She looks at the current that flows strongly downstream, the water that has come from Gundagai, and believes that her mother and father's love has travelled with it. Somehow, she believes they know.

When the women have finished preparing the boys, they hand over Wagadhaany's two beautiful sons. With one in each arm, and her body exhausted, she weeps with joy and love. Even though her babies' faces are scrunched up from crying, in them she can see traces of all the men she loves: her father, her brothers, Yindyamarra. All of them born by the bila. She dreams that one day soon her sons will meet these strong men who have gone before.

When the newborns are cleaned and fed, Wagadhaany is helped to her feet. The babies are placed in guluman-galang and Wagadhaany is ushered from the birthing place to where Yindy is waiting up the bank. As the women slowly walk, the children rush to see their new cousin. They clap their hands in excitement, having no idea there are two babies. They giggle and jump and gently push each other, vying for the closest view.

Yindy is standing tall and proud, but looking impatient to meet his child. When his eyes meet Wagadhaany's, she sees the happiness across his face, but then his broad smile is replaced by a frown. It must be because she looks so tired, she thinks. Then the frown becomes a look of confusion. Having two babies is not common in the camp.

The tears flow freely as she reaches his open arms. Before looking into the guluman-galang, he kisses her forehead and she wonders if he is as afraid of having two children as she was giving birth to them.

'Bula!' he exclaims loudly, and the old women can be heard laughing.

'Bula!' Wagadhaany repeats, looking at her two boys. 'Bula.'

As the sun streams through the grey box gums, Yindy holds his children up to the sky, one at a time. 'Marang ngarin,' he says to the sun. Just as Wagadhaany's father used to.

'Bila wurrumany-galang,' he says, looking back at his two sons. 'Ngarrang-bula, bila-bula.'

Wagadhaany's heart is full as Yindy speaks to their sons, reflecting on the significance of pairs: two water dragons, two rivers.

'Our Ngarrang, our Galari,' Yindy says.

And she knows he has named one son after the water dragon and the other after the river where he was born.

Ngarrang and Galari are cared for by the women when Wagadhaany has to go back to work. In the months that follow, their little brown legs become chubby, unlike those of other children in the camp. Wagadhaany likes that they have big appetites, and hopes they grow strong and brave like their grandfather. She loves seeing their little spirits grow; each is full of life, aware of everything going on around them. She misses them badly when she goes to the Bradleys' each day but does see their first crawl, and is there when they are strong enough to sit upright without any help.

Around the end of their first year of life her sons take their first steps, together, holding hands. Wagadhaany feels as if her heart might explode like it did the night they were born. She knows her boys share a close bond, even though she is separated from them for much of each day. And there are so many moments that she wishes her own gunhi could be there to enjoy. She wishes her brothers could see their nephews, teach them to hunt, just play with them.

'Look!' Galari points to a bird.

'Look!' Ngarrang repeats, as he always does.

'It's a dyirridyirri,' Wagadhaany says. 'White people call them willie wagtail. Those birds warn you of something, they protect you.'

She hopes the dyirridyirri isn't there to warn her about something happening to her family back in Gundagai.

'Dyirridyirri, dyirridyirri.'

She is amazed at how similar her sons are, not only in looks but also their voices, and the way they waddle after the little bird.

She convinces herself that today the dyirridyirri isn't a messenger, but has come to bring joy to her two sons.

Her happiness is dampened each time she returns to the Bradleys' homestead. On one visit Wagadhaany learns that it was David Bradley who insisted she return to work immediately after giving birth. Louisa tells her of an argument she had with David during which he'd stated that the meals wouldn't cook themselves, that the garden still needed tending and the linen needed washing. Even with new staff, there was always more work to be done.

'David reminded me that as James furthers his political ambitions, I will need to be more available for social events, more available to my husband,' Louisa confesses.

Wagadhaany can see Louisa's discomfort, but doesn't understand why she hadn't argued with her brother-in-law.

In the months leading up to the birth of her twins there had been many occasions, particularly when James had been drinking, when Wagadhaany overheard him and Louisa arguing. It always reminded her of how peaceful it was living away from the homestead, and how glad she was to be no longer sleeping there. One day, as she carries the linen upstairs to the master bedroom, she hears the phrase *Aboriginal rights*. Louisa is speaking passionately. Rather than making herself heard and walking straight into the room, Wagadhaany stays out of sight and eavesdrops.

'You don't know what you are talking about,' she hears, glued to her spot outside the bedroom door.

'It says right here in the *Wagga Gazette*,' Louisa continues with confidence, 'that New South Wales, *and* other colonies, have introduced the principle of the right to vote in parliamentary elections, that *all* men have the right to vote.'

'That's correct,' James says.

'But that means *all* men over the age of twenty-one!'

'That's also correct.' Wagadhaany can hear the smugness in James's voice.

'No! It means *all* men, not just the English ones but also the Aborigines. They have the right to vote too. Though of course, there is not any mention of women voting, I might add.'

Wagadhaany hears the newspaper being thrown down, onto Louisa's dresser perhaps.

'Don't be ridiculous! Blacks can't even read the voting papers. Besides, government is the business of men, not women, Louisa. It's that simple.'

Wagadhaany peeks around the doorway. Louisa looks furious, as if she might throw the newspaper at James.

'There is more,' Louisa says sternly, but calmly. 'It was legislated in 1850 that Aboriginal stockmen could be paid cash wages. That's five years ago, so why are we still paying them in rations? If they had cash they could buy what they wanted. And it would be good for the town's businesses too.'

'Louisa, Louisa,' James says in a condescending tone. 'This is the way it's done. And what would they spend it on anyway? More tobacco? Alcohol? We are doing them a favour giving them rations. It's the law of the land here that they're paid in rations.'

'James!' she exclaims, frustrated.

'Your anger is misdirected, Louisa. Anyway, you seem fine about not paying Wilma!'

Wagadhaany wonders if Louisa should have been paying her in money so she could buy food and other things for the camp. But Louisa doesn't address James's comment.

'Your ridiculous *law of the land* discriminates against Yindyamarra, Wagadhaany, and her father, Yarri. It needs to be changed.

If you are going to be mayor, I demand you fix this, at least here in Wagga Wagga.

'There have been massacres too,' she continues, 'of Wiradyuri who were just trying to survive on their own land.'

'They had it coming, Louisa. The Blacks aren't innocent, you do realise that? They have murdered our people, butchered our stock.'

'James!' Wagadhaany has never heard Louisa so furious. 'They were protecting their own land! Under British law, the Wiradyuri people are British subjects, and should be protected under that law, and have the same rights as the White settlers.'

James sighs loudly. 'Louisa, you don't understand. You are *one* woman, and from what I understand the *only* person in town of your faith, and probably the only person I know who has your concerns about the natives.'

'And that needs to change, James. Right now, there is no opportunity to speak about such matters in town.'

'Have you ever considered that perhaps you are not the one . . .' He pauses, choosing his words carefully.

'Not the one what?'

'Not the one who is in the right about these matters?'

As James moves towards Louisa, Wagadhaany steps back quietly, making sure she can't be seen.

'Perhaps it is God's will for the Blacks to eventually die out. Therefore, there is no need to legislate about them at all. Not before, not now, not ever.'

'Don't be ridiculous! That is the most absurd thing I have ever heard.'

Wagadhaany can hear Louisa walking around the room, agitated, so she retreats further into the hallway.

'And you know what else is absurd?' Louisa asks. 'That there is a new hospital in Kincaid Street, but Aboriginal people cannot go there if they are sick. Did you know that?'

James starts to speak but Louisa cuts him off. 'And *do not* bother trying to suggest to me that getting sick and not having medical help is God's way of saying they will all die out.'

'But maybe it is!'

'Tell me this, James, do you believe in Jesus?'

'Oh, don't be so silly.'

'Do. You. Believe. In. Jesus?'

'Of course, I do. On your first visit to my home in Gundagai, I told you we were a Catholic household. I may not go to church all that often, but I am a holy man, a good Christian, you know that.'

'Well, tell me what Jesus might think about your views on the Aborigines, of the laws that stop them getting equal wages, or having freedom to move around. What would Jesus do if an Aboriginal person was sick and needed a doctor?'

'I've had enough of this!'

Wagadhaany can hear James walking towards the door and she starts coughing to let him know that she is there, to have him think that she just arrived.

'Oh, be careful, Wilma!' he shouts as he bumps into her.

'James,' Louisa calls out, following him downstairs, and giving Wagadhaany a weak smile as she passes.

As she makes the bed, Wagadhaany wonders what James meant by Black people dying out, although she isn't sure she really wants to know.

Chapter Twenty-two

The next two years pass quickly for Wagadhaany. As the seasons come and go, the town of Wagga Wagga bustles with new people and new businesses, and there is greater activity on the Bradley property too. More Wiradyuri people have joined the camp and Wagadhaany has her hands full. Her boys are now three years old and getting into mischief all the time, always wanting to swim in the river, regardless of the weather. They are constantly being told to stay away unless they are with Yindy or one of their older cousins. 'Yamawa?' they ask. 'Why?'

In fact they ask questions all the time. 'Why is Aunty hugging the tree?' Galari asks, as Yiray leans into the trunk of the red river gum.

'Yes, why is Aunty hugging a tree?' Ngarrang repeats.

Wagadhaany laughs at their endless questions. She knows they get that from her, and she wishes they had the chance to ask their mumala and gunhinarrung questions too. She runs her hands through both her sons' hair, one at a time, and pulls them into her lap. They play with her long curls and snuggle into her breast.

'Aunty is giving love back to tree,' she finally says, kissing each of them on the top of the head.

'Yamawa?' they whine in unison.

'Because she took some bark to put on the fire, so the tree gave her a gift. And she is giving a gift back. The gift of a hug. One day, if you are ever sad, or need some love, you can hug the tree and get some of Aunty's love back.'

Both boys are wide-eyed.

'Is that true?'

'Ngawa! I have hugged lots of trees, and so has your babiin. So, now you know there is love all around you when you need it.'

'Wiray!' Galari doesn't believe his mother.

'Ngawa!' she laughs. 'We take something, then we give something back, and we call it the circle of life.'

She leans forward and draws a circle in the earth.

Ngarrang squirms out of his mother's lap and races to the nearest tree, almost throwing himself at the trunk, and stretching his arms around it. His twin does exactly the same thing and then kisses the tree.

'Ngurrbul, ngurrbul, ngurrbul,' he sings out. 'I'm putting love in the tree, Mama.'

'Ngawa you are, my son, you are.'

Such moments make Wagadhaany's heart sing. They help when she is so far away from her own parents. But they seem fleeting compared to her ongoing homesickness which sometimes makes her sad for days on end. Since her sons were born the heartache has become almost unbearable. Every time she looks at her boys, she thinks of her brothers and desperately wishes they could meet their new kin. She sees so much of her brothers' cheekiness in the twins, and never has she wanted to see her family more than she does at these moments.

'And me too,' his brother calls out.

Wagadhaany's heart overflows as her boys try to make their hands meet around the tree trunk. *I have double the love, double the joy*, she thinks. If only her sons could stretch their arms around the trees in Gundagai with their cousins, like she used to do.

As hard as she tries to be grateful for becoming a mother, each day she is reminded that she is without her own. Every moment she enjoys with her boys turns to sorrow at the distance between her and her miyagan.

Some mornings it takes all her strength to get up and into the day. Her sons make it easier and harder at the same time. They give her purpose, but they also remind her of her own childhood. At times, sadness clings to her for days. She wants her boys to know they are connected to ngurambang and miyagan outside of Wagga Wagga.

Whenever she can, she shares the stories she heard as a child. She tells her sons about the waawii and the days of her girlhood on the riverbank.

But as time passes and Wagadhaany retreats into herself more and more, Yindy takes over, telling his boys stories that he heard growing up, including about the Mirriwula, a spirit dog that would come out after dark. His sons listen intently, scared and excited at the same time.

'You must always be here with your mother or me before it gets dark.'

Wagadhaany loves the way their eyes widen. Her sons look frightened and intrigued at the same time. When they are older they will understand that she and Yindy are trying to scare them into behaving, into respecting their wishes, as parents wanting to keep their children safe.

'But Babiin, how will we know when the dog is coming?' Galari asks.

'You will see his red eyes in the distance, and the closer he gets, the bigger and bigger his eyes will get.'

Yindy opens his eyes as wide as he can and the boys squeal. They look at each other, trying to make their eyes wide too, and then they all burst out laughing.

Many a night, the three of them wait for Yindy to arrive home from the station. His long days out droving have not changed since he became a father; his family life is of no interest to the Bradleys, just his skills in the saddle and with the cattle. Their reunions at the camp become both the happiest and saddest times for Wagadhaany.

Time goes into slow motion whenever Wagadhaany thinks about her brothers, about wanting to fish, about dancing with her mother and holding her father's hand as a wide-eyed four-year-old girl. The sadness shows on her face.

'Don't cry, Mama. Yamawa sad, Mama?'

As the end of 1858 draws near, Yindy is home for what the stockmen have been told is a Christmas break. Just before sunrise one morning, Wagadhaany finds a quiet moment.

'Yindy,' she whispers, not wanting to wake the boys.

Her husband turns his head but doesn't open his eyes. She knows he is exhausted. He fulfils his duties on the station, and as a father, and never complains, and she loves him even more for that. She knows he is awake and listening but she needs to look in his eyes, and she needs him to look into hers. Now is the time.

'Yindy,' she says again.

He stretches his body out.

'Ngawa?' he asks, yawning.

He tries to reach an arm over to her without disturbing the boys. Their sons will be up and noisy soon enough. She acknowledges his effort but their bodies do not make contact. He turns to lie on his side to face the three of them.

Wagadhaany has been wondering about how to tell him she is marganduli again. She hopes he will be happy, that the double joy they have with their sons will only grow with another child.

'What is it?' he asks. When she doesn't answer immediately, he looks deeply into her eyes, as if they will tell him.

'I'm marganduli.'

Yindy blinks, unsure if he's heard correctly.

'I'm marganduli,' she repeats.

He looks at her as if trying to decipher her thoughts and, she imagines, his own. But when she sees the sparkle in his eyes and a smile sweep across his face, she knows that he is as happy as she is.

When Wagadhaany tells Louisa she is pregnant again, there is no dramatic reaction like the first time. Rather, Louisa is calm, accommodating, suggesting that Wagadhaany not work so hard around the house in the lead-up to the birth. Together they agree that Wagadhaany will continue to prepare and serve meals for the Bradleys and the stockmen, but the heavy cleaning duties will be handed over to the other servants.

'And don't you worry about David ordering you back. I've told him I will employ an extra person so that no work will be missed.' Wagadhaany is taken by surprise that Louisa does not expect her to come back to work at the homestead after she gives birth. She feels relieved for so many reasons, elated that she can just spend time with her newborn and sons, in the way she has always wanted to. She wants to know why Louisa is standing up to David now and not before when she was pregnant with the twins. But she doesn't ask. She understands that she can't change the past and must be grateful for the freedom Louisa offers her now. If only Yindy could get the same freedom. She may not be tied to the Bradleys but he still is, and so she still cannot leave Wagga Wagga.

With another gudha on the way, Wagadhaany's mind soon turns to her new responsibilities. Even though she continues to work at the Bradleys, Louisa has been less reliant on her for company lately. Wagadhaany is relieved, but unsure where Louisa's interests currently lie. Social commitments in the town in recent years have kept Louisa occupied and focused on things other than her work at the station.

When the first mechanical flour mill in the town opens on Fitzmaurice Street, Wagadhaany is fascinated by how excited Louisa is, and how desperate she is to look at the building. Something Louisa once spoke of as simply bricks and mortar now seems to make her eyes light up. Wagadhaany has seen the change in Louisa over time; she struggles for purpose in her day, and hasn't mentioned convicts or Aborigines for a long time. These days, Louisa is more interested in the development of the town, and on how to be part of the growing social scene. Wagadhaany's Quaker friend seems to have become the socialite wife her husband wanted all along.

Lately, Wagadhaany can hardly think of a single thing they have in common.

'It was built by Robert Nixon of Gregadoo,' Louisa says of the new mill. 'I think it's going to be hugely successful, don't you?'

But Wagadhaany isn't the least bit interested. She does not care about the flour mill. She cares that Louisa has changed. She cares that her words about helping people have been replaced with a focus on the opening of new businesses.

Where is the woman who had talked of teaching the children at the camp to read, the woman who shared intimate conversations about love and children and the desire for family? The friend who wanted to bake and garden together, to fight for equality? Wagadhaany only sees remnants of the old Louisa. She no longer feels any sense of sisterhood.

One month it was the new watchmaker; the month before a coach-builder, wheelwright, butcher, dressmaker, milliner and midwife. The midwife was the only person Louisa did not get excited about, though Wagadhaany suggested they should get acquainted with her.

As their lives become increasingly at odds, Wagadhaany feels less inclined to tell Louisa about her experience of pregnancy.

'Nooooo,' she screams into the night, her pain echoing through the camp.

She has lost count of how many long, excruciating hours have passed, trying to give birth. She can't feel the cold of the night as her body is burning; sweat drips from her. She can't remember the pain being so severe with her sons, and the aunties had promised her it would be much easier this time. *Were their eyebrows raised when they said that? Were they making fun?* She had put her headband on before walking to the birthing place by the river; she needed to feel her mother with her. She breathes in, she breathes out, she cries for her own mother, and vows she will never have another child without her by her side.

The bamali-galang are with her though, and she is grateful as they guide her breathing and make sure she is as comfortable as possible. In a lull between contractions she closes her eyes and focuses on the water lapping at the edge of the riverbank, the burbling that signals the current is strong. The sounds soothe her until the next contraction hits; it feels like the worst monthly cramp of her life. She doesn't know if she can breathe her way through this birth, she doesn't know how much more her tiny frame can take. It feels as if there is more than a baby inside her.

Then a sound emerges from her lungs that shocks them all.

'Wirayyyyy!'

It is so ear-piercing, the entire camp is drawn to the moment that Wagadhaany and Yindy's daughter comes into the world.

When Wagadhaany finally opens her eyes after the long, hard push, when she can see properly through her tears, she feels the cold night air on her burning cheeks, and above her, she sees a sky full of twinkling stars. When her daughter is placed on her chest, she knows they are both going to be fine. The stars seem to multiply like magic, more and more of them by the second, as if they have given birth tonight too.

'Miima,' she says, kissing her daughter on the crown of her head. 'After the stars.'

Yindy is waiting in the same spot he stood when the twins were born. She is glad there are not two this time. Two might mean double the love and double the joy, but it also means double the pain, double the effort, and as the boys are growing, they are proving to be double the mischief.

Dawn breaks as the women walk Wagadhaany up the bank after the baby is cleaned and welcomed the Wiradyuri way. Wagadhaany is wrapped in a possum skin, but her legs feel weak. Yiray holds her firmly by the arm. Yindy takes his daughter from her mother's arms, and kisses her gently on the top of her head. And then he gazes at her, falling in love with little Miima. Wagadhaany can tell his heart is lost forever to his daughter, and she weeps.

Before she knows it, her sons, now four years old, are latched onto her legs. They crane their necks simultaneously to see their baby sister. Wagadhaany pulls them to her and watches on, recalling the unmistakable look of love from father to daughter, the look she remembers seeing in her own father's eyes as a child. The look he had when he found her alive the night of the flood. The look on his face the night they said goodbye outside the Bradleys'; the look that expresses a depth of emotion that no words ever could. She imagines the loss her father must have felt the day she left, and hopes neither Yindy nor Miima will experience such heartache. As tears flood her eyes again, and Yindy whispers to their newborn, the only thing Wagadhaany wants now is to go back to Gundagai.

Chapter Twenty-three

Louisa pastes a smile on her face, pretending she is happy, over-joyed even, that James has finally become mayor of Wagga Wagga. After five years, his ambition, his self-belief and even his sheer arrogance have paid off. As the official ceremony begins, she knows her life is about to change. James has already warned her he expects 'appropriate behaviour'. And while he looks to be overflowing with pride, Louisa is left feeling desperate and lonely, on the verge of tears. Her immediate thought is to escape, and at the earliest opportunity, she does just that.

Hours later, ashamed and embarrassed, Louisa sits on the veranda reflecting on what her life has become. None of the aspirations she had when planning the move to Wagga Wagga have been realised. A cloud of failure hangs heavily over her as she acknowledges her lame attempts and lost opportunities, partic-ularly her inability to influence her husband into instigating any real social progress in Wagga Wagga. Nothing has changed for the local Wiradyuri, nothing at all, and her own attempts, her offers to read to the children and to teach them to read, were never maintained. She is conscious that her enthusiasm was short-lived, and accepts the blame that falls fully on her own shoulders.

More importantly, she berates herself for not being able to provide a comfortable, safe home for Wagadhaany and her children, let alone a better, equal life for Aboriginal people overall. And how deeply she misses Wagadhaany's companionship. Only after she let Wagadhaany stop working for her, for the Bradleys, after the birth of Miima, did Louisa finally understand how much the Wiradyuri woman meant to her, how bereft she feels without that sense of solidarity and support.

Female friendship is not the only thing that Louisa dwells on. The strength of love between Yindy and Wagadhaany has taught her that men can show love and respect for women, even without the trappings of the European way of life that so many believe is needed for happiness and success.

Most importantly, Louisa has seen love in an extended family, thanks to spending time with Yiray by the river. Yiray's family embraced Wagadhaany immediately, not knowing if they were blood related or not. It was enough that they were connected by land and language. *Imagine if English people here behaved like that, simply because they shared a history and geography. How much less competitive and more caring they would be.* She might even have been able to find more people to join her as Quakers if people were more willing to share stories and beliefs, as the women by the river do. Even the Quakers could learn from Wiradyuri people.

Louisa had learned from Wagadhaany that family for the Wiradyuri people meant much more than parents and siblings;

it included all those connected to you, not only by blood, but also by language, tradition, the land where you were born and raised, and by a sense of community that brings those needing a home into the fold. Louisa had been so focused on claiming Wagadhaany as family for herself, she had not realised that she was not hers to claim.

Along with James and David, she had dragged the young woman away from the people she loved most. It has taken the birth of three children for Louisa to understand that real equality would have allowed Wagadhaany to make choices herself, to have had the freedom to decide whether she wanted to go to Wagga Wagga or not. What had she done to the only woman she cares about, the only woman she has been able to confide in? Louisa misses her friend, and all the things she brought to her world.

'I have no-one!' she cries out loud. It shocks her to her core. 'I have no-one!'

She says it again and again, each time with less strength in her voice. Her isolation and loneliness weigh on her. More than ever she wishes she had a child to give her love to, and to give her a purpose beyond being James's wife. Each time they are intimate, she feels awash with hope, regardless of whether James has been drinking or if there is passion between them; in her mind, every act of lovemaking has been an opportunity to fall pregnant. Every time her monthlies appear, so too does the anguish of knowing she has failed again. The townsfolk must believe she is barren, useless to any man who desires fatherhood. She doesn't know of any women in town who are falling pregnant for the first time in their thirties, but she can't give up hope, for motherhood or for her marriage.

Louisa looks out, surprised to see that night has fallen and the dew has set in. Only when a bitter breeze sweeps across her cheeks does she realise that she is shivering. Upstairs she undresses, her motions mechanical, craving sleep to escape her feelings of loneliness.

It's the winter of 1859 and the *Wagga Wagga Express* is open on the kitchen table. Louisa pours her third cup of tea after a restless night. Today is a new day, and there is a sense of urgency, a need to take control of her day, of her life, and to find a worthy activity.

She turns each page with purpose, searching for a news story that might motivate her, guide her, so she can feel better about herself and about the society she lives in, in a town where as a White woman she has freedom, but few ways to exercise it.

Wagga Wagga School of Arts to Open. The headline lifts her mood immediately. She reads the article fast, searching for the important details. It will have entertainment and elocution lessons. There will be a library and a literary club.

As she continues to read, she feels uncomfortable at the announcement that the 'softer sex' may 'avail themselves of the invitation', but hopes that at least it might mean she will meet more of the town's womenfolk.

'This is it!' she says out loud. She will turn her efforts and energy to the new School of Arts and offer any help she can, hopefully in the library.

Later that week, she and James attend the opening. It's late July, and the winter weather is brutal. She is proud to be on

James's arm, and he looks dashing in his suit. She catches him admiring her as she takes her coat off, and feels her heart flutter as if they were newlyweds again.

As they enter the large room, she observes some of the town's most respected locals, including the School of Arts Patron, Mr William McLeay. She is more interested in making acquaintances with women, but the few in attendance all seem attached to their husbands.

'Where are all the other ladies?' she whispers into James's ear.

'They were invited, Louisa, but perhaps they know a woman's place is in the home. You are here only because you are the wife of the mayor.'

His words infuriate Louisa but she knows better than to challenge him in public. She will save that for later.

'Mr Baylis.' James extends his hand to the first police magistrate for the town. 'Congratulations on your appointment.'

Baylis looks past Bradley and tips his hat to Louisa. 'Mrs Bradley, so delighted you could join us. Not so many of your peers here this evening?' He too appears surprised at the lack of women. 'I am sure you are acquainted with Mr William McLeay. Not only is he a member of the Legislative Assembly, but he is also patron of our School of Arts, for which we are most grateful.'

'I hear you have donated a hundred volumes as a foundation to the library,' James says to Mr McLeay. 'A wonderful and generous gesture, I must say. I think my wife might have a few books of her own to donate.' He nods to Louisa, attempting to include her.

Louisa is happy to share her books, but would like to make any decision about her property herself. 'Of course, I would like to lend my support any way I can,' she says politely, wondering what James would think if he knew she'd already given many books to the children at the Aboriginal camp by the river.

'James, I hear you're involved in the new cricket club,' Mr Baylis says, making the swing of a bat.

'I have been known to bowl an over or two,' James says, throwing his arm over in a bowling movement. 'Of course, we are no Lords, but now that the roads are much improved and coach services are possible, I do believe that in time we should be able to attract teams from far and wide, maybe even from Victoria.'

In the months that follow, Louisa tries to get involved in the School of Arts. She donates books to the library, she offers to assist with literacy classes. She develops a newfound energy and devotes a lot of time reading everything she can about British law and the new colonies of Australia. At the library, she learns that Wiradyuri people should have been treated in every respect as Europeans by order of Governor Macquarie in 1810, except that years later he issued a new proclamation, placing extraordinary restrictions upon Aboriginal people as to where they can move, their rights to carry their traditional weapons and practise their own customs. She almost falls off her chair when she reads of the Crown Lands Encroachment Act of 1833, which protected Crown lands from intrusion and trespass. She groans out loud when she understands that the law effectively excludes Wiradyuri people from their own land.

She reads that in 1835, the concept of *terra nullius* reinforced the idea that the land had belonged to no-one prior to colonisation, which meant that Wagadhaany and all the people at the camp had no rights to own, sell or acquire land, other than through distribution by the Crown.

Louisa feels as if the thoughts in her head and the feelings in her heart might erupt at the injustice of these laws, but she maintains control and continues to read court case papers, government acts and House of Commons reports, bills and boards. The more she learns the more passionate she becomes about wanting to work for change, but she knows of no-one else with the same views. She studies all the information she can, trying not to draw too much attention to herself but wanting to be armed with knowledge before she embarks on any strategy, which she will need to design on her own. She decides she will try, one more time, to speak to James. He is the mayor now. Surely he must listen.

One night, Louisa speaks to James about what she has read but he is drunk and he becomes aggressive, complaining about her long visits to the library. So, she stops going.

With a full staff now running the homestead and James forbidding her from doing any domestic duties at all, Louisa spends her time visiting the latest specialist stores. She tries to forget her friendship with Wagadhaany by keeping busy with her duties as the mayor's wife, getting new dresses made for the numerous events she must attend: the opening of the first bank, the opening of the school on Tarcutta Street, where she helps occasionally when the one teacher is unwell. Without realising it, she has become what James had always expected of her. Any thoughts of working with the local Aboriginal people have all but disappeared.

That year, the profits from the station see the Bradley fortune increase and Louisa commissions the local cabinetmaker to build some new furniture. On one visit to his workshop she admires the craftsmanship in a baby's crib and her heart aches, knowing she might never have a child of her own.

Although she has avoided any form of organised religion in the town until now, reading the Bible alone to remind herself of her Quaker values, she decides to attend the opening of St Michael's Roman Catholic Church. She wants to meet people with faith, any faith. More than ever she feels the isolation of being a woman in rural Australia, and understands that sometimes religion is the only thing that can bring people together.

Meanwhile, she clings to her marriage and to a husband whose moods swing daily. Louisa decides that going to the Murrumbidgee Turf Club races with James will be good for their relationship. She needs to foster some romance and love between them again; she still hopes that she will conceive and that one day James will have the son he wanted.

'Do you remember the day we met?' she asks, as she watches him dress.

'What?' There is a hint of annoyance in his response.

'We met at the races. You commented on my parasol.' She feels a moment of nostalgia for that far happier time. 'Shall I join you today?'

James looks confused. 'You hate horseracing, and generally you hate the people who like it.'

'I don't *hate* anyone, James, you know that it is not within me to have harsh feelings towards another human being.' She is indignant, upset that her suggestion looks to be turning into

another argument. 'And how could I hate my husband? And . . .'
She hesitates.

James looks at her. For a moment there is a warmth in their
shared glance that has not been there for some time. 'I love you,
James. Horseracing or not.' She says it with such tenderness she
can tell he is affected when he pulls her close to him. 'I don't
really go for the horseracing, you know that.'

She feels her heartbeat quicken. It has been months since there
has been any intimacy between them and their lovemaking now
is frantic, desperate.

When she has dressed, she pauses to consider how much she
has changed. She has a house full of staff that she refuses to call
servants and she is going to the races. She is spending money for
pleasure rather than necessity. This is not the woman she was in
Gundagai. She recalls her conversation with Wagadhaany about
the transformation of the tree to the broom. What kind of transformation has she made?

At the races, Louisa tries to keep positive about her reasons
for attending, to be closer to James. She turns a blind eye to the
cruelty towards the animals she wishes she could protect, but
finds it harder to ignore the attitudes on display. Her husband
unashamedly flaunts his wealth, as do the other property owners.
She thinks they are a sorry sight, attempting to be aristocrats on
land they will never really own. She is glad that Wagadhaany and
the old women can't see her right now.

On the journey back to the homestead, she is silent. James
has become the opposite of the man her father was. She loved
her husband, she still loves him, but she doesn't like him. She
doesn't like his privileged ways of thinking, his prejudice against
the Wiradyuri people, his drinking, his manhandling of her.

But what is she to do? Even with some means of her own, where would she go?

A baby will give her – give them both – a new focus and purpose. A baby will bring them closer together. So despite his whisky breath and rough hands, she succumbs to him again that night.

Chapter Twenty-four

It has been almost a year since Wagadhaany has been to the Bradleys' homestead, having not returned after Miima's birth, and she feels nervous as she steps onto the veranda. When she enters the kitchen unannounced she is surprised to see so many Black faces.

'Who are all these people?' she says under her breath to her daughter, whose head is resting on her right shoulder.

She recognises some who had been at the Bradleys' when she had been there a year ago, but not the others. There are a few local Wiradyuri women, who she has seen before at the camp, but she doesn't know the others. There are also two White women. Reminded of the years she spent taking care of the Bradleys, and Louisa, she watches them quietly going about their work: washing, cleaning, cooking, setting up to serve the stockmen their meals. But never has she witnessed such organisation, so much busyness.

She wonders for how long things at the homestead have been so hectic, and is glad she didn't come sooner. Coming back has reminded her of her life at the Bradleys' both here and in Gundagai, and it shocks her back into the reality that she is not really free.

'Come in, come in. I've been waiting to meet your little girl.' Louisa makes room for them at the kitchen table. 'Though she is not so little anymore.' She smiles. 'May I?' she asks, reaching out for the baby, who Wagadhaany passes to her.

Wagadhaany is used to Miima being held by others; in the camp every newborn is smothered with love and attention, and she is grateful that there is always someone to hold her daughter, especially as she has been slow to recover from the birth.

'It's so busy here now, Louisa. The station has grown so much since autumn, when I was here last. The vegetable garden is full of pumpkins and potatoes now. I have never seen so many.'

'Yes, well the station has grown to the largest in the region, and there are more stockmen needing to be fed. And I am trying to grow as much food as I can to share around, like you do at the camp.' She pauses, smiles. 'Oh, I do miss you out there with me. Though even *I* am not tending the garden much these days.' She looks to the woman at the stove, who is stirring a huge pot of beef stew. 'And with more events in town, I found I needed even more help.' She puts Miima over her shoulder. 'There, there,' she whispers in the baby's ear before looking back to Wagadhaany. 'I don't have time to do everything I did before.'

'But so many servants?' There is judgement in Wagadhaany's voice, as if Louisa has become the sort of person she had always worked against.

'Helpers,' Louisa says, rocking little Miima. 'The truth is, Wagadhaany, I couldn't manage all of it without you, and David was livid that I'd let you go, he didn't want you to leave.'

She pauses. They both know that with Wagadhaany no longer around, he had no opportunity to brush past her, to stare at her with lustful eyes. Wagadhaany's skin crawls at the mention of his name, and she notices one of the servant women shivering and shaking her shoulders while another screws up her nose. Wagadhaany hopes that they are strong enough to fend him off.

'You do know that James is mayor of Wagga Wagga now, don't you?' Louisa says with a hint of pride. 'And the mayor's wife cannot be on her haunches in the garden or serving the stockmen their meals. It's just not the way things are done in this town, I have learned, albeit the hard way.'

Wagadhaany does not accept that Louisa believes what she is saying, rather that she is echoing her husband's words.

'One night, James said that if I wanted to behave like a domestic then I could live like a domestic. Honestly, he nearly made me sleep in another room. You do understand that marriage entails sacrifice and compromise.'

What Wagadhaany understands is that in Louisa's marriage *she* makes the sacrifices and compromises.

'And so I agreed to have more staff, more *helpers*. There have been a lot of changes since you left us. These women help me around the homestead, don't you, Dharru, Ginin and Ngamuwila?'

When Louisa rattles off the names as if she is fluent in their language, Wagadhaany is taken by surprise although she is not sure why. Louisa had called her by her own name from the very first day, so of course she would do the same with these women. And there are smiles between these women and Louisa too, and probably friendship as well.

'I help them gain new skills in the kitchen and the garden. Like *we* did. It's a partnership, really.'

Louisa doesn't add that she has made new clothes for the women, but Wagadhaany can tell they are all wearing Louisa's handiwork, and they move around the house freely, comfortably, so maybe they feel differently, maybe together they feel safer, happier there, than she ever did. Maybe Louisa is better at protecting them against David, or at least keeps them away from him. She doesn't know how to raise any of this, so lets her questions pass. But she does ask about equality, because that's the word that Louisa had always used.

'So they get the same pay now, the Blacks and the Whites? They get more than rations and clothes, and more than the boots that my Yindyamarra comes home with every now and then? These women are your equals now?'

'Almost.'

Louisa is vague, evasive, and while Wagadhaany tries to catch the eye of any of the workers, they remain focused on the tasks at hand. She hates being there now, feeling different again, like when she first arrived, with more privileges than the other Aboriginal women. She wants to leave immediately, to never sit at a table unless everyone is equal.

'Oh,' Louisa says, as if it's an afterthought, 'gold quartz has been found at Borambola Station. Well, that's what I've heard. And,' she continues, rubbing her cheek against Miima's, 'this could be very important for the town.'

All Wagadhaany can think about are the dinawan-galang killed in the name of gold. She knows the evil that greed can cause, and gold brings greed, and that's not good for any town. She gently takes Miima from Louisa and as soon as she finishes her tea, she leaves.

One morning, months later, there is a lot of activity at the camp. The women are singing as they weave and cook the food that has been caught by the men. It is the time of year when Aboriginal people are issued blankets from the government, and sometimes the men get tomahawks to assist with cutting firewood too. Wagadhaany has always thought it was an odd excitement, because blankets and tools were bare essentials. And often the tomahawks were to cut wood for their White masters anyway.

A huge corroboree is about to take place. Wiradyuri people from all around have gathered and a man known as King Peter is wearing a breastplate given to him by the Devlins, the family he works for. There are no Wiradyuri kings or queens like the English have, but Wagadhaany knows that when a Wiradyuri person is bestowed with a breastplate, everyone thinks it's very important. Wagadhaany is wearing the headband her mother gave her so many years ago, something she does more regularly now, and her boys are ready to dance as well. They are getting restless, and Miima is wriggling so much she nearly squirms out of her arms. She is grateful that Yiray is there to corral her sons while she searches the crowd in case some of her mayiny have travelled here. Maybe, she tells herself, maybe this time they have come. But she doesn't recognise anyone from Gundagai.

Everyone has gathered because King Peter, advised by a messenger for the mayor, has told them it is Queen Victoria's birthday, and even though it's *her* birthday, they will all get a gift, the gift of a blanket.

The corroboree goes for days, but the blankets do not arrive, and there is unrest at the campsite. The men are angry, the women are disappointed, and children just want to know where the gifts are. It doesn't matter that they are blankets and not fun things to play with, anything new is a treat.

On the third day the dancing and singing finally stops. King Peter stands to attention and demands he is listened to. It's a rare show of aggressive leadership and Wagadhaany wonders if this is the way that James Bradley commands the attention of the townsfolk. But no-one in the camp is concerned. They listen intently.

'Let's march to the courthouse!' King Peter exclaims. 'We should have our blankets.'

When they arrive at the courthouse in the middle of town, King Peter stands before them with a piece of paper. Wagadhaany doesn't know who wrote the words on it, and is surprised that King Peter can read them, but like everyone else she listens as he addresses the crowd of Aboriginal people, and the few White onlookers who appear curious about the ruckus.

'I protest the government. Queen Victoria on her birthday usually sends blankets for us. But we did not get the blankets, so we have come to the courthouse.'

When he finishes speaking, anyone who wants to say something has the chance to do so. It is the Wiradyuri way, that everyone is heard. So different to the White way, where only some men seem to have the right to speak in public about things that affect everyone. Wagadhaany is beginning to understand Louisa's unhappiness at the laws she talks about. Wagadhaany knows that White women and Black people can't vote, and an overwhelming sense of hatred for White lawmakers washes over her. She thinks of the Bradleys and then of Louisa, and as if her thoughts have summoned her, she sees Louisa standing at the back of the crowd. They haven't spoken since she visited with

Miima and as soon as they lock eyes there is warm recognition, and Wagadhaany's anger dissipates. They have missed each other.

After the crowd has dispersed – the march to the courthouse did nothing to bring about the blankets – Louisa makes her way over to Wagadhaany.

'Come and have tea with me,' Louisa says, 'like we used to. Please.'

Yiray takes the three children back to camp and Wagadhaany and Louisa walk to the homestead together.

'It has been a long time since your last visit, and in that time I have been working hard, Wagadhaany. Oh I know,' says Louisa, in response to a sideways look from her friend, 'I know what you are thinking, that I have said this all before. But this time it is different. I have been writing to the Quakers in Van Diemen's Land. I have been finding out everything that I can. I may be a wife, but that's not all I am. I have my own mission, and no-one – no, not even James – can stop me.'

Wagadhaany raises her eyebrow like the aunties did the first time Louisa met them.

'I know that questioning eyebrow, Wagadhaany,' she says. 'I am serious. I have heard too many stories of Aboriginal women being badly treated by White men working on stations, men who own stations. I can't stand by anymore, it must change.'

Wagadhaany sees a change in Louisa's spirits and thinks that maybe this time is different, as Louisa says. Even if it is, though, she finds it difficult to feel any positivity about it. Her sadness stays with her and there are only rare moments when she does not remember it.

Once inside, they sit down at the table. 'Just like the old days,' Louisa says, pouring tea.

Wagadhaany looks around. She sees through the back window that the staff are in the garden.

'It wasn't that bad, was it?' Louisa asks, traces of both confession and apology in her words. 'Working here? For you? And for the other helpers?'

Wagadhaany shrugs, and before she has the chance to answer, or to even change the subject to talk about the children, about how her boys are learning to dance, how her daughter giggles a lot, James arrives home. They can hear him whistling on the veranda, but as soon as he walks into the kitchen and sees the two of them sitting together, his mood instantly changes.

He rolls his eyes and huffs, stomps around, visibly displeased to see Wagadhaany there, and attempting to ignore her.

'Aren't you going to say hello, James?'

Without looking in her direction, he mumbles from the sink, 'Wilma.'

'Wagadhaany,' Louisa says. 'I bumped into Wagadhaany at the courthouse.'

He spins around angrily. 'What were you doing at the courthouse? Do I have to monitor everywhere you go? Who you see? What you say? Tell me why you were there!' The veins in his neck protrude angrily.

'I was in town,' she says, standing up. 'There was a meeting. The Queen's Birthday blankets haven't been distributed as they were meant to be. You're the mayor, surely you know about this.'

'I didn't! Blankets for the natives are not the business of someone in my position.'

'Maybe you could delegate this *trivial* task to someone who's in charge of such business?'

Wagadhaany likes Louisa's sarcastic tone, but it is clear James does not. He screws his face up, purses his lips, and snorts while he checks his pocket watch.

'Also, James,' Louisa continues decisively, 'we need to give the Aboriginal men some new boots and clothes, and provisions for their families.'

'What are you talking about?' James is getting impatient. 'They get a blanket, that's all we have to do under the law.'

'They didn't get the blankets, it seems, and besides,' Louisa stands tall with her hands on her hips, 'giving *one* blanket is *not* all we have to do. Our property is doing well, we should share the rewards with those who help us reap them.'

'That's not how business works, Louisa. Surely I don't need to explain that to you.'

Louisa ignores his condescending tone. 'Forget business, what about ethics? Morals? Doing what's right?'

Wagadhaany is worried that this discussion will turn into another violent argument. She sits quietly as Louisa goes upstairs. She is out of the room for only a few minutes but the tension is palpable until she returns with a bundle of letters and newspaper clippings.

'These were sent to me by the Quakers in Van Diemen's Land. I want you to read them.'

She tries to hand them to James, but he puts his hands in his pockets. 'It's called Tasmania now.' He speaks as if Louisa is a fool, but she reacts swiftly and calmly.

'Of course it is, renamed in 1856 after –'

'I'm not reading anything and, quite frankly, I really don't care what you were sent by anyone.'

His contempt for Louisa is embarrassing for them all. But Louisa continues undeterred.

'You should care!' she shouts angrily, her face flushed red. 'So much that is happening is unfair, James, unjust. The government is giving away thousands of acres of land to missionaries, to train Aboriginal people to be Christians and make them work. Did you know that?'

'Yes, and I agree with it.'

'And Aboriginal people are being sent to Van . . . Tasmania, for crimes that they are not necessarily guilty of because,' she says, pausing to look at some of the pages, 'they cannot defend themselves in court, or give evidence. They cannot be sworn in . . .' She flicks through more pages, adding, 'because in the eyes of British law, they are ignorant of religion.'

'Dear Louisa.' James's tone smacks of contempt. 'The Blacks are not competent witnesses in a court of law. Maybe if they learn some religion in the missions you so hate, they could swear on the Bible.'

Louisa continues, ignoring James's scorn. 'It says that sixteen per cent of income from Crown land sales is meant to be spent on the Aborigines,' she exclaims, exasperated. 'But all they get is a blanket, and this year they didn't even get that!'

'Do you know how much that equates to, Louisa? It's ridiculous to think we would be giving that amount to the natives. They would only spend it on liquor. Though they *could* buy their own blankets and stop complaining,' James scoffs. 'But the truth is, why should they get any money from the sale of Crown land? They don't *really* own the land, they don't work it, or farm it.'

'Their land has been stolen.' Louisa stops short of yelling. She calms herself and continues. 'It's Wiradyuri land.' She points out the window. 'We don't really own this; it is not yours, or mine. And those laws are British laws and should be illegal if they are not protecting Aboriginal people, who should be British citizens.'

Wagadhaany has not heard the word British so much before, but can't help but think it must mean something evil.

'I have the title deeds to this property.' James walks at pace towards the living room. 'If you need proof, if *Wilma* needs proof, I will get them.'

Wagadhaany does not want to be part of this conversation. She doesn't know what deeds are. And she doesn't need to see them.

'And who were the deeds provided by?' Louisa asks in a way that suggests the answer will only make her own argument stronger.

'The Crown, of course. Why do you make my life so hard, Louisa?'

'But how did the Crown *get* the deeds? That's my point. And why do you make *my* life so hard?' Wagadhaany thinks Louisa is very brave to argue with her husband in this way. 'Those acting on behalf of the Crown *stole* the land from these people,' Louisa continues.

'Oh for goodness sake, Louisa. The Blacks are just lucky we got here first, *before* the French.'

'Les Français ne seraient pas aussi stupides que les Anglais.'

'Don't speak French in my house, and don't ever bring *her* back here again.'

James storms out of the house, and it's a few moments before Louisa composes herself.

'I'm sorry you had to hear that, it happens quite a bit.' She says it calmly, and it is a change for Wagadhaany to see Louisa argue with her husband and appear so unaffected by it.

'What were those words I didn't understand?' Wagadhaany wants to know.

'That the Frenchman would not be as stupid as the Englishman!' And they both laugh out loud.

A few days later, as the sun falls behind the trees and Wagadhaany washes the children in the river, Yindy appears with three blankets. He is smiling from ear to ear.

'Where did you get those?' she asks him.

'Miss Louisa gave all the men extra blankets. And I got these boots. She sent some bully beef too.' Yindy is grateful, unaware of the conversation Wagadhaany had been witness to only days before.

'Miss Louisa gave us this also,' he says, pointing to another basket. 'A big boat called the *Albury* has pulled into the docking area and she said it was loaded up with flour, tea and sugar.'

Yindy speaks excitedly, but Wagadhaany shrugs her shoulders. She doesn't think that's anything to get too excited about. These things are not incredibly special, they are basic necessities and what he is due.

'Miss Louisa will be happy,' he says. 'Her sweet-smelling soap was delivered to her today too.'

Wagadhaany is convinced that Louisa is acting of her own accord in providing extra supplies to the workers. She is certain that James Bradley had no role in the distribution of them; he demonstrates no humanity towards Wiradyuri people. But to see Yindy happy as she unpacks some tea and sugar, well, that is enough for her.

Chapter Twenty-five

By summer the land is in need of rain and the Elders seek shade under the she-oak trees. But even the scorching sun doesn't stop Galari and Ngarrang from running amok, almost knocking over their mother who is holding their younger sister on her hip. The boys are about to turn five and are shooting up in height, their bodies long and lean like their uncles and grandfather. They are more excited than usual following a rare visit from Louisa, who has dropped off Christmas presents for all the children at the camp. The aunties had never seen such excitement, with books and wooden blocks and a ball the twins kick and throw and fight over. They start to wrestle over the ball and roll on the ground, all the way to Wagadhaany's feet.

'Be careful!' Yindy says. 'You take care, your gunhi is very important.'

He smiles at Wagadhaany while spreading casuarina leaves on the ground near their camp. He is serious when he speaks of her in this way, hiding his concern about her increasing sadness at being away from her own miyagan.

'Hey,' Wagadhaany says, as they continue to fight over the ball. 'Stop, give it to me.'

Galari rolls the ball on the ground towards his mother and clips his brother across the back of the head without her noticing. And they start to wrestle again.

Yindy watches as Wagadhaany lines the ball up and skilfully kicks it. Miima bounces on her hip and claps her hands, giggling.

'I'll get it,' Galari squeals, running after it.

'No, *I'll* get it!' Ngarrang challenges.

Yindy's heart is full. Watching his love have some fun with their children is a rare but beautiful moment, and he hopes he can recall her smile the next time he sees darkness overcome her.

'Rest here while we are gone. The snakes won't come near you as long as you and Miima are here.'

He double checks the lean-to he has built to shelter the two of them from the sun during the day. He worries about their safety, but as long as he has prepared the site and they do as he asks, he knows they will be fine.

The twins are excited about going out bush with their father. They have no idea how far they will walk though, thinking only of the adventure. Yindy has been waiting for this time with his sons, following the tradition he had with his father, to learn the ways of the land. He already knows there will be a lot of questions along the way, and a lot of complaints about tired legs. And that will be adventure enough for him.

They leave mid-morning and the first stop is at Wollundry Lagoon, where several billabongs are shaded by she-oaks. The boys are most fascinated by the silver banksia trees.

'This is the place of many stories,' Yindy tells his sons, who are trying to pull a woven fish-trap out of the water to see if any fish are inside. 'Let that go!' Yindy yells.

They let go of it immediately. Straightaway their attention is caught by something else.

'Look, Babiin,' Galari says, as he turns a leaf over to show its shimmering underside. Then quickly he says, 'Let's fish, I want to fish.'

'Ngawa, let's fish,' Ngarrang echoes.

'Not yet,' Yindy says, walking ahead, both boys following close on his heels. 'We are not here to fish, we are here for . . .' He looks around with purpose. The twins' eyes follow his gaze. He walks a bit further, bends and picks up a black stone. 'This.'

He holds out the lump of volcanic rock to his sons. They each take turns holding it, smelling it, shaking it, gauging how heavy it is in their small hands. 'This is the hardest rock you will *ever* find.'

The boys take turns at tapping it. Yindy takes it back, holds it up. 'And from it we make our tools.'

For as long as Yindy can keep their attention, the boys watch their father, learning how to make an axe head, step by step.

'It can also be used to cut a guluman from the tree so Mama can carry food,' he explains. 'And it can cut really big guluman-galang to make a canoe to fish in too.'

'Let's make a canoe,' Galari says.

'Let's make a canoe,' Ngarrang repeats.

'We need to make a handle for our axe first. Help me find a branch.'

The boys hurry off to look.

'This one,' Yindy says, finding one by a red river oak.

'It's as long as your arm, Babiin,' Ngarrang says.

'Come here.' Yindy stands the branch upwards. 'And it's almost as tall as you. Now we need some lomandra,' he says, walking to the edge of the lagoon and pulling some plants from the ground. 'And we tie the axe head to the handle like this.'

While Yindy demonstrates, the boys rest comfortably on their haunches. One day they will pass these techniques on to their own sons.

When the handle is secure, Yindy breaks off the bottom of the lomandra stem and hands half each to the boys. One shrugs his shoulders. The other says, 'What for?'

Yindy motions for them to put it in their mouth. They smile, look at each other wide-eyed and do as they're told.

With their new axe, they follow the edge of the lagoon back to the river. The boys are still brimming with excitement about this first big adventure with their babiin, and Yindy is determined his sons learn everything they need for survival, including respect for the land and all the creatures on it. When they come across some black ducks and water hens, Galari asks, 'How do we catch them, Babiin?'

Ngarrang echoes his brother's question.

'Budhanbang-galang don't like walga-galang or maliyan-galang, and they will duck when they are at risk of being dived upon. So, if you throw your boomerang so it flies over them just like a hawk or eagle, they will get scared and drop to the water, and then you can catch them easily.'

'I don't like hawks or eagles either,' Galari says, and Ngarrang agrees.

Being near the bila, the boys are keener than ever to fish.

'We want to catch wandha, Babiin.'

Yindy thinks it's the right time to cut a canoe and searches for a tree that looks ready to give one up to them. He feels the bark of each trunk to test it, tapping trunk after trunk. The boys mimic his actions.

'This one,' Yindy says, cutting the bark away. He works with a rhythm that mesmerises his boys, explaining each movement and his respect for the tree as he works. The sun moves across the sky as the time passes and when he is finished they are all impressed.

'That's a really big guluman,' Galari says, looking at the cut bark.

'Ngawa,' Yindy agrees. 'It is big enough for you, but never without me with you, all right?'

Both boys nod yes but it's hard for Yindy to tell if they are listening. Their eyes are fixed on the new canoe.

They head out on the river, Yindy and Ngarrang on the big canoe and Galari on a smaller one he cut and tied to the larger one. Later that day the boys take turns at riding alone. They fish and fall in the water, and there is laughter and joy. They catch enough cod for them all to eat well that night.

At the end of the day they are all exhausted, not because they have walked far, but because of what they have accomplished together. Yindy sleeps with one son on either side of him, and hopes Wagadhaany and Miima are safe on their mat where he left them.

In the morning, Yindy wakes first. His sons' bodies are twisted over his on both sides. He is grateful for this time away from the station while the cattle are rested. He lies still, staring up at the old river gums they are camped under, imagining their roots holding on to the earth.

When the young ones eventually rise, they eat damper, share a mouthful of billy tea and cover the coals with dirt before heading off again. They haven't walked far before the boys start complaining.

'My legs are tired, I don't want to walk anymore, this isn't fun.'

'Do you want me to show you how to make rope?' Yindy asks, hoping to distract them.

Neither son looks enthusiastic. They shrug their shoulders.

'Come,' Yindy says. 'This is a box gum. You pull the bark like this. Be careful, do it slowly, and it will come off easily.'

The boys are very good at pulling off the bark and they sit weaving it together.

Yindy leaves them for a moment to check a noise behind them, and when he comes back he realises the pair have wandered off. His eyes dart left and right. They're crouching down over a log. He walks towards them, reminded that he needs more eyes, more ears, more everything to keep them close and safe.

'Don't touch that, get away from there,' he admonishes.

He can't remember his own father having to tell him how to behave, or perhaps he didn't notice.

'Babiin,' Ngarrang calls. 'Look at this log.'

He and his brother are turning it over.

'Mabinya!' Yindy yells again. 'Don't touch it!' He runs over to them. 'Never turn a log with your hands, never. Do you hear me?' He looks them both in the eyes. 'Never, in case there is a snake underneath.'

The boys jump back in one movement. It almost makes Yindy laugh, but he wants them to learn the lesson.

'Always use your foot, like this,' he says, pushing the log hard and fast away from them, revealing the bugs underneath.

It is his job to teach them how to stay safe. He will always be their greatest teacher.

'I'm hungry,' Galari says, bored with his father's lessons.

'Me too!' Ngarrang replies.

'Here,' Yindy says, pulling a plant by the stem from the dry ground. There hasn't been rain for weeks. 'This is what your gunhi uses to make the dilly bags.'

It's still green, even without the rain, making it not only fire-resistant but good for eating. He places a stem in each boy's hand.

'Eat,' he says, putting his own piece to his mouth. 'This is garradyang. We can make fishing nets and lines with the stems too.'

He pulls up more stems and shows the boys how to make lines to fish with. They forget their hunger, excited about going out in their canoes again.

Soon the boys wander off, fascinated by a huge silver banksia. They pull at the bright yellow flower heads, disturbing some bees. Galari is stung and lets out a piercing wail. Yindy drops his net and runs over. He picks his son up in one swift motion as the boy starts to turn blue, and flicks the sting out of his son's arm. He paces around, looking for something to soothe the pain. He sees some bracken fern, breaks a stem off and rubs the leaves on the site of the sting, saying nothing.

In a few minutes his son has calmed down but now his twin brother is weeping quietly as well. Yindy thinks Wagadhaany has made them soft. But when Galari says, 'I'm better now, Babiin,' and gives his father a hug, and Ngarrang throws his skinny arms around his father's thigh, Yindy's heart melts. He too has become soft. Wagadhaany is to blame for that as well, he smiles to himself.

No sooner have the boys recovered, than Yindy starts gathering twigs and branches for a fire to camp by that night.

'Babiin! Babiin!' they call out, from the high branch of a river gum.

'A nest!' Galari points.

'There are lots of eggs, we should take some to Gunhi!' Ngarrang adds enthusiastically.

They both grab an egg in each hand and hold them up proudly for their father to see. But a magpie is about to swoop.

'Put the eggs back gently, now.' Yindy is trying not to sound alarmed. The boys do as they are told but aren't sure why. 'Now, I want you to slowly come back down here,' he says calmly but with authority, in fear for his sons' safety, and out of respect for the mother garru.

They find it harder to descend the tree than to climb it. And they are disappoined at having to put the eggs back.

'Why couldn't we keep the eggs? Gunhi would have liked the eggs,' Galari says.

'Yes, she would.' Yindy walks slowly towards them. 'But look!' He points to the garru now resting on the nest. 'That's the mother. Her children are in those eggs. If we leave the eggs, there will be more garru. And more garru means more eggs for later.'

'But what about for now?'

'For now, we have enough food.'

That night they sit by the fire to eat the snake Yindy has killed.

'I miss Gunhi,' Galari says.

'Me too,' Ngarrang responds.

'Look up,' their father says, indicating the stars. 'See the bilabang?' He points to the Milky Way.

'No, where? I can't see it.'

'There, over there,' Yindy repeats, 'that group of stars, with the white all around it, just there. Your mother and Miima are sleeping under the same stars as us tonight, so we are still together. And see there? That's Biyaami.'

'Where?' they sing out in unison. 'We can't see Biyaami.'

'In the sky, look, follow my finger.'

Yindy places one hand of each boy on his own and points to the outline of Biyaami. 'It starts with a boomerang, see the shape here? And there's the arm holding it high above his head. The other arm has a big shield, see? And we follow these stars down, and there we have Biyaami.'

'I can see him, Babiin, I can see Biyaami,' Galari says, excited.

'I can see Biyaami too,' Ngarrang adds.

'Biyaami is always looking down, watching over you and all of our family wherever we are, so we are always together. And your grandfather is flying high up there in the Milky Way, in the campfires in the sky, always looking down on you too.'

The boys listen intently. It's an important moment for Yindy, sharing his knowledge, his love and story with his sons. The Ancient Ones have always guided him, and he hopes that respect will encourage his boys to be the same.

'That is why you should always behave yourself, because the Old Ones, the Ancient Ones, are always watching over you with love.'

'When you die and go to the sky, can you still see?' Ngarrang asks. 'And can you still smell when you are in the sky with Biyaami?'

'You are just like your gunhi, with all those questions.' Yindy rubs Ngarrang's head. 'But it's time for sleep now.' He is tired, and doesn't have Wagadhaany's patience.

When they wake in the morning it is already hot. The boys have kicked off their possum skins but refuse to get up. Yindy laughs to himself at their joyful innocence, but they need to start their journey back.

'Look!' he exclaims, with a hint of laughter in his voice.

The boys race to their father's side. 'What?' they ask.

'Over there . . .'

Yindy stretches his lean arm to the west, towards a rise.

'I can't see it, I can't see it.'

To their great joy, Yindy lifts each of them onto a hip and nods in the same direction.

They frown, still not knowing what they are facing.

'Yerong,' Yindy says. 'See, the outline of a dog, over there?' The boys strain their eyes. 'Over there, we are walking in that direction.'

They walk for hours, until the boys complain of being tired and they set up camp for their last night. Yindy looks upriver; they are close to home. His sons will carry the lessons he has taught them for a long time to come. But now they are ready to see their mother again, just as he is. As he prepares the fire, he hears a cry from Ngarrang and mumbles to himself, 'What now?'

His son is on the ground, holding his ankle, and his brother is on his haunches, looking on with concern.

'He tried to push that log with his foot, Babiin, in case there is a snake underneath.'

Yindy smiles; his sons had listened.

'But I think he broke his foot.'

Yindy looks at the ankle. 'It's not broken, maybe a bit sore inside, but we can fix that. Stay here.'

He walks to a nearby gum that is shedding its bark, strips

some off, and thanks the tree for its generosity. He wraps the bark around his son's ankle, picks him up and carries him over to the fire. That night, he boils up some young leaves from a wattle bush he'd gathered along the way, and makes a billy can of soup.

On the last day of their trip they stumble across some water birds that have been killed in the cruellest of ways. Swans and pelicans have been bashed to death and left to rot on the river-bank, along with shattered ducks' eggs. Yindy takes his crying sons away from the river and makes sure they are safe before he sets about burying as many of the dead birds as he can. He recalls the stories he's heard of station owners telling their men to do this. When eaten with grass, moulting feathers form balls in the intestines of the cattle, which slowly kills them. The men who do the killing are called swan hoppers.

What kind of man could do this? Yindy asks himself.

And when he returns to his sons, they ask the same.

'Who did this, Babiin? And why?'

They howl louder. Yindy wants his boys to be strong, to be fearless protectors, but he understands their distress. He wants to be able to explain what has happened, but he can't find the words.

He holds his boys close, and they walk by his side all the way back to camp. As soon as they see the she-oak where they left their mother and sister, they look to Yindy, silently seeking approval. When he nods, they run as fast as their legs will carry them. He too wants to run, but he'll let them have their time first.

Chapter Twenty-six

'**C**ome quickly!'

Wagadhaany moves the children further away from the riverbank as the Marrambidya begins to rise rapidly. The rains have been falling for days. Debris rushes past; the current is strong and dangerous. The children are scared, and so is she.

Afraid of the devastation she knows flooding can bring, Wagadhaany almost chokes on her fears as her mind carries her back nine years to those dreadful nights when Gundagai lost so many souls to the raging waters. She tries not to recall the moment when the Bradleys drifted away and she was left clinging, cold, terrified and choked by the same fear gripping her right now.

There are no screams or yelling like that night in Gundagai. Rather, the people of the camp move quietly, strategically, purposefully. Everyone is looking after everyone else. No-one is left behind, but the Old People and children are moved to higher ground as a matter of priority. The camp dogs are barking, distressed by the crashing thunder and flashes of lightning.

Many of the men working on stations haven't returned to the camp. It is believed they are taking care of the cattle and the families they work for. The women are busy trying to establish a makeshift resting place until the weather changes. Older boys are helping, and Wagadhaany is grateful that Galari and Ngarrang are old enough, and smart enough, to behave themselves while their father is away. It is her concern for Yindy's safety that plagues her right now.

As she sits in her lean-to, the children huddle close. Her anxiety is overwhelming, and it takes every ounce of inner strength to remain calm. She sings the lullaby that Louisa taught the children when she first visited the camp.

'Bye, baby Bunting,
Father's gone a-hunting,
Mother's gone a-milking,
Sister's gone a-silking,
Brother's gone to buy a skin
To wrap the baby Bunting in.

'Sing it with me, please,' she asks.

The boys do so, even though they are not babies. The twins are now six years old. They cuddle into their mother and Miima, who at two years old is still a baby. They are entertained by the novelty of words they don't know and try to outdo each other by singing the loudest. Wagadhaany doesn't mind the noise; she needs them to be distracted enough not to notice the fear in her eyes.

When the children get bored on the third time around, their singing stops.

'Mama?' Miima cries, as Wagadhaany stares at the grey landscape, rocking back and forth. 'Mama?'

The girl's voice shakes. She and her brothers look at their mother, unaware that she wants to run out into the rain and scream away her fear, her anger, at having to hide from the flood, and her despair at having been away from her family for so many years. When Wagadhaany starts to cry uncontrollably, Miima, Ngarrang and Galari all follow suit. They howl with the wind that has picked up, causing the rain to fly sideways into their shelter.

All four rock together, which at least generates some warmth. As the rain continues to fall, Wagadhaany can see the full moon on and off as clouds move quickly across the sky. Eventually the children spread their bodies across their mother and each other, exhausted. But Wagadhaany stays awake, alert, waiting for Yindy to return, to rescue her from her memories of that awful night, and from her heartache.

As the rain and wind howl around them, she thinks of her brothers Jirrima, Yarran, Euroka, and Ngalan, and wonders how they would protect their own children in the same situation. She calls to Biyaami to take her home. It is time.

When the rain finally stops, the sky clears, the stars fade and the sun shines, as if to say, *It is going to be all right.*

There is movement in the camp. The dogs sniff around, and in the distance there are efforts to get a fire started.

'Are you all right?' Yiray asks, walking towards her, looking every bit as tired as Wagadhaany feels.

'Ngawa, are you?'

'Ngawa. And everyone is safe. Mamaba over there is trying to light a fire to get people warm again.'

There is a hint of a laughter in her voice, and they both look over to where a group of kids stand around watching as an Uncle tries to work magic and turn wet wood into flames. The Old People are sitting on logs, wrapped in possum skins, hoping to dry out quickly and waiting for a cup of hot billy tea.

'Where's Yindy? Have you seen him?' Wagadhaany's voice is shaky, but she is trying to keep herself together. 'Is he back yet? Are any of the men back?' She's only seen the older men walking around the camp.

'Look, down there! Is he there?' Yiray squints and points to a group of men cleaning up the original campsite, which now is all mud.

But Yindy is nowhere in sight.

'He's not there. Where is he? Why are the others back, and not Yindy?'

'He'll be all right, he's probably walking back now.'

'I need him back here, with us.'

During the long night, she had wanted him there because she was afraid of the flood, of what might happen to her and the children. But now she needs to see he is alive. Her heart is racing with fear.

What if he has been caught by the river and swept away? What if he has met the same fate as the Bradleys? The Marrambidya does not discriminate. It does not care what colour a man's skin is, it does not care how important you are to the people who love you, it does not care that one day it can provide you with life and the next it can take it from you.

'Can you watch the gudha-galang, please?' she pleads with Yiray, handing her Miima.

And before she has an answer she is walking towards the town. *Where is he? Why isn't he back? Please Biyaami, give me a sign he is safe.*

337

Her body is weak, her shoulders slumped forward, her hair messy. She has not eaten in the last day, more worried about sustenance for her children than her own wellbeing. Her feet drag along the ground. She feels hopeless and the deep mud and puddles do not help.

Some townsfolk nearby are busy mopping up after the flooding. Shopkeepers are sweeping water from the front of their stores and moving debris to the side of the road, seemingly unaware of her as she passes.

She is almost blinded by the mid-morning sun, and the Bradley homestead appears as a watery mirage. *But it is there!* She feels less anxious, more hopeful now that it is in sight. The last time she visited was the day of the courthouse protest and Louisa's confrontation with James Bradley. She does not care about James now, or Louisa; she can only think of one person, Yindyamarra.

Perhaps he risked his life to keep the horses safe, or was moving the cattle to higher ground. He is the best stockman they have, and would be the most reliable in a time of crisis. Maybe he was asked to protect Louisa; he would do whatever James and David Bradley asked him to. Or rather, instructed him to do. But surely Louisa would know that Wagadhaany would want him with her, with their children. Her head is spinning with scenarios of where her beloved was during the night, who he was saving when he wasn't by her side. She thinks of her father out on the river during the flood in Gundagai, her mother left with the children back at camp. This is the same. Yindy is the same as her babiin. Both heroes, both strong Wiradyuri men doing what the Ancestors have called them to do.

Her steps quicken the closer to the homestead she gets. Sweat drips down her face, mixing with her tears. She is hot from the long walk in the piercing sunlight, and disoriented from lack of sleep.

He will be there, he will be there, he will be there, she repeats over and over in her head, willing Yindy to be alive. Willing the man who has saved her sanity and her soul to still be alive. She still needs him to be a home for her heart when she is so far from her heart-land.

When she recognises his gait and sees Yindy walking towards her, she falls to her knees in relief. She is unable to get up, and in the minutes that follow she cries uncontrollably. Then he is there, picking her up off the ground.

There are no words spoken, only tears of love, of hope, of gratitude. They hold onto each other with an intensity Wagadhaany has never felt. When they finally break from their embrace, Yindy pushes her wet hair from her cheeks to behind her ears, just as he did on their first night together in the river.

Her eyes are dark with sadness, her heart is broken. When she finally speaks, she says the words that she has never said out loud, that she has never been selfish enough to ask. Words that will change the rest of their lives. 'Please, take me home to my miyagan. Please.'

Yindy's migay is broken; Wagadhaany's heart seems to be in so many pieces, he is both concerned and confused. As much as he wants to, he is not sure he can put the pieces back together, in their rightful places. But he knows he needs to act, to fulfil his duty to protect her and keep her safe. He is worried about the years she has spent missing her miyagan, even though his family has always been her miyagan too, even though they have created their own family with three children. He understands the power of being called home.

The time has come. There can be no more waiting, no more hesitating, no more hoping that she will wake up one morning and feel complete. The only way to cure Wagadhaany's sick heart is to take her back to where her spirit is. Back to where she can dance upon the earth that bore her. It is the only way he will ever be able to make her truly happy.

His heart is heavy as he looks at Wagadhaany sitting on the riverbank, watching their children. He wonders if he has ever truly seen her smile. He remembers the first look they shared when she served him food at the station, but in hindsight, he doesn't recall seeing a smile in her eyes. There has always been a darkness beyond her beautiful deep brown eyes, even though he found them alluring. He feels a pang of guilt that he has not rescued her earlier, and his desire to do the right thing now is overwhelming.

From that moment on, he sets about planning their escape; he from the shackles of the Bradleys, and she from the depths of sadness. He has no choice but to take the risk of being caught. Having his love so despondent brings more pain and punishment than he can ever imagine at the hands of Bradleys. He knows he is bound by the Whiteman's laws, but he is also bound by his own lore and culture. His name calls him to act for his family.

That night, as they lie in each other's arms, he tells her they will leave. Together, they will walk the long journey along the river, to her miyagan.

When her response is silence, he pulls her closer, as if they were still in the early days of their love. He whispers his plans to her. She should spend as much time with Yiray and the aunties as possible. The journey will begin soon, and then she will be home.

Chapter Twenty-seven

Since learning she is going home, Wagadhaany has walked through the days with elation flowing through her veins, with her heart feeling light and yet full with happiness. The many years of darkness and depression have been replaced with gratitude and hope, as she imagines what her life will be like back in Gundagai. She waits impatiently for the moment they can leave Wagga Wagga.

It is with trepidation that she walks up the drive to see Louisa, but she needs to say goodbye. She has little idea what the homestead looks like these days, nor what greeting might await her today. She recalls their conversation years before, about the tree transforming into a broom, and wonders what transformation, if any, she might find today.

As she reaches the door, Wagadhaany reflects on the secret she must keep. She wants to trust Louisa, but she and Yindyamarra agreed that she would not tell her about their leaving Wagga Wagga. Yindy will be breaking the masters and servants law and the risk they are taking is already high enough.

You are my family now, Louisa had said. And for Wagadhaany, family is everything. You protect family. You nurture family. You do everything to make your family happy. She hopes that after all this time, Louisa has come to understand what family means to her, and will understand why Yindy must take her home.

She knocks gently, not expecting Louisa to answer the door herself after seeing so many servants on previous visits.

'Wagadhaany!' Louisa exclaims. 'It's so wonderful to see you.' She throws her arms around her. 'I have missed you.'

Louisa's enthusiastic reaction causes Wagadhaany to take a step backwards.

'Come, come, sit! I've just made scones, let's have a cup of tea.' Louisa moves swiftly in the kitchen. 'It really is so good to see you. Did you walk? Where are the children? How is everyone at the camp?'

The questions come thick and fast, and Wagadhaany smiles. How easy it is for her to be there now as a visitor, as Louisa's friend.

'How did you manage in the storm? I was thinking of you, terrified here, of course. I just haven't had time to visit.'

They sit in the kitchen for hours, Louisa insisting on hearing about every single person she has ever spoken to at the camp. Wagadhaany realises that she has missed the affection Louisa truly has for her, and for her people. It has been there from the moment they met, during all the time she worked for the Bradleys, but she understands now that her suspicions about Louisa's motives had blinded her to it. She wants to tell Louisa that she now sees her caring and commitment, and that she is sorry for being so guarded. But she doesn't say any of that.

When Louisa runs out of questions, there is a long silence. The house appears deathly quiet.

'Where is your help, Louisa?' Wagadhaany eventually asks. 'I've only just noticed there's no-one else here.'

'I am alone today.' Louisa takes the cups to the kitchen sink as if to prove she is the only one to do the work now.

'Why? Since when? Is everything all right?'

'Oh yes, Wagadhaany, I am fine, though disappointed in myself.'

'But why do you choose to be alone? And why are you disappointed?'

'Sometimes we don't always keep our own actions in check, we don't realise we are saying one thing and behaving in another way. You taught me about being true to my word, and reminded me of my intentions coming here to Wagga Wagga when you asked me what I had actually done. And right you were to ask.'

'I did?' Wagadhaany is pleased that she has achieved something, even if she never set out to do it.

'You asked me how I could have servants, when it went against everything I believed in. And everything I really wanted in life. I didn't want servants, and today I have staff. I pay them. And I try to treat them as equals. Small steps, Wagadhaany, can lead to bigger changes.'

'And yet you didn't stop David Bradley making me come with you to Wagga Wagga.'

'Wagadhaany, I must tell you something. You are right that David made you come. But it was me, too. You gave meaning to my life after the flood. When David explained about the Masters and Servants Act I believed him. It was something that, well, was accepted. I should never have accepted that at all. But I was selfish, happy you were coming to Wagga Wagga with us. I was relieved, even though I could have talked James into letting you stay in Gundagai, because I wanted you to be with me.'

Wagadhaany is lost for words, struck by the pain of knowing the truth. Her head starts to spin a little, and she shakes it, trying to clear it and her initial feeling of doubt about what she may have heard. She frowns and stares fiercely at Louisa, and breathes quick, sharp breaths in shock. The one White person she thought was good was no better than all the others. She slows her breathing, forcing her anger deep inside. She knows there is no point in ending this visit with Louisa or herself in tears. It takes some seconds but she calms herself while Louisa is still talking, still trying to justify her behaviour.

'I can see by your face you are upset, Wagadhaany, but I never treated you like a servant! Did I?'

'No, but Mr Bradley did,' she replies, unwilling to let Louisa get off that lightly. 'And you watched him.'

'I'm so sorry. I was blinded by love, he was blinded by arrogance *and* ignorance, and neither of us could see the damage it was doing to you.'

Wagadhaany is certain that neither of the Bradley men were remotely concerned about her wellbeing, but she reminds herself that she is going home soon, so there is no point in upsetting Louisa now.

'I gave myself a good talking to, Wagadhaany. It's easy to do that when you are alone and no-one can hear you acting crazily.' She laughs, but they both know how true those words are. 'I thought deeply about my Quaker values, and what I have seen in this town, and back in Gundagai, and about what I have been party to since marrying James.'

With one hand on her chest, Louisa says seriously, 'I come from a proud Quaker family.'

'I know, Louisa. I have always known that. You don't have to explain that to me.'

345

'No, I do need to explain. I need you to understand what *I* have come to understand. It's taken me years to understand myself. You must believe me when I say I have never – Quakers have *never* – supported slavery. We have denounced it for centuries in America and Europe.'

Wagadhaany does not know where America or Europe are, but she does know the meaning of slavery. She has heard the Old People use the word when talking about station owners like James Bradley.

'The English who come here use Aboriginal people as cheap or free labour, and while they might not call it slavery, in my books it's not far off. I thought I was helping by having the women here, but I wasn't. And when some of them were handled by the stockmen . . . well, I wanted that to be the end. But the reality is the station is too big for me alone to cook for the men, and tend the garden and so on.'

'So you still have servants? Where are they?'

'When the stockmen are away droving, I tell the women to stay home. I pay them what I can, and they can take vegetables from the garden. And I make clothes for the children, and sometimes I ask them to bring the little ones here so I can read to them. And when the men are here, I am nearly always close by, so they *never* have an opportunity to hurt any woman, not here, not while I am alive and breathing.'

'But what about Mr Bradley?'

'Oh, James has no idea. I could not do any of this if he was around. But he is away so much now because he *is* the mayor.' She rolls her eyes at Wagadhaany.

'But it's such a big lie, Louisa.'

'I know, but as I told you, marriage is a compromise, and I've made a compromise with myself, letting go of one value to hang onto another. It is for the greater good, Wagadhaany, I am sure of it.'

'How is your life now that you are *the mayor's wife*?' Wagadhaany rolls her eyes as well, as if it's their secret code.

'I am on show a lot of the time, but I manage. And in terms of my Quaker work, it's still a battle in terms of turning my intentions into reality. James hates it when I talk about social justice, and I still can't convince him that the servants were in fact slaves. He refuses to listen to me when I talk about it.' Louisa stops abruptly. 'But I *did* remind him he married a Quaker, and that he fell in love with a woman who knows her own mind. He'd prefer a more subservient wife, and I'd prefer a more tolerant husband. I know I'm repeating myself but marriage is a compromise.

'We both know that James is far from perfect. He has a bad temper when he drinks, but deep down he is not a bad person. If we are completely honest with ourselves, we are all flawed. Some more than others.'

Wagadhaany shrugs her shoulders.

'The truth is, he loves me, Wagadhaany, and I love him. And there is a physical attraction that I cannot deny. We need each other. He is really all that I have to hold onto, in so many ways.'

And in those words, Wagadhaany finds the answer to the questions that have plagued her for years. How could she and Louisa possibly be friends? What do they have in common? The answer is simple: they have mostly respected their differences, tried to accommodate each other's needs. Above all, they share the human emotions of love, loneliness and loss that have connected them daily, often without them even being aware of it. And finally, they share the feelings that come with loving a man.

'But,' Louisa adds, 'having you surprise me like this, drink cups of tea and talk to me, these are the moments I truly cherish. And that I miss.' She rests her hand on top of Wagadhaany's. 'Please come more often.'

Wagadhaany's heart feels heavy. She will not be visiting for cups of tea and eye-rolls ever again. Today is her farewell to Louisa. She feels awkward. Louisa seems to be waiting for a response.

'Do you still want to have children?' she stammers, hoping that Louisa doesn't notice the change in her voice, and also hoping the question does not upset her.

Louisa sighs deeply before answering matter-of-factly. 'I have come to accept that I cannot have children. It might be me or it might be James, but either way, it is not God's will for me to become a mother.'

'I'm sorry,' Wagadhaany says softly. She doesn't know what else to say.

'Oh no, please don't be. I'm all right. Truly I am. A new room was added to the school some time ago. I spend a lot of time there now, helping out where I can. I am not trained, of course, but I am teaching the children to read.'

'You are very good at it, and the children at the camp love you reading to them.'

Louisa accepts the compliment graciously. 'Thank you. I have found a maternal role of sorts in the classroom, where I can be with *lots* of children.' She looks out the window. 'I have learned to be happy.'

'You sound happy, Louisa,' Wagadhaany says, though she is not convinced that Louisa is as content as she claims. *How can she be, when she admits to loving a man who does not allow her to fulfil her own dreams or be true to her values? More importantly, how can she accept not being a mother when that is what she dreams of most?*

'There is no point being anything other than positive. Of course, it is hard, very hard, and I was sad for a long time. I blamed James, he blamed me. All that blame and disappointment . . .'

A wave of guilt rushes through Wagadhaany. Louisa had been so helpful and understanding each time she was pregnant, and it must have been hard for her, knowing that her dream of holding her own child would never become a reality.

'I am so sorry, Louisa.'

'You are the kind of mother *I* wanted to be. And when I stopped being stupidly envious, I was happy for you. I *am* happy for you. And so,' she places her hand back on top of Wagadhaany's, 'there is nothing to be sorry for. It is no-one's fault. It is God's will and I accept that He has bigger plans for me.'

Louisa's belief in her God must be like her faith in Biyaami and the Ancient Ones, Wagadhaany imagines, and so she doesn't doubt her or judge her, even though she still feels sorry for her.

'The school gives me purpose and I will continue to chip away at James with my ideas. Who knows, maybe *one* day, he will see the way.'

'Mr Bradley is not a Quaker though.'

'No, he is not, he is Catholic, but he also believes in God and the Son of God, and I often have to remind him to follow the example of Jesus.' She smiles. 'But he always has an answer for me: Jesus wasn't a businessman, Jesus wasn't the mayor.'

'Mr Bradley *can* be charming sometimes,' Wagadhaany offers, remembering his boyishness when he was first courting Louisa.

'He can be, but he forgets that. If only he understood that human beings are all the same. When he bleeds, he bleeds red, just like the Aboriginal stockmen who work for him.'

Wagadhaany sees a transformed woman, one who is clearer in her thoughts and words, aware of what she is capable of.

'Sometimes I think my dreams were too big. Change is impossible in a place where women do not have the vote, where we are treated as extensions of men, not as individuals in our own right. If only all the townsfolk were Quakers, don't you think?'

Maybe Louisa is right. *But what if the entire town lived by Wiradyuri values of miyagan, yindyamarra, ngumbadal, murrumbang? What if the White people put family, respect, unity and love before business and cattle?* Louisa has dreams, and she has values. Right or wrong, she is stronger and more capable than the woman Wagadhaany met in Gundagai. Whatever happens once she leaves, Louisa will be all right.

'I must go now,' Wagadhaany says, standing. 'Louisa . . .' She pauses. The words *I am leaving* sit uncomfortably on the tip of her tongue. Before her is the one White person she has come to know well, and grown to love. She is overcome by the thought of most likely never seeing Louisa again. How can she walk away without saying a proper goodbye?

'Yes?'

'I am happy you are teaching at the school, and teaching Mr Bradley. I think you have found what you call your mission.'

'Perhaps I have. Yes, perhaps I have.'

For the first time ever, Wagadhaany leans in first and gives Louisa a hug. As she rests her head on Louisa's shoulder, she feels tears beginning to rise. The words want to come out. She wants to say goodbye. She wants to say thank you. She wants to whisper that she is her miyagan too. But she doesn't. She can't. She hopes that somehow Louisa can read her actions as well as she reads the books she brought to the camp. She steps back, sees the look of gratitude on Louisa's face and turns to leave.

'Wait.' Louisa hands her a parcel of biscuits. 'These are for the women. Tell them I will visit again soon. And we can have your billy tea and talk some more.'

'They would love that. *I* would love that.'

Smoke rises from the fire where everyone has gathered for a corroboree marking a new life, and the farewell of a family.

Yindy walks with his sons into the middle of the circle. They wash the cleansing smoke of the gum leaves over their bodies, then turn around and lift their feet and let the smoke wash over those too. To his left are Wagadhaany and Miima, his two-year-old daughter lifting her tiny feet in imitation of her brothers' actions. Wagadhaany wears her feather headband and breathes deeply. This singing is their goodbye to those they love here. It is the end of their life in Wagga Wagga for now. When the new day dawns, their journey along the Marrambidya to her heart-land will begin.

Chapter Twenty-eight

In the cold of the morning Yindy can see his breath in the air. Mist rises across the campsite. They must depart quietly so as not to risk being spotted by locals. Many in the camp are still sleeping; this is how he and Wagadhaany planned it. The corroboree and feast the night before is all the farewell they needed.

The twins are fooling around and making more noise than they should. Yindy needs them to calm down. Their escape from Wagga Wagga must be silent and swift, and they need to cover as much ground as possible before full light.

His mother waits for him, arms folded tightly across her chest. Her posture suggests she is cranky, but he knows her well enough to understand that her heart will be breaking, and that her arms are keeping her heart within her chest. It is the goodbye he has dreaded most, the one he has pushed to the back of his mind, knowing how difficult it will be for her to see him leave, to watch her grandchildren walk away. His own heart is heavy as he considers the pain he is causing her. But that weight is lifted every time he sees the joy in his migay's eyes when she talks of being back in Gundagai.

One by one the children hug their grandmother. She picks each up and whispers into their ears. Miima is too young to understand what is happening, but she cuddles with love and enjoys the attention. They walk over to the aunties, and as much as the twins want to wake their cousins, Yindy glares at his sons in a way they know means they are not to.

But then his daughter lets out a noisy wail as her Bamali Yiray hugs her too tight. Realising they are going somewhere, she wraps her tiny arms around her bamali's neck, refusing to let go, not wanting to say goodbye.

'Yindy,' Wagadhaany says, pulling him to her, 'that was me saying goodbye in Gundagai, only I wasn't a child, I was a grown woman.' She is sobbing too. 'This is the only miyagan Miima has ever known.'

He understands that one day he will need to bring their daughter and sons back here. The sense of belonging to your birthplace never leaves you. Their children may leave Wagga Wagga, but Wagga Wagga will never leave their children.

When Yindyamarra says his goodbyes, his mother's arms are forcibly removed from around her son by the aunties and he walks away slowly, choking back tears and the sadness of the farewell.

The family heads east, Yindy leading the way, flanked by his sons. Wagadhaany carries Miima, who has fallen asleep.

Using the trees as indicators, Yindyamarra leads them upstream, remembering everything the older men have taught him about reading the landscape. When Wagadhaany wanted their boys to learn to read the books Louisa brought to the camp, he would ask himself, *What good is it to read books if you cannot read the land you live on?*

They follow the Marrambidya into the morning sun. The boys are slow, touching everything, wanting to look at wagiiy-galang and ngumbarrang-galang and ngurragawundil-galang. They kick over logs with their feet the way they have been taught. They entertain themselves, competing to see who can see what first, singing out the names of birds and animals at the top of their lungs: gugubarra, wilay, gugaa, ngarrang, wandayali. As much as it pains Yindy to stop his sons having fun, he keeps shushing them for fear of being heard. Although they have been walking for hours, they are still not far enough away from Wagga Wagga to relax.

Yindy panics when Ngarrang shouts, 'Gadi!' and Galari screams in fright at the top of his lungs. Ngarrang drops to the ground, laughing. There is no snake in sight, and while Yindy wants to laugh, he can't. He is worried about being caught, about their dreams being squashed because they were careless. He is worried about what will happen to him if he is caught. He looks at Wagadhaany with a frown and shakes his head. He puts his hand firmly on the shoulder of the young joker and says, 'We need to keep moving.'

As they walk, Yindy thinks about the men at the station. At this time of day he is usually with Mudyi, working with the other stockmen. *They will know by now that he isn't there, but will they have guessed he has left for good? Will they look for him immediately, or will they wait a while?* He can't know what they will do.

As the sun moves to the western sky, he knows the day is drawing nearer to dusk, and his children are tired. With Galari on his shoulders and Ngarrang on his back, his body is feeling the strain. When he turns to look at Wagadhaany he sees her exhaustion also.

'Let's rest,' he says, lifting his sons to the ground one at a time.

'Here?' Wagadhaany asks, her voice tired.

He nods. Close by is the fresh running bila, where his sons are already waiting in anticipation of some fishing.

'Look!' Ngarrang points to a scar tree. 'Guluman!'

'Ngawa.'

Yindy is proud his sons are trying to read the landscape, and he's pleased he is walking in the footsteps of others who have passed this way. He wonders if they were seeking their freedom as well.

'Come,' he calls.

Together, father and sons collect branches and sheets of stringybark to build a ganya, while Wagadhaany gathers kindling for a fire.

'Fishing?' Yindy teases his sons.

They can barely contain their excitement and are at the water's edge within seconds. Miima waddles down behind them but is quickly shooed away by her brothers. She starts crying.

'Come here,' Wagadhaany calls out, and her daughter waddles back, rubbing her eyes.

Within minutes, Wagadhaany is showing Miima how to weave grasses. When Yindy catches a glimpse of them from the riverbank, he wishes he could spend the rest of his life here, in this sanctuary.

It is not long before the sun disappears and Yindy asks his sons to help him make a fire. They take turns to keep the drill stick spinning until the fire takes hold. Dry grass is piled on until the flames are hot enough to cook their fish. The boys are proud of their catches and of being able to feed their mother and sister.

'I love the bila,' Galari says.

'*I* love the bila,' Ngarrang echoes.

'Bila!' Miima mimics, pointing to the river.

Wagadhaany bursts out laughing. Yindy has never heard her laugh so heartily. It's as if in one day their life has completely changed, their spirits lifted, all because the weight of homesickness has left her heart. And he has never been happier.

That night is the beginning of the rest of their lives and Yindyamarra, while already missing his clan, is focused on what lies ahead. As they sit around the fire, he tells them stories of how all the rivers are connected, how Biyaami created it that way. He draws a map in the sand to show the river system as he knows it from years of droving, and from what he remembers coming from his birthplace on the Galari as a child. He tells the stories his own father told him growing up. He recalls what the men at the camp shared with him over the past few years.

As the children wriggle and fidget, they still look at their father. And Wagadhaany listens with new interest, as if this is the first time Yindy has spoken to her of these things. There are no interruptions, no wild dogs barking in the background, just one man and the people he loves most, together, safe, living the way they want.

Yindy smiles as he shares stories about the creeks, the swamps and the lakes he camped by while droving, where he caught fish in the summer, wambuwuny in the colder months and smaller animals like lizards and water birds in spring. His sons are wide-eyed, but it's Wagadhaany's eyes that he really notices. There is a softness to them he hasn't seen before; the darkness has faded since they decided to leave Wagga Wagga. He has always found her alluring, strong. Even with the lines around her eyes now showing the signs of age and the hard physical work she has done over the years, she is still the most beautiful woman he has ever set eyes on.

As he drifts off to sleep, Yindy recalls the song lines, the connection to landscape, and when he sees a shooting star, he is reminded that his Ancestors will get his family safely to Gundagai.

At dawn, he is up and his sons are waiting for the next adventure. He is surprised that Wagadhaany is still asleep, her arms wrapped around Miima. When she finally wakes it takes her some time to rise.

'Let's stay here,' she says to his surprise.

'But I thought you wanted to get home.'

'I do. But when we get there, it will be like the camp in Wagga Wagga, with all the ganya-galang and gudha-galang, and all my aunties like your aunties wanting to be with us all the time. It will never just be us, like this, ever again.'

Yindy is concerned about staying where they are. Will they be safe from the authorities? He thinks about the Black stockmen and he knows they will never give up one of their own. He thinks about the White stockmen who hated him and who would never take themselves down the camp by the river to look for him. He also believes that the red-faced Charlie would never think he would be brave enough to try to run away, so they won't look for him just yet.

'Yindy?' Wagadhaany breaks his focus. 'The bamali-galang – no peace. Can we stay?'

He looks at the sparkle in Wagadhaany's eyes and his heart melts for the woman he loves more than life itself. He tells himself they will be safe there a little longer.

357

Yindy finally laughs. 'You have never said anything truer. If your aunties are like mine . . .' He shakes his head with the widest of smiles, thinking about Prickly Aunty and the hard time the other women give her. 'You are right, this is our last chance for peace. But let's ask them,' he says, nodding towards the boys, who are keeping their distance from, but watching intently, a little bird.

'Ngarrang! Galari!' he calls out.

They barely register his voice.

'Ngarrang! Galari!' he calls again, with more authority.

The pair jump to attention but say nothing, just look at their father, waiting for instructions or chastisement. He smiles to himself; there is so much of his own childhood in his sons – their inquisitiveness, their mischievousness, their fear of getting into trouble.

'Do you want to stay here a little while longer?'

'Ngawa! Bila!' the boys scream with excitement, knowing they'll be able to fish again.

Their excitement fuels Miima. She struggles to get out of her mother's hold and waddles over to her brothers, clapping her hands and giggling.

'I think you have your answer,' Wagadhaany says.

The following days bring a sense of peace and freedom neither Yindy or Wagadhaany has ever known. They rise with the sun and the birds, and focus only on their children and each other. They are all full of enthusiasm and energy during the day, fishing, swimming, learning how to make rope. Miima learns new words as Wagadhaany tells her the names of all her special cousins and other family she will soon meet.

Yindy feels like his life is complete; they are finally free of the shackles of the White people forcing them to live a certain way, in certain places. To live a life that was never explained to him by his Old People.

But on the third day Yindy's fears take over. By this time, Charlie and the Bradleys would surely know he wouldn't be coming back. He knows they need to keep moving, and so they start walking again.

As they travel further, the children want to walk less and rest more.

'We can't stop, we must keep moving now,' Wagadhaany says to her sons, who moan.

Finally, after many hours, Yindy listens when his sons say they want to sit and eat quandongs from the trees they use as markers along the way, when they want Yindy to tell them a story at a scar tree. Every stop, every story, every fruit picking and eating moment adds time their journey, but the further away they get from Wagga Wagga, the more he feels he can relax and relish these moments. He breathes in the time they are enjoying together, free to eat and sleep where and when they want.

Galari and Ngarrang walk ahead, skimming rocks across the river at times, turning logs with sticks, half-climbing trees. Yindy has his eye on them constantly, conscious that Wagadhaany and Miima are trailing behind.

'Yindy.' He hears his name faintly from behind. 'Miima needs to rest.'

Wagadhaany isn't complaining, but he can see by her posture that she needs to rest too.

He nods, signalling there is just a little way to go so he can look for a suitable campsite, but he waits until she is by his side and they walk together. Wagadhaany is humming, lost in thought, while Yindy carries their daughter. The twins walk in a zig-zag fashion ahead of them.

'Mabinya!' he sings out. 'Stop! Come!' He waves them back to where he has put Miima on the ground. 'We will camp here.'

The pair turn around.

'Can we swim?' they plead.

'Wiray, not until I can be there with you, the current is too strong.'

'Can we sit at the edge of the bila?' Galari asks.

Miima claps her hands and bounces on her bottom, excited too.

'At the edge, do not go in. Do you hear me?'

'Ngawa. Ngawa.'

'And watch your sister,' Yindy instructs his sons as they walk down the riverbank.

Miima follows, and when they get to the edge of the water, they walk straight in.

'Bila! Bila! Bila!' Miima points to the fast-flowing water, reminding her brothers of their father's warning, but both boys just look at her with contempt. They don't want her there, and they certainly don't want her telling them what to do.

'MABINYA!' Yindy yells.

The boys jump so high with fright he can't help but laugh. Wagadhaany is amused as well, but he finds his authority again. 'Didn't you hear what I said?' he yells.

'Ngawa!' the twins answer in unison.

'Why don't you try to catch us something to eat? A man must feed the women in his family.'

The two boys nod and busy themselves finding the nets they made a few days before.

Yindy watches as his sons walk to the water's edge. They stand on a rock, staring into the river. He imagines they are looking for their dinner and smiles as they squat, trying to catch fish but missing every time. He shakes his head as his daughter approaches and her brothers again shoo her away.

'Stay there,' Galari orders Miima.

'Yeah, we don't need a girl coming with us,' Ngarrang adds.

Miima clumps some wet sand together in her tiny hands and throws it towards her brothers. The mud doesn't travel far, and Yindy laughs at her effort. It is hot, very hot, and he knows she wants to go for a swim too. He can't take his eyes off her; she is the image of her mother.

As Yindy helps Wagadhaany prepare the ground and shelter for their camp, he feels again his new sense of contentment. His fears of being caught have subsided. They have come so far. Maybe Louisa Bradley talked James Bradley down, or maybe Charlie didn't have the tracking skills to find them. Either way, he knows they are free.

His beloved will soon be reunited with her miyagan and her spirit will be renewed. His children will get to know their clan. Most importantly, Wagadhaany will be home.

The days that follow are joyous, fun, without fear or dread. Yindy feels like they are living the life his Ancestors lived for years upon years. He has travelled the countryside droving the cattle and he knows that this is new country for him, that teams have never come this way. The land has not been worn.

He relaxes into the days. The boys cut a guluman large enough to go fishing in and they catch enough cod to feed them all. Wagadhaany spends time with Miima, teaching her as best she can how to move her tiny feet and dance. She makes her daughter a headband, just like the one her own mother gave her, which she has worn every day since they left the camp. Her bond with her daughter continues to grow as they search for ochre, which they will carry with them along the journey.

Yindy's heart swells seeing the two together; they remind him of his sister and mother.

'We're going fishing!'

The boys appear from nowhere and race right past their mother and sister, running to the water's edge.

'Ngalamarra!' Miima squeals, pointing to the river, to her brothers. 'Ngalamarra!'

She points to her father, who is so proud his two-year-old daughter has learned so many new words.

Wagadhaany shrugs. 'What do you think we talk about all day, while you men are off without us?'

He shrugs back, laughing.

'We talk about *everything*!' she says, with a twinkle in her eye as if it's a warning.

'Guluman?' Miima asks, wanting to go on the river with the boys.

Yindy laughs. 'Nwaga, come.'

She follows him like his shadow, stepping into each of his footprints as if it's a game. He counts and she repeats; ngumbaay, bula, bula ngumbaay, bulabu bulabu, marra. When they reach the river, he wades in with her on his hip, then lifts her into the makeshift canoe.

'Guluman,' she says, wriggling into place.

As he pushes the craft against the strong current, Miima puts her tiny hands over the sides and splashes him, laughing. Wagadhaany is watching from the riverbank and Yindy can see the resemblance in their dark eyes and hair, and their beautiful, cheeky smiles. He pushes Miima's hair behind her ears and she shakes her head, giggling.

The freedom of being in control of how they spend each day has been life-changing. When they leave the next day it will be by choice, not out of fear.

As they eat the day's catch by the fire at dusk, Yindy says, 'I had thought it would take many more sunrises than this to get you home but I feel,' he looks to the low moon in the sky, 'that we are not far away now.'

'I want another day like this. I want the sun to rise again but it hasn't even set properly yet.' She laughs.

He leans over and kisses her forehead. She may have had three children, but she is still the young woman he fell in love with by the river under a blanket of stars and a rush of nerves. His love for her has never wavered and tonight, as they get closer to their destination, he feels he loves her more than ever.

'I used to sleep like this with my cousins,' Wagadhaany says to her children as they lie down to sleep. Miima is wedged between her and Yindyamarra, and the twins are on either side of them. 'Our legs would get twisted up together, and we would giggle until my babiin, your grandfather, would sing out for us to be quiet and go to sleep.'

The kids twist and giggle until Ngarrang ends up in tears. His crying makes Miima giggle, and suddenly they are all laughing. Yindy raises an eyebrow at Wagadhaany but stops himself from saying, *You have made our boys soft, but the girl, she is clever.*

'Sleep now,' Yindy says.

The sun is barely above the horizon but Wagadhaany is already up, preparing damper before they start the final stretch of their journey to Gundagai.

'Go and wash your faces,' she instructs the boys. Miima follows them to the river. 'But don't go in the water,' she yells. 'Stay on the edge, and watch your sister.'

'I'll finish here up here,' Yindy smiles, as he rolls up their possum skins.

And then it happens.

'Mama! Babiin!'

The cries that come from Galari and Ngarrang chill Wagadhaany's blood and pierce her ears. Yindy drops the skins and runs to the river. She runs as fast as she can behind him.

'Where's Miima?' she screams. 'Where's your sister? Where is she?' She grabs Galari, shaking him. 'Where's Miima?' She can hardly breathe with the choking fear.

'Down there!' Ngarrang points.

But the girl is not in sight.

'Where?' Yindy yells frantically, running into the water.

'She wanted to go in the guluman,' Galari says, shivering. 'She wanted us to put her in it. She was pointing and laughing, and then she cried when we didn't do what she wanted. Mama, she wanted us to.'

'Nooooooo! Miima!' Wagadaany follows Yindy into the river,

slips, regains her balance and keeps walking, all the while calling out for her daughter. Her only thought is to see Miima safe. But the current is too strong, she is being pulled with it, and she knows that by now Miima will be a long way downriver.

'Yiiiindyyyy!' she screams, panic rising from the pit of her stomach.

He turns, looks at her briefly but doesn't speak. He pushes his body swiftly across the current, then wades to the bank. He climbs up the slope and starts to run downstream. As the twins sit howling, Wagadhaany watches as Yindy jumps over branches and leaps great lengths, until she can no longer see him at all. Yindy will find their daughter. He is Wagadhaany's hero, and he will be Miima's hero too. She tells herself that he will save her. He will bring her back and then they can start walking home again.

'Mama!' the boys cry.

She wades back to the bank, steps out of the water, pulls them against her body and starts to sing. She calls on Biyaami to protect her daughter, to bring her back to them safely. She rocks back and forth, tears streaming down her face.

Eventually the boys move away from her, watching and waiting for their father. She walks in circles, looks in all directions, disoriented, angry, afraid. She squints into the sunlight, desperate for any hint that Yindy is returning, that they are both returning.

'Babiin!' Galari cries out, pointing downriver. 'He's coming!'

He sounds happy and Wagadhaany's heart fills with hope. Relief washes over her. She runs to where the boys have been on lookout. Yindy is carrying the guluman. And then she sees the limbs of her daughter, draped over the sides of the guluman, dangling, lifeless.

Wagadhaany sits with her knees pulled in tight, slowly rocking back and forth, back and forth, back and forth, as if rocking her baby daughter to sleep. Yindy is on his knees behind her, leaning into her, ready to catch her. She wails over and over and over. *Yamawa? Yamawa? Yamawa? Why? Why? Why?*

Every heartbeat is painful.

Her vision is blurry, as if there is never going to be an end to the tears. It feels like someone is standing on her chest, trying to stop her heart beating all together. She wants to die like her daughter, her little star, her Miima. She doesn't want to live with this pain that is strangling her.

'Mama?' Ngarrang whispers in her ear, putting his arms around her neck. 'Please don't cry.'

His voice is soft, gentle and his pleading cuts deeply. He is too young to comprehend the meaning of death, or know what grief is. She can't look at him, or Galari, not yet. They are too young to blame, but somewhere within, that is what she feels.

The day turns to night, turns to another day, and Wagadhaany hasn't slept, hasn't stopped crying. She lies on her side, with Miima wrapped in a possum skin, curled up as if she is still in the womb, as Miima once was. She remembers the night she gave birth and how the night sky lit up for her baby daughter.

'I want to get you home, we need to get Miima home,' Yindy says. 'I will carry her back with us.'

She does not look up, she does not know where to look. She shakes her head. 'You cannot carry her, it is too far.'

'We must go,' he says quietly, his giiny breaking with every word.

'How can I move my feet forward, how?' She stares into the distance, her face blank, her eyes red and teary. 'I left Gundagai with heartbreak, empty inside, and I return the same way.'

She continues to rock back and forth, thinking again of the night she gave birth to Miima by the river. The bila gave her life, and now it has taken it away. The same bila that gave her so much joy with Yindy has devastated her. She wants to walk into the Marrambidya right now and not walk out, to stay there until her spirit meets her daughter's.

After a long time she speaks again. 'My mother once told me that death means going back.' She wipes her nose with the back of her hand and takes a deep breath. 'That when someone dies, they are no longer here in the real world, but they have life in the spirit world.' She stops talking, blinks away her tears.

For a fleeting moment she feels for the Bradley brothers. Now she knows what it is like to have lost someone to the force of the Marrambidya. And for the first time, she truly understands the loss suffered by Louisa. This ache inside is what the death of a loved one feels like, and the only thing that will bring her out of this chasm of despair and hopelessness is her responsibility to care for her surviving children. If not for them, she would wish only to sleep and never wake again.

She takes the ochre she and Miima collected together, and prepares her daughter for burial. Yindy readies the boys, and together they send their daughter and sister to the Wiradyuri Ancestors who will be waiting for her. There are no words, only wailing and interminable heartache.

Yindy gently takes Wagadhaany by the arm and urges her to walk. She is disoriented, unsure how her feet can be moving forward while she is leaving her daughter behind.

Wagadhaany wishes Yindy had not woken her. She is exhausted, her whole body in pain, every part of her aches. Nothing can heal her broken heart. Still, she forces herself to rise, knowing she will soon be with her miyagan again. Her only incentive to keep walking is the thought of her parents' arms around her again. But not even the thought of their reunion eases the devastation she feels.

They walk in silence, grief stealing any fun, any conversation, any chance of enjoyment. At dusk, a soft pink sky attempts to break through the clouds. Wagadhaany stops still. Yindy, Galari and Ngarrang continue to walk ahead, but her feet are rooted to the ground. She knows this is her birthplace, she can feel it in her bones. She recognises the slope of the land, and even though the grass is dry, not deep green, each tree seems to be welcoming her back. She feels lightheaded, dizzy, and for a fleeting moment her pain subsides. She has arrived. She is home.

She walks slowly in a circle, taking in the landscape, looking for her miyagan, for anyone she resembles, but there are few people to be seen. Her heart beats fast at the thought of reuniting with her parents. *But where are they?* She wants to scream that she is home, that she has returned.

She sees Yindy talking to some local men. They are pointing, giving directions, looking at the setting sun as if determining the time. He comes back to her, disappointment etched on his tired face. She is too frightened to even contemplate what might be wrong, too scared to imagine any more death.

'They say your miyagan, many miyagan-galang have left, moved to a place called Brungle. There is something called a mission there, where Aboriginal people live.'

Wagadhaany doesn't understand. She can't comprehend that after all she has been through, all the years she has waited to come back to her birthplace, to her miyagan, that they are not here.

She collapses to the ground, and Yindy drops to his knees to catch her.

'Maybe they are lying,' she sobs. 'Maybe my miyagan *are* here.' She looks up, scans the area, sees Yindy's tear-filled eyes. 'How do we know it is true, that they have gone?'

Yindy pulls her up, his sons helping, their hands around their mother's thighs.

'I believe it is true. Those men,' he points in the direction of the ones he had spoken to, 'their own miyagan-galang have been moved on as well. It is happening everywhere, to all our people.'

His chest rises and falls, and she knows he is concerned for her, for them all.

'We should go to this Brungle, there is no reason to stay here,' he says.

She feels her heart break again, when she had thought nothing could bring her any more pain. She shakes with the agony of all that has happened, losing her daughter then finding her family gone to a place she has never heard of. It is too much for her spirit to bear.

'I can't go on. I can't,' she weeps, and she collapses again.

'Mama.' Galari throws his arms around her neck. 'Don't cry, Mama, we will help you, come.'

He takes her left hand, motions his twin to take her right, and together they manage to lift her back to her feet. It makes her want to cry harder, the recognition that she must go on for her sons. She forces herself up, Yindy assisting from behind.

'Come.' Yindy is gentle with her as she slowly puts one foot in front of the other, unaware of the direction or the pace at which she moves. Her mind is a fog, her body numb, as they walk towards the place they call Brungle.

She has no idea how much time has passed or how far they have walked, but Yindy and her sons are still holding onto her. They have found the mission.

She feels a wave of acknowledgement wash over her, as a breeze drifts gently over her skin. Her Ancestors are with her. And the land has the same low-lying hills as Gundagai even though they are no longer following the powerful Marrambidya. Yindyamarra's instincts have brought them safely to this place, she knows, but she must take these final steps alone.

Her breathing becomes faster, stronger, as do her steps.

She breaks from Yindy's hold when she sees ganya-galang in the distance, and people milling about. They are dressed in Whiteman's clothes, but are unmistakably Wiradyuri. There are women with children, and men smoking. Yindy and their sons look at her, hopeful that this is the place, her people, their people.

And then she sees him, her babiin in the distance. Her legs move faster, carrying her heavy heart forward. Tears are falling down her face. She is desperate to reach her parents, to throw her arms around them and finally feel safe again, feel at home.

She wants them to tell her that things will be all right, that the years of homesickness and heartache weren't real, that her daughter Miima is still alive. That they can all live together now, free from being controlled and working for White people, and that her children will have a better life.

The closer she gets, the harder she sobs, and although her tears won't stop falling she can see her babiin's face: sad, disappointed, disempowered. Even at a distance her father looks old and weathered, as broken as she feels. And it breaks what is left of her heart.

When they fall into each other, they are overcome by the years of yearning to be reunited. Their embrace marks the end of one journey and the beginning of a new one.

During the long minutes they hug, the universe all but stops, and then there is cheering and screeching, laughter and weeping.

'She's home!' her gunhi screams, running across the mission. 'She's home.'

Wagadhaany puts her arms around her mother and clings to her. She will never let go of what she loves *ever* again.

'Come this way.'

When her gunhi ushers her behind a huge she-oak, Wagadhaany is confused. Why is she being hidden?

'What are you doing?'

'We aren't alone, we don't live alone here. Someone is watching over us every day.'

'Someone watching? Where?' Wagadhaany looks around to see who that might be.

'Over there,' says her babiin, 'he has his own hut. He is called a mission manager.' Her father nods in the direction of the manager's hut.

'Let me look at you, properly.' Her gunhi steps back, her hands still on her daughter's shoulders. There are tears streaming down her cheeks. She pulls Wagadhaany in close again, tightly, as if no-one will ever pry them apart.

Wagadhaany notices the greying hair on her gunhi's temples, the lines around her eyes and along the corners of her mouth. She looks tired and thin, not as she remembers her when they lived on the river and ate well from the land. She doesn't say anything though, just watches and listens.

'You're home, you're home, you're home.' Her gunhi hugs her tighter. 'It will be all right now. I am your mother, and I tell you it will be all right.'

Wagadhaany doesn't know how she can tell her gunhi about Miima. She looks into her mother's eyes and sees the love only a mother can have for a daughter, the love she has for Miima.

As if her gunhi can read her mind, she says, 'The Ancestors will take care of everything, my girl, they will.'

Yiramiilan pulls her daughter to her chest again and they stand motionless for a long time, oblivious to everyone who has rushed to their sides.

Suddenly Wagadhaany feels a tug. The aunties are there, and also miyagan wanting to properly greet the girl who was sent away. They want to welcome her back too, meet her husband and children.

When mother and daughter are finally broken apart, Wagadhaany can see there is as much love today as there was on the day she left so many years ago.

For the first time since Miima passed, she smiles. She is spun around and around by her brothers and cousins and second and third cousins. And all the balgabalgar-galang surround her, crying and hugging and cheering. This is the love of family she wanted her baby girl to experience, to be immersed in. This is the love that will bring her own spirit back to life.

Chapter Twenty-nine

Life in Brungle

Every morning for the past few days Yarri has greeted the sunrise with gratitude, looking in the direction she first appeared. Every sunrise he thanks Biyaami for bringing her home. He has stopped being bitter about the years he lost while she was with the Bradleys, and instead relives the joy of their reunion, the relief he felt at seeing her again, the happiness that every day since has brought him.

His heart swells watching his grandsons find their own identities within the clan. Shy when first introduced to everyone, they are now thriving on all the attention.

Most importantly, he is grateful for the man Yindyamarra, the one who brought their daughter back. He looks to the campfire where the one who has protected Wagadhaany is now sitting with the other men, the young ones at their feet. He sees the pain in Yindy's eyes, aware of the responsibilities and sense of loss borne by a man who is grieving the loss of his own daughter, and having to be a strong patriarch at the same time.

Yarri is sitting alone, contemplating how much he has missed out on, when he is startled by Wagadhaany sneaking up behind him. They haven't had much time to talk privately since she arrived; her return has been exciting for everyone. She appears on her own, and he looks to the skies with gratitude once again and waits for the endless stream of questions. Her face has aged, but he can tell his daughter's inquisitive mind is still ticking over. Somehow, he will need to explain why they are living in Brungle.

'Babiin, tell me why we are here. Why would you leave our home?'

'We had no choice.' He coughs. 'We lived for a while on the edge of town in Gundagai, near where we lived when you were with us, but we were told that the White people didn't want us there. So, they moved us here, with other people from Tumut, just along that way.' He points in the direction of the other town. 'They are our people too, but they didn't want to move either.'

He shrugs, shakes his head and coughs again. He feels resigned about his life now, but hopes his daughter can't see it. He still wants to be her hero, the strong babiin he should be.

'Tell me about the mission manager.'

He takes a deep breath, understanding he must tell her about their life now.

'Your mother calls him the mission monster.' He shakes his head. 'He is from the government in the city and he controls *everything*.'

'What do you mean *everything*?'

'He tells us what we can eat, where we go, even who people here can marry.'

'How can someone control your heart, Babiin?'

He shrugs his shoulders. 'It is the Whiteman's law we live under now. They have their laws and we have ours. And they are very different.'

They look to where the children are gathering for their lessons, in a hut they call a school. Yarri is not sure how this school will make their lives better, but they have been told that to be a good parent you must send your children there.

In the distance his wife is waving her arms as she speaks to the manager's wife.

'Your gunhi gets wild whenever he is around. She always stands up to him. It scares me and makes me laugh at the same time. I think she scares him a little too.'

'Some things haven't changed then.' Wagadhaany smiles.

When Yarri sees the warmth and love in his daughter's eyes his heart melts. 'But you know he cannot control our breathing, and we are alive and here together again, and that is all that matters right now, for me anyway.'

He takes his daughter's hand in his, as he did when she was a child and they strolled the streets of Gundagai as the town was being built.

Galari and Ngarrang appear, panting from running around. They sit at their grandfather's feet, taken by the sound of his deep voice. He rubs them both on the tops of their heads. His heart bursts with joy just having them near. Their presence goes some way to easing the pain of being without his daughter for so long.

'They have your high forehead and long legs,' his daughter says, smiling at him again.

'I am sorry you came home to this place, to these laws, and that now your children have this life too. Maybe Wagga Wagga was a better place for you all.'

'No, Babiin, nowhere is better than being with you and all my miyagan. I don't know what the future holds, but right now I want to be here, with you. This is where I belong.'

He feels a tug on his arm.

'Tell us a story, Mumala,' Galari says.

'Ngawa,' Ngarrang adds.

'Let me tell you about the waawii . . .'

When he sees the twinkle in his grandsons' eyes, he grins widely. Knowing there was a granddaughter who should be here with them is heartbreaking, and he wishes desperately that he could take away his daughter's sorrow, but for now he must focus on his grandsons.

As all the gudha-galang gather around, he tells a tale of the bunyip.

Wagadhaany looks on. In time she will understand what mission life means. He hopes that it doesn't break her spirit.

As the sun hangs high in the sky above them, the moment is precious. And it is his. He looks at his daughter and his heart swells. She is home.

'Now let me tell you a story about your Wiradyuri miyagan, the people of Marrambidya.'

Glossary of
Wiradyuri Words

With thanks to Dr (Uncle) Stan Grant and Dr John Rudder and all their significant work on Wiradyuri language reclamation. *A New Wiradjuri Dictionary: English to Wiradjuri/Wiradjuri to English* (Restoration House, 2010) forms the foundation of the language used in this novel. I have also used the Wiradyuri Dictionary app (with language spoken by Dr Stan Grant, Elizabeth Grant and Midnight Brydon). In my novel I have chosen to use the spelling 'Wiradyuri' as there is no 'j' in our language alphabet. The 'j' sound is made by the letters 'dy'. 'Wiradjuri' is commonly used by most today, and is recognised by the government, as noted in *A Grammar of Wiradjuri Language* by Dr (Uncle) Stan Grant and Dr John Rudder (Restoration House, 2014). Many Wiradyuri words have multiple meanings and some words have many different spellings. I will be learning for the rest of my life.

babiin – father

bagabin – a beautiful bluish flower

balang – head

balgabalgar – Elder, group leader, chief, ruler, leader

bamali – aunty

bila – river

bila wurrumany – river son

bila yarrudhanggalangdhuray – river of dreams

bilabang – Milky Way, billabong

bila-bula – river pair

binbin – belly

birig – ghost or spirit

biyaami / baayami – the great spirit

bubul – buttocks, backside

budhanbang – black duck

budhang nyiwarri – black sweetheart

bula – number two, a pair

bula ngumbaay – number three

bulabu bulabu – number four

dharang – general term for any kind of snake

dharraay – please

dharru – bee

dinawan – emu

dyirridyirri – willie wagtail

euroka – the rising sun

gaagang-gumbal – older brother

gabaa – white man, stranger

gadi – snakes

galang – many

Galari – Lachlan River

ganya – shelter, house or dwelling

gari – truth

garradyang – fibre

garru – magpie

giigandul – prickly silver wattle with a silver flower

giiny – heart

ginan – kind, gracious

gudha – baby or child

gugaa – goanna

gugabul – Murray cod

gugubarra – kookaburra

gugurmin – a very dark place in the Milky Way, said
to be an emu

guluman / gulumba – wooden container

gumbal – brother

gunhi – mother

gunhinarrung – grandmother

gurgur – very deaf

jirrima – mountain

kuracca – white cockatoo (in honour of Kerry Reed-Gilbert)

mabinya – stop, wait

mamaba – uncle, grandfather

mamadin – wife, husband (spouse)

mandaang guwu – thank you

marambang ngulung – handsome face, beauty

marang ngarin – good morning

marang yariya – good evening

marganduli – pregnant

marra – number five

marradir – rock

Marrambidya Bila – Murrumbidgee River
marrumbang – love, kindness
mayiny – people
mayilgan – death
migay – young woman, girl
miilgi – large drops of rain
miima – star
mingaan – older sister
minhi – younger sister
mirri – dog
mirrigan – dingo
mirriwula – devil dog, ghost dog
miyagan – kin, family, relations
mudyi – friend, mates, companions
mulbirrang – eastern rosella
mulyan – eagle
mumala – grandfather
ngalamarra – fishing
ngalan – a light
ngamurr – daughter
ngamuwila – desert pea
ngarrang – water dragon, lizard
ngawa – yes
ngindhu – you, one person
ngumbaay – number one
ngumbadal – unity, union
ngumbarrang – bug
ngurambang – country, home
ngurambula – spotted bowerbird
ngurragawundil – small beetle

ngurrbul ngindhu – love you
nyinmaay – penis
waadyin – White woman
waawii – bunyip, large water snake, legendary water creature
wadhagung – rabbit
wagadhaany – dancer
wagiiy – ant
walga – hawk
wambad – wombat
wambuwuny – grey kangaroo
wandayali – echidna
wandha – fish
waringinali – cousin
Way! – Quiet! Be quiet!
wilay – brushtail possum
wurrumany – son
wunaagany – cousin
Yamandhu marang? – Are you good? Are you well?
yamayamarra – help, assist
Yamawa? – What for? Why?
yarraman – horse
yarran – sacred tree
yinaa – woman
yinaagang – young woman, girl
yindyamarra – respect, be gentle, be polite, to honour
yiramiilan – sunrise
yiray – sun
yiri – light
yullara – long-eared bandicoot
yuwin ngadhi – my name is

Historical Note

Heroism in the Great Flood of Gundagai

There has been much written about the Great Flood of Gundagai, and my work aims to complement all that is already in print.

It's important to note that *Bila Yarrudhanggalangdhuray* is a fictionalised account of what transpired in June of 1852. My goal in writing this novel was to highlight the heroism of the Wiradyuri men who braved the dangerous floods to bring locals to safety: Yarri (also known as Yarrie, Yarra, Yarry or Coonong Denamundinna), Jacky Jacky (also known as Jackey Jackey or John Morley, after Joseph Dillon Morley, who adopted him following the death of his mother), Long Jimmy and Tommy Davis. I felt compelled to write their story into the national literary landscape to reach the broadest possible audience.

Many readers will recognise the name 'Jacky Jacky' as it was commonly used by Whites in place of an individual's own Aboriginal name. Over time, 'Jacky Jacky' jokes have appeared as part of 'Australian humour', but these attempts at humour are always derogatory, racist, and they often stereotype Aboriginal men.

It was many years after the flood before Yarri and Jacky Jacky received any recognition for their heroic acts. In 1875 they were given an engraved breastplate each and granted a lifelong pension from the settlers. Yarri passed away at around the age of 70 in 1880 in Gundagai hospital. Jacky Jacky died in 1908 at 72 years of age.

In 2017, on the 165th anniversary of the Great Flood, the Gundagai community unveiled a bronze sculpture on Sheridan Street, of Yarri and Jacky Jacky with a canoe. Sculpted by Darien Pullen, the unveiling brought national attention to the men.

In 2019, both men were awarded posthumous bravery awards for what the then Governor-General Sir Peter Cosgrove described as 'considerable courage'.

It is important to note that Yarri, while a hero in the flood, was also reported to have killed a 16-year-old Aboriginal woman by the name of Sally McLeod, near Gundagai in 1852. On 15 September the *Empire* newspaper reported that there were warrants for his arrest, with the hopes he would be imprisoned:

HORRIBLE MURDER.—Intelligence has just been received at the Crown Lands Head Quarters, Tumut, through the Tumut blacks, by Mr. McKenzie, the Crown Lands Commissioner, for the Murrumbidgee District, of the most diabolical murder of a half-caste girl, named Sally McLeod, by an aboriginal named "Yarree," or "Coonong Denamundinna," son of Bobby King, of Adelong country. The girl was about sixteen years of age, and possessed considerable personal attractions, spoke English well, and was baptised in infancy. She roved about occasionally with the blacks, under protection of her uncle, one of the Tumut tribe, but was more generally at the residences of the white settlers, who were kind to her. It appears that Yarree decoyed her away to be his "gin," but repenting of the act, or disgusted with him, she made her escape, with a view to reach Darbalara, where she had always met a kind home; when the murderer overtook her below Tarabandra, on the Tumut, and satiated his revenge, by her murder. The blacks having described to Mr. McKenzie where Yarree had buried his unfortunate victim (under a tea-tree in a tea-tree scrub), about 15 miles below headquarters, Mr. McKenzie at once started with his sable friends to exhume the body for identification, &c., notwithstanding the really dreadful state of the weather and flooded state of the country, and has, besides, issued warrants for the apprehension of the murderer in every possible direction—even as far as Yass, out of his district—by which prompt and energetic measures there can remain little doubt but that Yarree will ere long be in safe keeping. The girl was the daughter of Mr. McLeod, of the Tumut district, who is at present in Argyle with Mr. Hindmarsh, buying bullocks for the Melbourne market.—*Goulburn Herald*.

We don't know if Yarri did or didn't commit this heinous crime as there appears to have never been a conviction. I chose to create a fictional Yarri whose role in the rescue could allow him to be a symbol of extraordinary and largely unacknowledged heroism at the time.

Today there are many tributes honouring Yarri and Jacky Jacky:

1960: Wallace Horsley (grandson of R.F. Horsley, who was rescued by Yarri) erected a sculpture of the hero in front of the family property.

1961: The Horsley Family presented a sundial to the people of Gundagai to honour Yarri. It sits on the grounds of the Historical Museum of Gundagai.

1969: Arnold St Clair depicted Yarri and Jacky Jacky in a mural in the Criterion Hotel, Gundagai.

1980: The Historical Society of Gundagai commemorated the centenary of the death of Yarri by erecting a plaque in the front of the local museum.

1984: Yarri Bridge was opened by the Honourable Terry Sheahan.

1990: A plaque was unveiled in Gundagai, in Yarri Park.

1990: A monument was erected in North Gundagai cemetery. The headstone reads, 'In memory of Yarri, Hero of Gundagai.'

2017: A Gundagai community committee, including members of the Wiradyuri community and descendants of those saved by Yarri and Jacky Jacky, erected a bronze sculpture in Sheridan Street, Gundagai. The nearby plaque reads, 'The Great Rescue of 1852 . . . in honour of the Wiradjuri heroes.'

2019: Yarri and Jacky Jacky received posthumous bravery awards.

Brungle Station

Brungle Station in the Tumut Plains region was set up in 1888 following complaints from residents of Tumut and Gundagai about Aboriginal people living on the outskirts of town. The Aborigines Protection Board (APB) believed that Brungle, being halfway between the two town centres, was the best setting and would deter 'the natives' from loitering in or around the towns.

Brungle Station, which became known as Brungle Mission though it was not a mission run by the church, was then gazetted in 1888 with a purpose of assimilating Aboriginal people so that they could live a 'superior' White life. The station was overseen by the APB and managed by a station manager. There were eleven station managers between 1890 and 1954, when the station officially closed in February.

Googedee Aboriginal School was established for Aboriginal children at Brungle Station in 1888 and it was later amalgamated with the Brungle Public School, against the wishes of the local Brungle residents. In 2018 Brungle Public School celebrated its 150th anniversary with cultural activities and speeches from past students at the school.

For the purpose of this novel, Brungle Station opens before 1861 to allow for a timelier return of Wagadhaany to her family.

A great resource for information about the Brungle Mission is *Brungle, Tumut and Region: An Aboriginal History*, compiled by the Brungle Tumut Aboriginal Community and National Parks and Wildlife Service.

Quakers

Many of the earliest British settlers in Australia were Quakers. In 1832 two prominent English Quakers came to Australia with the support of their congregations. According to Quakers Australia, 'Although their main concerns were the treatment of the convicts and of the Aborigines, they also travelled around Australia contacting as many Quakers as they could. This resulted in the formation of a formal Quaker group in Hobart, where they were mainly based, and later, groups in other States.'

The foundation of this novel always centred on the relationship between Louisa and Wagadhaany after the flood. But it was on learning about the Quakers' interest in Aboriginal people and convicts that it became clear to me that Louisa's character would embrace those values and ideals, giving her a greater sense of purpose (realised or not) and the want for a deeper connection with her new friend and the local Wiradyuri people.

You can find the Quakers Australia website at www.quakers australia.org.au.

The Masters and Servants Act

The *Masters and Servants Act 1840 No. 28a* ostensibly protected the rights of both masters and servants. In reality it protected the masters. A servant was not allowed to disobey their master, be absent from work for any length of time, or leave their job without permission. The punishment was harsh: a servant could have their wage confiscated or be imprisoned.

It is likely that the Masters and Servants Act applied to Aboriginal people in theory. Though it is uncertain, it is highly probable that the legislation played out in practice, too. It is fair to assume that the Wiradyuri people lived in fear of it.

Resources

The author notes that this is not a comprehensive list. Please visit www.anitaheiss.com for a full list of resources used as research for this novel.

A New Wiradjuri Dictionary, compiled by Stan Grant (Snr) and Dr John Rudder. Wagga Wagga, Restoration House, 2010.

Aboriginal Women's Heritage: Wagga Wagga. Dept of Environment and Climate Change NSW, 2007.

Aboriginal Women's Heritage: Brungle and Tumut. Dept of Environment and Climate Change NSW, 2007.

Blood on the Wattle: Massacres and Maltreatment of Aboriginal Australians since 1788, Bruce Elder. Frenchs Forest, New Holland, 2003.

Land of the Wiradjuri: Traditional Wiradjuri Culture, Paul Greenwood. Wagga Wagga, New South Wales Riverina Environmental Education Centre, 2014.

Wagga Wagga: A History, Sherry Morris. Wagga Wagga, Council of the City of Wagga Wagga, 1999.

Wagga Wagga Community Heritage Study Volume 2: Thematic History. Heritage Council of NSW with City of Wagga Wagga, 2013.

Wiradjuri Heritage Study for the Wagga Wagga Local Government Area of New South Wales, compiled by Go Green Services in conjunction with the Community of Wagga Wagga. 2002.

Wiradjuri of the Rivers and Plains, Iris Clayton and Alex Barlow. Port Melbourne, Heinemann Library Australia, 1997.

Wiradjuri Plant Use in the Murrumbidgee Catchment, compiled by Alice Williams and Tim Sides. Wagga Wagga, Murrumbidgee Catchment Management Authority, 2008.

Yarri: Hero of Gundagai, Allen Crooks. Gundagai, NSW, 1989.

Author's Note and Acknowledgements

In January 2018, I started learning my Wiradyuri language as I entered my 50th year on the planet. The experience of being home on country with my miyagan was life-changing. Being back on my homelands was a gift, and it allowed me to reflect on the life my Ancestors led, particularly in and around Wagga Wagga, where our classes at Charles Sturt University and barefoot along the Marrambidya Bila were held.

It was during this time that I learnt that Wagga Wagga was known as the place of celebrations – not the place of many crows, as it had long been misinterpreted. And my time there over the next two years, and since graduating the course, has always been a form of celebration for me.

Hearing language fall easily from the mouths of my teachers, Dr (Uncle) Stan Grant, Letetia Harris, Lloyd Dolan, Yarri Lambshead, Professor Sue Green, Peter Ingram and Debbie Evans, while enjoying the stories and support of Elders like Uncle Pat Connolly, Bidyadya Elaine Lomas (Aunty Swannie),

Aunty Gail Manderson and Aunty Bonita Christian-Byrne, was a privilege.

Continuing to learn language remains a celebration and connection to Wiradyuri mayiny, to the ngurambang, and to a culture once denied our mobs. For me it is a reclamation of sovereignty, and a chance to be part of the process of rebuilding our mighty nation. But it's also a journey I am fortunate to share with many others.

It was while I sat wrapped in the love of the yinaa-galang in my course and listened to the words and wisdoms that Uncle Stan Grant and his protégés shared, that I came to a deeper understanding of myself, and how blessed I am to be able to gather, share, learn together in a way my mother couldn't.

As part of that journey of learning, I stood in the floodplains in Wagga Wagga one Sunday, and I tried to imagine life there for my Ancestors. I realised very quickly I had to honour those Ancestors who for millennia had lived, loved, and nurtured the land and each other. And I wanted to pay tribute to those who carry on culture, knowledge and language still today. I felt I had a responsibility as an author to write our Wiradyuri heroes – our men and women – into the Australian narrative where they had been ignored or forgotten for too long. When hearing the story of Yarri and Jacky Jacky and their heroism in the Great Flood of 1852 in Gundagai, it became clear their story was a fitting place to start.

I may be the author of this book, but it is filled with the love, the knowledge, the wisdom, the support and the yindyamarra for Wiradyuri life and values of so many others. It is with a heart full of gratitude that I thank Uncle Stan Grant and Dr John Rudder for their extraordinary work in documenting our language.

An extra special mandaang guwu to Uncle Stan and Aunty

Betty also for their unwavering love and support on this journey, not only to me but to all of us. And Uncle Stan's unfailing generosity and patience in teaching those who choose to learn.

To my Wiradyuri yinaa-galang – Rebecca, Teesh, Bec and Reggie, Candy, Helen, Nokes, Cheryl and Bronwyn – ngurrbul ngindhu always.

This manuscript had the support of generous readers and smarter people than me, whom I wish to thank. From the early days of the project till now, I have valued Miriam Crane's counsel on the story of Gundagai and this work as historical fiction generally. I would also like to acknowledge Peter Smith (Chair) and the entire Yarri and Jacky Jacky Sculpture Committee for their work in bringing the lives of our heroes to national attention.

For feedback and thoughts on the various stages of the manuscript I thank Miriam Crane, Rebecca Connolly, Lloyd Dolan, Aunty Elaine Lomas, Letetia Harris and Yindy, Jessica Bulger, Kerry Kilner, Angela Gardner, Ian Horsley and Aunty Sony Piper.

Mandaang guwu to my cousin Luke Penrith for allowing me to use his artwork of the gugaa on the cover. Thank you to Samuel Dalgarnowebb for early research (as part of an AustLit internship) and Carol Williams for research assistance from afar.

Libraries are the homes of so much knowledge, not only on the shelves but behind the counter. So thank you to staff at both Gundagai Library and Wagga Wagga Library for your support along the way.

Many thanks to Leanne Collingburn and Chelsea Zwoerner (Norton Rose Fulbright Reconciliation Action Plan Working Group) for their much-needed assistance with historical legal research as part of truth-telling in the novel.

For original commissioning and editing thank you to Roberta Ivers and Janet Hutchinson, and to Cass Di Bello, Bronwyn O'Reilly, Dan Ruffino and the extraordinary team at Simon & Schuster, gratitude for helping me share this important story.

To my agent and friend Tara Wynne, Caitlin Cooper-Trent and all the team at Curtis Brown who take me, my work and my purpose seriously, I am always grateful.

I acknowledge that my role at the University of Queensland affords me time to work on significant projects like *Bila Yarrudhanggalangdhuray* and my heart is full of gratitude to my colleagues in the Aboriginal and Torres Strait Islander Unit for their unswerving support.

Finally, to Mum – for always being there, role-modelling dignity, commitment, love and respect. This is for you.

Read on for an excerpt from *Dirrayawadha* (*Rise Up*), another
groundbreaking historical novel about resistance, resilience
and love during the frontier wars by Anita Heiss.

A n i t a
HEISS
Dirrayawadha

'A story of courage ... Anita Heiss is a remarkable writer'
TONY BIRCH

From the award-winning author of *Bila Yarrudhanggalangdhuray*

Chapter One

'There are too many white ghosts here,' Windradyne whispers to his sister Miinaa, and she is thankful to hear her natural tongue after a day of trying to speak only English at Cloverdale. She is exhausted mentally and physically as she tries to settle three restless gudha-galang for the night. The eldest, Giyalung, is an astute six-year-old, Yarruwala, a confident five-year-old, and Ngawaal, a boisterous four-year-old.

Miinaa's accommodation consists of a small room with a single bed pushed against a stone wall. The full moon can be seen through the window above the bedhead this evening, and the sunrise will wake them in the morning. Even though other windows at Cloverdale have curtains, she prefers the natural light – it reminds her of sleeping under the stars before she arrived at the Nugents' property. There are lumps of wood fashioned into something to sit on in one corner and a small lamp offers a dull light as she puts the children's meagre belongings neatly in one spot.

Windradyne's own children live with their mothers along the Wambool Bila, as do the rest of their miyagan. Other families are scattered across Wiradyuri ngurambang. Some live and work on land granted to, and now legally owned by, white settlers. The arrangement that Miinaa has at Cloverdale is unique, and not something many others want. Some see it as becoming like the white ghosts. But Windradyne just wants his minhi to be safe.

'This is what the Gubbna Ghost wanted, back when he drove that carriage to our ngurambang many, many nights ago,' Windradyne says, with a bitter tone. 'When they built that road over our trading routes, when the white men in rags and chains came here as their punishment, they brought punishment upon us as well. Making us live *their* way.'

Miinaa was a younger girl when the white ghosts first arrived, but she recalls the day that the Gubbna Ghost raised a piece of red, blue and white material and renamed her homeland a settlement, calling it 'Bathurst'. She remembers vividly the first time she ever saw a white ghost: his coat was the colour of blood, and when he removed that coat, she thought he was peeling off a layer of skin. She had to blink hard before realising there was another layer of cloth there, and then very, very white skin beneath that. She felt silly that day, but then she felt sick.

Those earlier times, of seeing convicts arrive, threw her into emotional turmoil she'd never known. Seeing them beaten if they did not work past exhaustion shocked her and the other yinaa-galang, but they came to learn it was important for the white ghosts to finish the road, so that more of their kind could arrive. And that the people giving the orders were often far, far away.

It was back then that she first realised her gumbal, Windradyne, was a leader; that it was his role to meet the leader of the white ghosts, the one they called the Gubbna. He took that meeting with two other men, and they were given some food and tomahawks and a piece of yellow cloth in exchange for a possum skin cloak.

Her thoughts are broken by the sound of Ngawaal giggling.

'The gudha-galang are restless tonight,' she says, smiling, grateful for the laughter of the children, the only joy in her long day. 'They've had a good feed of wambuwuny, thank you,' she says to her brother, who is known as a skilled hunter among their own. She observes him as he watches the children; she notes his strong features. Some yinaa-galang say he is marambang ngulung, but she never strokes his ego. She also thinks it would be strange to tell your brother he is handsome.

Miinaa has a much smaller frame than Windradyne; she hasn't the height of her brother, but is lean like him. Her dark hair falls down the length of her back and is tied together loosely with a piece of calico to keep it off her heart-shaped face. Her full lips curve upwards tonight after many hours in the vegetable patch today, and she thinks sleep will come easily to her tired body.

As Windradyne plays with the children, she admires his strong Wiradyuri features, similar to most of their men, and she can see both Yarruwala and Ngawaal are growing to have the same body shape and looks: broad shoulders, muscular arms and legs, and thick, black curly hair. Windradyne has his hair pulled back tonight, and his beard is plaited in three sections.

She hopes the young boys who look up to Windradyne will have the same physical strength, and walk with the same fierce pride and confidence, when they're older.

But Miinaa also sees a side of him that many don't – the gentle, loving man, not afraid to show ngurrbul to the younger ones in their Clan. And it warms her heart when he visits them at Cloverdale straight from hunting, bringing with him wild turkey or geese for everyone to enjoy, or when he takes the gudha-galang out fishing.

Tonight, the children seem extra happy to see their uncle, and he tickles Ngawaal, making the child chuckle loudly. When the youngster pulls on Windradyne's plaited beard, he mocks pain and falls to the ground groaning, making them all laugh.

'Why you have this, Mamaba?' Ngawaal asks, pulling on his own chin. 'And why this many?' He holds up three fingers.

'One for each of you gudha-galang.' Windradyne tickles the young fella some more.

Their laughter warms Miinaa's heart. There hasn't been much to smile about of late, as the Nugents' station continues to grow, with more convict workers, which means more work for her, cleaning, cooking, tending to the needs of her miyagan but also the owners of Cloverdale, Andrew and Susanna Nugent, and their children, Oscar, Edward and Lalla. Yesterday, she had to darn all the socks of the men on the station, and threading a needle was an exercise in patience she didn't enjoy.

'And why this?' Ngawaal asks his uncle, touching the red cloth wrapped around his forehead and tied at the back.

Windradyne picks the gudha up and rests him on his lap. 'This says I am a warrior.' He watches the young one, whose eyes focus on the cloth as he runs his little hands along the band, concentrating on the sense of touch. 'You come from a long line of strong Wiradyuri mayiny, and you will grow into a big, strong man one day. You'll be next in line soon enough.'

'Your gumbal is the next warrior in line,' Miinaa says, pointing to Yarruwala.

'And then you!' Windradyne lightly pokes Ngawaal in the belly, making him wriggle about.

'*Me?*' he asks enthusiastically. Miinaa's heart fills when she sees pride in the child.

'Yes. Your name, Ngawaal, means power and force. And you carry your name within you.' Windradyne rests his palm on the boy's chest for a moment. 'It is part of your identity.'

'I *am* powerful!' The child beats his chest and chuckles.

The five-year-old pipes in. 'What does *my* name mean, Mamaba?'

Windradyne's grin tells Miinaa that he's happy to be sharing culture with the children. 'Yarruwala means very strong and almighty.'

'Ha!' Yarruwala boasts to Ngawaal. 'I am strong, and *almighty*.' He flexes his barely-there muscles.

Miinaa knows their sister will want to be front and centre of the activity, and seconds later she's there, forcing the two boys out of the way, pushing her face up close to Windradyne's.

'What about me? What does *my* name mean?' she asks excitedly.

'Your name means that you are very, very smart.'

'I'm very, very smart,' she says proudly in the direction of the boys, her blue eyes lighting up her face.

Miinaa and Windradyne glance at each other knowingly. It is never spoken of by the adults who know the dark girl with the blue eyes was born from rape. Her mother's role with a settler was often exploited, and then one day she was abused in the most heinous way, her spirit never the same after the brutal attack. Before the child was born it was agreed between the Clan that the happy-go-lucky girl would only ever be told she was loved, that she had grown from love, and would always be loved. Giyalung had been nurtured and protected in the communal way the Wiradyuri had raised all their gudha-galang, generation after generation, for tens of thousands of years. She is one of the reasons they have ended up at Cloverdale – it is added protection for the young girl. For all of the children.

Miinaa understood the look of grief and anger in Windradyne's eyes whenever Giyalung asked about her own story, though; it reminded them both of the violation, and the need to avenge it. The fire that stirred in his belly was stirring in hers as well.

'I'm smart,' the girl says again, satisfied, without asking anything else, and crawls into the bed sheets next to Yarruwala, while Ngawaal climbs back onto Windradyne's lap.

'Where's the line you said?' he asks, pulling on Windradyne's plaits.

'What line?' Windradyne doesn't want to sound cranky, but Miinaa knows he's tired and that the plait tugging will be annoying him. He takes Ngawaal's hands in his own and holds them still.

'You said that I was in line after Yarruwala. Where's the line?' The child looks around the cramped space.

'Ngawa, Windradyne, where's the line?' Miinaa laughs, and her brother shakes his head and rolls his eyes.

'It's not a line you can see, silly.' He rubs the boy's head. 'It means that you're the next man in the family to do an important job.'

'What job?' The boy's eyes are wide, as if what is expected of him in reaching manhood is something to look forward to.

'Your job will be to teach your sons and their sons the same stories, the same responsibilities that you will learn as you grow up to be a man.'

Ngawaal springs from Windradyne's lap and stands tall, chest out, ready for the call to manhood and yet too young to understand what that call will look like in years to come. Cloverdale and Wiradyuri ngurambang is set to change dramatically.

'What's *your* name mean, Mamaba?' Ngawaal asks.

Miinaa smiles. It's a long time since she's heard his birth name, and she looks forward to his answer.

'Well, the name I had when I was your age was Wiinymaldhaany, and that means fire maker.'

'But, Mamaba, why does everyone call you Windradyne?'

'You ask a lot of questions, Ngawaal, and I'm too old and too tired for any more talk.' Windradyne lifts the young boy from his lap.

'Into bed now.' Miinaa ushers Ngawaal who climbs willingly between the sheets, squishing into his sister's back. Yarruwala is then pressed up against the wall where he is trying to get to sleep. The three tussle for a few seconds before quietening down.

Ngawaal rolls over and faces the adults, eyes wide open. 'Mrs Nugent said when you are tired, you say it's time to sleep.'

'Then it's time to sleep,' Miinaa says, tucking the sheet tight under the thin mattress so the child can't escape easily, as he is prone to do at night.

'Come,' Miinaa says to her brother and nods in the direction of the far corner, where she places the lamp on a tree stump used as a table. Windradyne follows, rolling his shoulders as he walks.

As they sit, Miinaa whispers, 'What's wrong, gumbal? Why so much worry in your eyes?'

He shakes his head and sighs, taking his time to answer. 'I don't know how much longer we can be welcoming, friendly to the white ghosts. We have tried for long enough, but there is no yindyamarra from them.' He looks over to the bed. 'And then, even when we are kind, they treat our women . . .' His voice trails off, but she doesn't need him to say anything more.

'I know.' Miinaa agrees with him generally, but feels the need to defend the one family that has always shown her Clan yindyamarra. 'But the Nugents have treated us as friends. They've acted kindly towards us.'

'They treat us kindly, ngawa, but, Miinaa, they just treat us like we're human, how we *should* be treated. We shouldn't think of it as special. It's how *everyone* should act towards each other. With kindness, with ngurrbul, and ngawa, always with yindyamarra. But that's not the case with the other white ghosts.'

Miinaa understands the point her brother is making. She knows that since the white-skinned tribe arrived, things have never been equal. There has been some courtesy and exchanges of knowledge and trading of goods and food, but she has never felt the same about life on their own ngurambang.

But the Nugents, the Irish people she works for, the people who have given them a room in their house, who let her Clan move freely on what is now regarded as *their* land – these white ghosts are learning the language that Miinaa and Windradyne have spoken since birth. In her heart she believes that *this* family is different.

'They may not understand our connection to ngurambang, but they do listen when we talk, when we tell them things they should know,' she continues.

Windradyne nods in agreement, then says, 'But the rest of the white ghosts, they don't care though. They don't listen, and they don't want to know.'

'I know, gumbal,' she nods. 'But the Nugents are trying to do it the right way. We're showing that sharing is our way of doing things too. Surely, learning about each other will help us understand each other better.' It's a question as much as a statement, and there's hope in her voice. It's a hope that her brother does not share. Windradyne believes that hope is a luxury in a landscape that is rapidly changing in ways that do not benefit his own people. Even Miinaa is learning that hope can be a wasted emotion.

But hope is all she has these days, as she watches her brother get more frustrated, angrier, overwhelmed by the changes happening around them daily: more white ghosts, more foreign animals and plants, more pressure on their own food supplies, more movement off their traditional lands as they are fenced off for the invaders to control. More of everything except control of their own daily lives, because that has declined since the first white ghosts arrived. Even speaking language now they mostly do in private, forced otherwise to speak the white ghost language around them.

'Windradyne?' she prompts. Her brother is bowed over, with his head in his hands.

He sits upright. 'It's true the Nugents are walking with us, but why can't all the white ghosts show the same yindyamarra?' His voice has started to rise and Miinaa puts her finger to her mouth, nodding in the direction of the gudha-galang, who are finally asleep. He nods, and speaks more quietly.

'It's one thing to welcome a few of these ghosts, to show them our campgrounds, and where to find food; to be hospitable and caring as you would be to visitors to your home. But it doesn't mean they can take *over* our home, *our* ngurambang. We never agreed to that; we never said that was all right, that we approved. We never *gave* them what is rightfully ours.'

'I know, gumbal, but we're here, at Cloverdale. We're safe and the gudha-galang are happy.' The children are always her main concern.

'Ngawa, but I think Andrew and Susanna Nugent feel they owe us, because one day I showed them where the creek and the rivulet met, and then they built here.'

Miinaa is not sure about her brother being responsible for where the Nugents built their house, but she lets him continue.

'And, ngawa, we're all safe and happy, but you're here to work, to help raise their children. Others are simply being pushed off their land, moved away, having to find new places to camp along the bila. Most are not as lucky as you and the gudha-galang here.'

Even though she has to live the white ghost way, Miinaa knows her quality of life is better than other yinaa-galang on stations nearby, because the Nugents are kind to her. Mrs Nugent is teaching her and the gudha-galang the language of the ghosts and they work together to grow potatoes and cook for the family and the employees.

'I guess it's good, too, that the Nugents are the Irish tribe,' Windradyne says, adjusting the lamp to make the room darker as Ngawaal's eyes are still open. 'I understand them to be better than the English tribe.'

'Why?' Miinaa shrugs. She'd never noticed much difference between the ghosts, other than that some have yellowish hair, or light brown hair, and that Susanna and her children all have reddish hair, and some of them have freckles. But they all go red in the sun, because their skin is pale white – not like the colour of the whitest clouds, but still so pale she thinks many of them look sick.

'Mr Nugent said the Irish are different to the English, and they have tribes inside their own tribes too, like we have clans within our tribes. But the Irish clans aren't miyagan, they're religious clans who go to the same church where they pray to their creator god.'

Miinaa is fascinated, impressed that her gumbal has listened and learned from Andrew Nugent, one of the few white ghosts he has confided in over time.

'The Nugents belong to the Catholic tribe and the other big Irish tribe are the Protestants.' He stumbles over the foreign word but it doesn't matter because Miinaa doesn't understand the Irish tribes anyway, though she knows about the Catholics and has heard Susanna mention the Protestants before, with a cold tone.

'How does it work, with the two tribes?'

'Apparently they don't get on,' Windradyne says, 'and they're all controlled by the English tribe. And there are two different areas of land separated by galing.'

'Like a bila, maybe, like the Wambool?'

Windradyne shrugs. 'I don't know, but Andrew says he came to this land because the English are trying to control the Irish, and their ngurambang as well.'

'So, the Irish are still white ghosts, but they are *better* than the English ghosts?'

'Ngawa, because it is mostly the English ghosts who are making the rules here and causing havoc on our ngurambang, on our mayiny. We know the Darug have already tried to fight back. But we need many, many spears to fight against the white ghost firesticks. We know over the ranges the people have fought back against the English, but the fighting hasn't ended either.'

Windradyne frowns.

'What is it, gumbal?'

'I hope what happened over the mountains with Pemulwuy will not happen here.'

'It might,' she says. 'He was a warrior like you. And they shot him!' Miinaa's shoulders slump as she reflects with yindyamarra about the warrior from Botany Bay that they had all heard about. They knew him as Pemulwuy, a Bidjigal man who led the resistance for his own people. There had been bloody battles fought in Parramatta and on Dharawal ngurambang at Appin. She's heard heartbreaking stories of people massacred or left wounded. Stories that Pemulwuy's head had been cut off and sent to another country over the seas, a vast body of water she can only imagine. Such brutality would never have crossed her mind, had she not heard it from her own brother's mouth. A story so vile she threw up what little was in her stomach that day. There were already too many stories that scared her; she didn't want, couldn't cope with any more.

Windradyne's words break into her thoughts.

'Word has travelled to our camp by those who have walked carefully over the ranges,' he says, straightening his spine, 'that down in Sydney-town, where the white ghosts are taking over all of the ngurambang with force, moving all the Clan off their homelands, and worse,' he pauses, 'the warriors Cannabaygal and Durelle have been murdered too.' Windradyne hangs his head in silence.

Miinaa puts her hand on her brother's shoulder.

'I don't want to hear any more.' Tears form in her eyes. She stands because she is too restless to sit any longer. The men

Windradyne speaks of were warriors like her brother, and her greatest fear is losing him the same way.

Windradyne rises from his slumped position, takes a deep breath, and looks up towards her. 'They—' he gulps, then resumes. 'They cut off the men's heads, and left their bodies hanging from trees. They are savages,' he says, teeth clenched, trying to contain his anger only because he doesn't want to disturb the children.

Miinaa almost loses her balance at the image that flashes past her eyes. She squeezes them shut tight and shakes her head, wishing hard for what she sees to disappear, but the horrific scene remains in her mind long into the night, until she finally falls into a restless sleep. It will be many nights before she can dream of better things.

Gugar Dreaming

Luke Penrith is a passionate, proud Aboriginal artist. He lives and works on Wiradyuri Country, his great grandmother's Country, in central NSW. Luke's artwork is modern contemporary. He believes working in a single medium restricts his artistic process as each idea manifests its own individual style. Luke paints on canvas, then transfers his designs to many different mediums, such as home décor, sporting activewear, and streetwear. He also loves interior design, sport, gardening, fine food and travel.